ALSO BY MELISSA GOOD

Dar and Kerry Series
Tropical Storm
Hurricane Watch
Eye of the Storm
Red Sky At Morning
Thicker Than Water
Terrors of the High Seas
Tropical Convergence
Storm Surge: Book One

Storm Surge:
Book Two

Melissa Good

Yellow Rose Books
Port Arthur, Texas

Chapter One

DAR SPRAWLED IN the leather desk chair, her bare feet propped up against the desk and her elbow resting on its surface. She listened to the voices on the conference call with barely contained aggravation, shifting forward suddenly only to relax again, as another voice took up the argument.

She picked up her glass of grapefruit juice and sipped from it. The astringent beverage was cold, and she swallowed a few mouthfuls before there was a gap in the discussion and she saw her chance to dive in. "Hey!"

The phone almost visibly shuddered. "Yes, Dar," Alastair said, after a moment. "Listen, I know things are tough where you are, but we're getting a lot of pressure here from a lot of people."

"Too bad," Dar said. "Have any of you been listening to what I've said the past twenty minutes? It's 8:00 a.m. I got back from the work site at 3:00 a.m. We just got things moving there."

"Now Dar," Hamilton chimed in. "Settle your shorts. Nobody said you weren't working hard. We just made some promises to the government and they want to know when we're gonna keep them."

"I can't see why we're delaying," another voice chimed in. "This is big. We've got a great opportunity here."

Dar glanced plaintively at the ceiling. "What the hell's wrong with you people?" she asked. "Did you not see the hole in the side of the Pentagon on CNN? Do you not know what goes on in that building?"

"Now Dar," Alastair sighed. "Well...listen folks. Today they're doing a big ceremony, and I've got to go get ready for it," he said. "I know your people there are working like anything, Dar. I understand it's important to get things going there. I know you've got a personal responsibility for the place. But damn it, I need you here."

Dar turned her head and glared at the phone. "So, what part of yes, I'm making arrangements to get to the city today wasn't clear? Did that whole five minute spiel from me at the beginning of this call not mean anything to anyone there?"

Alastair sighed. "I was hoping you'd be here this morning."

"I was sleeping this morning," Dar said. "And frankly, you all can kiss my ass. Anyone who thinks they can do this better, c'mon. Bring it."

"Dar, no one said that."

"Then everyone shut up and go do something productive." Dar turned and slammed her hand on the desk, raising her voice to a loud yell. "Instead of tying me up when I should be!" She turned, to find Kerry unexpectedly standing behind her. "Yelp."

"What was that, Dar?" Hamilton asked. "Cat get your tongue?"

"Nothing." Dar leaned back in the chair and let Kerry rub her shoulders. "Are we done?"

Long silence. "Well, I guess I'll see you here later today, huh, Dar?"

Alastair asked. "The mayor was just on the line, something about an office at the pier...any chance of looking at that first?"

"Sure," Dar said. "Done now?"

"Goodbye, all," her boss sighed and gave in. "I'll do what I can here. Going to be a rough day." He clicked off the phone and it echoed a little, then the room was once again silent.

"He sounds pissed."

"He wants me to be there making him look good," Dar said. "Screw that, Kerry. We had work to do here. "

"Uh huh. And we'd better be taking a train to go there." Kerry informed her. "'Cause, sweetheart, they're not letting anyone fly without ID," she said. "If we get packing, we can catch a train in an hour, and be in New York in three more after that. We end up in Penn Station. "

"A train," Dar mused. "Think we can get tickets? Probably pretty busy. No one wants to fly."

"Already got them." Kerry kissed the top of her head. "C'mon. Let's just get there. I'll give Dad a call." She held a hand out to Dar. "Shower? We'll save time together."

"Hedonist."

"Takes one to know one."

"HM." DAR STROLLED back down the aisle and resumed her seat next to Kerry. "I think I like trains," she concluded, folding her hands over her stomach as she regarded the inside of the somewhat narrow first class car.

"I suspected you would." Kerry looked up from her laptop, that she'd been diligently typing on. "There's windows to look out, and lots of mechanical stuff around to explore. I'm not sure I like the motion though."

"The wiggle waggle?" Dar stretched her legs out. "It's not bad."

"Mm. It's making me a little queasy." Kerry continued typing, tucking the bud in one ear more firmly into place. "At least we can stay in touch riding on this." She held a finger up then she clicked her mic on. "LA Earthstation, what was that? Who's asking you for that bandwidth?"

Dar rested her elbows on the arms of her chair, taking the time to sit back and consider an action plan for when she reached the city. Tough situation. She reached down into Kerry's briefcase and drew out a small pad, taking a pencil from her shirt pocket and hitching one knee up to rest the pad against it.

She could have hauled out the big laptop she'd been given, but it seemed too much trouble to do that just to take a few notes. "Okay."

"Okay?" Kerry glanced up.

"Talking to myself."

"Oh. Well, you know, all the traffic we took off the satellite back to the network is being filled with requests from the city." Kerry shook her head. "They're stuffed again."

"I figured they would be." Dar spent a moment doodling on the pad. "So let's see. We have the pier office to worry about, right?" She scribbled a note. "What's our best option for that? We don't have much on that side of Manhattan."

"You do, hon. You're forgetting the Intrepid Air Space Museum you managed to wheedle a contract out of after you visited the last time," Kerry reminded her.

"Mm. Not a big pipe." Dar groused.

The train hummed along, and a service person appeared with a tray. She started down the aisle, smiling at the travelers and offering them champagne flutes filled with orange juice. A few people took them, but most seemed glum and withdrawn huddled near the windows or with radio headsets covering their ears.

Kerry wondered if it was always like that or a reaction to what was going on. She accepted the glass from the server with a smile, and waited for her to pass by before she took a sip of it. "Oh. Hello." She blinked. "Mimosa. Wasn't expecting that."

Dar set her own down on the table between them and cleared her throat. "Fizzy."

"Miami exec, this is the New York office," a male voice quietly said. "Mr. McLean is asking your ETA."

Kerry checked her watch. "New York, we're looking at two hours to Penn Station," she said. "Is there anything we can do from here?"

"No ma'am," the man said. "There are a lot of people here from the city and state and he was asking."

"Well, we're moving as fast as the train lets us," Kerry said.

"I'll let him know, thanks," the man said.

"God we do need someone on the ground there," Kerry muttered. "Let me check who we've got accounted for." She typed into her keyboard and sighed. "Someone with some initiative."

"Send an email to Hermana Jones," Dar said. "Tell her to meet us at the Rock." She continued scribbling on her pad.

Kerry paused, and looked at her. "Hermana Jones? Who is that? Name is not familiar to me."

"My friend who now runs the Queens data center?"

Kerry blinked. "Oh. You mean...um... What was that funny name that sounded like a part from Intel?"

"Scuzzy."

"Scuzzy." Kerry opened her mail. "That's right. You met her in Manhattan, didn't you?" She typed the message, trying to remember if she'd ever had occasion to talk to the woman. The data entry side of the house really wasn't her area, and she decided she probably hadn't.

She remembered Mariana having a heart attack about Scuzzy though and Dar's mischievous laughter when Hermana had turned out to not only be a worthwhile addition to the company, but was promoted to center manager to boot. "Why did you do that?"

"Huh?" Dar looked up but was distracted as the forward door to the train opened and Andrew sauntered back in after being absent for a good part of the journey. "Hey Dad."

"Hey, rugrat." Andrew sat down in his seat across from the two of them. There was a line of single seats along one set of windows, and double seats along the other, and there was ample room for Dar's father to stretch out his long legs in front of him. "This here is a nice train. I like it."

He was dressed in a company logo sweatshirt, the arms pushed up past his elbows and a pair of carpenter's pants. His scarred face took in reflections of the passing sunlight from the window, as he watched the countryside go by.

"I like it too," Dar agreed. "Thanks for coming with us, Dad. I thought maybe you'd want to stay back in DC with the guys."

"Them people pissed me off," Andrew told her.

"Our people?" Kerry leaned forward a little. "What did they do?"

Andrew glanced up as the server came by and offered him the tray. He took a glass and sipped it. "Jesus P Fish there's alcohol in that." He set the glass down. "No, kumquat, not your fellas. Those are good folks there. Ah was just getting ticked off because everybody's runnin' round in circles and nobody wants to own up to how bad things got screwed."

"Dar, Hermana just answered. She said 'Hell yeah!'" Kerry seemed bemused. "This should be interesting."

"You'll like her." Dar made another note on her pad. "Dad, it's only going to get worse where we're going. That's all civ."

"Wall, somebody's got to keep you kids out of trouble."

Kerry almost laughed, caught between answering a question posed to her on the bridge and processing what was going on around her in that slightly disjointed way she'd had to develop over the past few days.

What was it she'd called it? Acquired Attention Deficit Disorder? "Okay, that's good news guys. Go on into the city, and get down to the office. We'll meet you there, and set up a command center." She released a breath. "Newark Earth, any luck with your power? We could use those trucks in the city."

"Ms. Stuart, this is the New York office again. Mr. McLean would like Ms. Roberts to call him, please."

"Dar, Alastair wants you to call him." Kerry muted her cell. "Okay, New York, message passed. Can you clear some space for us when we get there? Is there a big room we can take over for logistics?"

"Should have brought some of them fellers with us," Andrew commented.

Dar stopped writing and looked at Kerry. "Okay. Give me a second to draw a cell phone." She remarked dryly. "What in the hell does he want that can't wait an hour and forty five minutes?" Dar turned her head toward her father. "Mark will bring the RV with him after they finish up the install at the Pentagon."

"I have no idea, sweetheart. I'm just the messenger," Kerry said. "Borrow Dad's phone."

The attendant came back through. "Sir, can I offer you some breakfast?" She addressed Andrew. "We have cheese omelets, waffles, or cold cereal."

"You all got any hot dogs? Ah already had my egg things at o'dark hundred."

Dar chuckled, and shook her head. "Better have something. We're going to get swept up in a pile of crap as soon as we get there," she warned her companions, giving the server a glance as the now harried woman turned to her. "Omelet for us." She indicated Kerry and herself.

The server moved on, and Andrew handed his cell phone across the aisle to her. Dar took it and flipped it open, frowning a little before she punched in Alastair's number.

"Miami exec, this is Newark Earth." Kerry's ear bud crackled. "Good news. We just heard from Con Ed, they're expecting to finish retying us in around lunchtime."

"Great." Kerry smiled.

"Course that means we know it's really probably sometime tonight," the Earthstation acknowledged. "But soon as we're back, we'll send the trucks to the office with you."

"Alastair, we're on the way. What the hell more do you want me to do?" Dar was saying. Then she paused. Then her free hand hit the arm of her chair in muted frustration. "Because I don't have a goddamned driver's license! You want them to put me in as cargo? For Christ's sake, Alastair it would have taken us three hours to get on a damn plane this morning anyway!"

"Easy honey." Kerry patted her arm.

Dar abruptly cut the call off and closed the phone, tossing it over to her father. "If he calls me back tell him to kiss my ass."

Andrew caught the phone in one big hand and eyed his daughter dubiously. "What's that feller's problem? Thought you two got on?"

"He's losing his mind." Dar folded her arms over her chest. "I think the pressure there is getting to him. Goddamned politicians." She glanced at Kerry. "No offense to your mother."

"Who tried to hijack me into a senate investigation? No offense taken, sweetie," Kerry responded in a mild tone. "But he is our boss. You sure you should be hanging up on him?"

Dar reclined her chair and put her pen and pad away. "What's he going to do, fire me? He'll be lucky I don't belt him one when I see him."

Kerry patted her arm again, and went back to her conference call. After a moment, she found her hand captured, and her fingers interlaced with Dar's. It was inconvenient for typing, but she made no move to disengage, pecking at the keys with one hand as she studied her screen and faintly shook her head.

Crazy day.

THE THREE OF them stopped short after exiting the train platform, finding themselves in a circular lobby with people moving around them in pretty much all directions.

It was disorienting. The last part of the trip into Manhattan had mostly been underground and so they'd arrived in the station without a real sense of being in New York at all.

"Now where?" Kerry looked around. "I don't think I've ever been in this station. Where are we in relation to the office?" She took in the numbers of National Guard troops with submachine guns cradled in their hands and serious faces. "Wow."

Dar looked around as well, resisting the urge to reach up and cover her ears at the harsh, echoing clatter from the trains, the people, and the announcements bouncing off all the faux marble walls and the hard stone floor. "Loud."

"Yeah." Kerry raked her hair off her forehead. "Okay, so..."

"South." Andrew had been studying the walls. "We can take that little train up there. C'mon." He shouldered his overnight bag and headed off down one corridor. "Ain't no point going outside just yet."

Hesitating a moment, Dar and Kerry followed him. They made their way down a side corridor until they reached an area with ticket dispensing machines and turnstiles. "I remember this," Dar said. "Hope my experience this time isn't as much of a pain in the ass."

"Mm. Subways." Kerry fished some folded bills from her pocket and studied the machine. "Let's get a pass. Who knows how long we'll be here?" She inserted the bills and punched in her order, rewarded with a square of cardboard dropping into the dispenser.

She removed it, then rejoined Dar and Andrew who had already gotten theirs. "Not really conducive to luggage, huh?" She regarded the turnstiles.

Andrew took her bag and threw it up on one shoulder. "City folks livin' like water rats down here. Ah swear."

Dar did the same with her bag and they made their way through the turnstiles and into the subway station track area. "Uptown, I guess." She indicated a passage and they walked down a set of steps to a lower level with tracks on each side, and a somber group of fellow travelers waiting for the train.

Dar set her bag down and looked around. No one was talking much and there was a feeling of oppression she didn't remember from her last visit.

Andrew had put down the bags he was carrying and was standing with his hands in his pockets his pale blue eyes regarding the crowd.

The loudspeaker crackled suddenly, and everyone around them jumped a little. Kerry tried to picture where she was in the city and realized she was under Madison Square Garden. "Wow," she murmured. "Guess people are a little shell shocked."

"What's that, kumquat?" Andrew asked.

"Just thinking." Kerry felt a gust of wind hit her in the face. It smelled of dust, iron, oil, and a sense of time that made her aware of the age and the history of the walls around her.

Different than Miami. Different than Michigan.

New York was one of those few cities in the United States whose bones showed. That raw skeleton born in the turn of the last century's industrial revolution that had laid a foundation buried in the stone Manhattan was built on that was often covered over, but never replaced.

How many of those bones were exposed now on the southern tip of the island?

But there was no real time to think about it because in a moment, the train was there poking its nose out of the tunnel and screeching to a halt in front of the platform in a rush of humming silver. Kerry grabbed her bag and waited for the door to open, glancing aside at Dar as she did. "You okay?"

Dar had her bag held in both hands in front of her, and she turned her head and peered down at the questioner. "I'll live," she said. "It's not a long trip. Only a couple of stops."

They entered the train along with the rest of the waiting people. At midmorning it wasn't that full. Everyone got a seat, waiting in silence until the door alarm sounded, and the door slid shut. They lurched into motion, but not before a national guard soldier entered the car from the door between them, and took a seat at the front facing them.

His face had a smear of gray dust across his cheeks, his uniform was half covered in it, and his eyes were bloodshot. He exchanged nods with Andrew though, and then leaned back with his hands resting on his rifle as the car rumbled through a station.

"You going to call Alastair?" Kerry asked. "Let him know we're here?"

"Nope." Dar stolidly watched the walls flash by in the shadows. "I'm going to walk up behind him and smack him in the back of the head when we get there."

"Ah."

"Then we'll get to work."

"Mmph. Alrighty then."

THEY EXITED THE subway right under the building where their offices were located. "What time is it?" Dar asked, as she studied the selections of street exits the station offered.

"Eleven." Kerry edged closer to her partner, as the crowd flowed around them. "Are those the stairs there?" She pointed.

"Good as any." Dar started toward it. They crossed the hallway and started up the steps, emerging from underground into an overcast sky and a surprisingly uncrowded street. "There." Dar pointed at the entrance to the tall, distinctive building nearby. There were several men standing outside, and after a cursory glance, they moved aside to allow them to enter.

Dar ignored them. She entered the revolving glass doors into the lobby and headed immediately for the elevator stacks with Kerry and Andrew following close behind her.

The inside of the building was stunning. Kerry glanced around as they stopped in front of the elevators. It was in an art deco style, and every inch of it spoke of class and money. The people inside though, weren't bustling around much. They were standing in small groups, talking or watching the televisions mounted on the far walls.

Kerry caught a glimpse of one. "Ah." She followed Dar into the elevator car. "The president is here today."

Dar punched the floor button. "Good. Maybe they'll all go mess with him and leave us alone." She waited for the doors to close then leaned against the back wall.

They were alone in the elevator and as it ground gamely upward, a pensive silence fell.

"Know what I was thinking?" Kerry asked, after about twenty seconds of silence. "I was thinking that given what happened here earlier this week, I'm pretty sure I don't like being in a building as famous as 30 Rock and sharing it with NBC."

Dar gave her a wry look, then patted her shoulder as the doors opened and they were on their floor. Obviously their floor, as the elevators opened out into a lobby with a curved wall of glass with their logo chiseled into it in all its staid and definitely boring corporate detail.

A big reception desk guarded the opening curved in the same shape and made of polished teak. Behind it a young woman was standing, a headset on her ears, her head bent and cocked to one side and her hand on the buttons of a big console phone. "Sir…sir…please, hold on a minute…sir…I'm sure I don't know if…sir, please stop yelling at me. I'm trying to…"

Dar went over and tapped her on the shoulder, making the girl jump almost into the glass wall. "Gimme." She held out her hand for the headset, glaring at her until the receptionist surrendered it in bewilderment, staring around and spotting Kerry and Andrew standing there.

Her mouth dropped open.

Dar put one ear muff to her ear and got the mic in position. "Who is this?" she asked sharply. "Mister Dobson? What do you want?" She paused. "Let me give you some advice. Turn on a goddamned television set. Half the city is down."

The receptionist's eyes almost came out of her head. Kerry stepped forward and put her briefcase down, giving the girl a smile.

"I don't give a damn. Tell your boss if you don't stop calling and harassing my people I'm going to put him last on the list of things to worry about behind the pushcart vendor outside and some taxi driver going by. Understand me?"

"Ma'am…" The receptionist bravely held her hands out in a placating gesture. "He's a big customer."

"I don't care," Dar mouthed back at her. "Roberts," she said into the phone. "Dar Roberts. I'm the only person in the damn company who can help him, so stop pissing me off and get off the phone." Her voice rose into a yell. After a pause, she nodded. "Thanks. Goodbye." She released the line and handed the girl back her headset. "Here."

The receptionist took them as though they were going to explode. "Uh…"

"Hi." Kerry distracted her. "We're from Miami. They're probably expecting us inside." She held her hand out. "Kerry Stuart."

"Uh." The girl merely pointed at the entrance.

"Thanks." Dar picked up her bag and motioned them inside. "Let's go."

Andrew picked up Kerry's luggage and followed her, giving the receptionist a polite nod of his head. "Lo." He ducked inside and waited for Kerry to catch up, then they both hurried to catch up with the visibly annoyed, stalking CIO ahead of them. "Tells folks off real nice, don't she," he conversationally said to Kerry.

"Best in the world," Kerry acknowledged, with a wry smile. "Nobody does that better than Dar."

Dar turned and walked backwards, giving them a dire look. "You better be talking about my phone skills and not anything more intimate." She turned back around and kept going, turning left down a corridor and whisking past various, mostly empty, offices.

Kerry felt herself get lightheaded as a deep blush colored her face, not helped in the least by Andrew's deep chuckle. "Someday I'll learn not to do that," she muttered. "She gets me every time."

She could hear the sound of raised voices and she quickened her steps, catching up to Dar just as her partner stiff-armed a large, heavy mahogany door open. The sounds got a lot louder as they entered a big conference room full of people.

Four men were faced off opposite Alastair, all talking at once. Three more were surrounding Hamilton, who had both hands up and was arguing forcefully. Two or three more men were standing around, aides apparently, and they were the only ones who looked up as they entered.

Then they went back to watching the disagreement, dismissing the new arrivals.

"You made a commitment to the mayor," one man said. "This ain't no joke anymore. I need an answer on when that office is going to be up."

"That and the president's office said you'd get things working. What's happening with that? You've been telling me for two days you've got a plan. Where is it?" an older man asked.

Dar tossed her bag toward the wall and went right to the table slamming her hand against it and creating a loud, startling sound. "Excuse me."

Alastair turned immediately, recognizing her voice. He spotted her behind the table, and a look of utter relief appeared on his face. Even Hamilton looked glad to see her, and they quickly abandoned their opponents and circled the table to join her.

The other men followed, staring at them. "What's this?" the oldest of them asked. "We have no time for more interruptions, McLean. You've stalled long enough. I need results! The governor's expecting an answer!"

"Well, Dar. Glad you made it. Glad you're here," Alastair greeted her, ignoring the man for the moment. "I was just explaining to these fellas..."

Dar stared right at him, until his voice trailed off and he fell silent. Then she turned and looked at the rest of the men long enough for them to start to fidget a little. "Everyone sit down, please," she said, resting her hands on the table.

The older man looked annoyed. He started to say something, but Dar stared him down until he pulled out a seat across from Alastair and sat down, motioning for those with him to do the same. "All right, lady. Make it fast."

Kerry settled into a seat to Dar's left, and Andrew ambled around and took the chair on the other side of her. The rest of the men grudgingly took seats also, leaning forward and looking at Dar.

"Thank you." Dar remained standing, resting her weight a bit on the hands she still had resting on the table. She looked at the older man. "Can you please introduce yourself so I know who the hell I'm talking to?"

Hamilton put a hand up over his mouth, his eyes twinkling a little. Alastair merely clasped his hands and worked to keep a benign expression on his face.

"Ivan Falcuzzi," the man said, shortly. "I work for the governor.

Who the hell are you?"

"Dar Roberts," Dar responded matter of factly. "So let me get my plan out on the table sthen we can stop all the horse crap and actually get something constructive done." She drew in a quick breath, and started talking again before she could get interrupted. "You don't really have to tell us your problems, Mr. Falcuzzi." She straightened. "We know what the problems are."

"Then why aren't you doing something about it?" the man asked bluntly. "We were told you people would fix things. Things ain't fixed."

"I was fixing things," Dar responded. "We've been fixing things since this situation started. Tell me what you'd have liked us to do here before you let people back in the city, before we could travel, before we could get anything shipped in to help you, or before we made sure the military was going to keep running so nothing else could happen to anyone else?"

Falcuzzi lifted his hand. "Wait a minute."

"What did you expect us to do?" Dar enunciated each word separately. "What in the hell do you people think we are? Any of us here look like Poodle the Magnificent? Think we have rabbits we can pull out of our asses?" She leaned forward again. "I appreciate that you are frustrated Mr. Falcuzzi, but you are not one tenth as frustrated as I am to come in here after working round the clock for three days and finding you in here blowing hot air for NO GOOD REASON."

He opened his mouth, then shut it again.

"WE WILL FIX ALL YOUR DAMN PROBLEMS," Dar hollered at top volume, "IF YOU GET OUT OF HERE AND LEAVE US THE HELL ALONE!"

He stared at her. "You got any idea who you're talking to?"

"You have any idea how little I care who I'm talking to?" Dar countered. "You're keeping us from doing our jobs. Get out of here, and we'll deliver whatever it is Alastair promised we would. I don't have time to talk to you any more."

Falcuzzi studied her for a moment, then he glanced to the side, where Andrew was seated, his big, scarred hands resting on the table, folded together. His mouth pursed, then he shrugged and stood up. "All right," he said. "At least you ain't pitching me any excuses." He made a curt gesture to the rest of his gang. "But if I were you lady, I'd make good on that fixing business. Know what I mean?"

"Gentlemen," Hamilton stood up, recognizing a legal cue when he saw one, "as our dear CIO has so eloquently said, we know what we need to do. Now take your distinguished selves on out the door, and let us get on with it." He opened the door. "I'll walk you on down."

The men filed out. The last three, big men with very little in the way of necks, made a point of looking around before they walked out, tugging their jacket sleeves straight as they left and closing the door behind them.

The conference room became quiet. Dar rested her weight on her elbows and glanced at Kerry. "Got any Advil?"

Kerry grimaced in sympathetic understanding and leaned over to rummage in her briefcase.

"Well, Dar." Alastair put his hands on his chair arms, and sighed.

"I'm really glad to see you." He eyed his scowling CIO. "I know I've been a pain in the ass all day. You going to kill me?"

Dar stood and went to the credenza, poured herself a glass of water and used it to chase down the pills she was juggling in her right hand. "I'm not going to kill you Alastair. Too many crappy things have happened to too many people in the last few days for me to get pissed off about a couple of phone calls."

Alastair twiddled his fingers on the chair arms. "You sure sounded pissed off at the politico's boys."

"I don't know or care about them." Dar came back and sat down, exhaling. "I know and care about you." She caught her boss's eyes widening in surprise. "So I'd rather take my cramps out on them since they weren't doing anything productive for us anyway."

"Ah."

Kerry reached over and gave Dar's back a little rub. "We have a short list of critical tasks, sir," she addressed Alastair. "The emergency office and some kind of coverage downtown are top on the list. Is there anything else they're pressing us on?"

"Well." Alastair eyed them both warily. "I don't want to get your shorts back in a twist now."

"Alastair, please." Dar smiled briefly.

"We do have a little longer short list," Alastair admitted. "Some things came up today, and I guess they thought they'd throw everything at us and see what stuck."

"Bring it on." Kerry took her laptop out and put it on the table. "Dad, you want some coffee? I'm going to find some tea."

"Naw," Andrew said. "How bout I get your's and Dardar's bunks squared away. I figure you got a lot of stuff you got to take care of," he offered. "Ah'll find out what's going on round here anyhow."

"Thanks, Dad," Dar said "That'd be great."

Andrew stood up and slung his own bag over his shoulder. He stepped behind them and patted Dar on the shoulder then collected their bags and ducked out the door. "Better find me that coonass, too, 'fore he gets into trouble with them folks," he muttered as he left, his words echoing softly.

That left the three of them. Kerry focused on getting her laptop started up, as Dar and Alastair regarded each other.

"Here we go again," Alastair said, finally.

"Here we go again," Dar repeated, with a sigh. "Got any rum?"

"Eh?"

Chapter Two

"FIRST THINGS FIRST." Dar had her hands in her pockets, as she studied the conference room wall. Once sedately weave covered, it now sported various plans and blueprints spread out from end to end. "Kerry, who do we have here from services?"

"I've got three people here, Dar. They're the support folks for this office," Kerry said.

Dar ran her finger along the coastline of Manhattan. "Okay. So let's get them out to the Intrepid. If this is to scale, and it's correct, we'll need a fiber spool and someone who can terminate it. We got that?"

Kerry reviewed her notes. "I don't think so," she admitted. "We contracted out the fiber install here. I don't think that's our access either."

"Okay." Dar moved to the other end of the map. "Let's start from a place I know they'll let us into. Have the guys take the biggest spool we have, make sure it's rubberized, and have them start at the mayor's damn offices and move toward the Intrepid. Maybe I can work on getting us access while they do that."

"Will do." Kerry leaned over her laptop and put her headphones in.

They were alone in the conference room. Alastair and Hamilton had gone to join the rest of the New York staff in watching the visit of the president, leaving them in peace to get things rolling.

Dar didn't feel like rolling anything. The pills had taken the edge off her cramps, but only the edge, and her body was aching so badly she felt like curling up in the corner of the room and forgetting all about the long list of problems facing them.

She suspected Kerry knew that. Her partner kept watching her, and giving her little rubs on the back, and looking like she wanted to tuck her into bed somewhere.

Dar would have given a year's salary to be able to let her.

"Dar?"

She turned around and leaned one shoulder against the wall, finding Kerry gazing back at her with wry sympathy. "Yes?"

"The guys are on their way in the company van. They said they hope they'll let them down there," Kerry said. "Can I get you some tea?"

Dar held her hand out. "Gimme your cell." She waited, and caught the phone as Kerry tossed it. She pulled a piece of paper from her pocket and keyed in a number, then held the phone up to her ear. "Yes. Can I speak to the governor please? This is Dar Roberts. Yes, I'll hold."

Kerry got up and came over to her, circling her with her arms and resting her cheek against Dar's shoulder. She felt Dar exhale, and looking up, saw the wry expression on her face. "What can I do for you, my love?"

"What more can I ask of you besides loving me?" Dar responded, with a gentle smile. "Hello, yes?" She returned her attention to the phone. "Governor, you said you could remove roadblocks. You ready to make good on that?"

Kerry kissed her on the upper arm and gave her a gentle squeeze. Then she moved around behind her and started massaging Dar's lower back, making small circles with her thumbs on either side of her partner's spine.

"Are you telling me you can't clear them through there? Get someone to help us?" Dar's voice rose and took on a darker edge. "What in the hell do you expect me to do, bring guns and force our way into the telco demarc?"

Kerry started humming "New York, New York" under her breath as she worked on her aggravated boss's tall frame.

"You people are as useless as tits on a boar." Dar clapped the phone shut and almost tossed it across the room, remembering at the last minute it wasn't hers to destroy. She handed it back to Kerry and growled, leaning with both hands against the wall. "Son of a bitch."

"Easy, babe," Kerry soothed her. "We'll find a way. "

A soft knock came at the door. They both paused then sorted themselves into a semblance of decorum as Dar cleared her throat. "C'mon in." She resumed studying the wall, but didn't hide a smile as Kerry kissed her hand then let it go just as the door opened.

A woman with dark golden skin and dark hair entered, wearing a colorful jacket and leather pants. "Hey!" She spotted Dar. "Dar from Miami! How are ya!"

Dar chuckled and stepped forward to take the extended hand. "Hello, Scuzzy," she said. "How are you doing?"

"Well," Scuzzy stuck her hands in her pockets and shrugged, "not so great, you know? It's been tough the last few days."

"I know," Dar said. She half turned. "Scuzzy, this is Kerry Stuart, our Vice President of Operations." She could see the quirk in her partner's brow. "Ker, this is Hermana Jones, from the Queens data center."

"Hello," Kerry extended her hand, "nice to meet you."

"Oh hey!" Scuzzy took her hand and shook it vigorously. "That's been you on the phone that whole time, huh?"

"Mostly, yes," Kerry agreed. "It's been a long couple of days."

Scuzzy released her. "Everyone here's pretty shook up, you know? It's been tough. My brother's FDNY."

"Oh no," Kerry said. "Is he okay?"

"Yeah." Scuzzy nodded. "He was uptown saving some lady who got stuck in her car or something. He was all pissed off that he didn't get down there until them buildings fell down. Then he wasn't so pissed anymore, just mad about all the other guys."

They were all silent for a moment, and then Scuzzy shrugged. "My mama wants to send that lady a basket of flowers, you know?" She glanced around. "But they weren't so lucky here, huh? I heard about the big cheese."

"They weren't," Dar agreed. "But we've got a lot of other things to worry about too. That's why I asked you to come down here, to see if you could help us out." She turned to face the map. "You up for that?"

"You kidding?" Scuzzy asked. "Meeting you in that subway changed my whole freaking life. You want me to do something? Whatever, you know?" She glanced at Kerry. "Sorry, I know that sounds crazy."

Kerry's green eyes twinkled. "I know exactly what you mean," she demurred. "Dar certainly does have that effect on people." She patted her partner on the side. "Let me get back to the conference. Do I take it we get no help from the governor?"

"Jerk," Dar said. "No." She looked at Scuzzy. "But you might be able to help. Here's the deal." She turned to the map, finding the pier with one long finger. "The city's putting in a command center here."

"The pier? That old creaky place?" Scuzzy seemed dubious. "You got to be kidding me, right?"

"Wish I was," Dar said. "They want communications. There's nothing down there, no phone lines, nothing."

"You ain't kidding. I had a cousin used to live under the terminal," Scuzzy stated. "There ain't nothing but rats under there, I'm telling you."

Dar eyed her. "Nice," she said. "Well, I've got some guys going down there to run a big cable from there, down to the Intrepid, the air museum, where I was going when I met you."

Scuzzy nodded. "All right."

"Problem is, we have to get it into where we have an office there, and get them to let us connect it up," Dar said. "In the electrical rooms."

"Oh man." Scuzzy made a sound with her mouth like a mouse screaming. "They ain't going to let you in there to do nothing like that. Not those guys down there. They don't like nobody messing around down by the docks."

Kerry, who had been listening, now spoke up. "We could pay them to do it," she suggested. "It'd be worth it if that would get it done."

"How many fiber optics technicians you figure work off the side of the Hudson, Ker?" Dar put her hand against the wall and leaned on it. "Who haven't already been sucked down into the financial district?"

"Ah."

"Y'know." Scuzzy had been looking at the map. "I got an uncle I could maybe call," she offered.

Dar's lips twitched. "I was hoping you did."

"He does some business down there, you know?" Scuzzy explained. "He's in real good with those guys. You want me to call him, see if he could maybe help us?"

"I do." Dar went over to the conference table and perched on its edge. "Scuzzy, we don't mind paying whatever service fees they want, understand? This is important. We have to get the city emergency center up so those people can do what your tax dollars are paying them to do."

"Gotcha." Scuzzy pulled out her cell phone, a bejeweled item with three or four things dangling off the edge of it. "No problem. Lemme see what I can do here, okay?" She moved to one side, and started punching buttons. "Uncle Jazzy, Uncle Jazzy where are ya in here..."

Dar folded her arms over her chest and turned her head, giving Kerry a wry look. Kerry merely smiled back at her charmingly, letting her chin rest on her hand. "Got that tea?" Dar finally asked, with a mild grimace. "Or a hammer to hit my head with?"

"Absolutely." Kerry got up and slid her laptop over, handing the ear buds to her partner. "Listen in while I'm out doing your every bidding." She winked at her partner, and ducked past, going to the door and slipping outside into the hallway.

Dar sighed, and put one bud in her ear, doing her best to ignore the cramps that were getting on and stomping all over her last nerve. It was even making the back of her eyeballs ache and she swallowed, feeling a little like she was going to throw up.

Like life wasn't a pain in the ass enough as it was, right?

"Miami exec, you on? This is Miami ops."

Dar clicked the mic. "Miami exec here," she dutifully responded. "Go ahead Mark. How's it going out there?"

"Boss, we're doing pretty well," Mark said. "Especially since a freaking truck just showed up here with linemen from three of the phone companies dumping into that closet. They're in there giving our guys a break now."

Dar managed a smile at that. "Well, I'll be damned," she said. "That is good news." She spared a wistful thought of the bus, and the crew they'd left behind. The two other community buses were here, and parked downstairs but it wasn't the same thing. "Listen, do we have any fiber guys there? I'm going to need one."

"Hold one, boss." Mark clicked off.

Dar was glad enough to remain silent. She checked her watch to see if she could take more painkillers, sighing and rubbing her temples when she realized she couldn't. She turned and looked out the window, finding her eyes drawn to the east, where a dull plume of smoke was still rising between the skyscrapers in the distance.

Sitting here, she realized, she could have seen the whole thing happen. Had the people here wondered if they were next?

Dar sighed, hearing Scuzzy talking at the other end of the room. She got up off the table and sat down in the nearest chair, resisting the urge to put her head down on her arms as the cramping worsened. She focused on Kerry's laptop instead, moving aside the window with her mail to study her desktop background.

It was a picture of a sunset from the boat. She vaguely remembered it, a lazy Saturday out on the water that had ended with a freshly caught fish dinner and Kerry leaning back against her on the bow snapping shots of the sky.

Dar could almost smell the salt tang on the air and feel the warmth of Kerry's back pressed against her as she rested her chin on Kerry's shoulder and gently blew in her ear.

"Dar?"

The hand on her shoulder nearly made Dar jump out of her skin. She turned to find Kerry standing there with a faintly concerned look on her face, and a cup of steaming tea. "Ah. Sorry. I zoned out for a minute." She took the cup and set it down. "Mark's finding us a fiber man."

"You were a million miles away there." Kerry sat down next to her, glancing past at the still talking Scuzzy, who was now pacing back and forth, gesticulating with her free hand. "You okay?"

Dar took a sip of the hot, minty, honey laced beverage. "Not a million miles," she disagreed. "Only about two thousand or so. I was thinking about the day you took that picture." She pointed at the screen.

"Wishing I was there again right now."

"Mmm." Kerry settled the ear bud in her ear and gazed at the red orange scene. "That was the day you caught the grouper," she said. "What a gorgeous night that was, too. So many stars. The sky was so clear."

"You found so many loony animals in the sky I ended up tossing you overboard," Dar added grinning.

"And I ended up tangled in seaweed half scared out of my mind," Kerry concluded. "I wish I was back there now too."

"Hey, Miami exec? This is Miami ops." Mark came back on. "Found one guy who can do splicing. That what you need?"

"Sounds good, Miami ops. Put him on the train," Kerry answered. "When are you heading up here? We're really short on techs and really heavy on sales folks here."

"Hey, I got him." Scuzzy came back over, and the pace picked up again around them. "He says he's interested in doing business with us, yeah."

"Great." Dar half turned to face her, catching Alastair entering the room with a frown on his face. "Alastair, get your checkbook ready."

Her boss stopped in mid step, and blinked. "Eh?"

"We need to start doing business here," Dar said. "The old fashioned way." She motioned to Scuzzy. "Meet Scuzzy."

"Hey. How ya doin?" Scuzzy held her hand out. "Nice ta meet ya."

Alastair took her hand automatically, his pale blue gray eyes going wide. "Charmed." He looked over at Dar. "I'm sure."

Dar smiled briefly at him. Then the door opened again, and one of the sales staff poked their head in, and a flashing alert went off on Kerry's screen. In the distance, a siren went off.

And it still wasn't time to take more drugs.

"DAR." KERRY LOOKED up from her laptop, and across at her visibly miserable partner. "I'm sorry, sweetie, but they're going to need you to go down there." She grimaced in sympathy at Dar's hunched over posture.

"Fuck." Dar had her eyes covered with one hand, having just swallowed a second set of pills. "Why?"

Kerry felt as emotionally miserable as Dar was physically. "They won't let them in the demarc room at the Intrepid. Not even our local people." She got up and circled the table, putting her hands on Dar's shoulders and beginning a gentle massage. "Want me to go? If you tell me what to look for, and I take Dad, maybe we can do it."

"Stupid fucking bastards. What do they think they're going in there for with a three hundred pound spool of fiber optics? Wiring the admiral's urinal?"

"Does the admiral have his own urinal?" Kerry returned the wry attempt at humor. "I'll go down there. Let me get some usefulness out of my PMS before I'm as miserable as you are."

Dar sighed. "I'm in hell." She straightened up. "We'll all go down there. If I don't kill someone we can stop by a bar I know near there and get me some alcohol and see if that helps."

"Aw, honey." Kerry kissed the top of her head. "You're making me crazy watching you be so miserable." She wrapped her arms around Dar from behind, resting her cheek against her hair. "I wish I could do something besides ache for you."

"Life sucks." Dar sighed mournfully. "Someone once asked me if I wasn't pissed off I was born a woman instead of a man. I told them absolutely. For about four or six hours every goddamned month."

Kerry chuckled wryly. "Buy me a beer at that bar?"

"Buy you the bar if you want." Dar gathered herself and stood up. She followed Kerry around to her laptop and waited for her to start to shut it down. Then she came up behind her and wrapped her arms around her, returning the hug and the emotion behind it. "We get this office up, you and I are going to our hotel, and chilling."

Kerry glanced at her watch. It was almost 2:00 p.m. and she figured it would be at least two hours before they had an even chance of getting the problem on the river resolved. That would make it four. "We can schedule more stuff from there," she agreed, "and at least get comfortable."

"What have we done to get someone into lower Manhattan?" Dar asked. "That's going to be a lot tougher than fixing this damn office of the mayor's."

"I called my contact at AT&T. He's arranged to get us credentials down there. I haven't told him what we're doing. I just said we might be able to help somewhere."

"Mm."

"Well, it's true." Kerry closed her laptop. "Just not how he's going to think of it." She went still, taking a moment to savor the warmth of the body pressed against her back, finding herself rocking gently as Dar did.

How crummy and unbearable it would be if Dar wasn't here, she mused. No matter how lousy they both felt. "I love you." Dar didn't answer. She hugged Kerry a little harder and nibbled the edge of one of her ears.

Then they both sighed at the same time, and Dar released her so she could slide her laptop into its case and zip it shut. "Let me call Dad." She grabbed Kerry's phone and opened it, half turning as she heard footsteps outside the door. "Grrr."

"C'mon honey, remember where we are," Kerry murmured. "They've had it really rough."

"Rowr." Dar's eyes narrowed, but she subsided, juggling the phone in one hand as they waited.

The door lock worked, then opened, and Alastair came inside, shutting the large wooden panel after him and leaning against it. "Y'know, I could get to not like people after a lot of this." He studied them. "You two off somewhere?"

Dar's brows twitched. "We're going to the emergency office. Try to get the cross-connects done and get those people off our backs at least." She paused, holding the open phone in one hand. "Wanna go with us?"

"Yep." Alastair didn't even hesitate. "One more person calls this office from somewhere in New Jersey and tells me they're down I'm going to take my Longhorns coffee mug and stick it right up their behind."

Kerry's eyes widened. "Wow."

"I didn't think so many people these days didn't read the newspaper. Or watch the evening news. Or have CNN in their houses. Or lived in such a bubble," Alastair said. "I simply don't understand it. The blacksmiths on my damn ranch know more about what's going on in the world than some of these folks."

"You mean, they really didn't know what happened?" Kerry asked, in an incredulous tone.

"Apparently not." Alastair sighed.

"C'mon." Dar was at least glad for this startling distraction to her cramps. "I think you could use a beer too." She indicated the door as she put the phone to her ear. "Let's get out of here for a while. I need some fresh air." She paused. "Hey Dad. Meet you downstairs?"

"Air," Alastair agreed, waiting for them to exit and following along. "Don't much care if it's fresh or not at this point."

Dar hung up as they got to the elevator, pausing to exchange a brief smile with the receptionist. "Sorry if I startled you earlier. It's been that kind of day."

"Oh." The woman smiled back. "Actually, what you did was really cool," she said, "and I forgot to say thanks."

"What did you do?" Alastair asked, as the doors slid open.

"Told a customer to kiss my ass." Dar entered the elevator and impatiently waited for them to follow before she punched the door button. "Dad's downstairs at the bus."

"Ah."

Kerry leaned against the back wall of the elevator, swallowing a little as it descended and she felt the familiar pressure against her inner ears. It reminded her of their last diving trip on the boat, where Dar had taken the Dixie out deep to a wreck in nearly 140 feet of water.

They had descended in the blue, clear water until the wreck had morphed out of the depths, half on its side, filled with ghostly schools of fish robbed of their brilliance by the depth.

Gorgeous and spooky, startling when a huge grouper came nosing around from the gloom around the wreck, and reeking with mystery they could barely get a few minutes to look at. The loneliness of the wreck's position, settled in its bed of white sand had triggered her poetic side and she'd thought about the site frequently since.

What story was behind it, she mused?

"Ker?"

"Huh?" Kerry looked up, to find the elevator doors open and her partner gazing back at her with mild bemusement. "Oh. Sorry." She pushed off the back wall and scooted out of the car, feeling a little embarrassed. "Daydreaming."

Dar patted her on the back as they walked across the huge lobby and out the side door, to a large parking area complete with two of their buses were. There were a few people around them including Andrew, and they walked quickly across the lot to join him.

"Hamilton's gone down to represent us at the big shindig," Alastair commented. "I figured it wouldn't do for me to be showing the flag there with all this stuff yet to be done."

Dar gave him a wry look.

"Glad I'm not trying to fly out of here today," Kerry muttered. "I'd be stuck on the tarmac at LaGuardia until the circus leaves town."

Alastair gave her a wry look.

"Kerry had an unfortunate ground hold the last time the president was in Miami," Dar explained. "She got stuck in a 737 in the middle of July for six hours with no air conditioning. It made an impression."

"I can still smell the inside of that airplane, matter of fact," Kerry said. "Closest I ever came to going postal in public."

Alastair grimaced, "That does sound painful." He dredged up a smile up as they arrived at the bus, and people turned to greet them. "Hello, folks. How's everyone doing?"

"Lo there." Andrew cocked his head and regarded Kerry and Dar. "How are you kids doing?"

"I've been better." Dar didn't bother to dissemble. "Let's get a cab and get down to the pier. The faster we do that, the faster Alastair can go preen for the press."

"Well, hey." Her boss turned around, startled. "I didn't mean you should go make me into a hero, Dar. For Pete's sake!"

"Don't worry about it," Kerry whispered to him. "She's just in a really bad mood."

Alastair frowned. "I'm in a really bad mood too. Should I say mean things?"

"If you want to." Kerry exhaled, blinking into the cool air. "I don't think she meant to be mean. It's been a long couple of days and she doesn't feel well."

Alastair grumbled under his breath, but kept his comments to himself and stuck his hands in the pockets of his khaki pants instead.

"C'mon then." Andrew pointed to the curb. "Dardar said you all's got some folks down at the flattop giving you a hassle?" he asked Kerry, as they steered between the buses and headed for the road. "What's that all about?"

Dar hailed a cab and they got into what was fortunately one of the minivan versions. "I need to go to the Air Space Museum, please," she said, crisply.

"S'closed, lady," the man said.

"I know. I need to go there anyway," Dar told him. "It's business. We don't want a tour."

The driver took off without another word, pulling into the traffic stream with a typically supreme lack of regard for anything including other cars and his own safety.

"What's that all about?" Andrew asked. Kerry sighed. "Well, see, they decided to put the new emergency response center down at the pier, Pier 92 I think Dar said."

"All right." Andrew's brows knit a little. "Seems like a funny place to put something like that, ain't it?"

"Well," Kerry's lips twitched, "I have to say if I was thinking of doing an emergency center in Miami, that port we were in is the last place I'd pick, but I'm sure they have their reasons. Anyway, they need things to connect and the only place we have something close enough that's got a good link to our systems is at the Intrepid."

Dar let her head rest against the window, wishing fervently she was several thousand miles away in a quiet, dark room, with a cup of hot chocolate and nothing more to do than read a magazine. She didn't really feel like making the effort to get out of the cab and get involved in all the chaos she knew she would have to and, for once, didn't mind the traffic making it take longer to get somewhere.

She let Kerry's quiet voice go past her, not really hearing the words or the answers to them, aware only of the warmth of Kerry's fingers curled around her hand, her thumb idly rubbing against Dar's knuckle in absent caress.

Kerry probably didn't even realize she was doing it. Dar remembered when they first started dating, when Kerry was so very self conscious about touching Dar in public—though she'd never been in private.

Now, it was second nature to her, and to be honest, second nature to Dar as well. She liked the warmth of the touch and the affection in the gentle squeezing. It soothed her ragged temper a little, and allowed her to put aside her discomfort in favor of this tiny bit of physical pleasure.

Outside the window, the city moved past. Though traffic was heavy, she noticed the frenetic pace of the cars seemed subdued, and the people on the streets were as well. Men and women were gathered around storefronts, talking. There were few trucks on the road.

They passed a crossroad, and she watched two men simply standing, looking at each other in front of a subway entrance, seemingly frozen in place. A woman was sitting in front of them on the edge of the road, her feet resting on the tar surface itself, her arms wrapped around her knees.

In her hand, she clutched a sheaf of papers. Dar could see something square on them that looked like a picture, but she was struck by the expression on the woman's face, dull, and lost and so full of grief it was hard to look at her.

It brought back to her, suddenly, what had happened a few days prior, and she felt small thinking about how she'd been bitching to herself only a minute ago and wanting to be somewhere else.

"Dar?"

"Hm?" Dar turned her head and regarded Kerry's face. "Sorry. I was thinking of something else."

"I got a message from my contact at AT&T. They've got credentials for us. He's dropping them by the office." Kerry glanced behind her, as Dar did the same. They looked at each other then Kerry shrugged a little. "For what it's worth."

"We'll use them." Dar settled back as they started moving faster, heading across town toward the Hudson River. "Okay. Did we get a handle on what the roadblock is at the Intrepid? Are we running into labor issues already, or is it something security related?"

Kerry's eyes looked apologetic. "Sorry, don't know. All they said was it wasn't working."

"All right." Dar rested her elbow on her knee. "Then we'll get it working."

"One way or t'other." Andrew remarked, from his seat behind them. "Let's get this here show on the road. I've bout had enough of people fussing."

"You got that right," Alastair agreed. "It's time to get things rolling."

Dar and Kerry exchanged glances, and Kerry leaned closer, lowering her voice. "We're the only ones who are actually going to do anything aren't we?"

Dar chuckled dryly, and shook her head. "Guess we'll find out."

Chapter Three

SECURITY AROUND THE Intrepid was heavy. Kerry edged to one side as they got out of the taxi, seeing a line of National Guard in front of the entrance to the Museum. There were also large orange traffic barrels blocking any vehicle access. To the right hand side she could see the ramp that led up to the pier entrances sealed by yet more guard vehicles. "Wow."

Dar settled her backpack onto her back and cinched the straps a little tighter. She paused to study the front of the structure, spotting a cluster of vehicles and a barrier that was surrounded by people. "Over there." She started for the spot, quickly joined by Kerry as her father and Alastair trailed a little behind them.

Scuzzy was there, and spotted them as they approached. "Oh, hey," she called out. "Now we're talking."

Dar kept walking toward her and the guardsmen who were gathered around turned to watch them approach. She had about ten steps to decide on her approach, and with the cramps and her exhaustion, she decided on mellow just as she reached Scuzzy's side. "Good afternoon, gentlemen," she greeted the guards courteously. "Sorry we're causing a commotion."

The guard nearest her, apparently in charge, had opened his mouth to respond, his body tense and shoulders squared off, but blinked and paused at her words.

Dar smiled at him, cocking her head slightly as she stuck her thumbs in the straps holding her backpack on and shifted her own posture. "I know you've got a big load on your shoulders here. I don't want to add to it. What can we do so I can provide what you need to let me do what I have to do?"

Kerry merely stood there, her hand on the strap of her briefcase looped over her shoulder, as she watched her partner use one of her rarest strategies, her innate charm. She often wondered why Dar didn't use it more often, since it was compelling and irresistible, and she wasn't just saying that because they were lovers.

She could see the man wavering, in fact. He'd been all set to respond to anger, to aggression, to a yelling civilian out to make his life miserable, and faced with that gentle smile and those pretty blue eyes he had no idea how to get the adrenaline out of the way of his testosterone fast enough to respond.

She understood. In the few times they argued, more often than not it was that charm that made her anger evaporate no matter which one of them won or lost the fight. Even now, Kerry felt herself responding to it, her body relaxing and a smile edging her lips as she watched Dar's face.

"Well," the man said, "this is a secure area."

Dar nodded. "I'm sure it is. That flattop's a big target, and there's a lot of history both inside and on her decks. No one wants anything to happen to it." She went on, "I don't want anything to happen to it. "

"Okay." The man leaned back against the truck blocking the entrance. The other guardsmen also relaxed, moving their guns down and turning aside a little as it became apparent these civilians were not about to physically storm the barrier. "So what is it exactly you people need to do? This lady here was explaining it but it didn't make any sense to me."

Scuzzy frowned. Kerry winked at her, and gave the waiting, grubby looking techs a smile. "Why don't you guys go relax for a few minutes over there. I think they have sodas over at that hot dog stand on the corner."

"Thanks, ma'am. Great idea," the taller one said. "It's like a nightmare under those piers running this stuff." He turned and pointed at the big spool of rubber coated wire, the strand a full two inches wide. It trailed back behind them, snaking across the ground and underneath the rampway toward the depths of the inner pier structure. "I live here, but man I saw rats bigger than my brother under that thing."

"I'm up for lunch too," Scuzzy said. "C'mon you guys. I'll buy." She tilted her head in Dar and Kerry's direction. "You want something?"

"We're fine for now, thanks," Kerry answered for both of them. "But the next round we're having after this I'm buying."

Scuzzy grinned. "You got it. " She jerked her head at the two techs.

They set their gloves on the top of the spool and trotted quickly to the nearby crossing light, waiting for it to change before they headed across toward the pushcart vendor.

"Well, it's like this." Dar half turned and pointed over toward the pier. "The mayor decided to put his new emergency management office in that building over there."

The soldier nodded. "Yeah, we know. They've been coming back and forth and going crazy over there since yesterday. Trucks full of stuff," he said. "What's that got to do with you and this thing?" He thrust his thumb behind him, toward the Intrepid.

"It's the closest place I can connect the mayor's new office to so they can have computers and phones," Dar explained. "I have a connection in there because we run all the IT for the gift shop, and the museum."

The guard thought about that. "Oh," he said. "So you want to run that cable in there for the mayor?" He turned and looked up the ramp, where the entire top was filled with official looking cars. "How come no one said so? For Pete's sake."

"Well, you know it's pretty crazy for them up there," Dar regained his attention, "just like it is for you and for us too. It's hard to keep track of everything that's going on, but we want to get them connected so they can work. We have identification."

Kerry glanced at her partner, wondering if she was forgetting that she, in fact, did not.

The guard nodded. "Okay, I need to get my lieutenant here to sign off on it, let me radio him and have him come up. Sorry to have caused you some heartache, ma'am, but I know you understand what's going on here."

"I do." Dar kept eye contact, and injected a good dose of sincerity into her tone. "We'll move over here and wait, and you let us know when you're ready." She held her hand out. "Thanks."

The man took her hand and they exchanged clasps. "Can I get your name?" he asked. "Lieutenant's going to ask. They probably need to run a check."

"Sure." Dar motioned Kerry forward. "I'm Dar Roberts, and this is Kerry Stuart. We're with ILS."

The man scribbled down the names. "And those guys?" He indicated the bemusedly watching Andrew and Alastair.

"We're just footmen," Alastair spoke up, in a mild tone. "We came to help move that big round thing."

Andrew chuckled, and handed the man a bit of pasteboard card. "Thar," he said. "Ya'll don't half understand me when I talk up here anyhow."

Thus prompted, Alastair handed over his own business card. The guard took it and tucked it into his clipboard then moved over to the truck and stuck his head inside, picking up a radio mic and talking into it.

They walked over to the spool and sat down on it, the techs having laid it flat on the ground to keep it from rolling anywhere. "Dar," Alastair peered over at her, "how come you never talk nice to me like that?"

"You don't have a gun," Dar responded, deadpan. "Besides, with how I feel right now it was either be nice, or pick up that pipe and end up getting arrested. I figured nice was more productive." She rested her hands on the edge of the wooden spool and sighed.

Alastair was facing the pier, watching all the activity. "So," he said. "We roll this big thing inside the aircraft carrier, then what?"

"Then we hope the fiber tech coming here by train gets his ass here in time to terminate it to a patch panel I have no idea if we have inside, with connectors I don't know if he has with him and we can't get at your average hardware store or Radio Shack, and then connect that patch panel to another patch panel with cables that don't exist yet."

"Ah."

"Sounds like a Navy kinda plan," Andrew commented, with a faint chuckle under his breath. "Good to be out of that damn office though."

"Amen," Alastair said. "Is there anything we can do to fix any of those variables, Dar? Someplace we can get those things while you're charming the fatigues off all the boys?"

Dar turned her head and looked at Kerry. "Did we source those yet?"

Kerry checked her PDA, scrolling through messages with a flicker of the LCD. "Ah." She tapped on one and read it. "Yes, we did. We found a place that can make the patch cables, and has the bits and pieces for the patch panel." She tilted the device so Andrew could see it, as he pulled a half pencil from his shirt pocket and wrote down the address on the back of one of his cards.

Alastair craned his neck to watch. "Where is that? Long Island?"

"Yes," Kerry agreed. "It's nowhere close. I'd better send one of our guys for it so..."

"Ah, Ah, Ah." Alastair stood up. "Good grief. I'm the CEO of the biggest tech company on the planet. Don't you think I can find Long Island?" He motioned Andrew to stand up. "C'mon, Daddy Roberts. Let's go find us some bits and parts."

"All right," Andrew agreed. "Dar, you be all right here? I think these fellers are going to be okay."

"We'll be fine," Dar assured him. "Thanks for taking care of that for us. Sooner it gets here, sooner we can get this connected." She watched her father and boss walk off, heading for the corner to hail a cab. "Why do I feel nervous all of a sudden?"

Kerry leaned her head against Dar's shoulder. "Honey, I'm sure they can handle this." She exhaled. "Besides, we really need the stuff. I sent a list to the vendor, and he said he had it, but he didn't deliver and wasn't about to start."

"Nice."

"Can't really blame him." Kerry kicked her feet out a little. "We're not really local here. He didn't know me from Adam."

"With your voice, if he didn't know you from Adam I'm scared to be buying fiber from him," Dar remarked dryly. "Okay, here comes our boy. Let's see where this gets us." She got up as the two men approached.

The lieutenant was an older man, with grizzled gray hair and stocky body. He looked tired and harassed, which put him in league with everyone else in the city, she reckoned. "Lieutenant. Thank you for coming to talk with us."

The man nodded briefly. "Ms. Roberts, I've had a call from the mayor's office. We'll give you the access and anything else you might need. Sorry to hold you up. Everything's crazy here." He glanced at the pier. "I don't know what the hell's going on."

The other guard looked somber and apologetic.

"Please. Don't apologize, we know how stressed everyone must be." Kerry picked up the conversational ball. "We appreciate that you took the time to get everything sorted out. Is it okay for us to proceed now? I'll get my guys back from the hot dog stand."

"Sure," the lieutenant said. "John, give these folks an escort back to where they need to be, and a few hands to help move whatever this is." He gestured to the spool. "Ladies, have a good day." He turned and walked off. After an awkward moment, the other guard hurried after him, leaving Dar and Kerry alone with their spool again.

"Well," Kerry exhaled, "that was easier than I thought it would be. Want me to go get the gang?"

"Sure," Dar said. "I'll sit here and wish I was under a bus."

Kerry stroked her arm. Dar's face was a little pale, and she could see her biting the inside of her lip. "Honey, why don't you go to the hotel? I can handle this," she urged. "C'mon. You look like hell. It makes no sense for you to sit here and suffer. Go relax and get a heating pad or something."

Dar paused then looked mournfully at her. "I can't." She tilted her head and indicated the returning techs. "My macha won't let me. C"mon." She got up as the techs approached. "All right, folks. Let's get this rig rolling. They're letting us in."

"Your macha can kiss my ass," Kerry growled, earning her a raised eyebrow look from her partner. "I should have made your Dad take you back to the hotel."

"Hey, good deal," Scuzzy said. "You knew how to talk to those guys for sure, Dar from Miami."

The techs put their shoulders to the spool and got it upright, then pulled their gloves back on. They started rolling the spool carefully, laying out the fiber wire behind them as they maneuvered down the slight incline to the entrance of the museum.

The guardsmen drew the barricades aside and two of them came over. "Can we help?" the first one asked, a tall blond with a scar across his mouth. "Where you going?"

The techs looked at Dar. "That way." She indicated a tight path around one edge. "Down that ramp, between those two posts, and then stop by that second hatch panel." She stood back as the guard and the techs wrestled the spool of wire forward. "What was that about my macha?" she asked Kerry.

Kerry stuck her tongue out.

They followed the techs down the ramp and through the truck barricades, past the visitor entrance down to the walkway alongside where the big carrier was anchored. It was quieter here, since the museum was closed, and the sound of the Hudson lapping against the old pier was much louder.

It smelled rank. Kerry's nose wrinkled, as she glanced past the pier toward the shores of New Jersey. Above that, she could also smell the scent of iron, and grease and sun warmed metal, and they stopped just before a big metal housing from which extended thick black cables that ran into a hatch onboard the ship.

Dar studied it. "We need to figure how much we're going to need in slack, and cut it," she said. "That spool can't fit in the hatch."

The techs straightened up, and peered at the ship uncertainly. "Wow," the younger one sighed. "Didn't bring my measuring tape."

Dar ducked to one side and looked, trying to measure with her eyes. She shook her head. "Need to extend inside too." She headed for the lower gangway, which was chained off and led to an open shell door in the ship's side. "Let's see for how long."

After a quick look around Kerry followed her, and after a moment, the rest of them did too. They waited for Dar to unlatch the chain and let it fall, then they all trooped across the gangway, its surface flexing under their weight as they made for the entrance.

Dar didn't hesitate. She stepped over the edge of the shell door and entered the ship, ducking inside the next watertight door and into a larger open space.

Kerry got a flashback, suddenly, to the cruise ship. It had the same smell of age and old oil and she rubbed her nose as she carefully stepped over the door sill and followed Dar into the shadows. She found herself in a narrow hallway and spotted Dar ahead of her, sticking her head into an open doorway. "Dar?"

"In here." Dar squirmed into another compartment, this one admitting some light from outside. Kerry poked her head in, and saw the cables running in the opening. "Oh. That's the hole from outside."

"Uh huh." Dar turned and followed the cables to a pipe on the far wall, and tipped her head up. "Oh crap. I forgot it was two decks up."

Kerry looked up at the pipe, aware of the techs behind her. "Hang on guys, Dar's tracing the cable path."

"Dar's wishing she was curled up in a ball in the bilge, actually," her partner sighed. She went to the pipe and stuck her hand in it, then pulled it out and studied her extended fingers. "Might have space," she muttered. "Okay, we need to find either a thin cable, or stiff rope."

"Okay." Kerry backed up so the techs could hear. "Did you get that, guys? We need some cable — I guess Dar wants it for a pull string."

"Got a spool of Ethernet in the truck," the nearer tech offered. "That work?"

"Perfect." Dar's head appeared from around the doorway. "Get it, and I'll show you where the demarc room is. We can run a pull cable down here, and pull the fiber up once we get it across from the pier. Ker, while they do that, let's see if we can find a hank of rope."

"Rope. You got it." Kerry backed up so Dar could exit the space and then followed her as she started a methodical exploration of the pretty much deserted ship. They moved out of the tightly confined hallway and into a bigger space, with a tall ceiling that spanned the interior of the ship. "Wow."

"Hanger deck," Dar interpreted the exclamation. "Watch your step. There might be tie downs on the decking."

"Aye Aye, Captain Dar." Kerry shifted so she was walking in Dar's footsteps and put a hand out, hooking one finger on her partner's belt loop. "Did Dad sail on one of these?"

"He did," Dar answered, as she wandered around the big space, peeking behind boxes. "C'mon, they have to have a damn coil of rope in here. Who the hell heard of a Navy ship without rope?"

"What about over there?" Kerry pointed to something vaguely circular on the wall. "Is that rope?"

They walked over to the wall and looked up. On the metal surface was a hook, and from the hook a loop of thick rope was coiled, with a float fastened on one end. "Perfect," Dar complimented her, then for good measure, she turned and kissed her on the lips. "Absolutely perfect."

Kerry rested her hands on Dar's hips, gazing up into her eyes. After a long pause, they kissed again. "This has to be one of the last places on earth I'd ever expect to be doing this," she admitted, when they paused for breath. "But you know, it's kinda sexy."

Dar's eyes took on a twinkle in the half light. "Sure is. Making my cramps feel better too."

They rubbed noses, then reluctantly parted, as Dar turned to face the wall and started to take the rope down. "However, business first."

"Pfft."

KERRY'S CELL PHONE rang, sounding loud and jarring against the steel she was surrounded by. With a muffled curse, she pulled it out with her free hand and flipped it open, putting it to her ear as she squirmed around into a marginally better position. "Hello?"

"Kerry? This is your mother."

Kerry blinked at the steel wall inches from her face. "Oh. Hi," she said. "Where are you?"

"I have just returned home. Are you terribly occupied? I was wondering how things were going for you there."

How were things going? Kerry felt the cold surface chilling her back through her shirt. "Well." She grimaced as the edge of the pipe she had her arm extended up into bit into her skin. "We're making some progress."

"Are you? Wonderful. Where are you now?"

Kerry heard a curse echo softly down the interior of the pipe. "Lying on my back on the deck of a decommissioned aircraft carrier with my arm shoved up a pipe covered in axel grease," she responded with complete honesty. "You?"

Absolute silence. Kerry wiggled the tips of her fingers in the vain hope of feeling a bit of cable impacting them. Above her, through the pipe's metal confines she could hear Dar cursing, the soft grunts traveling down with wry accuracy to her ears.

"I don't understand," Cynthia finally said. "What exactly are you doing?"

"Well." Kerry squirmed a little and extended her fingers a bit more. "It's a long story. I'm helping hook up the emergency management office for the City of New York. In a really material way."

"Ah. I see."

"Ker?" Dar called down. "Anything?"

Kerry stretched and wiggled, closing her eyes as she wished the end of a cable probe into her hand. After a moment, she relaxed. "Sorry hon, no," she called back. "Not a damn thing."

"Shit."

Kerry returned her attention to the phone. "How are things there?" she asked. "Since they're sort of crummy here."

Her mother sighed, "I'm very disturbed. That's why I decided to call you. When I got here, one of my aides informed me that we have had several incidents of people being beaten."

"Beaten?"

"For being....well, I suppose they were thought to be from abroad."

Kerry heard footsteps and turned her head to see Dar's tall body slipping into her torture chamber. "Hey," she said. "Say hello to my mother."

"Hello Kerry's mother." Dar dropped down into a crouch. "Listen. There's something in the middle of that damn pipe that's stopping the probe. I can't get it to go any further."

"Hang on, Mother." Kerry put the phone on her chest. "So what's the plan?" She watched Dar's face, which had liberal streaks of grime on it. "Is there any way to clear whatever the obstruction is? Can you get inside the pipe anywhere?"

"I can," Dar said, "but it means I've got a good chance of ripping up whatever else is in there. I think it's a damn cable tie that's blocking it."

"A cable tie?"

"Yeah." Dar sat down and braced her elbows against her knees, grimacing. "I feel like such crap."

Kerry gazed compassionately at her. "I wish I could give you a hug, hon, but I don't think this axle grease being all over you is going to make you feel any better." She put the phone back to her ear. "Sorry, Mother. Did you say someone was attacked?"

"I can see you're very busy Kerry. I will be glad to fill you in later, if you want. Please go take care of poor Dar. She sounds terrible," her mother said. "I have another call to take, so we can speak later."

"Okay. I'll call you when I'm somewhere more comfortable," Kerry promised. "Goodbye." She closed the phone and clipped it back on her pocket to free her hand, which she then put on Dar's leg. "Cable tie?"

"Yeah," Dar repeated, gazing at her dirt covered hands. "One of the big half inch ones, turned sideways."

Kerry pictured it and made a face. "How in the hell do we get past that? Why the hell would someone put it in there, anyway?"

"Figured nothing else would need to go in the pipe I guess, or it twisted...who the hell knows?" Dar sighed. "Maybe if I can find a rod long enough, I can put some kind of edge on it and cut through it." She blinked a few times. "I tried to find an outside hatch or something...anything to bring the cable through somewhere else, but I couldn't."

Kerry eased her arm out of the pipe, her skin covered in black goo. She sat up and flexed her fingers, looking around with a vague sense of despair. The light was a bare fluorescent fixture, a pale, dim glare that hurt her eyes and made the metal space even more depressing. "Dar, I'm sorry."

"For what?" Tired blue eyes regarded her.

"Sorry I can't make this better," Kerry admitted. "Sorry we're here. Sorry we can't leave and go rest."

"Me too," Dar agreed. She rested in silence a moment more, then she started hauling herself to her feet. "Jason," she called into the hallway. "You back?"

"Yes, ma'am." One of the techs appeared immediately. "We measured the rope you threw over to the pier, and we've got enough cable, ma'am. You want me to tie the end of the rope to the end of the fiber? John found a hardware store too, so he's going to go get some flexible ducting."

Dar paused, one hand on the metal doorsill. "He found a hardware store near here?"

Jason nodded his tow colored, curly head. "Little place. Not like a Home Depot or anything, but they got stuff." He glanced over at Kerry who was carefully keeping her greased up forearm away from her clothing. "Wow. That looks gross," he blurted, then looked abashed. "Sorry ma'am."

"It does look gross," Kerry agreed. "I feel like a plumber on a bad day."

"Jason." Dar spoke, suddenly, her eyes a trifle unfocused. "Tell John to get to that hardware store. Get a metal rod, long as he can find, and a stick soldering iron, the narrowest one they have, plus a spool of metal wire."

"Uh." Jason pulled a small pad out of the back pocket of his khakis and started scribbling on it. "A metal rod, ma'am? How big?"

"Half inch. If they don't have rods, get the narrowest conduit they have," Dar said. "Eight or twelve foot length if you can get it."

"Gotcha, ma'am," Jason nodded. "And you want a soldering iron?"

"A soldering iron," Dar confirmed. "And a 16 or 14 gauge extension cord at least twenty five feet long. Got that?" she asked. "And a bar of soap."

"Got it." Jason trotted off. "Not sure what I got, but we'll get it. Be right back."

Dar went to the open hatch and perched on the edge, taking in a breath of diesel tinged brackish water air, letting her hand drop to rest on the coil of rope. She glanced up as Kerry came over to join her. "Ugh."

"Ugh." Kerry sorted through Dar's hair, pulling it out from under her collar and riffling it in the light breeze coming through the hatch. Looking up the river this way, everything looked so normal. She could see the other piers, all old and rusted, and the buzz of activity on the rooftop parking lot of the furthest one down the way that was the emergency center.

A few small boats moved quietly past, police boats with slowly flashing lights. They were too far away to see the two figures in the opening, but they cruised past, obviously watchful. In the distance, the air was hazy and from the right she could hear the muted sounds of the city.

Jason finished tying the rope to the cable, and waved at them. He stood by the spool, and started unwinding it as Dar sighed and stood up again, taking hold of the rope and starting to haul it in. "Watch it."

Kerry took a step back, holding her grease covered arm out to one side and out of the way. "Want more Advil?"

"Yes." Dar stolidly coiled the rope as it came in, making a neat circle on the deck. "Please."

With a nod, Kerry turned and headed out of the small space, glad to take a break and stretch her legs. She moved down the hallway and into the hangar deck again, aware of the slowly fading light as the sun edged toward the west and left the outside in a haze of blue.

She entered the small office-like room they'd stored their bags and gear in. It had a desk against the wall and filing cabinets on either side. The furniture was functional but plain, and there were banners on the wall celebrating the many functions and trials the Intrepid had gone through.

"Ugh." Kerry paused, as she remembered not to touch her bag with her right hand. She opened the latches with her left, and fished inside the leather sack, finding her bottle of Advil and pulling it out. She removed her bottle of water along with it, and latched the bag shut again, turning to head back out of the room.

Her cell phone rang. She almost reached for it, then stopped again, and cursed. "Son of a..." She went back to the desk and put the bottles down, then grabbed the phone. "Kerry Stuart."

"Hey, Kerry. It's Mark."

Could be good, could be bad. "Hey, Mark. What's up?" Kerry sat down on the edge of the desk. "We're making some progress here in case anyone's asking on the call." She wrinkled her nose at the smell of the axle grease.

"They found our two guys here."

Kerry felt her own breathing stop. The tone of Mark's voice held more explanation than any words could have, and she bit the inside of her lip feeling a deep pang of loss for these unknown to her techs that had, at some level, traced up an org chart to her name. "I see."

"They were in that part that got hit," Mark added, after a moment's silence. "About all they could identify were their badges."

Oh my god. "I'm sorry, Mark. Did you know them well?" Kerry wasn't really sure of what to say, or really of what she was saying. It just sounded like random words.

"I didn't. The guys here did though." Mark sounded somber. "Danny's pretty trashed. I sent them off to hang out for a while. My guys are handling the stuff."

Kerry exhaled heavily. "Okay," she said. "Have you told Mariana yet? "

"No. Called you first."

Only right. "Send me their names," Kerry said. "I'll call her. We'll get the process started." She felt profoundly sad. "And contact their families."

"Okay. Will do," Mark said. "Sorry to bring such totally sucky news. Stuff's going pretty good here otherwise. We got a few more circuits in. Those telco guys really helped."

"Good," Kerry murmured. "Glad to hear that, anyway. Let me get hold of Mari so she can get the ball rolling. I know she was sending some people here to talk to the staff. I want to make sure she sends some folks there too."

"Okay boss," Mark said. "Talk to you later."

Kerry closed her phone and simply sat there for a few minutes. The senselessness of it all overwhelmed her and she closed her eyes, sparing a bit of her soul and thinking of the split second of terror and heat and pain the techs must have suffered.

There was no sound, no indication of any one approaching, but Kerry was suddenly aware of Dar's close presence, and she opened her eyes just as her partner's hand touched her cheek and she looked up at her in question.

"Had a feeling you needed me," Dar said bluntly. "What's wrong?"

Kerry leaned against her touch. "Humanity," she answered. "I think the whole fucking species sometimes is just one big screw up."

Dar ignored her grease covered arm and settled against her anyway, putting an arm around her shoulders and pulling her close. "Present company excluded."

Kerry turned and buried her face against Dar's shoulder, allowing herself that little time out before the nightmare continued to roll on.

ANDREW STUDIED THE small bit of cardboard in his hand as he maneuvered down a steep set of stairs bracketed by old fashioned brass railing. He got to the bottom of the steps and was pleased to find a train waiting, its doors open. "Figure that's the one."

"You're probably right," Alastair agreed. "And with the bridges and tunnels still tied up, this is the fastest way to get where we need to be. Damn nice to have rapid transit that's both, isn't it?"

Andrew made a low grunting sound. He led the way into the train and they found a couple of seats near the front with enough room for Andrew's long legs and got themselves settled. "Hope them kids are getting on all right" he said.

Alastair folded his hands over his stomach. "You know, I don't think of them as kids."

"You ain't their father."

"That's very true," Alastair admitted. "I've got my own handful back home, but I'll tell you what, they're nothing compared to yours."

Andrew chuckled and sat back, tapping his thumbs together in front of him. "How many you got?"

"Three," Alastair responded promptly. "Two girls and a boy. Two of them are married, and I've got three grandkids." He glanced at his traveling companion. "I think Dar said she was an only child?"

One grizzled eyebrow twitched, as Andrew peered back at him. "Ah do believe that one was sufficient," he paused, as the doors closed, and the train prepared to leave the station. "Though mah wife and I did think about another, it was tough on her."

"Ah." Alastair nodded. "My daughter had trouble with her first. He was born breech."

"Wall." Andy glanced out the window as the train moved through the underground tunnels that burrowed into Manhattan Island and into Penn station. "Dar came right way round, but wasn't no small baby and mah wife ain't big." He glanced down at his long legs. "I do believe that's likely mah fault."

"Dar does take after you, no doubt," Alastair agreed. "Spitting image, matter of fact. I remember meeting you the first time and being struck by that." His PDA chirped, and he removed it from his pocket, opening it to review. "Excuse me."

Andrew was content to turn his head and watch the windows change from underground darkness to the late afternoon light. He was glad they were off doing something useful, though it was possible they could have done some good back at the flattop.

He pulled the list of things from his pocket and studied them again. They appeared to be something like electrical parts, but he figured Dar certainly knew what she was looking for. He watched the landscape go by for a moment more then removed his cell phone from his pocket and opened it.

There were only a few numbers in the speed dial, and he selected one and keyed it in, putting the phone to his ear and waiting for it to be answered. "Lo there."

"Ah, my husband," Ceci replied. "Where are you?"

"'Nother damn train," Andrew said. "Goin out to get Dar some special cables and some such. What are you up to?"

"Well," Ceci said. "Believe it or not, my family called, either to find out whether we were all right, or if we were part of the insurrection, hard to say. My sister sends her regards."

Andrew made a slightly snorting noise.

"Well, she does," his wife responded mildly. "How are Dar and Kerry doing?"

"Them kids are having a time," Andrew said. "Ah don't think Dar's feeling well, and ever'body's chewing a piece of them all over. Makes mah eyeballs itch," he grumbled. "People here are pretty shook up though. Bad stuff."

"I saw on TV," Ceci murmured. "Andy, you stay away from that place, okay? They've still got buildings falling down around everywhere and I don't want you near any of them."

"No problem," Andrew said. "Right now me and th...Dar's boss are on this here train heading for Long Island. Ain't nothing keeling over out there, and Dar's over at that old flattop off the Hudson fussing with them bolts and nuts there."

Ceci chuckled wryly. "No matter what the situation, she ends up with the Navy."

"Eh," her husband smiled briefly. "Got salt water in her even if she didn't end up no swab." There was something of that he was happy with. The sea had been a passion of his since the first time he'd seen it, opening wide in front of him after an eternally long two months in basic training up at Great Lakes.

Huge. Beautiful. Full of deep greens and blues and rich with salt like nothing ever before in his life had been back in Alabama. He'd loved everything about it, even the rough motion in weather, and the agonizingly small amount of space he'd been assigned for someone his size.

Finding his daughter with the same love in her heart had charmed him. Some of the best times when Dar was growing up had centered around the beach, and the sea and the underwater world they all shared.

"She certainly does," Ceci interrupted his musing. "But that's not helping her there now. Anything we can do from here? Can I use my nonexistent family influence and insult someone for her? Browbeat some government official? Offer to paint the president in the nude? Wait. Scratch that one."

Andrew chuckled in reflex. "Y'all do say the damnedest things."

"It's hard being here and just watching," Ceci admitted. "At least you're there on trains getting gizmos. All I can do here is watch CNN and try to imagine what scandal Miami will be involved in next in this whole thing. You know that airport Dar landed in was where all those terrorists trained in."

"Ah heard."

"I feel like they're going to close the border at Orlando."

Andy chuckled again. "You just keep your head down there on Dar's island. We'll fix this joint up best we can and head back soon as we're able," he promised. "Got to go now. Ah think this train's fixing to tunnel again."

"Call me back later, sailor boy."

"Yes' ma'am. G'bye." Andrew shut the phone and leaned back, tapping it against his knee as his brow furrowed into a frown. "Know what?" he addressed Alastair. "This here world surely does suck sometimes."

Alastair looked up from his PDA. "Sure does," he answered after a brief pause. "Wish we could find another one sometimes."

KERRY REMOVED THE contents of the brown paper bag and set them down on the piece of metal wall near where Dar was working. They were up on the second level now, in the space where the cable would have to come up.

There was no opening in the space except the small oval door hatches, and it was close inside, full of the scent of grease and silicon. Against one wall was a large patch cabinet painted with thick coats of paint to match the inside of the ship. The door to it was open exposing a plethora of connections, and there was already a shunt opened in the side to receive the new cable.

Dar was standing near the wall where the pipe emerged, a long piece of thin conduit in her hand and a soldering iron in the other. "Let's see."

Kerry set out the various supplies, glad she'd taken the time to go and get most of the grease off her skin so it wasn't getting all over the place. She could still smell it though, and cast a brief, wistful thought toward a nice long shower with lots of soap to scrub with.

Dar leaned the pipe against the wall and concentrated on the soldering iron, using a tiny screwdriver from the tech's tool kit to unfasten the plastic grip and remove it. She experimentally fit it into the end of the pipe, glancing up as Jason stuck his head in the hatchway. "I think this will work."

Jason eyed her. "Yes ma'am," he responded dubiously, "if you say so. Is there something else we can do in the meantime? Any prep we can do for the fiber guy?"

Dar looked around. "I need some 110 cable in here. Can you rig that while I'm duct taping and twining us into a solution for this pain in the ass problem?"

"Sure." Jason disappeared.

Kerry took the opportunity to sidle closer. "What are you doing with that hon?"

"Trying to resist the urge to bash it against the wall," Dar responded. "It's probably good they're leaving us alone in here. You're the only person I want around me right now."

Responding to the compliment, Kerry pressed her cheek against Dar's shoulderblade, then kissed it.

Dar put the pipe back against the wall and looked at the plug of the soldering iron holding it up against the opening. It was obviously too big to fit inside. She went over to the makeshift shelf and pawed among the supplies. "I need wire nuts."

"Wire nuts," Kerry repeated. "Is that something I need to send the guys back for?"

"No." Dar removed a pair of cutters from the toolbox. "I'll just tape the damn thing." She cut off the end of the plug, then removed the extension cord from its wrapping and cut off the female end as well.

Kerry merely stood back and watched, her arms folded across her chest.

With the cutters, Dar clipped the cord in the middle of the two wires, and pulled the ends apart. She then stripped off the ends exposing the copper. She repeated the process on the end of the cable connected to the soldering iron.

Setting the cutters down, she took one of the ends from each cable and twisted it together, taking a piece of the duct tape and wrapping it around the ends. She repeated the act with the other end, then she wrapped all of it together into a neat bundle. "There."

"Okay." Kerry glanced at the pipe. "Did you want to put that through the pipe there before you connected that? Cause the other end won...sorry, sweetheart."

Dar was banging her head gently against the metal wall.

"You did such a pretty job though." Kerry picked up the other end of the extention cord and examined it. "You can do that with this end too if we cut it off, right?"

"I want ice cream," Dar sighed.

"Me too. Should I cut this off though? I got the idea." Kerry picked up the cutters. "You want to put the cable down that pipe, then plug it in, right?"

"Right."

Kerry clipped the plug off and retrieved the pipe, carefully threading the end of the cord through it and pushing it down. She continued until she got to the taped part, which she wiggled in and coaxed onward, glancing at the bottom of the pipe and smiling as she saw the end of the cord emerge. "There."

Dar fit the soldering iron into the end of the pipe and took the tape, strapping the device in as tightly as she could. "Thanks," she eyed Kerry, "my brain is a little off right now."

Kerry walked to the other end of the pipe and drew the cable out. It extended a good foot outside the pipe. She took the cutters neatly cutting the end and pulling it apart as she'd seen Dar do.

Electrical work was definitely not a general part of her skill set. In fact, she hadn't thought it was part of Dar's since her partner had contacted electricians on the few occasions they had issues either at the condo or the cabin.

However, this seemed simple enough. She picked up the plug she'd cut off and split the ends there then looked at it. "Dar, does it matter which one connects to what?"

"One of the cables has a white line," Dar answered. "White to white. Brown to brown."

"Oh." Kerry examined the cable, and proceeded. "Cool."

They worked in silence for a few minutes until Dar had the soldering iron fastened to her satisfaction. Then she set the pipe aside, coming over to Kerry's side to watch her finish taping the ends of the cable. "Good job."

"First time I've ever done that," Kerry admitted. "Now what?"

"Now we wait for 110 power." Dar carefully leaned the conduit against the wall. "Then we plug that in, I stick the pole down the pipe and with any luck, I use the soldering iron to melt the cable tie."

Kerry studied the pipe then turned to look at her partner. "Dar, that's really ingenious."

"Thanks." Dar sat down on a metal shelf. "I could have tried to shear through it with a blade, but chances are I'd cut through some of the damn cabling in there and that's the last thing we need." She exhaled as Kerry came over and put her arms around her neck, cradling the side of her face and kissing her on the cheek. "Mm."

"You're so damn smart," Kerry whispered in her ear. "I wanna be you when I grow up."

Dar let her forehead rest against Kerry's collarbone. "Know what I want?"

"More Advil?"

"That or a gun," Dar sighed. "Cause I don't think this day's ever going to end."

IT WAS COMPLETELY dark by the time their train pulled back into Penn Station halting with a jerk and a screech and the hiss of hydraulic doors preparing to open.

"Well." Alastair stood up and opened the storage bin over the seats. "That wasn't so bad."

"Nope." Andrew also stood, stretching out his long frame before he carefully lifted a box from in front of his feet and cradled it. "Glad that place wasn't but a minute from the train. That feller was looking to close up on us."

"Wasn't very friendly was he," Alastair agreed. He pulled down another big brown sack and followed Andrew as he stepped off the car and back into the lower levels of Penn Station.

"Jackass," Andrew grunted. "Like he was doin' us a favor selling this stuff." He paused to let a woman with a large child stroller move past then continued.

"Then asking twenty questions about what we're going to do with it." Alastair frowned. "What in the hell did he think we were going to do with it? Install fiber optics in our hotel room?"

"Jackass."

It was a bit quieter now, the rush hour just getting passed, and when they climbed up the brass lined stairs to the concourse there seemed to be more National Guard in the area than passengers. A number of the guards with large dogs on leashes were nearby.

Everyone walking by looked a little nervous. But the dogs merely sat there, tongues lolling, waiting to be called into whatever action they were apparently trained for.

At least it was less chaos. Alastair tucked the bag of gewgaws under his arm and was glad of the noise reduction. He gave the guardsmen a pleasant smile as they crossed the open concourse and headed for the hallway that would eventually take them to the escalator and outside.

"Long day," he commented. They entered the main part of the station, a large, high ceilinged space with several branch corridors and plenty of signage pointing to trains and subways in three different directions.

"Got that right," Andrew agreed as they headed up another hall. He glanced to one side and then paused. "Goin' to get me a hot dog. You want one?" He indicated a shop to one side.

Alastair looked past him to a cluttered gathering of fast food marquees, all crammed into one low ceilinged space. "Why, sure," he said. "Been a long time since lunch."

Andrew went inside and set his box down on a table near the hot dog counter. He removed his wallet from his back pocket and advanced on the woman behind the counter, turning his head as he stopped. "You want one with all them things on it?"

Alastair set his bag down on the box and pondered the menu. "Chili dog," he said. "Might as well hold up my end of the Texas stereotype."

"Gimme two of them there things, and some taters, and a couple of cokes," Andrew addressed the woman.

The woman studied him. "You want two chili dogs, French fries, and two sodas?" She hazarded a guess.

"Yeap."

"No problem." The woman turned to take care of the order, leaving Andrew to loiter in front of the desk. Near the back a man was starting to clean up, putting chairs up on tables to sweep under them, carefully avoiding the two tables of guardsmen finishing up their dinner.

Andrew briefly pondered bringing some dogs back for Dar and Kerry, but figured they'd be stone cold before they got out there, and a mess to boot. He turned and leaned against the counter, folding his arms over his chest.

Alastair took a seat and rested his elbows on his knees. Having a chili dog in a train station didn't even seem odd after the last few days. He could barely even remember how the morning had started and he found he was mostly looking forward to some kind of success before the night ended.

He suspected there would be one. Dar generally created success, which was one of the reasons he trusted her the way he did. He also suspected she was probably waiting on their return, but he figured a five minute stop for hot dogs probably wouldn't skew the pitch one way or the other.

His cell phone was off. He intended it to remain that way until they were back at the port, when there was some chance he could actually report on whatever status whatever politician on the other end was asking for.

Right now, tired as he was, he gained a glimmer of understanding of the undisguised sigh of exasperation that Dar sometimes uttered when she was being hounded for something. Sometimes, you could do what you could do, when you could do it.

"Here." Andrew handed him a cardboard box, which had a hot dog and a paper dish of fries in it with a little plastic pseudo fork poked in them. "Figure that is good as any till we finish up." He took a seat at the table and bit into his dog.

Alastair followed suit tilting his head a bit as he realized the guardsmen were watching them. He wondered if they looked particularly suspicious or something. He glanced at both himself and Andrew, then at their burdens, which he'd shifted carefully to the floor so they could eat on the table.

Hm. Two guys, in a train station, with a brown box and a brown bag full of electrical parts, and one of the guys was wearing combat boots and a face full of scars. He watched the guardsmen in his peripheral vision as they all started looking their way and whispering.

Andrew shifted a little, so that he was facing Alastair and could see over his shoulder. His eyebrows hiked up a little.

Alastair took another bite of his hotdog. "Not bad," he commented, wiping his lips on a napkin and hoping the guard would find some other thing to interest them.

"S'allright," Andrew agreed. "Two things I always did like t'eat round here is hot dogs and pizza pie. Had liberty here once and mah whole SEAL team went and got us ten of them big pies and we nearly got ourselves sick to death with it. Still like it though."

Alastair chuckled. "Have to say when I was in the Army, the most interesting place we ended up having liberty in was Fargo, North Dakota. Those people know how to party, I'll say that." He thought the conversation had died down over at the other table, but didn't want to be obvious and look.

"Army, huh?" Andrew gave him a wry grin.

"I'm from Texas. It's a family tradition," Alastair admitted. "Granddaddy was in, Daddy was in, I did the ROTC rounds in college...I kept it to one hitch, though. After that I decided I liked climbing the corporate ladder better than the one in the obstacle course." He finished off the last bite of his hot dog and poked among the wedge cut fries, selecting one with the little forklet and tasting it. "What made you pick the Navy?"

"Didn't like hiking around with them big old packs," Andrew said. "And ah figured at the least I'd learn me to swim in the Navy. Don't do that much in Alabama." He paused, studying a fry. "Wanted to see something but dirt roads and candy assed rednecks."

Alastair glanced casually over at the guardsmen, who were now studiously looking in another direction. "I got to see a little bit of Korea," he mused. "Then I got posted in Italy and Belgium. That wasn't so bad. "

Andrew stood and took his cardboard tray over to the trash and disposed of it. He glanced at the guardsmen as he finished. "Lo there, you all."

"Hello." The one nearest him nodded respectfully. "Something you need from us?"

"Nope." Andrew shook his head. "Hope you all have a good night now." He returned to the table and picked the box up while Alastair disposed of his tray and came back to join him. They exited the food stop and headed across the concourse toward the exit.

"You know, I don't think I ever heard you mention what you did in the Navy before," Alastair commented, giving his taller companion a sideways look.

Andrew chuckled a bit. "Didn't want them fellers asking me what all was in these here boxes cause I don't have not one jack clue what it is," he admitted. "Figgured if I started flapping my jaw about what I done they'd mind themselves."

"And they did." Alastair clapped him on the back. "Good decision. Because frankly, though I paid for them, and I can pronounce the names, damned if I know what this stuff is either." They got to the escalator and rode it up, passing from the claustrophobic concourse into the street that was quieter than they expected, in a city that now seemed exhausted in a strange kind of way.

"Taxi!" Alastair waved one down. "Let's see what your kids have gotten us into." He handed his bag to the driver, who set it in the trunk along with Andrew's box. "And if we're very lucky, it's beer time."

"Won't be luck."

"Not with your kid, no. You're right. It sure won't"

"OKAY, HANG ON." Kerry wriggled under the pipe again and got her eyeball to where she could see up it, poking her slim flashlight into the space and turning it on. "See that?"

"Got it." Dar's voice came down tinnily. "Get your face out of the way in case something comes shooting out of this damn pipe."

"Yes, Grandma." Kerry edged over so she could keep the light in place, but removed most of her head from the danger zone.

She could hear Dar maneuvering the pipe into place overhead, and just as she reached up to scratch her nose, a big clump of pipe crud came tumbling down landing near her ear. She could hear a soft curse, and in the tone, she sensed her partner's frustration both with the tedious project and the cramps she was still suffering from.

Dar wasn't usually that unlucky. Kerry suspected it was the stress of the situation that was tying her up in knots and making her monthly cycle worse than usual, and she herself had the same thing to look forward to any minute now.

"Okay, I'm heating up the iron," Dar called down.

"Go for it, babe." Kerry tapped lightly on the pipe with her flashlight. She was tired, and hungry, and the worst part of it was knowing that even when they finished this crazy jury rig, all they could do was pull the cable into place.

They still had to wait for the fiber terminator to come in, and finish the connection so they could get it working.

Kerry's nose twitched, as she smelled the odd scent of heating metal. She peeked up the pipe and saw a hint of motion in her flashlight's glare, now outlining the blockage that was preventing the cable from passing.

Sure enough, the light reflected off dusty white plastic, a zip tie wrapped around the cables already in the pipe, its end extending across and bending against the far pipe wall. Kerry could just see the tip of the soldering iron approaching the tie and she had to smile again at the ingenuity of her partner.

Who would have thought of using a soldering iron? She was pretty sure she wouldn't have. Kerry pondered a moment as to what she would have done, given the limited options. Used a knife on a stick?

Not try getting it through?

Would she have gotten someone, a construction worker, to come in and cut through the pipe so she could access it?

"Watch out," Dar warned. "I'm about to start melting things."

Kerry gazed up at her overprotective spouse. "Okay, I'm clear."

She edged her head out of the way, cocking her ears as she heard Dar curse again. She felt sorry for the two techs, trapped in the small space with her irritated partner. "Easy honey. We're almost done."

She could smell burning plastic. "I think you got it, Dar. I can smell it."

"Maybe that's my brain cells frying," Dar responded, her voice echoing softly.

Grumpy grumpy. Kerry licked her lips, and peeked up the pipe again, seeing a wisp of smoke showing in the light. A moment later, the tip of the soldering iron jerked to one side, and a piece of curled, blackened white plastic plummeted down and smacked her flashlight before she jerked her hand out of the way and it landed on the ground. "Hey! It's out!"

"Wooeffing hoo," Dar grunted, soft clanking noises and dust bunnies issuing down the pipe as she removed her makeshift tool. "I'm going to send the pull cable down."

Kerry removed the flashlight and shut it off, laying there quietly and enjoying the cool breeze from the opening, resisting the urge to close her eyes. She could hear the cable snaking its way down the conduit, and a moment later, the RJ45 end covered in tape plonked its way onto the metal deck near her head. "Yay!"

She got up and took hold of the cable, pulling it gently until about two feet of it was outside the conduit. Then she turned and took hold of the cable Dar had pulled in through the hatch, carefully tying the end of the fiber to the Ethernet cable and pulling it taut. "Dar?"

"Yes?"

Kerry jumped, as the voice sounded right behind her head. "Yow!" She reeled backwards off her crouch, waving her arms until Dar grabbed hold of her and let her regain her balance. "For Pete's sake!"

Dar chuckled tiredly. "Left the guys up there to haul this thing up. I vote we go and get something hot to eat, and a beer."

Kerry stopped moving and slumped back against her. "Ugh. I love you."

"Likewise." Dar hugged her, then let her go. "Feed the wire up there, and let's haul. Maybe by the time we get back, our fiber man'll be here, and we'll be in the home stretch."

Kerry eased the end of the fiber into the pipe, and Dar knocked against it. After a moment, it started to move, snaking it's way slowly up from its pile of coils on the floor up through the pipe to the second level.

Dar watched it, and dusted her hands off. "Things are looking up," she said. "We might get outta here tonight."

"Piece of cake now," Kerry agreed. "All we need is some ends." She jumped a trifle as her end was smacked, and scooted for the door. "It should go smoothly now, right?"

"Right."

Chapter Four

DAR WAS GLAD enough to feel the springiness of the gangway under her feet as she preceded Kerry toward the pier. Around her, the city seemed muted, sounds of sirens audible and the soft roar of traffic only barely.

She could smell the pungent scent of the water, but above that, on the wind now blowing from the sea, she could smell the burning, acrid scent of destruction, and the taint left a strange taste on the back of her tongue.

The darkness hid the billow of smoke still emerging from the Trade Center site, but if she looked up, and off to the horizon, she could see the stars being obscured by it.

"So where do we go from here?" Kerry asked, her hands tucked inside the pockets of her jacket. "All we need is the terminations, right?" She caught up to Dar and walked alongside her, their steps sounding an odd echo as they moved off the gangway and onto the concrete pier.

"Right," Dar said, "and to integrate the datastream, but that's trivial compared to everything else on the physical layer."

Kerry removed one hand from her pocket and tucked it through Dar's elbow. "You sound so sexy when you talk like that."

"Ker-ry." Dar gave her a sideways look.

"C'mon hon. I have to take my fun where I can find it tonight," Kerry responded wryly. "Let's walk down to that bar you mentioned, and see if we can get some nasty bar food or a pizza and a beer. Hell, I'd even take a hot dog right now."

"Me too." Dar exhaled, feeling some of the tension in her unwind. The last big hurdle was done, and she was actually looking forward to finishing out this particular task and getting on with the much larger one ahead.

They walked along the pier toward the gates, which now had some lurid, orange lights outlining the guard vehicles blocking the way. As they got closer to the gates, the sounds of arguing voices were heard and they stepped up the pace by silent accord.

"Hope that's not Dad out there," Kerry muttered. "I thought those guys were okay with us."

"If it was Dad, they wouldn't be yelling," Dar responded. "Let's see what's going on."

They got to the gates, and ducked through the opening to find a half circle of armed guardsmen facing off against three young men in jeans and windbreakers. All were carrying backpacks. Two of them were tow-headed and fair skinned, the third was dark skinned, and had black, straight hair.

The guardsman in charge, a different man than when they'd entered, was on a radio, giving the trio dark looks as he talked into it. "Not sure what to do with these guys, sir," he said, just audible to them.

"They've got all kinds of tools and some crazy story."

"Uh oh." Kerry slowed. "Maybe we should stay back."

Dar hesitated, taking in the angry stances and the weapons and almost decided Kerry was right, until their forward motion took them into the floodlights and the young men spotted them.

They weren't familiar to her, but apparently she was familiar to them, because the look of relief on all three faces was almost comical.

The closest one called out, "Ms. Roberts! Tell these guys not to shoot us!"

"Then again, maybe not." Kerry released Dar's arm and followed her into the light. "Looks like they're ours. Mark's guys, probably."

"Probably." Dar sighed, continuing past the trucks toward the crowd. "Don't shoot, gentlemen."

The guard in charge turned, startled to find them behind him. "Holy shit hang on...I've got some people inside here." He pulled the radio from his mouth. "Who are you people? What are you doing inside that gate?"

"Someone didn't leave handover notes." Kerry sighed. "Jesus."

"Now I wish it was my father out here." Dar grimaced. "Okay, hold it everyone. Let's discuss this before people start getting hurt," she said. "Let me start from the beginning."

"Let me start from the beginning," the guard captain said. "Let's see some identification from you people."

Uh oh. Kerry removed her identification case from her pocket and stepped forward, holding the leather case out to the man. "Okay, here's mine. We've been in here since this afternoon, one of your colleagues allowed us in after he checked us out with the mayor's office."

"What?" The man grabbed her folio and glanced at it. "No one said anything about people being inside there. Who are you people?"

"I'm sorry if they didn't leave you word," Kerry said, in a calm voice. "But we came in here around three o'clock. We've been working inside the ship this whole time." She took a step closer to him, aware of Dar's alert presence at her back. "We don't want to cause you trouble. These people here are employees of ours."

"Boy, we're glad to see you, Ms. Stuart," the tech said. "They sent us from Washington. They said you needed us."

"Shut up," the guardsman ordered. "Go stand over there, both of you. I don't know who you are, and I'm not buying some crazy story that you got let in here earlier. Don't you people know what's been going on around here?"

Dar just walked past him, catching Kerry's arm as she went and gently hauling her along with her. She stopped where the techs were, all of them visibly relaxing. "You our fiber boys?"

"Yes, ma'am," the talkative one said. "I'm Shaun Durhan, this is Mike Thomas, and Kannan Barishmorthy."

Dar had her hands in her pockets, and was regarding them mildly. "Dar Roberts," she finally said, then glanced to her left. "Kerry Stuart.

The men all blushed a little. "Yeah, we knew that," Shaun said. "Glad you came out here. They were really starting to hassle us, especially Kannan."

Dar glanced at the third man, her brows contracting. "Kannan?"

She knew the name, vaguely. Mark had spoken well of him, she remembered, one of their H1B Visa candidates she recalled signing off on. "Why?"

"They often joke that some people do not understand geography," Kannan said in a quiet voice. "However I did think most knew the difference between the Middle East and India."

"Don't count on it." Kerry glanced behind her, where the guardsman had now taken her identification and ducked inside his command car with it and his radio. "My mother said they'd been expecting some problems in Michigan with a backlash."

"Expecting?" Kannan eyed her. "Ma'am, there were two men from my home country already killed there, beaten in their shops from people thinking they were Arabs."

Kerry remembered the call earlier, and bit off a curse.

"Well." Dar exhaled. "I'm sure having a bunch of them living in Miami without being detected didn't help anything." She looked around. "It would be like one of them living here. How could you tell? Half the cabbies in the damn city come from that part of the world."

"Well there...what are you folks all doing out here?" Alastair shifted the bag in his arms. "Waiting for us?"

Andrew was right behind him with his box, glancing alertly around at the guard, the command car, and the small group waiting outside the gates. "We got trouble now?" He came up next to Dar and cocked his head in question. "How're you feeling, Dardar?"

"Frustrated." Dar craned her head around to look at the command car. "You can give those things to these guys. It's their gear." She indicated the techs. "You three might want to fish through there and make sure we got everything."

The techs took possession of the bundles and knelt next to them on the ground, opening up the bag and peering inside it. "Kannan, this is your stuff." Shaun handed it over. "Let me get the box open."

"Ah, yes. Thank you so much." Kannan sat down on the ground and removed his pack, swinging it around and setting it down next to his leg.

"Hey! What are you people doing?" The guard commander circled his truck and approached them. "What's going on here? Who are you two?" He pointed at Kannan. "Get those things away from that guy—he's one of them!"

"One of them what?" Kerry turned in confusion. "He's our fiber tech. What's wrong with..."

"Shut up. You're probably in it with him. All of you, a bunch of t..."

Kerry got in front of him. "They're also part of our company. Look, can't we just call the command that was here earlier?" She held up both hands, then realized he wasn't going to stop and couldn't get out of the way in time before she was shoved hard to one side. "Hey!"

"Get out of my way. You men, over here. Bring that..." The guard commander hauled up short as Dar suddenly surged into rapid motion, coming right up into his face with her hands raising up into fists. "What the hell do you...hey!"

Dar had him by the front of his shirt. "You stupid little piece of shit!" She yelled at top volume. "What in the hell do you think you're doing pushing around the people who pay your fucking salary?"

"Oh boy." Alastair moved nervously forward. "This is going to end badly, I can tell."

The guard reeled backwards, then reached for the gun hanging off his back and started pulling it around only to find himself lifted up off his feet and shoved through the air back against his truck as his rifle was taken from his hands in a single, smooth motion. "Why you..."

"Hold UP!" Andrew barked, taking the safety off the gun and cocking it. "Paladar, you get back."

Dar took a single step back, her hands at her sides, fingers twitching.

The other soldiers belatedly started forward, only to halt when Andrew slowly moved his head in their direction.

"Put them damn things down," Andrew ordered. "And you still yourself, mister." He addressed the guard commander. "'Fore I shoot you in the nuts and save us all the trouble of you spreading out them know-nothing genes."

The other guardsmen hesitated, then put their rifles down on the ground and stepped back.

Kerry eased forward, and got her hand around Dar's arm. "Hey." She rubbed her thumb against her partner's heated skin. "I'm okay. He's just an idiot."

The guard commander at least had the sense to stay where he was, sitting on the ground with his back against his truck. "You're all ending up in jail," he said. "You better put that gun down, buddy. This is no game."

"No, it aint," Andrew agreed. "Most times when I been holding one of these here things, it weren't no game and not so much as when you can't tell who you got on the other end, a friendly or a target." He stared, unblinking, at the man's face. "Like now."

The guard captain went very still, only his breathing evident in the rise and fall of his shirt.

"Now," Andrew said. "These here people are here to do something for the gov'mint. You are going to get on that there radio and get your CO over here, so you can 'splain why you ain't letting them do what they need to do. Right now."

"Okay." The guard captain held his hands out. "I'm just trying to do my job."

"No you ain't. That feller there today was doing his job. You just ain't got no sense, and don't want to listen to nobody," Andrew disagreed. "So get yourself up and get on that comm, 'fore I do it and get them collar bugs turned to half stripes for you."

The guard got up and reached in the open window. Andrew shifted the rifle audibly and he paused, then slowly pulled his hand out with the radio mouthpiece in it. "Can I ask who you are?"

"No you may not," Andrew told him. "But ah will tell you that if ah don't know someone who will bust you, ah know someone who knows someone. Just get on that thing and get someone with a brain ovah here."

The man hesitated.

"And if you all don't believe that, ah'll just let mah little girl here beat the tar out of you and take pitchers," Andrew continued mildly with a straight face.

The guard captain keyed the mic. 'HQ, HQ...this is Hudson Midtown. Over."

"Thought that might do it." Andrew turned his head slightly. "You kids want to get on back in case someone does something jackass here?"

"No," Dar replied.

Kerry shook her head in agreement, half turning as Alastair eased up next to them. "We're all jackasses, right?"

"Without question," Alastair agreed. "I've never been a jackass, in fact. But you know, the Commander is right. Let's get back a little."

Both Kerry and Dar just looked at him.

"No, huh?"

Dar finally relaxed, her shoulders easing and her hands uncurling. "Let's see if we've got everything." She gave in, and stepped back from the half ring of uncertain guardsman, and her father's threatening, brace legged form.

The techs were all crouched near the ground, eyes wide. "Wow," Shaun muttered, as they joined the three of them. "This is getting crazy."

"Getting?" Kannan looked upset, and tense. "Never have I felt so scared, you know? Intimidated by my own nationality being in question. It is terrible. I feel like I am walking target for people to think badly of."

Kerry felt her heart finally starting to settle back down in her chest. She felt a trembling weakness in her legs and she leaned against Dar for support as much as in comfort. "He didn't even know who you are. He didn't even care," she said. "Jesus."

"Asshole," Dar said, quietly.

"You all right?" Kerry murmured, leaning close to her.

Dar didn't answer for a moment, then she exhaled. "Well," she said, "at least my cramps are gone." She glanced down at Kerry. "I just saw red."

Kerry bumped her shoulder with her head. Then she looked down at the techs. "Kannan, I'm sorry. I know what it's like to be judged on something you don't have control over." She knelt next to him. "Is there something we can do to help with that? We might as well get started, since I think we're stuck here for a little while."

The techs were willing to be distracted. Kannan pulled his bag over and took out a tool kit and set it on the ground, then removed a handful of bits and pieces from the paper bag. "Not too much light here." He looked up at the orange lamps.

"I have a flashlight." Shaun paused removing it from his pack. "Want me to hold it?"

"I will." Dar held her hand out for it. "Let's get done what we can. Then the beer is on me."

The techs smiled timidly at her and started to get to work. Dar turned the light on and focused it on the sidewalk with its odd scattering of technical debris, glad of a chance to stand still, the sense of thrumming anger only slowly fading from her awareness.

Kerry's shoulder was pressed against her knee. Dar slowly turned her head and stared past her father's form, at the soldiers who were staring back at them.

Assholes.

KERRY PUT HER hands on her hips as they listened to the guard commander, casting a glance behind her where the three techs were now seated in a ring of bright white light from the headlamps of four guard vehicles.

"Listen, I know how damned crazy this all is," Dar said. "But you people need to think before you start wailing away on folks you don't even know did anything."

"Ms. Roberts, I understand what you're saying," the guard commander replied. "But to be honest, there's no time to think right now. Just react. I know you know what I mean."

Dar sighed. Andrew sighed. Alastair grunted and shook his head.

"I'm really sorry we...no, I didn't leave notes for Josh there about you people being inside," the commander went on. "I got called out on a bomb threat, and three men were arrested with parts in a backpack, a lot like what your guys there looked like."

They turned to look at the three techs who were working contentedly on the sidewalk. "I mean, what the hell were they supposed to think with all that? What is it? Do we know? We're not mechanics," the guard commander asked, plaintively.

"Commander, we understand," Alastair spoke up. "You're trying to get a job done; we're trying to get a job done. We're on the same side, y'know."

"The guys that did that," the guard commander pointed in the general direction of the disaster site, "lived among us. Tell me how we can trust anyone?" He let his hand drop. "I can't. I know you're all right because the mayor's office said so, but those people come walking up here with backpacks and a wild story, and one of them looking like one of those guys who did that, what can you expect?"

Dar exhaled. "Kannan's from India," she said. "It's not even the same continent. Are you telling me anyone who doesn't look like Kerry here is eligible to get shot now?"

The guard commander lifted his hands and let them fall. "I don't know. You hear the news. People are getting shot and beat up all over because everyone's so angry they want to lash out. Me too. Us too. Maybe I would shoot someone like him if I had a doubt, if I thought maybe something else was going to happen. Yeah," he answered, honestly. "I would."

"Wow," Kerry murmured.

"You asked," the commander said. "But anyway, if you say he's okay and these guys are okay, then I have to go with that because the mayor says you are okay. But you could be lying."

"We're not," Alastair said. "These people are employees of ours. They have government clearances." He shifted his gaze to Dar slightly, and caught the equally slight nod of her head. "We all do. That's how the mayor knows we're all right.

The commander shrugged. "I don't have that information when people are walking toward me. I'm not saying it's right; I'm not saying people aren't going to get hurt in this who are innocent; I'm just telling you what the truth is. We don't know, and we can't afford to risk erring on the side of caution anymore."

They were all briefly silent. "Gotta wonder why the heck we're here trying to help then," Alastair said. "Because these people's lives are worth a hell of a lot more than making sure the mayor has a phone and a connection to the internet."

The guard commander now looked a little embarrassed. "Anyhow. I'm sorry this happened, Mr. McLean. I've talked to Josh, and I made sure everyone in this area knows you people are here. Maybe they can get some badges or something. I don't know. I don't know what the answer is right now."

Shaun had gotten up and now he cautiously approached the group. "Ms. Stuart?"

Kerry turned toward him. "Hey. You guys finished prepping?"

He nodded. "We're done, and we've got the gear packed up."

"Okay." Dar ran her fingers through her hair. "Dad, you want to take Kannan back into the ship where the other guys are waiting and let him get that fiber done, and we'll go up the ramp to prep the office side. That work for everyone?"

"We'll send a couple guys in with you just in case anyone else's gotten in there," the commander said. "No more screw-ups on this end tonight."

They walked back over to where the techs were packing up and getting their bags together. With a faintly anxious look, Kannan followed Andrew toward the gates, as the rest of them trooped on toward the ramp leading up to the new offices.

"He going to be okay, ma'am?" Shaun asked Kerry. "He's kind of freaked out about everything." He shifted his pack on his back. "I would be too, I guess."

"He's in good hands," Kerry told him, feeling a little freaked out herself. "Dar's father is a retired Navy Seal. They're not going to mess with him. Let's get this done and get the heck out of here. It's been way too long a day."

"Yes, ma'am."

"Wonder if they'd deliver pizza to this damn emergency office," Kerry said. "Or I'm going to have to call that damn bus to come down here before I pass out."

"Ma'am?"

A PALE SLICE of moonlight peeked through the clouds, illuminating the peeling iron and concrete of the pier with grudging nobility.

"Can I speak to the governor, please?" Alastair leaned against the railing, his back to the city. "Alastair McLean here, from ILS."

In front of him, the tarmac of the port's driveway stretched out to either side separating him from the front of the pier that was dusty concrete and steel. The glass doors were spidered with cracks and partially plywooded sections.

Behind the doors he could see Dar, her arms crossed over her chest talking to two men in blue coveralls. At a desk just inside the door, Kerry was perched, likewise talking to two men in guard uniform.

It was near midnight. He was exhausted. At the moment he wanted nothing more than to get on a plane to Houston and leave all the messy, uncomfortable, gritty details of it all to Dar, and he was almost too tired to be ashamed of himself for that.

"McLean? That you?"

"It is, Governor," Alastair said. "Just wanted to tell you, we got your emergency office up. My people are making the last connections and bringing up systems now."

"Yeah? About time," the governor said. "You people took long enough."

Alastair exhaled. "Well, you know, sometimes these things take time," he said. "As you may realize, it's not that easy to get things done in the city right now."

"I'm not looking for excuses. Just get it done," the man said. "Now if you don't mind, I have to call the White House. Good night."

Alastair closed his phone and juggled it in one hand. Then he walked across the road and into the terminal, the doors creaking reluctantly open to admit him inside. "How's it going, folks?"

Dar glanced at him. "Just waiting for Mark to call me back and confirm the routing integration," she informed him. "But we've got a good signal. We just need to push their routes."

Her boss nodded sagely, as though he understood what she was saying. "Well, wish I could say it was much appreciated by the governor, but I just got yelled at for taking too long. Hell with him," he said. "Let's gather our folks up and get out of here, if we're done."

One of the coverall suited men put his hands on his hips. "If it's any consolation to you, we're grateful as hell to you people for coming in here and getting us going," he said. "All we've been getting from the politicos today is pointless jaw flapping." He looked cross. "All of them in here wanting this, wanting that, but when its time to throw a little influence around, forget about it."

Alastair smiled at him. "Thanks," he said. "But we're used to being abused, aren't we Dar?"

Dar rolled her head around and looked at him, one eyebrow hiking up. "I've had enough abuse for one day," she announced. "The governor can kiss my ass." She looked up as Kerry's cell phone rang and waited while her partner answered it. "Hope that's Mark."

Kerry gave her a thumbs up.

Dar exhaled, just as the two men at the desk started clapping and cheering. "Woo effing hoo," she said. "It's done."

Alastair studied the two men who were high fiving each other. The activity in the room which had been subdued now perked up, and a flow of workers poured from the break room behind a broken wooden door and approached the endless rows of banquet tables set up for use.

It was done. Now that he stood there and looked at the room, with its peeling steel columns and dirty walls, it seemed anticlimactic considering the effort and the struggle that they'd gone through.

Crazy. After hearing what Dar had done, with a soldering iron, and watching the young technicians sweat over the tiny glass strands of the fiber in a process so alchemic, he almost felt like he'd been watching some magic rite.

The techs emerged from the break room, and headed toward them. They were smiling, as they pulled their packs up onto their back and headed for the small group near the door.

"Ready to go back to the hotel?" Kerry folded her phone and clipped it to her belt. "I think we're finished here." She tucked her hand around Dar's elbow. "I need a drink. Finally."

"Let's go," Dar replied quietly. "I'm about done in myself. Alastair?"

Her boss snorted tiredly. "Lady, you got to be kidding me. I was done before sundown." He indicated the door. "I see Papa Roberts out there, so let's get ourselves someplace more comfortable." He glanced at the techs. Fellas, did they make arrangements for you?"

The techs exchanged glances. "I don't think so," Shaun admitted. "They weren't really specific about what we were supposed to do when we finished. I think they expected us to be here all night so maybe it wasn't a concern." He looked shyly at Dar. "We thought we'd have to run the big cable too."

Dar managed a return smile. "Glad you didn't have to."

"Well, c'mon with us then, and we'll get you sorted out." Alastair decided. "You fellas did a great job tonight, and you, at least, deserve a nice bed and a shower." He turned and regarded the door. "Now. As to finding a taxi."

"No probl'm." Andrew had entered, and was loitering near the door. "Them fellers down the ramp said they'd take us in their truck. Ah think they're just trying to poligize."

"I'll take it." Alastair shooed them toward the door. "Let's go troops. Shops closed for the night." He gave the men inside a wave, then followed the group out the door. They turned and started down the ramp, in the cool dampness of a fall night that despite the late hour, wasn't really all that quiet.

Emergency sirens still sounded. They could hear trucks on the lower level pulling up and the clank of forklifts unloading.

Dar let the sounds move past her. She was almost at a point where she was so tired she wasn't really cognizant of where she was, and the ability to care about what was going on was fading fast. She felt Kerry's hand clasp hers, and focused on the comfort of the contact willing the ride to the hotel to be over and the long day to end at last.

She was glad, in a distant way, that they'd brought the office up. Knowing the bigger task that faced them though put this in meager perspective. She wondered, briefly, if the governor was expecting them to go right from this to reviewing downtown without a break.

Probably he was. Probably he could put his head between his legs and kiss his own ass, too. Dar bumped Kerry lightly with her shoulder, smiling tiredly as she was bumped equally gently back.

The guard post was now very quiet with only two of the men standing by the barricade with their rifles, The rest were hunkered down behind the truck, legs sprawled out and a pizza box nearby. As they approached, the two men on guard alerted the others, and by the time they reached the bottom of the ramp, the guard captain was there to greet them.

"You folks finished up?" he asked.

"Yeap." Andrew did the talking for them. "We're fixing to get out of your space now. Got all them people up there happy, time to move on."

"John, bring that truck up and give these people a ride to their hotel," the captain said. "And listen, sorry again about that mixup earlier, Commander. Things are so mixed up here, we're just trying to be safe." He glanced over at Dar. "So much is going on."

Dar frankly couldn't have cared less at this point. "No problem." She waved it off. "Let's get the hell out of here."

They got in the personnel carrier and it rumbled off turning onto the roadway and heading for the nearest cross street, a blinking yellow traffic light fluttering overhead. The driver leaned on his wheel and glanced at Andrew. "Where're we going, sir?"

"Doubletree Metropolitan," Alastair provided, then settled back in the hard, bench-like seat as the truck turned and headed east. "Boy. What a day."

Dar was leaning against the door on the other side of the vehicle with Kerry between them. The window was shaded but she was able to look out and see the buildings go by with blinking lights and vivid neon decorating the mostly empty streets.

"Ms. Roberts?" Shaun spoke up from the back seat. "So, are we going to stay and help out with whatever else is needed tomorrow? My folks were asking. They're kind of nervous I'm here."

Dar stirred herself to some kind of skewed alertness. "Yeah," she said, after a pause. "Tomorrow we have to go down to the Trade Center site and see what we can do about putting the country's financial infrastructure back together."

Shaun leaned forward and put his hand on the back of Dar's seat. "For real?"

Kerry half turned her head and nodded at him.

Shaun sat back. He blinked a few times, then exchanged looks with his coworkers. "I'm going to tell my ma you're sending me to Niagara Falls."

"Very good idea," Kannan agreed. "Or maybe to Buffalo, so we can get some wings."

Kerry managed a faint laugh. Then she let her head rest against Dar's shoulder and tried to forget the cramps she was now experiencing. "Barrel over the falls sounds good right about now," she muttered. "Hope the hotel has room service."

"They better." Dar sighed. "They damn sure better."

THEY DAMN SURE did. Dar ruffled her hair dry as she exited the bathroom to find Kerry sprawled on the bed with her arm wrapped around a pillow and a cup of rum laced chocolate nearby. Her forehead had that little wrinkle it got when she was in some discomfort, and Dar fully empathized with her on that subject.

"Ugh." Kerry reached over and picked up the cup, lifting herself up enough to take a sip from it, then putting it back down. "Life sucks."

Dar draped her towel over the chair and climbed into the king sized bed, laying down behind Kerry and slipping one arm over her as she blew gently in her ear. "Could be worse."

Kerry leaned back against her. Despite her current discomfort, she could appreciate the wonderful feeling of that solid connection and was very glad she could simply lay here with Dar wrapped around her and not have to move, or think, or yell at anyone.

Wonderful. "What a long, freaking day."

"Ultimately a successful one. I'm glad we saw that connection through. At least we won't have that on our plates tomorrow morning."

"Only thing I want on my plate tomorrow morning is some French toast," Kerry sighed. "But somehow I don't think we'll get that lucky."

"Advil kick in yet?" Dar asked, sympathetically.

"Not yet. But I think you're enhancing its attempt," Kerry told her. "It's nice to just lay here. I'm trying not to think about having to get out of this bed tomorrow morning and go do again what we did today only in a much worse place."

Dar exhaled. "I feel like we busted our asses all day and ended up getting the finger from the city. I appreciate they've having a crisis here, but we're not the cause of it."

Kerry folded her arm over Dar's and exhaled. "Yeah. It's a weird attitude. I think it's because they're so pissed off at what happened, and they can't lash out at the people who did it. So they're taking it out on everyone else."

"Peh."

Kerry smiled. "Hey, we're going around saying we're being mean because we're having our periods. Cut them some slack, okay?"

Dar chuckled dryly. "I never needed that as an excuse," she demurred. "Though it sure didn't help today. I felt like doing some surgery on myself there for a while."

Kerry grimaced in reflex. "Ouch."

"Mm."

"Do you think we can get the financial stuff going, Dar? Is it going to be more of what we had to do today? That was kinda nuts," Kerry said. "I mean..." She went briefly silent. "I don't know what I mean."

Dar pulled her a bit closer and felt her eyes drifting shut. "I don't know," she answered. "If it's as big a cluster there as I think it is, maybe we don't have to do anything. Or maybe we have to come up with some wild ass scheme no one's thought of yet."

"Ah."

"Or maybe someone else will be brilliant for a change."

Kerry felt her own eyes closing, and she relaxed against Dar's warm body, setting aside the aggravations of the day and letting them go for the moment. Far off, she could hear the late night sound of the city, but that too was fading, and before she could take another breath she was asleep.

Dar was awake a bit longer, savoring the peace and quiet after the long day. She felt Kerry's body go limp against her and her breathing even out and hoped they'd be able to get through the night without any calls, or demands, or...

Screw it. She reached over and turned Kerry's phone to silent. Then she closed her eyes, and tugged the covers up over them.

Chapter Five

"OKAY, SO WHERE are we." Kerry blinked into the pallid dawn light coming in the window, half distracted by the scent of coffee nearby. "Mark, your three guys are here in the hotel with the rest of us."

"Cool, yeah," Mark answered. "I got an email from Shaun last night," he paused. "He sure was glad to put his head down on a pillow."

"Me too," Kerry agreed. "So, what's the status right now? Who's here, who's on the way here, and what kind of gear is everyone bringing."

There was a soft knock at the door. Kerry went to mute the mic, but stopped when Dar appeared from the bathroom and waved at her, heading over to answer it. "Who the hell is knocking this early?" She grumbled under her breath.

"What was that, boss?" Mark asked.

"Nothing. Go on." Kerry sighed. She leaned forward a little, grimacing as a cramp gripped her.

"Anyway," Mark cleared his throat, "so we've got six guys and me in the truck, and we're like one, maybe two hours out. I left a bunch of guys there, a half dozen showed up from different accounts yesterday to help out so I thought it was okay to take off from there and head over."

He sounded a touch nervous. Kerry half smiled, understanding the feeling from her first weeks working for Dar, and having to lay out her own decision making. "Great plan," she said. "We need you here badly."

Mark didn't answer for a moment, and then he chuckled. "Thanks boss. So we've got the camper, and we'll pick up the SAT units and the power trucks on our way down there. Where do we go?"

Ah, good question. "For now, come here...well, to the Rock," Kerry clarified. "We have to find out where the best place is to start working. I know we'll need stocks of cable and patch equipment, do you know if we've got that on the truck?"

"Hang on, lemme check."

Kerry muted the mic and hissed a small curse as another cramp hit.

Dar came back over to the desk where she was seated and emptied the contents of a packet on the table. "Ah. I'm legal again." She flicked her slim billfold with one finger and pushed the folder of identification cards around. "You don't have to worry about me being deported."

"That's a relief." Kerry managed a smile. "Though I have to admit razzing the admin at the office was pretty funny."

"It was." Dar sat down and extended her long, mostly bare legs across the floor. "Gut still hurting?"

"How'd you guess?" Kerry made a face, resting her chin on her hand. "I feel like dog poo."

"Been there."

"No kidding." Kerry turned her attention back to the phone as she heard rustling against the remote microphone. "I'm surprised we haven't gotten called from Alastair or anyone yet this morning."

Dar picked up her newly reunited cell phone and opened it, triggering it on and watching as it obediently started up. After a quiet moment, it started buzzing and rattling loudly, making her jump. "Yah!"

"Holy crap!" Kerry blurted.

Dar dropped the phone and it danced across the table in truly spectacular fashion. "Any ideas how to bulk delete voice mail messages?"

"Okay, boss." Mark came back on the line and paused as he heard the noise on the other end. "What the heck's going on there?"

"Um...not much." Kerry grabbed the phone and tossed it to its owner. "So what's the scoop?"

"Let me put it this way, you got any pull with those guys at ADC? We used all the stuff they sent rebuilding the space at the old P, and we ain't got any more."

"Ugh," Kerry uttered. "So we don't have patch panels or anything like that, right?"

"Right."

She sighed. "What do we have?"

"Got some routers, some little switches, a couple spools of STP, couple spools of UTP, another big roll of that fiber the guys used last night, and a handful of RJ45 plugs."

"My mother could probably do a three dimensional art project with that," Dar commented, her eyes fixed on her now rattle free phone as she thumbed through the alerts and messages. "Want some coffee?"

"Well...I'd say let's get ordering, but you know what Mark?" Kerry sighed.

"We got no idea what to order," Mark supplied. "I know. I thought of that when I got up this morning and took over the driving again. I think we gotta get eyeballs on it then figure it out."

Kerry muted the mic. "Coffee sounds great, except it's going to make my stomach ache worse." She moaned.

"Figured you'd say that. I had them bring tea too. Want blackberry or honey lemon?" Dar didn't even look up from her phone. "Mark's right. Let's wait for him to get here, then we will all go down to the Trade Center and see what we've got to work with."

"I love you."

Now Dar looked up, and smiled. "Blackberry?" Her eyebrows lifted. "And we've got some warm muffins. You up for that?"

Kerry merely rested her chin on her fists and gazed at her partner.

"Take that as a yes." Dar set her phone down and sauntered back over to the room service tray.

"You hear that, boss?" Mark queried. "Hello?"

"Sorry." Kerry wrenched her attention back to the phone. "That sounds like a plan, Mark. Dar was just saying we should wait for you to get here then all go down together. You think you'll be here by eight? It's just ten past six now."

"We can probably do that unless we get held up nearer to where you are," Mark replied. "They going to let us in there?"

"We've got passes." Kerry didn't elaborate. "All right, you guys head on up here. We'll meet you at the office." She waited for the line to drop then closed her phone. "What else do we need to do? Why do I feel like I'm so damned behind the eight ball today?"

Dar came back over with a plate containing a buttered muffin and a steaming cup of tea. She set them down next to her partner's laptop and leaned over, giving her a kiss on the top of her head. "I love you too."

Kerry leaned against her. "Oh honey, I sure know that," she murmured. "Thanks for breakfast."

"No problem." Dar straightened up and went to retrieve her coffee, pausing to watch the silent television screen full of frenetic activity and destruction. More people. More rubble. More talking heads. The scroll at the bottom spat a never ending series of numbers that she had to force herself to realize meant human beings either missing or dead.

It was strange. The whole thing had started to take on a surreal glaze and it was hard to concentrate on the facts that seemed to come at her from the screen in so many different directions. She watched shots of the president down near the still smoking rubble yelling into a bullhorn, an American flag flapping in the wind nearby.

Behind him a fireman sat on a flat, twisted piece of iron, his head down and his elbows resting on his knees in exhaustion.

Dar nodded to herself a little, then went over to the small table and picked up half a corn muffin, taking a bite of it as she tried to focus her mind on the task at hand. She glanced at her new laptop, open on the table, and watched the network metrics, a slowly healing graph of yellows morphing to greens rather than blotches of solid red.

The company was recovering. Things were starting to move back into normal patterns, and along with that her list of tasks shunted aside for the emergency were starting to build.

The world had held still since that morning. Now, she had a sense, that her world, if not everyone else's, was starting slowly to turn again and she had to admit a trace of impatience that she found herself tied up here, working a problem not remotely her own, heading toward a hopefully successful end that probably would get little notice and less credit.

Uncharitable, probably. Dar chewed her muffin and turned to watch the television screen again with a thoughtful expression. "Ker?"

"Hm." Kerry looked up from her laptop.

"Can we get a list of our customers who are still out of service here?" Dar asked. "Let's see what synergy we can get with restoring services to them at the same time we're relieving our obligation to the government."

"We don't have enough to do?" Kerry's tone was, however, merely quizzical rather than accusing. "Sheesh."

"Let's just say we have a responsibility to them, and I'd like to walk out of here with a sense of accomplishment beyond some rubber chicken," Dar replied. "Getting the job done for the markets, but leaving our own customers high and dry ain't my way of doing business."

Kerry smiled. "I want to be you when I grow up." She stood up and popped the last of her muffin into her mouth. "Well, the day's not getting any younger, so I guess I'll go get my shower and start getting ready."

"Be right there with you." Dar sat down to finish her muffin, leaning back and watching the dawn light slowly growing in the window, turning her back to the TV screen.

KERRY LEANED BACK against the driver's partition in the courtesy bus, watching the street roll by outside the window. "At least the traffic hasn't built up so much again."

"You got that right, ma'am," the driver agreed. "People are still in shock, I think. I was talking to a man who came by the bus earlier. His son worked in one of those investment offices up near the top of one of the towers, and he kept saying he was going down there to visit him real soon now."

Kerry grimaced a trifle. "It's hard to take it all in," she murmured.

"Can't imagine it myself," the driver agreed.

They were traveling east, heading toward the disaster site. Kerry eased forward and knelt, resting her arms on the front console as she started to see a dusting of ash on the streets, and the cars, and the buildings.

It was not that strange to her eyes. It resembled a light coating of snow more than anything. As they passed, she could see some shops open, some closed, some in an in-between state where the rolling garage doors were half open and people were standing outside, talking or sweeping the ash.

The bus stopped at a stoplight, and she watched one man carefully sweeping his sidewalk clean of the stuff and putting it into a tiny pile. He then knelt and pulled out a dustpan and hand brush, and whisked the ash into a small plastic bag, standing when he was done and looking at it.

Would he throw it away? Save it as a memory of the horror? Or sell it on Ebay? Kerry watched him put a twist tie around the top of the bag and take it inside, ducking under the half drawn door and disappearing.

Could go any of the ways. Kerry sighed. The bus started moving forward again, and on the right hand side they passed a fire station. The big doors were wide open, and she looked inside only to find it completely empty of either trucks or people.

A prickle ran down her spine. She looked at the sign above it. "Ladder 11. Hope they're all okay."

The driver glanced at the empty station then looked at her. "Ms. Stuart, beg your pardon, but no one here's okay," he said. "No matter if they walked out of that mess or not."

True. Kerry saw the coating of ash getting thicker as they turned left on to Houston Street. "What insanity."

Dar came up behind her and looked over her shoulder. "Mess," she said succinctly. "Are we going to end up east of the site?"

The driver nodded, as he turned the big bus right. "Yeah, that's what the cops told me to do. Take the FDR around the end of the island and come up from there. Too much destruction on the west side, and besides, they've got Battery Park there wide open."

Now through the walls of the bus, they could hear sirens, though as yet all they could see was the outline of Staten Island across the water. A pensive silence fell over the bus as everyone picked a window and stared out of it.

"Mark still behind us?" Dar asked in all that quiet.

The driver glanced in his mirror. "Yeah, he's there."

Dar watched out the window at the thick plume of smoke rising from between the buildings and the debris that was starting to line the road. "Jason, break out the case of radios, please," she ordered quietly. "And the masks."

"Yes, ma'am."

"Everyone stay calm. This is going to be hard," Dar added, after another brief pause. "Stay focused, and remember that everyone here has been through a hell of a lot worse nightmare than we're about to experience."

Alastair came up behind Dar and gazed past her, his face quietly grim. "Know something, Dar?"

"Wish you'd turned the White House down?"

Alastair's lips pressed into a humorless smile. Then he turned and went back to the side window, seating himself on a stool and staring outside.

Kerry slowly stepped down from the bus, the third one out after Dar and Alastair had exited to deal with the gun toting guardsmen who had flagged their convoy to a halt. She stood quietly for a moment, the wind at her back as she slowly scanned the area around them.

They had been pulled to a halt on State Street, just across from Battery Park. The roads were eerily silent covered in thick white gray dust and debris with cars and trucks parked every which way. She could look right up Broadway and see more automobiles, more dust, and windows blown out with curtains being sucked out and fluttering in the breeze.

She could smell burning rubber, diesel oil, and the strong scent of the water. Fireboats and barges were churning offshore and a ferry was passing by, its decks packed with uniformed figures.

Small groups of police, firemen, and other workers were clustered around. Some were sitting in the grass of the park; a few resting against trees facing away from the city and toward the water.

Mark came up next to her, his arms folded over his chest as he stood and looked around. "Man."

"Yeah." Kerry half turned, as a car with a siren blaring turned the corner and headed up Broadway, the sound echoing between the buildings and then fading.

"We going all the way up there?"

"Depends." Kerry leaned forward slightly to watch Dar and Alastair with the guard. Dar's body posture was still relaxed, so it didn't look like the situation was getting confrontational. "Let's see where they'll let us go. I told our telecom friends we'd be trying to get over here before we left the Rock."

"It's like a ghost town down here," Mark commented grimacing. "That was tacky bad. Sorry."

"Don't worry about it." Kerry walked across the street and into the park, carefully skirting around a pair of firemen sitting in the grass.

One of them looked up at her as she passed. "Hey," he called out. "Where'd you come from?"

Kerry stopped and went over to him, kneeling down in the grass and letting her hands rest on one knee. "That bus over there." She indicated the waiting caravan. "What about you?"

"Me?" The fireman looked exhausted, and his face was coated with the gray dust outlining red rimmed eyes. "I'm from Connecticut. What's the bus for?"

"It's our company bus. We're going to try and help get communications back up and running down here," Kerry readily explained.

The fireman snorted. "Good luck." He picked up his radio lying beside him and let it drop. "Hear more static than talk on these things."

"All these tall buildings," Kerry agreed.

"Ker?"

Kerry turned to see Dar motioning her over. "Well, time to go back to work. Nice talking to you."

"Same here." The fireman nodded.

Kerry got up and crossed the grass glancing both ways in reflex before she crossed the road. The dust under her boots felt like a light, powdery sand. She joined Dar and Alastair who had moved closer to the bus. "We set?"

"Not quite," Dar said. "They're trying to move heavy construction rigs in—cranes, whatever—we can't pull the trucks down yet. They told us to park them up here until we can move closer."

"Nice fellah," Alastair commented. "Thought we were going to have a dust up again, but this guy seemed like good folk."

"Okay," Kerry said. "So we walk up from here? Is that what you're saying? I know John and the telcom folks are up nearer the site."

"We walk." Dar turned and faced the bus, lifting her hand and waving. "We should pull the sat and power trucks up on that side street there. Get them out of the way." She stared at the bus as Andrew appeared from behind it and headed her way.

Alastair put his hands in his pockets and regarded the scene. "I have a feeling this is the most pleasantness we're going to see today," he said giving Kerry a sideways look. "Shall we go get our togs? This stuff looks nasty." He kicked a bit of the dust with his boot.

"Sounds like a good idea." Kerry turned and cupped her hands around her mouth. "Everyone get your overalls and masks! Sync up radios!"

A swarm of activity started around the bus as the driver got out and popped open the underneath storage and techs started to drag big cases out and open them. Kerry joined Dar near the door to the bus waiting their turn to pick up equipment.

"Dad's getting the trucks parked," Dar said. "You ready for this?"

"Dar." Kerry leaned briefly against her. "How in the hell could anyone be ready for this? I've already got a knot in my gut that has nothing to do with having my period."

Dar looked around and grunted.

"Ma'am, I think this one will fit you." One of the techs approached Kerry with a coverall and handed it and a mask to her. "We didn't have many this small."

"Thanks." Kerry smiled wryly. "I think."

Dar eased past him and rummaged through the bin on her own, removing a set of the clothing. "On the other hand, I have to fight the wolves for mine." She came back to where Kerry was standing, leaning back against the bus and starting to pull the coveralls on. "Someone get the tool belts out! " she added in a loud yell.

Kerry picked a spot against the bus next to her and got her first boot into the leg opening of the thick, dark green garment. The fabric was tightly woven and tough, and it reminded her a bit of a military flight suit.

Not tremendously attractive, even with the company logo bold on the chest and across her back. She snapped the wrists closed that thankfully were, in fact, her length, and bent to unlace her boots tucking the legs into them and lacing them back up again.

She stood up and examined the mask Dar had handed her, a full face unit with lavender filter cartridges poking out both sides of the bottom. She fitted it to her face and found it relatively comfortable.

"Not bad." She removed it and let it hang around her neck, as Dar handed her a smaller, mouth only mask. "What's that for?"

"Wind's right," Dar said. "I figure we can leave these big ones off until we're pretty close, but it doesn't pay to take chances. You see that stuff? Ten bucks it's full of silica particulate." She pointed at the dust in the streets.

"Powdered glass?" Kerry remembered the fireman and his red rimmed eyes. "Ouch."

"Not to mention asbestos." Alastair had come up next to them, clad in his own green outfit. "Nasty stuff."

Andrew circled the bus from the other side already draped in a tool belt and bearing a pack on his back. He had a mask gripped in one big hand, and to all appearances absolutely knew what to do with it. "You gals." He addressed Dar and Kerry seriously. "Keep them damn masks on. Hear?"

Dar had just finished clipping a utility belt around her, and fastening her radio to it. "Got it," she said. "You too." She adjusted the radio and clipped the transmitter to her lapel. "Check." She keyed it. "Check. Mark?"

"Here." Mark's voice crackled back. "I did a radio scan. We're clear on this frequency. Most of the rest of them are using lower band. I've got the base repeater up and going."

"Run radio checks with everyone." Dar looped her credentials around her neck and settled them under her collar. "Then let's meet up near the head of that street there." She pointed.

"Broadway," Kerry supplied.

Dar looked at her. "Really?"

Kerry nodded. "It's where it starts. Kind of like where US 1 begins in Key West."

"Huh," Dar muttered. "Okay, we'll go try and find your Telco folks and see what we can do in that area, then we can come back and see what's left of our technical office down here. It's just south of the Exchange."

"Sounds like a plan," Alastair said. "I told the gals to see what they could offer those poor guys out there after they get set up." He indicated the firemen. "Can't be easy."

They started toward the edge of the park, as Mark's voice crackled and echoed doing his checks. The guardsmen glanced at them and waved as they went by. They paused at the end of the park for the entire group to gather.

Dar gazed down the street and acknowledged the sense of nervous dread in her guts. This was something past her experience.

Something past all of their experience, save maybe her father. She looked at him as he came up to stand next to her, pale eyes flicking back and forth as he watched everything around them. "Dad?"

He focused on her. "Yeap?"

"Glad you're here."

Andrew reached out and clasped her shoulder, but didn't say anything in response.

"We all here?" Dar asked, assuming the leadership role. "Everyone geared up and got radios? Listen up." She turned to face them. "Stay together. No one goes wandering around anywhere. This is a dangerous place."

Everyone sobered and regarded her seriously.

"I don't know what we're going to have to do. If it's something I think is too dangerous, we're not going to do it. Everyone understand me? No one is risking their lives for someone's stock options."

Everyone nodded. Even Alastair.

"We're not heroes." Dar pointed past them. "Those guys over there? They're heroes. They went into those damn buildings while they were falling around them to try and get people out. A lot of them are missing. We're not here for that. "

One of the techs raised his hand. "Ms Roberts?"

"What?" Dar put her hands on her hips.

"We get the point," the tech said. "And that's really cool. But we all saw you on television hanging out of a ten story window putting kids in a basket." He looked past her. "So can we go see how we can help out?"

Kerry scratched her nose to give her an excuse to muffle the smile on her face.

Dar sighed. "Let's go." She turned and started up the street, with her little army behind her, walking carefully around lumps in the road that could have been anything.

KERRY DECIDED AFTER a few minutes of quiet walking that the settling of dust over everything reminded her not so much of snow, but of the underwater landscape she and Dar so often explored together.

The dust had that kind of silt, grungy appearance to it. It draped over everything — the sidewalk, the cars, anything on the sidewalk — just like it did underwater over discarded concrete blocks, and forgotten anchors.

The odd gust of wind from behind them stirred it just as an errant fin would. She'd only gone half a block before she'd put her smaller mask on, convinced she could taste the stuff on the back of her tongue.

There were workers and firemen, an isolated few, walking the other way, but they all looked exhausted and none of them paid attention to either their surroundings or the passing techs. Some had breathing masks, some had full face units like they did, a few had nothing at all protecting them and were rubbing at their eyes with the backs of their hands.

It was quiet. Far off, she could hear the sound of heavy machinery, the faint hoots of a big truck or something backing up, and the sudden, unexpected sound of metal against metal that rang in the middle of her ears, making them itch.

It was surreal. If she looked behind her, she could see the clear blue sky of an autumn day with wind riffling over the waters of New York Harbor. But ahead of her, she felt like she was going down into a dungeon as the air seemed to be getting thicker and more hazy, and the ravaged building fronts rose high on either side of them.

"Put your masks on," Dar ordered her voice startlingly loud.

Kerry removed her small one and replaced it with the full face mask, adjusting the straps as it put a surprisingly comfortable veneer between her and the scene. The constriction of her vision almost seemed welcome, and after a minute she realized it wasn't really very different from putting on her diving mask.

They turned a corner and headed west. Rising up in front of them were fire trucks and cars, beaten and half destroyed.

"Wow."

Kerry glanced to her left to see Nan with her mask on. "Hey."

"This is unreal," Nan said. "I feel like I'm in a sci-fi film."

The sunlight filtered through the haze outlining the destruction in a peculiar beauty. Kerry pulled her small camera from her pocket and paused, focusing and snapping a quick shot of it. "It's definitely unreal."

They walked along the center of the small cross street and at the corner turned right and faced north.

Everyone stopped in their tracks. The people in front only barely avoiding being crashed into by those following until their eyes could take in what they saw and freeze their steps too.

"Holy shit," Mark said, after a few moments of silence.

DAR FOUND IT hard to absorb what she was seeing. The entire end of the street was blocked by a huge pile of twisted debris. Heavy smoke was coming out of its depths and chunks of ruin tumbled down toward her amidst the wreckage of cars, trucks, and vans.

Kerry put a hand on her back, easing closer. "I saw this on television but my God, Dar."

"Yeah." Dar looked around. "Don't think we can get through that way. I guess we better...well, hell. I have no idea where we should go. Want to give your buddies a call, find out where they are?"

"Sure." Kerry unclipped her cell phone and opened it, finding the number and dialing as she switched her headset to the phone from her radio.

Andrew and Alastair had walked a little further down the street and now had stopped next to an ambulance that had been flipped on its side and burned almost past recognition. They studied it and shook their heads.

"This is fucked up," Mark finally commented. "This is really, really fucked up."

"Yeah," Dar said. "It is."

"This is crazy," Mark said. "They should just move all the freaking banking stuff out to Wyoming. We've got lots of power and bandwidth there."

Dar pondered that. Could they?

"Look at this place. Holy shit." Mark shook his head. "Man. I can't believe it."

Dar mimicked the motion and studied the scene.

The shops on either side of the street were blown out. Windows had imploded, driven inward by the blast of roiling debris the tall buildings had funneled down away from the collapse—no where to go but out and down—scouring the area raw.

It smelled. Even through the mask and the filters she could smell rot mixed with electrical burn, and garbage from the surrounding areas that hadn't been touched since Tuesday. Bags, covered in dust were on the sidewalk, buzzing with flies.

A puff of air brought a stronger scent to her—one of death—and she barely stifled a gag.

She realized she didn't want to be here. Dar never minded reality and considered herself a straightforward person, but there was such a thing as being too much in the moment, and she thought this might be one of those times.

"This is one bad thing."

Dar turned to find her father at her shoulder. His voice was slightly muffled by the mask, but the somber look in his eyes wasn't. "It's hard to take in," she admitted. "It's like a bad sci-fi movie."

"Yeap," Andrew agreed. "Real bad things are hard to look at and take serious." He went on reflectively. "Cause your mind says, nah, that can't be. Can't be so."

"But there it is." Dar studied the smoking, twisted debris. "And the more I look at it, the more I wonder what the hell we're doing here."

Her father snorted a bit.

"We can't fix any of this, Daddy," Dar told him. "This is broken past my ability to make it right."

Andrew studied her. "So what're you all doing here?"

Dar folded her arms over her chest. "Good question."

"Dar." Kerry came back over. "Okay, they're one street back down and further in front of 2 World T..." She paused. "Where 2 World Trade Center was. There's a damaged subway entrance there." She pointed to the street they'd just come from. "There, and then the first left."

"Lead on," Dar told her.

They trooped back down to the corner and headed back the way they'd come, turning again at the corner Kerry indicated and walking down this wider street full of wreckage.

The building faces here were ravaged. Parts of the brickwork had been scoured off, and the fronts were crumbled in and sagging. One of the roofs nearby was draped in metal debris, dripping down into the street and forcing them to circle it to get past . The metal stained in a dark rust color made Dar's guts shiver.

Once past that, she could see a group of men clustered at the corner near a set of stairs going underground. As they approached, the men at the edge of the group turned and shuffled, splitting apart to allow two figures through from the center.

The one in front headed right for Kerry. "Kerry Stuart, you're a welcome sight."

Kerry extended a hand. "Hello, Charles." She could see his red rimmed eyes behind the shield of his mask. "Did you find your brother?"

He hesitated then shook his head. "They're still looking at the hospitals in Jersey. A lot of guys were found over there today," he said. "Glad you could come down here. We were going to see how far we can see underground. Maybe there's clearance enough to get to the line pipes."

"Okay." Kerry half turned. "I brought some help."

Charles nodded briefly. "Any help's welcome." He gave the rest of them a distracted look. "Do you have…oh, yeah, you do have flashlights. Great. We can get going then." He gestured toward the half wrecked staircase downward. "See what we can see."

Another man walked over in a vest with Verizon on it. He had a small breathing mask on his mouth, but no other protection. "You people ready?" he asked. "We got a lot of other things to do, y'know? I got people chewing my ass right and left here."

"Let's go." Charles motioned them all forward. The group by the stairs was a mix of Verizon staff, his own staff, a few people in different color protection suits with Sprint's logo, and one with MCI WorldCom on the shoulder.

They all looked at the newcomers in question. Charles gestured vaguely at them. "ILS sent a team to see what they could to do help," he said. "I figure the more help the better." They started carefully down the steps that were full of dust and debris, the railings half collapsed. "Be careful folks."

"Took them four hours to clear them this good," one of the other men said. "We're crazy to be going down here."

Everyone turned on their flashlights and the space erupted into a dancing, bobbing light show as the beams reflected against all the dust in the air, and what they were walking down into. Kerry felt like she was descending into some cave, and she felt Dar's reassuring hand rest on her shoulder as they picked their way downward.

One of the Sprint techs was right in front of her and he turned as they slowed waiting for the people in front to continue. "Jake Davies." He offered a hand. "Thanks for coming down. We got some cell sites up and running on generator, but it's tough."

"Kerry Stuart." Kerry returned the grip. "We've got some satellite trucks and generator vans with us."

The men closest to her half turned, their ears perking up. "Yeah?" one asked. "We could sure use those."

"Everyone could," Dar answered. "Once we finish seeing what the needs are, then we can talk about who gets what." Her voice indicated lack of debate on the subject.

The men looked at Kerry then looked up at Dar.

"She's the boss," Kerry remarked. "Want to go on down? I think they're waiting for us."

The men turned and headed down the steps with Kerry and her group behind them. It was very dark, and the ground was very uneven. She reached the bottom of the stairwell with a sense of anxiety as the flashlights danced around the dark interior.

"Holy shit," one of the men said, as they moved a little further inside. His light shone on the walls that had big, gaping cracks in them, tile scattered all over the floor and sliding around with a brittle sound as boots kicked them.

They moved past the turnstiles cautiously. "We sure this ceiling's all right?" one of the men from Sprint asked. "There's a ton of concrete over our heads."

"Look at that!" another man said, shining his flashlight down the second set of stairs. A huge metal column was piercing the ceiling extending down and bisecting the steps halfway down.

"Wow." Charles shook his head. "I don't know about this."

"Aw, c'mon you little girls." The Verizon man headed down the steps.

"Now there's a right jackass." Andrew started to push past Dar and Kerry, only to have his daughter casually block him with one arm. "Scuse me, rugrat."

"Dad. Relax." Dar started down the steps. "If asses need kicking, I'm capable of that."

Kerry was glad of the banter, since the area around her was giving her the severe creeps. Aside from being dark, it stank, and, despite the filters, her eyes were watering from the smell. Her imagination was painting almost anything in the corners, and she was halfway afraid of looking too closely in the glare at what might be there.

She instinctively edged closer to Dar, hooking one finger in her partner's belt as she followed her down the second set of stairs deeper into the earth under the collapsed tower, down to the platform that was the subway.

There she had to halt, as Dar had halted, because everyone else had.

The flashlights couldn't do the scene justice. "Hang on." One of the Verizon men went over to one side and worked a latch on something, accompanied by a long, screeching sound that made everyone jump.

A floodlight flickered on, dim with age. "Shit for batteries," the man muttered. "But it's better than nothing."

The light blared down the tracks showing the destruction. A subway train car was at the end of the platform, its top crushed in, the tunnel ceiling collapsed on top of it.

They were all silent for a moment. "Hope that was empty," Kerry murmured.

On the other side of the tracks, the entire tunnel was collapsed on top of the platform blocking any further travel in that direction. The tunnel leading east, away from the towers, was still intact, but a light shown down it displayed debris covering the tracks as far as the eye could see.

A rain of debris suddenly came down from the ceiling, rattling down on the tracks.

"Shit," the Verizon man said. "This ain't going nowhere. We can't even get to the intake blocks." He ran his flashlight along the back wall. The concrete and steel pylons were cracked and bent and somewhere, a faint hissing noise was going off.

"No," Charles said. "Dead end."

Another silence. "Probably a lot of them," the Verizon man finally muttered. "Let's get outta here. Waste of time." He took a step backwards, as another rain of debris came down. "I tolja it would be. We should get back to the damn work site and do something productive."

Rude or not, Kerry was totally in sync with the idea. She kept thinking she heard things moving in the distance, and she could feel her heart racing as the shadows seemed to move closer. She backed up and got on the steps, swallowing hard to keep her stomach down.

The upper level was almost bright by comparison. Hazy sunlight was coming down the steps to the outside world, and Kerry made a beeline for it, relaxing only when she knew her head was out from under the cracked ceiling and she could see sky above her.

"You okay?" Dar asked, climbing up the steps at her back.

"Yeah," Kerry answered after a brief pause. "Just freaked me a little."

Dar patted her back in comfort, as they exited onto the street, faced with the pile of wreckage and the sound of sirens blaring suddenly.

They both jumped. Dar turned in a circle, her eyes scanning the area.

"Shit. Now what?" The Verizon man hauled up out of the stairwell after them, looking quickly both ways. On the next street, a police car growled by, it's lights cutting the dusty air as the officer inside aimed a high beam light on one of the building fronts.

The Verizon man relaxed. "Looter." He guessed. "Bastards." He looked around again. "We should get the hell..."

"Away from here? I agree." Dar turned and counted quickly, making sure all her team had come out from the subway. "Tell you what. We've got a tech office a block or so over. No lights but we can sit and talk about what we can do there."

The group gathered around her, most looking a bit shaken, and even Andrew assuming a somber expression on his face.

"You said you had sat trucks?" Charles asked, finally. "I thought I heard you say that, Kerry." He turned to look at her. "Right?"

"We do," Dar answered for her. "So let's go put our heads together and figure out a plan," she suggested. "Maybe we can start from the other end, at the Exchange, and see where that takes us."

After an awkward pause, Charles nodded, though the rest just looked at Dar. "Sounds like a good idea," he ventured. "Sorry, I didn't...I don't think we were introduced."

"My manners are slipping." Kerry shook herself out of her funk. "Sorry, Charles. This is Dar Roberts. Dar, this is Charles Gant, the technical executive on our account." She paused, as she took in Charles' wide eyed expression and the sudden, startled looks from the other men.

It would have been funny, if it had been any other situation. Kerry couldn't appreciate the humor at the moment. "Let's go folks. You can gawk later," she said. "We need to get out of here."

"Git." Andrew started herding them toward the cross street. "Just git."

Another siren started screaming behind them, and they retreated around the corner, just as a second joined it, and then a third, rending the air as though the sound were chasing them.

Chapter Six

KERRY SAT QUIETLY in the corner, perched on a wooden table shoved against the wall. They were inside a fairly small room in the back of the New York Stock Exchange, a space filled with pipes and racks that was both stuffy and dank at the same time.

There was a rough, wooden table in the center of the room and at the moment, Dar and Alastair were seated at it along with some of the guys from Verizon, Sprint, MCI and AT&T all clustered around a set of yellowed blueprints spread on the scarred plank surface.

The rest of them, Kerry, and the techs, and the lineman from Verizon, were back against the walls. Kerry knew she could have squeezed in next to her partner, but she was content to stay where she was and leave the wrangling to someone else.

They had their masks off this far from the destruction, but she could still taste the dust and the smell on the back of her throat and she found she really wanted to be out of here and done with it.

Maybe it was the juxtaposition of the pressure to bring up these banking systems put against the smell of death and the look in the eyes of the firefighters she'd seen. She felt almost ashamed they were putting out as much effort as they were do to what they were doing instead of helping all the people around them who had lost so much.

She hiked one knee up and circled it with her arms, briefly debating if she should ask Dar if she could go back to the bus and get back in touch with the rest of their organization, working to get the rest of the problems and outages sorted out.

As if divining this, Dar turned and looked back at her, one dark brow hiking up.

It felt like her mind was being read. Kerry gave Dar a wry look then glanced at her watch and lifted her own brows in question.

Dar held up her hand then turned back to the discussion at the table.

Kerry settled back against the wall, wishing she'd thought to bring a bottle of water with her. "Going to be a long day," she commented to Mark, who was perched next to her.

"Yeah," Mark agreed. "I'm not really into this."

"Being here?" she asked, lowering her voice.

"This part." Mark indicated the building with a circle of his finger. "I was cool with being at the Pentagon. That was cool, helping those guys out. All I'm getting from this place is a 'what can you do for me' vibe."

Kerry glanced past him, where the technicians who supported the building were standing around, arms crossed with dour expressions on their faces. "I think I'd rather be helping the people who can't even get back to their homes here."

"Exactly," Mark agreed. "I mean, don't get me wrong. I know this is important, but like, when you see people scraping up body parts from the street it kind of puts it in perspective."

Kerry grimaced. "On second thought, I'd rather be in here than seeing that."

Mark eyed her. "Sorry about that," he said. "I didn't really see it either. Just heard the guys talking outside."

The room they were in had power. The whole building did, driven by generators that were being fed by a line to a tanker barge tied up off the end of the island. All the other buildings around it were still dark and the apartments that ringed the area likewise, but this place, and one or two others, had lights glowing through the windows still caked completely with dust.

"I'm not even sure how we're going to help with this. All they're doing is arguing who should get the resources we've got first." Kerry shook her head. "If I was Dar, I'd be yelling already."

The door opened and Andrew entered, a backpack on his back. He removed his mask and crossed over to where Kerry was seated, easing the pack off and setting it down on the table. "Lo there."

"Hey, Dad." Kerry was glad to see him. "Where'd you go off to?"

He opened the pack and handed her a bottle of Gatorade. "Back to that bus thing of yours," he said. "Got tired of all the yapping here." He took out a bottle for himself then offered one to Mark. "Got some folks outside doing more yapping, some of them gov'mint types."

"Great." Kerry opened the bottle and gratefully took a sip. "Thanks for the drinks. My throat is coated with that dust."

"Yeap." Andrew leaned against the table. "What's Dardar up to over there?"

Kerry had lost track of the conversation. "Talking to them about resources, I guess," she said. "Everyone thinks they're priority one. Same story as usual."

Andrew crossed his arms and took a sip of his own drink, shaking his head as he listened.

"GENTLEMEN." DAR RESTED her forearms on the table. "We've been around the block with this a dozen times. We need to get moving on it."

Charles lifted his hands and let them fall. "Well, that's mostly because we keep coming back to how in the hell do we start," he said. "I've got a demarc here with a thousand lines that go no where."

"Look." The Verizon man stood up and put a dirt smudged finger on the blueprint. "Just like I told everyone else around here. This ain't no magic. Just because you people think you got some kind of priority here don't make the truth any different."

"Hey, it's your damn last mile," the MCI representative said. "What are you going to do about it?"

"What do you think?" The Verizon rep shot back. "We lost a whole fucking switching center. You think I got one in my back pocket? Tell your big shot customers they gotta wait, like everyone else. We gotta find a place, we have to pull conduit...shit. It'll be six months to get service back to everyone down here."

He stood up. "I'm outta here. I've got things to do. C'mon boys."

He motioned for his crew to join him. "So long."

"Then we'll bypass you and light the building up ourselves," the MCI rep said.

"Yeah?" The local man snorted. "Don't try it, buddy. We're all union here and any of my people will tell you to go kiss their asses. You people are gonna wait until we're good and ready." He strode out with his men behind him, slamming the door on the way out.

Dar sighed, and rested her chin on her fist. "Just what the situation needed. More assholes."

The door opened again, and one of the other AT&T men came in. "Charles, the governor's rep is outside. He wants some answers."

"Maybe he should ask one of the jerks who just left for them." Charles pushed back from the table in disgust. "Jesus." He got up. "I'll be right back. I don't' know what the hell I'm going to tell this guy, but I'll think of something."

He left, and took his assistant with him, leaving the rest of them to sit around the table in pensive silence.

"Okay," the Sprint rep said, after a long pause. "So, what are our options? I've got twenty customers leaving voice mails for me every ten minutes."

"We all do," the MCI rep agreed. "Except you people." He glanced across the table at Alastair and Dar. "Bet you're glad they're not your customers."

"Well now." Alastair settled back in his chair. "You're right. I don't have a dog in this hunt. We'd be happy enough to be one of your customers calling and bugging you, but as it happens the folks in Washington did hear we have some experience in this type of thing and asked us to stop by."

"Really? Chuck didn't say that."

"Not sure he knew," Alastair admitted.

"So." Dar picked up the ball. "Let's discuss what the possibilities are. If there are any."

THEY CLUSTERED INTO the demarc room, only six of them this time as the rest waited outside. Dar was there along with Mark, the reps from the three telcos, and one of the techs who worked in the Exchange.

Kerry found a bit of wall to lean against between Alastair and Andrew. "What a mess."

"You could squeeze in there if you wanted to." Alastair pointed at the room. "See what's going on."

"Nah." Kerry shook her head. "This is Dar's ballpark." She paused, the word triggering a memory. "Ballpark. We were supposed to play our first practice game today."

"Eh?"

"We joined a corporate softball league. Today's Saturday right? We were supposed to all meet at the park today and see how bad we all are at playing ball." She let her head rest against the wall. "Sorry I'm not there. I'd even enjoy striking out and falling on my ass right now."

Andrew patted her shoulder. "Can't last forever, Kerry. We'll be getting on home soon, for sure."

Kerry rubbed her eyes. "I hope so."

"This really stinks, doesn't it?" Alastair asked. "What in the blazes are we all doing here?"

"S'what I asked Dar," Andrew said. "Leave these here people to fix their own problems. They give me a hive." He added, "don't 'preciate nothing nobody does for them, like it's owed."

Kerry thought about that. "Well," she said, after a moment. "I think maybe they do. I think they expect everyone to go the last mile for the city, because of what happened."

"True enough." Alastair allowed. "But does that mean we throw off all our own responsibilities to take on theirs?"

Andrew and Kerry looked at Alastair. "I think that's your call, isn't it?" Kerry asked. She studied the older man's face, which was tired looking and smudged with dust. "Can we just walk away from this?"

Alastair thought for a moment, his eyes going a little unfocused as he considered the question. "Sure would be nice to go home, huh?"

Kerry flashed back to that underground nightmare, and the strong desire it had spurred in her to turn and run, and keep on running right back to the warm sun and blue skies waiting for her back home.

Home. Miami was home now in a way Michigan had never been. "It would," she replied softly. "It's not that I don't want to help those guys in there. I don't think it will end up being worth anything to us."

"Hm." Alastair rubbed his nose. "Not sure we should expect any worth out of it. There is something to be said for public service. We don't always get a return on an investment, at least not in the short term. I have a feeling if we turn our backs on these bastards, we'll suffer in the long term." He paused. "Not fair, really."

"Jackasses," Andrew muttered.

"Let me go see what's going on." Kerry pushed away from the wall and headed over to the doorway, more to give Alastair room to think than because she thought she would be of any help inside. She eased into the space, spotting Dar's tall form to one side as her partner pointed out something.

She could sense the tension in the room. With a gentle "excuse me", she edged behind the Sprint rep and came up behind Dar, finding a spot between her and the wall that was just about the right size for her to fit into.

With a gentle clearing of her throat, she fit into it.

Dar sensed her, stepping back and draping an arm over her shoulders with a complete lack of self consciousness. "Hey Ker."

"Hey." Kerry hoped the layer of dust on her skin masked the mild blush. "How's it going?" She studied the demarc, rows and rows of telecom cards in shallow racks festooned with tags in a rainbow of different colors.

Dar shook her head. "Hard to say where to even start," she admitted. "It's not just communications with the rest of the exchanges. Data comes in here from all over the world."

"Yeah," the tech from the Exchange said. "That's what I was trying to explain to those other guys." He walked over to the wall. "This stuff's just here in the financial district. It's all local point to point." He indicated one rack. "This goes to the banking system. This goes to the major trading houses in, like, forty cities."

He slapped the wall. "None of it's working."

The MCI rep put his hands on his hips. "I don't think we can do this. Even if we bring in a full sat setup, there's not enough transponder space up above to handle the traffic."

"They'd never let you anyway," the Exchange tech said. "The trading houses, and the other exchanges...the foreign ones, they've got security on this stuff big time."

Charles exhaled. "That's true. Most of those tie lines are ours. I've already had a call from London and Hong Kong."

"We had enough trouble getting space on the sat to relay our mobile cell units down here," the Sprint rep said. "They're jammed."

"They are." Kerry spoke up. "We've got a majority of the transponder space up there and we're using it for our customers."

The men turned and looked at her, then looked back at the maze of wires. "So what the hell are we doing here?" Charles asked. "Let's tell them we can't do it. What can they do? I'm already toast and I don't have an ass left...begging your pardon..." He glanced at Kerry. "For them to chew anymore."

Kerry looked at all the tags, then she glanced up at Dar. "What are our options, boss?"

Dar regarded the mass of wires. "Our options? Our options are which direction we're going to drive the bus out of here on our way out of town, unfortunately. We can't fix this."

The rest of the men nodded in simultaneous agreement.

"No way?" Kerry nudged. "Nothing at all we can do? I sure got the impression from the White House that this was really important. "

"It is important," the Exchange tech spoke up again. "If the market doesn't open, that's a huge amount of money tied up that can't go anywhere."

"Can't they do it by hand?" Dar asked. "Y'know, computers are a lot younger than this building."

"You got to be kidding me," the tech said, in chorus with Charles and the MCI guy.

"Guess not," Kerry murmured. "Dar, there has to be something we can do. Even to bring up basic services. Isn't there?"

Dar removed her arm and put both hands in the pockets of her coveralls, tilting her head to one side as she gave the question its just due. Everyone waited respectfully in silence, until she cleared her throat and shrugged slightly.

"Think of something?" Kerry could tell, by the body language alone, what the answer was.

"Won't fly," Dar demurred. "The only way we could help out is if we get a trunk line from here over to Roosevelt Island. That's our closest node." She went on. "You'd have to do it underground."

"Impossible," the Exchange tech said, immediately. "Especially not without the union guys. I can't even get in a manhole without paying them through the nose."

"We'd never get the clearance," the MCI rep said. "He's right. That's all Verizon right of way and there's no way they'll let us run cable in there. Not taking money out of their pocket. I wouldn't either." He added. "If it was me."

Charles looked thoughtful. "Okay, it's impossible," he said. "But what if we could do it? What would that get us? It gets us to your network. That's private. We all know it."

"You're riding on it right now." Kerry reminded him mildly. "I'm tunneling you between your headend to your office here."

"Sure, but you can't do that for all of us, and all of this," Charles said. Then he paused, when Dar didn't respond. "Can you?"

Dar merely shrugged again. "No point in wondering, since it can't be done," she said. "But theoretically, if we could do it, and get the pipe over to my node, I might be able to do something useful with it."

There was a moment of silence, as the men all stared at Dar, who kept her hands in her pockets, a thoughtful expression on her face.

"Are you shitting me?" The MCI rep finally asked.

"No," Dar replied. "Excuse me." She removed her hands from her pockets and patted Kerry on the shoulder. "Be right back," she advised, as she slipped past, and ducked out the door.

The men turned around and looked at Kerry, who folded her arms across her chest. "Don't ask," she said. "But if she says it's possible, you can take that to the damn bank."

"Yeah." Mark spoke up for the first time. "But if we can't get that cable from here to there, it's crap."

"Yeah," the Exchange tech said. "Crap."

Charles sighed. "Well, I can call Verizon. I think someone high enough in my company is probably related to someone high enough in their company."

"Their name Bell?" The MCI rep asked, wryly. "Better start digging. You're gonna need him."

KERRY WAS GLAD enough to drop into a soft, leather chair safe in the confines of the bus and surrounded by her colleagues. "Buh." She let her head drop back. "Glad we're here."

"Glad the wind is blowing off the water." Dar finished stripping out of her jumpsuit, tossing it over the back of the chair opposite Kerry before going to the bar and pouring herself a glass of juice from the waiting carafe.

"You got that right." Mark was toweling his face off. "This is some nasty shit. "

Kerry slung one leg over the arm of the chair and squirmed in the corner, letting her head rest against the soft leather. "You're right. That was nasty."

"It was." Dar sat down in the chair next to her, extending her long legs across the floor of the bus and cradling her juice between her hands. "Glad it's over."

"Is it?" Kerry asked.

"Well, for now," Dar clarified. "Until they come back and talk to us about getting action on that cabling I don't' see a reason for us to go back in there. Do you?"

Kerry shook her head emphatically. "I can live the rest of my life not going back in there given my choice, thanks. I'll be having nightmares about that underground for a month."

Dar reached over and curled her fingers around Kerry's arm, gently rubbing the inside of it with her thumb. "Sorry."

"Not your fault," Kerry muttered. "I could have stayed upstairs."

The door to the bus opened, and Alastair entered, putting his mask down and closing the door behind him. "Son of a bitch."

Dar's eyebrows hiked.

Her boss unzipped his dust covered overalls and removed them, sitting down on the nearby barstool to remove the legs.

"Can I get you something, sir?" The bus attendant zipped over, alertly

"Scotch. Double," Alastair said. "Straight up."

"Yes, sir."

"Governor's office get you again, Alastair?" Dar asked.

"Stupid son of a bitch." Alastair took the glass the bus attendant handed over, and gulped down the contents.

"Wow." Mark edged over to the counter nearby, giving his CEO a look of healthy respect. He opened a glass covered case and removed a sandwich sitting down to take a bite of it. "Want one of these, Mr. M?"

Alastair set his glass down with loud clacking sound. "I gotta tell you, ladies and gentleman. I'm about to pull this company out of here."

He got up and crossed over to where the chairs were, detouring long enough to grab a sandwich before he sat down across from Dar. "Son of a bitch."

Dar gave him a wry look. "Welcome to my world."

"Lady, you can keep it. I should tell that damn governor to take his threats and shove them up his ass."

"Threats?" Kerry frowned. "What on earth does he have to threaten us with? None of these are even our circuits." She got up and went over to the counter, selecting two sandwiches. "Sheesh."

"Hungry, boss?" Mark asked, giving her two fisted selection a quizzical look.

Kerry merely gave him a look as she retreated back to her chair stopping on the way to deliver Dar's sandwich. She sat down again and took a bite from the roll, glad of the tang of the horseradish sauce taking the taint of dust from her mouth.

"Thanks." Dar licked a bit of the sauce off her fingers.

"He said if we didn't come through on this damn Exchange issue, he'd cancel all our state contracts," Alastair said. "Can you believe that? In the middle of all this? I asked him if he didn't have enough problems without us pulling out and taking the rest of his offices down."

"I think he's just panicked." Dar chewed her mouthful of prime rib thoughtfully and swallowed it. "I think the federal government is all over him, and he's punching at whatever is in reach." She took a sip of her juice to wash the sandwich down. "Besides, we committed ourselves to help out here. "

"We did." Alastair agreed mournfully. "Sorry about that."

"I'm not," Dar replied.

Kerry tilted her head to one side and regarded her partner. "Really?" She asked. "You like being here?"

Dar shook her head. "No." She licked another bit of sauce from her thumb. "I hate being here. But if those people get their heads out of their asses, and get that cable run, we can do something to help." She glanced at Alastair. "Did you explain that to him?"

"Do you think they can do it?" Kerry nibbled the edge of her sandwich.

"There's no technical reason they can't," Dar said. "If they have the cable, and they're the damn phone company so they should have the damn cable, and they can find their way into the subway which goes right over onto the island, they can do it."

Alastair extended his legs and crossed his ankles. "Seems like a lot of work for two days. I did mention to the governor we had a dependency on those folks, but he wasn't hearing any of it. Said I should get it done myself."

Dar rolled her eyes.

"Hey, it's your reputation that got us into this." Her boss reminded her. "I wasn't the one who called the government and volunteered us."

"Like I did?" Dar shot back. "You're the one who told me to go do it. I could have told Gerry we didn't have a chance at fixing this."

Alastair paused and thought, then shrugged. "Well...you know you're right. I did," he said. "But you never do listen to me, so why did you this time?"

"Children." Kerry cleared her throat. "Can we table the snipe fest? We've already got enough issues here to deal with."

"Doesn't she work for you?" Alastair pointed at Kerry, staring pointedly at Dar. "Insubordination?"

"Don't **I** work for **you**?" Dar grinned suddenly. "What's your point?"

Alastair chuckled wryly after a brief pause. "Damned if I know. Someone get me another scotch." He waved a hand at the bus attendant. "All right. So you're saying if those folks do manage to get some agreement then there's a chance this can happen?"

Dar got up and went to the white board on the far wall of the bus. It was covered in scribbling, and she picked up an eraser and wiped it off. "Okay." She grabbed a marker and started drawing. "Let me just sketch this in."

Kerry took the opportunity to finish her sandwich. It was good. Her body was craving protein, and it really hit the spot.

Dar was drawing in a reasonable facsimile of Manhattan with the Hudson and East rivers on either side. Her hand made easy, sure motions and after a moment, she was finished. "We're here." She made a mark near the tip of the island. "Mark, hand me that subway map over there will ya?"

"Sure." Mark hopped off the barstool he had perched on and brought the map over. He handed it to Dar then stepped back out of the way.

"Thanks." Dar opened the map and spread it on the bar, studying it for a moment. "Okay." She turned to the whiteboard again. "Here's where we were today." She marked a spot on the map. "That's Cortland Street. Here's the disaster site." She marked a large square. "Here's where the triple pop was, and Verizon's Central Office."

Kerry watched in fascination while sipping her drink. Dar's sense of space had always intrigued her. She'd seen her partner draw underwater diagrams with a three dimensional precision that was amazing. Now, she laid out the diagram with absolute sureness.

"Now." Dar moved on to the east side of the island. "Here's Roosevelt Island. The subway comes in here and then the line that goes through there comes back around this side down to here." She tapped her marker on the map. "If they bring it up Lexington Avenue, to Central Park, they can come down the tunnel here, and they'll end up not that far from our node."

"That's a hell of a long way." Alastair protested. "Not that it looks that far on that board, but Dar, I've been on that side of the city. You're not talking about a trivial effort here."

"I know." Dar juggled the marker in her hand, flipping it end from end. "You didn't ask me if it was reasonable or likely...just if it was possible."

Kerry was about to voice her doubts about the possibility of it happening at all when her mind flashed back to a rainy night in the Carolinas and her jaws clicked shut.

It was possible. Dar wouldn't have bothered discussing it if she thought it wasn't. Whether or not those other guys could achieve it was another question, but it was a question Kerry wasn't sure she should be asking.

It wasn't their problem.

"That's a crazy amount of work." Mark spoke up. "If those guys have the reels, then maybe, but I don't think they can get through all that red tape, Dar. I heard those guys from the phone company talking and they're not into it at all."

"Well." Dar went to the bar and sat down on a stool. "Governor or no governor, I'm not going down there and do it for them," she said, quietly. "This is their city. It's their customers. I'm not crawling around in a tube kicking rats out of the way on their behalf."

Kerry nodded in relief. "Dar, I'll go wherever you go, but I don't want to do that either. Being under there today freaked me out."

"Right there with you," Mark said.

Alastair sipped his scotch. "I can work with that." He decided. "Let me get hold of Ham and we'll go see that damn jackass again."

"Somebody call me?" Hamilton Baird entered the back of the bus, wiping his hands off on his handkerchief. "Why, hello there you all. Gentlemen. Ladies." He glanced at Dar. "Maestro."

"Just talking about you Ham," Alastair said. "Dar's got a plan. We've got to go sell it."

"Now that's different," Ham drawled. "Ah got to tell you, Dar, I heard from those people down at Crisis on the Bay, or whatever they're calling that junk shop on the Hudson, and they do think you're just the cat's meow."

"Thanks," Dar said.

"Did you really do something with a welder?"

"Soldering iron." Kerry supplied. "It really was pretty spectacular and brilliant, but that's pretty typical of Dar."

Dar looked at her, eyes widening a little.

"Do tell?" Hamilton half turned toward her, a humorous tone in his voice.

"When we're done with the chit chat, we've got a jackass to go see," Alastair said.

Hamilton paused at the sandwich tray. "Do I have a New York minute to swallow this like a civilized man or should I have this lovely young lady put it in a blender and make it a smoothie for me?"

"Eat." Alastair waved a hand at him.

Hamilton picked up his sandwich and his drink and wandered to the front of the bus where a television was playing. After a moment, Alastair got up and followed him.

Mark dusted off his hands. "I'm gonna go see what routers I've got to mess with left back there." He unlatched the back door and disappeared, leaving Dar and Kerry alone in the small seating section.

They were both quiet for a moment, just looking at each other. Then Kerry got up and moved over to Dar's chair, taking a seat on the arm and leaning along the back.

"Children?" Dar rested her head against Kerry's shoulder. "You crack me up."

"Sorry." Kerry ran the fingers of her free hand through Dar's hair. "My brain is running in circles. Can they really do this, Dar?"

"Probably not," she conceded. "It would be like us running a cable from the office in Miami to our house. Possible, but pretty damn unlikely."

"Can they get it to our office at the Rock? We could take some of the traffic there, and not go all the way across to Roosevelt." Kerry suggested. "It's a little closer."

Dar considered that. "Which one of us is spectacular and brilliant?" she asked. "I forgot all about that. I have extra capacity at the office. We might be able to take part of the traffic there." She closed her eyes. "But I was serious, Ker. They have to step up, just like we had to step up yesterday and get the job done."

Kerry kissed the top of her head. "I love you," she replied, simply.

Dar smiled.

"Anything we can do to help though?"

"I knew you were going to ask that." Dar remarked. "Let's get Scuzzy up here and see if she knows someone we can talk to. I met her on a subway. Maybe it's a sign." She reached over and put her hand on Kerry's leg. "Want to hear my ulterior motive?"

"That if they run the cable up to our uplink, we can piggy back our customers down here on it? Starting with our tech office?"

Dar chuckled under her breath, a soft, light sound that echoed inside the bus. "Busted!"

Kerry started laughing too, her body finally giving up its tension as her headache faded and her blood sugar stabilized. The sense of horror from the disaster site moved to the back of her mind and the optimism that was more natural for her returned.

Dar turned her head and brushed Kerry's lips with her own, ignoring the rest of the folks on the bus that were within earshot.

Shocking. Kerry returned the kiss, caressing Dar's face with gentle fingers. But who cared?

The whole world was different now.

Chapter Seven

KERRY RESTED HER chin on her hand as her other hand moved her mouse clicking on another email. "Go ahead, Air Hub. I think it sounds like everyone has everything pretty much together."

"Roger that, Miami exec. Traffic isn't back to normal, but it's steady, and I think we can handle the additional service requests."

"Miami exec, this is Herndon." A female voice broke in. "We're getting calls from sites affected by the Pennsylvania outage. They want a status."

Kerry tapped on the mouse. "Do you have someone on now?"

"Yes, ma'am." Herndon answered. "Docson Pharmaceuticals."

"Put them on."

There was a moment's silence. "Put them on the bridge, ma'am?"

"Yes," Kerry said. "I only have two ears and one set of vocal cords. Put them on."

"Uh...yes ma'am. One second."

Kerry released her mouse and picked up her cup of hot tea, taking a sip of the mint and raspberry flavored beverage as she waited for the customer to come on the line.

She was in the last section in the bus a small, discrete office barely the size of her bathroom in the condo, but furnished in solid teak with the most comfortable leather office chair she'd ever encountered.

Plush and expensive, it was designed to provide a marginal business purpose for the courtesy bus and, in the case of strange and utter emergency, it allowed whoever was using the bus at the time—always senior officers of the company—to perform whatever office it was they held in dignified good taste.

She liked it. It was private. There was a smoked glass wall that separated it from the rest of the bus, and a door she currently had shut. The glass kept it from being too claustrophobic, but the shading kept it from being a fishbowl and it was soundproofed to a moderate degree.

"Standby." Herndon warned her. "Mr. Eccles? You're on the line with Kerry Stuart, our VP of Operations. Go ahead."

The only thing it lacked was enough space for Dar to be in there with her. "Go ahead, Mr. Eccles. What can I do for you?" Kerry spoke into the mic.

"Ah, okay, yes. Ms...ah, Stuart was it?" A male voice came from the speaker, along with faint static.

"That's right." Kerry saw a popup start to flash, and she clicked on it.

Hey Kerry – got a minute?

Kerry typed into the box. *Go ahead Mari.*

"Well, listen. I need to know what's going on here. I've tried to get hold of my account rep, but he's not answering, and the support center said there's no one available down there so..."

Kerry clicked on another box as a text message passed through their internal messaging system rather than to her phone.

Scuzzy knows a guy. She smiled at the words. "Well, Mr. Eccles, I'm very sorry, but you'll have to be a little more specific on the question. There's an awful lot going on right now. I am sure you can appreciate that we have many issues we're working on, including yours."

She waited for the answer while she typed a response. *Scuzzy's going to be worth a promotion by the time this is over*

She'll end up a regional director. Can't wait for the conference calls with her on them.

Kerry stifled a laugh, appreciating Dar's wry humor. Then Mari's box started flashing with a new incoming message, and she clicked over to it.

Kerry, I've got a request here from the FBI to provide them with all our employment records.

Kerry's head jerked up. "What?"

"Well, I...what?" Eccles answered. "What did you say?"

"Sorry." Kerry typed furiously into the machine. "Go ahead. I have quite a few things working here right now."

"As I was saying, our offices have been down since Tuesday. I'm the first one to understand that there's been terrible things going on, and I assume your people are busy, but my business is at a standstill and I need to know what's being done for us."

What? Dar's response came back.

What should I tell them? Mari asked.

"Hang on a minute, Mr. Eccles. Let me call up the support system and see what I can find out for you." Kerry said, as she typed. *Mari, I'm getting Dar on this. She's with Alastair, and I hope also with Hamilton. They really need to handle that request. Who's it coming from?*

I'm on the way there. Dar's message somehow sounded as indignant as Kerry knew she was.

Bring Alastair and our lawyer. Kerry advised her. "Okay, Mr. Eccles, what I have here on your outage is that you have three circuits down..."

Her cell phone rang. "Hold on a second, maybe that's news." She put the mic on hold and opened her phone without looking at the caller ID. "Kerry Stuart."

Okay, gotcha. Mari typed back. *I halfway understand the request, Kerry—it's become very obvious to a lot of people just how involved we are in the government, but I'm concerned.*

She's concerned? Kerry took her eyes from the screen briefly as she heard a slight buzz on the phone. "Hello?"

"Ms. Stuart? Hello? This is Danny down at the Pentagon...I'm trying to get hold of Mark. Do you know where he is?"

The door opened and Dar entered the small room, bringing her restless energy with her. "Who's asking?"

"Danny, last time I saw Mark he was inventorying the routers here. Can I get him to call you? I'm on a few things right now." Kerry blocked out the distraction of her partner with difficulty.

"Oh, sure. Sorry about that," Danny said. "They're all of a sudden chewing me to move some of our rigs and I don't want to disconnect anything."

"Let me see that." Dar circled the desk and squeezed behind it with her, leaning over to peer at Kerry's screen. She clicked on Mari's box and typed into it.

"Okay, yeah, I'll have Mark call you." Kerry promised. "Bye." She hung up the phone and picked up the mic. "I'm on the bridge, hon. Don't start yelling."

"Idiots." Dar growled while reading the screen.

"Okay, sorry about that." Kerry keyed the mic. "Mr. Eccles, according to our system…" She paused, as Dar's typing removed the view from her screen. "Sorry, hold on one more minute." She clicked the mic off. "Sweetheart, I need to see my stuff. I'm in the middle of something here."

"I know…I know…just one second," Dar muttered. "Freaking idiots. I'm having her give them Hamilton's number. He's earning his salary today, that's for sure."

Kerry took the opportunity to take a sip of tea. Despite Dar's interruption in her flurry of communication, she didn't mind having her partner hanging over her. It gave her a chance to rearrange her thoughts, and the warmth of Dar's breasts pressing against the back of her head didn't hurt either.

"There. Sorry. Want me to pass that message to Mark?" Dar kissed the top of her head. "Since I messed up your flow here?"

"That would be awesome." Kerry took possession of her laptop. "Now let me go and give some BS story to this guy about his circuits. Do you think they'll look at the Philly ones any time soon?"

"All the techs are here," Dar said. "Want me to send him a sat truck? Is he big enough?"

Kerry called up the account and studied it. Then she sighed. "Honestly, no," she said. "Let me see what I can do to placate him."

"Okay." Dar gave her shoulders a squeeze, then edged out from behind the desk and got the door open. "Let me know if you need anything else, okay?"

"Absolutely." Kerry resisted the urge to come up with something else on the spot. "Thanks babe." She waited for Dar to close the door then she went back to her mic. "Okay. Where the hell was I?"

DAR SHUT THE door to the bus and emerged into the area defined by the bus, the sat trucks and equipment vans that had accompanied it. In the middle of the open space, they'd set up a rough wooden worktable, and on it was spread the underground map with a handful of techs and Scuzzy all looking at it.

She rejoined them and the techs cleared a space for her. She was about to delve back into the underground puzzle when her conscience poked her. "Where's Mark?"

"He was just here," Shaun said. "Just a second ago."

"Mark!"

"Whoa, whoa…right here, Big D." Mark appeared from around the back of the bus. "I got that stuff you wanted me to look for…what's up?"

"Pentagon was calling for you. Something about moving a rig." Dar replied briefly. "Call them. Tell them not to bug Kerry if they want you.

She's not your sitter."

"Okay boss, you got it." Mark reversed course and headed for the bus. "My cell's gone wonky. It keeps losing sig. I'll tell them to text me on the PDA."

Dar returned her attention to the map, satisfied she'd taken one annoyance off her partner's plate. "Okay." She pulled out another schematic of the office building where their office was located. "Let's say, by some miracle of political voodoo they do manage to get a wire in this direction."

"Y'know, they could," Scuzzy said. She leaned on the table with both hands, appearing pleased to be involved. "Those union guys, they ain't that bad, you know? They want their stuff the way they want their stuff, if you know what I mean."

Dar nodded. "Matter of fact, I do know what you mean. But I don't lay bets on people I don't know. So all we can do is have a few plans in our back pocket." She tapped the blueprint. "As I was saying if they do manage to get up here, then what? How do we get the signal upstairs? Riser?"

Shaun hunkered down over the plan, leaning on his elbows. "Here's something labeled electrical room. I think."

"But are there any openings between the room and the lower basement?" Kannan added, folding his long, slim arms over his chest. "I am thinking that will be the largest of the problems. I do not think they will let us put a hole through the wall."

Dar drummed her pencil against the plans. "I think we should relocate back to the office...at least half of us anyway. We can start figuring out what to do about the connection while some people stay here and work on this end."

"You really think these guys are going to do this?" Shaun asked. "I was talking to one of those Verizon techs. He didn't sound too enthusiastic."

"I don't know," Dar answered honestly. "But I do know if they do decide to come through, and we're not ready for it, we'll look like a bunch of jackasses. That's not on my agenda for today."

"Ah. Yeah." Shaun blushed a little. "Sorry."

"Lo there Dardar." Andrew had slipped between the bus and the sat truck and came up next to her. "What's the problem with them fellers? All these people round here looking to help, and all they're doing is pushing back."

He stuck his hands in his pockets, and cocked his head. "Don't make no sense."

"It doesn't really." Kannan agreed. "I don't understand it myself."

"You guys don't understand, yeah, that's right." Scuzzy spoke up. "These guys—like the tunnels, and the buildings and everything—they've been these guys like, home plate, you know? Like, my cousin, he's a guy who works in the tunnels. His pop, he was a sandhog. You know what that was?"

"Fellers work underground." Andrew supplied.

"Yeah, but here, that's like, something special." Scuzzy told them. "This whole place, this whole city? It's built on what's underground. So they take it real personal about all them spaces. "

Dar now folded her arms. "You know something? I get it."

"Yeah?"

"Yeah." Dar said. "I get it, because our entire company is built on a foundation I laid. I take that really personal also. But right now, they need to either get their heads out of their asses and be part of the solution, or be the ones who are going to answer to the damn politicians when their banks won't open on Monday. I'm not covering for them."

Scuzzy nodded. "That's pretty much what I told my cousin to tell those guys. 'Cause you know what? They ain't into seeing their pictures in the Times, you know?"

"Let's hope so." Dar pulled a pad over and started to scribble on it. "So. Let's see."

"Ms. Roberts?" A strange voice broke in.

Dar looked up, to find Charles somewhat timidly sticking his head around the corner of the bus. "Yes?"

He took that as permission to approach. "Listen, we're having a meeting with the city and union folks...would you mind stepping in and giving your view on the situation?" He asked. "There's some skepticism as to what our goals are."

Dar's brows lifted slightly.

"Okay, they all think we're nuts," Charles amended hastily. "I'm not having much luck convincing them otherwise. I thought maybe you'd have a better chance at it." He looked hopefully at Dar. "Please?"

Dar let him wait for minute, then shrugged and dropped her pencil. "Have it your way," she said. "The rest of you folks—let's get packed up to move back uptown. I don't care which lot of you stay here to work on the Exchange, sort it out among yourselves and be ready to head out when I get back."

"Yes, ma'am," Shaun said. "Will do."

"Let's go." Dar gestured for Charles to precede her. "I don't know if I can talk any sense into them, but I guarantee they won't have any question about what our goals are when I'm done." She glanced behind her as she felt a presence, not really surprised to find her father strolling along at her heels.

"Well, we're sure not getting any help from the politicians on this one." Charles shook his head as he walked quickly ahead of her. "They want us to fix the problem, but they don't want to help us do it."

"Now." Andrew mused. "Why is that, ah do wonder?"

"Maybe we can ask them that when I'm done with the rest of those guys," Dar said. "Should be an interesting answer."

"Should be."

KERRY WASHED DOWN a handful of Advil with a swig of water, then set the bottle down and shaded her eyes, listening to the chatter on the bridge without looking at her screen. Her cramps had returned with a vengeance. She was glad all she had to do was keep her ear glued to the activity and not do something more strenuous like move equipment around at the moment.

She knew there was a lot of activity going on around the bus. She could hear thumps and bangs, and voices through the thin aluminum walls. There was a flurry of coming and going through the bus's three doors, and the rumble of the truck engines of their little caravan was rattling the window near her shoulder.

"Miami exec, this is Vancouver hub."

"Go on." Kerry kept her eyes closed.

"Okay, we're finally back to normal traffic patterns. We released the last bandwidth advance for the airport." The Canadian hub reported. "Everyone's rather chilling out we think."

"Good to hear," Kerry murmured.

"Miami, this is Houston ops."

"Go ahead."

"Miami, we're running into some pretty big issues with new contracts that were due to start this week and early next." A male voice answered. "We've been told pretty much not to expect any circuit acceptance or demarc changes in the foreseeable future."

"In Houston?" Kerry's brows knit.

"Anywhere," the man answered. "We were told all the line techs — for telco and power too — are being sent to New York to help out there, and anyway, some are going regardless because of all the work available."

"We had the same issue in Washington believe it or not," Kerry replied. "What is up with that? How many techs do they think they're going to need here? It's not that big an island. I realize there was a lot of damage done but there are only so many guys that can fit in a manhole."

There was a bit of silence when she finished.

"Well, okay, but what are we supposed to tell all these clients?" The voice from Houston asked finally. "I'm running out of excuses."

Kerry drummed the fingers of her free hand on the table. "Yeah. That's a good question. Rather than answer every one of our hundreds of thousands of customers, I think we should probably put out a note to everyone."

"Miami exec, are they really serious, that no one is going to get connected until whenever?" Another voice asked.

"Another good question. We have some of the head guys of the different companies around here, let me go round them up and see if I can find out. It could be that a lot of the local companies are putting everything on hold because they're not sure what's going to happen."

"That would be great, Miami exec," Houston said. "We sure could use the help, or at least, something we can tell all these people. We were supposed to bring thirty two branch offices of the local credit union here online, and the guy in charge there's my wife's brother-in-law. He's calling me every five minutes."

"Gotcha." Kerry reluctantly got to her feet. "Okay, folks, I'm going offline for a few. I'll try to get us some answers."

"Hey Kerry?" Mariana broke in. "Where are you guys?"

Kerry paused. "Battery Park," she answered, finally.

'How is it down there?" Mari asked. "I know we saw on the television, but..."

How was it? Kerry let the silence lengthen as she tried to come up with an answer. "It's like a nightmare. The wreckage up close...it's overwhelming. The dust is overwhelming. The smell is horrific. "

"Wow." The man from Houston murmured.

"We went underground to see if we could spot any of the cables and I could swear I heard all those souls screaming."

Now there was dead silence on the bridge. Kerry took the moment to breathe, swallowing the lump that had come up in her throat. "So anyway," she continued, after the tightness relaxed, "Let me go see what I can find out from those telco guys. I'll be back in shortly."

She disconnected the mic and let it drop on her laptop taking a moment to lock the screen before she eased wearily out from behind the desk and went to the panel door. She opened it and went through, glad the interior of the bus was now quiet.

The floor of the bus shifted slightly, she paused and then continued on toward the outer door hoping the motion was just some last loading and unloading, and not anything more ominous.

The haze in the air seemed to have gotten thicker. Kerry wondered if it had, or if it was just her impression. Most of the sun was blocked out, and as she watched, a layer of dust was settling on the table Dar had set up in the center of their technical encampment.

She felt the breeze blow into her face, and realized the wind had changed, and that accounted for the thicker air, and heavier dust. "Crap." She turned and went back into the bus, picking up the mask she'd left near the bar and adjusting it over her head.

It felt gritty, and uncomfortable. However, she tightened the straps and returned to the outdoors, turning her head to look around for the others she expected to find somewhere outside.

It was too quiet, though. Kerry walked around the bus, then around the satellite trucks sitting silently aligned with it. She opened the back door to trailer Mark had hauled, but it, too, was empty. "Where in the hell is everyone?"

Past the truck she could see clusters of workers seated in the park with their backs to the wind as they huddled over paper wrapped sandwiches. Nearby on a table she spotted three of the company coolers, and cups that were clutched in many hands, and then, at last, she could see one of the bus attendants heading back toward her. "Hey, Sharon!"

The attendant skewed her route and ended up next to Kerry. "Oh, hi, ma'am. Did you need something? I was giving those guys some of our sandwiches. They really don't have a lot of supplies down here yet."

"Do you know where everyone else is?" Kerry asked. "And absolutely, give those guys whatever we've got. They look exhausted."

"Well, you know I was wondering that myself," Sharon said. "I was inside cleaning up and then I came out here and everyone was gone. Maybe they went back to the site?" She glanced over her shoulder then sneezed.

"You should have a mask on," Kerry told her. "This air's thick with who knows what."

"I know," Sharon said. "I'm going inside to get one now. It just started to get bad again. I got sidetracked listening to those men talk about that place. My God, Ms. Stuart, they were here when it happened. One of those firemen said bodies were dropping out of the sky all over the place."

Kerry grimaced. "Yeah." She pulled out her PDA and opened it. "Well, let me find out where the gang is. I thought we were trying to get out of here." She typed a quick message to Dar and sent it. "Ah, here are some of the guys now."

Shaun and Kannan were headed toward her, masks firmly settled on their heads and collars turned up on their jumpsuits. Kerry waited for them to come over, then motioned them over to the bus and pointed on the other side of it. "Let's get out of the wind."

"Great idea," Shaun said.

They followed her to the far side of the vehicle and pulled their masks off. "Ms. Stuart, I am very apprehensive here," Kannan said. "My brother has just called me, and has said there are many instances of people from my country being hurt here."

"Here?" Kerry looked around. "What's going on?"

"Everywhere," Shaun said. "Jerks in pickups with guns shooting out convenience stores and some guy got gunned down on the street because he had a turban on. I heard it on the news."

"What?"

"It's true," Kannan said. "My family is very upset. They do not wish me to stay here."

Kerry nodded. "Absolutely," she said. "Where is your family? We'll get you there." She felt her PDA buzz and opened it. "Hang on."

Hey Ker.

I'm in a meeting with the telecom people. Wasting my time mostly. What's up?

DD

"Well, isn't that handy," Kerry muttered. "Hold on a second guys, I need to ask Dar something."

"No problem, Ms. Stuart," Kannan said. "I am glad to be back here, with our vehicles. I am going to go inside our camper there, and perhaps do some wiring while we wait." He headed off toward the camper Mark had brought, but not without glancing around carefully before he crossed between the bus and it.

"That totally sucks," Shaun said.

"It does." Kerry agreed. "Where's his family? In Virginia?"

"Arizona, I think. That's why they're so freaked. One of the killings happened there." Shaun informed her. "So maybe his family should take off and go somewhere else, huh?"

"Could be." Kerry tapped into the PDA. *Good timing. I was just on the wire with Houston, and we're getting complaints from all around that we can't get circuits completed. Can you find out if that's a knee jerk one day thing, or if we're in real trouble? Where are you? It's getting creepy here. We should get out of this damn dust cloud.*

She hit enter. "Where were you guys? With Dar?"

"No." Shaun shook his head. "We were with some of the Verizon guys, trying to make friends with them. We were in one of the manholes a little bit away from here, just helping them out and stuff."

"Did they say anything?"

Shaun shrugged. "They're just linemen. They're...I don't know, it's hard to figure them out. I think they're pissed because of all the destruction and all that, but they also were almost sort of jazzed because of all the OT they'd be making."

"Welcome to humanity," Kerry remarked dryly. "The one truly consistent trait of the species is self interest. But if that's the case, why are they pushing back so hard in helping us? If they want OT, we're sure offering a lot of it."

"They aren't." Shaun shook his head. "They don't give a squat about it, in fact, they thought the idea was sort of slick, to run a cable up the subway. It's their bosses who are being such a...a PITA."

"Uh huh." Kerry mused. "I wonder why."

"Maybe they want a payoff." Shaun suggested. "I heard it was like that here."

Kerry's PDA buzzed. "Hang on." She tapped the new message.

Charles is calling his head office. He'll let me know. These Verizon bastards won't budge.

Kerry tapped her stylus on the edge of the PDA, then tapped a response. *Offer them a payoff. I was talking to Shaun, and he said he talked to the linemen. They're fine with running the cable.*

The message came right back. *You're kidding me right?*

No. Kerry typed back. *It's New York, Dar.*

We're a public company and I'm an officer of it, Ker. Dar responded. *I could get thrown in jail for that.*

Kerry somehow doubted it. *Then tell Alastair to do it. He's there, right? Dar, I love you but please don't tell me ILS has never paid a bribe to get something pushed through.*

ILS has. I haven't.

Despite it all, it made Kerry smile. Ruthless, smart, quick thinking, driven...and yet, there was a line that Dar wouldn't cross. It was a beautiful thing, really. *Okay. Just a thought. I can't really think of what else is holding their management layer back, if the line boys don't care. I thought it would be them, the union guys who would be balking.*

Good point. Dar responded.

"Hey, guys?" Kannan came running back out. "Did we fix it? Did Ms. Roberts do this already? I am amazed!"

"Huh?" Kerry's head jerked up. "We haven't done anything. Why?"

Kannan skidded to a halt, his thin face crumpling in confusion. "I have just heard, on CNN, that they have tested the systems successfully, for this Exchange? Is that not what we were supposed to be helping with?"

Kerry and Shaun exchanged deeply puzzled looks.

Kerry opened her cell phone and dialed it. "Are you sure?"

Kannan spread his arms out and lifted his hands slightly. "That is what the news said. I am sure of that."

The phone crackled, ringing once and then crackling again as it was answered. "Dar?"

"Yeah." Dar's voice sounded slightly muffled. "Hang on, I'm going outside." She paused a moment. "Go ahead. What's up?"

"Kannan just heard on CNN that they successfully tested the Exchange computers to work on Monday. Are we doing this for nothing?" Kerry asked.

"Huh?" Dar said. "Ker, I'm in the Exchange. We're in the technical center. Trust me. Nothing's being tested here. They just lost power to the data center and there's no AC. Nothing's even turned on. And listen, I do appreciate the suggestion before; it's just not my style."

"I know hon," Kerry said. "So if nothing's working, what did they test?"

"The public trust?" Dar asked. "I haven't a clue. Hang on, Alastair? Kerry just said they announced on the news that they tested the Exchange systems and they were all good to go for Monday. You know what's up? What? No? Okay." Her voice got louder. "Ker, we don't know squat here. I'll try to find out."

"Okay sweetie." Kerry sighed. "I'll do the same. Maybe I'll call my mother. Maybe she knows something. It's getting really cruddy here. We moving out anytime soon?"

"Soon as I get back there." Dar promised. "Hang in there, love."

Kerry exhaled. "I'll do my best. But do me a favor huh? Kick their asses and don't hang around to take names. We should get out of here. "

"Will do," Dar said. "Talk to you shortly."

She hung up the phone. "Dar says they're not testing anything." She told the techs.

"So...the news was a lie?" Kannan asked.

Kerry shrugged a little. "I don't know. I don't really know what that's all about." She indicated the trailer. "Let's go see what else they say about it."

"Weird," Shaun said. "But hey, we've got Oreos and milk in there...if you don't mind paper cups."

"Lead on." Kerry found the thought of the familiarity of Oreos appealing. "Let's see what else they're putting out on the news. Maybe aliens have landed. Who knows?"

Chapter Eight

"LOOK, WHAT YOU'RE asking is nuts." The stocky man threw his hands up and let them drop. "Lady, even you know it's nuts. Run a cable up to midtown? In the subway? Where the hell you think we're going to get the cable? Macy's?"

Dar stared him down. "You're a phone company. You don't have cable? What the hell do you use then, tin cans and strings?"

"Not that much cable!" The man protested. "You know how much that stuff costs?"

'Well, sir...' One of the other Verizon reps cleared his throat. "We got that cable. In Jersey."

The man whirled. "Shut the fuck up. Who asked you?"

"If you have the cable, why shut him up?" A tall man in a rumpled tie and suit spoke up from the back. "Why the stall? This isn't some fucking game, buddy. "

The man from Verizon turned back to him. "Who the fuck are you?"

"Aide to the governor," the man said. "Who maybe wants to know why someone's holding up a critical promise of his."

The man didn't seem fazed. "Yeah? He can kiss my ass. Him and his let's squeeze the union bullshit," he said. "I'm not putting my guys down those holes for you. I don't give a crap what you promised."

Ah. Dar revised her opinion for the third time in less than five minutes. At first she'd suspected Kerry was right, and the man was looking for a payoff. Then she'd decided he was probably really looking for an excuse not to have to bust his ass.

Now she figured he might just be an asshole with a grudge. "Listen." She brought the room's attention back to herself by standing up. "Let's can the bullshit. What's at stake here is a lot bigger than any of us. No one wants to be on CNN explaining why they deliberately harmed the nation."

"Aw, c'mon with the crap already." The Verizon man rolled his eyes.

"She's right," the governor's aide said. "Matter of fact, I'm going to call the cops in and have your ass arrested. Maybe you're in it with the terrorists. Sure sounds like it to me."

"Would you shut up," the man said. "You ain't calling no one. And you lady, even if we did have that stuff there's no way we could lay it out in time. It ain't possible."

The governor's aide opened his phone and dialed. "Hello? Yes. Is this Agent Jackson? Yes, this is Michael Corish from the governor's office. Yes, thanks, I am. Listen, it's come to my attention we could have someone here who might be of interest to you. Can you send a few boys over to the Exchange?"

Everyone looked at each other, then back at the aide.

"You will? Great. I'll wait here for them. Thanks." He closed the phone and regarded the man from Verizon. "Hope you like body cavity searches."

The man's jaw dropped a little. "What are you crazy? I'm not a terrorist!"

"Doesn't matter," the man said. "You're in the way, and I'm going to remove you." He turned to the man who'd spilled the beans about the cable. "Now. You want to help us out here, or go with your friend?"

The man swallowed.

"You're bluffing!" The other man exclaimed.

"No," the aide replied. "I just called yours. Here we have a room full of people who all have one goal, which is what our government wants." He gestured, taking in the other telco men, and Dar and her group. "They're working hard to do what we need, and your stupid pig-headedness is blocking that. You're worthless. We don't need you."

"Listen! Who do you think ya are, anyway? My uncle..."

The door opened and a man in dark, paramilitary looking clothing entered. "Mr. Corish?"

"Here," the aide said. "It's that fellow over there. You might want to question him on his background."

The agent nodded, and unclipped the strap on his sidearm. "Let's go buddy. Don't make any trouble for me." He advanced around the table, the rest of the crowd parting before him as the man from Verizon backed up against the wall.

"Hey! Wait...I d...didn't do nothing!"

The agent grabbed his arm and swung him around, slamming him against the wall as he pulled a set of handcuffs from a case in the small of his back. "Then you've got nothing to worry about, right?" He snapped the cuffs on and got him in a solid grip around one bicep. "Thanks, sir. We'll take it from here."

"Thanks for coming so soon, officer. I, and of course the governor, really appreciate it," Corish said. "Let me get the door for you." He smiled as the man was dragged out, then he slammed the door and looked around at the room. "Where were we?"

"I'll help," the other Verizon man said quickly. "I know where we've got that cable. But I'll need someone to pull some strings for us to get it on a barge over here."

"I think I can help you with that," Corish said. "Let's go outside and make a few calls." He glanced around. "The rest of you better be ready to move once we get this accomplished. I don't want any more excuses."

He left, taking the chastened Verizon man with him, closing the door behind them both.

"Holy shit." Scuzzy whispered.

Hamilton crossed his arms, looking as nonplussed as Dar had ever seen him. He turned and looked at her and they both simultaneously shook their heads. "Well," Ham said. "Not to put too fine a point on it, but now ah do understand in full that old Southern saying that goes something like...ah do declare!"

Andrew had been sitting quietly in the corner, and now he snorted audibly. "Mah neck of them Southern woods they said "Somebitch!"

"I can't believe that just happened." Charles pushed his chair back from the table.

Dar stood up. "Well, it did." She veered toward the practical. "So that means you all need to get your line folks in here and get ready to hook up to one end of that damn cable. We'll go prepare the other end. "

Charles nodded slowly. "I'll get my guys in here. Roger, do you have a big router we can all use? I don't see much point in running separate links on this end if Dar's just going to combine them on hers."

The MCI rep opened his cell phone. "Let me see what they got on the truck. I think we do," he said. "Sam, I've got a service trunk going up to the roof, you want to tie your cell temps in there?"

The Sprint rep nodded. "We can do that. Yeah," he said. "Tell you the truth, folks, I don't much know what's going on with the FBI and all that, but I'm glad we're moving forward with this. Sitting still and listening to people pissing on each other is not my idea of a good time."

"Mine either." Dar agreed. "Let me go pack up my crowd and get back up to midtown. I've got three sat trucks, anyone need them? I'm reserving a fourth one for our technical office. I need to get them online for some critical backhaul."

"I'll take one," Sam said. "I can use the back channel for the cell sites. I hear they're going to start letting people back down here, at least on the east side, tomorrow or maybe Monday."

"I'll grab one for our business office," Roger said. "Thanks Dar. Any little bit helps."

"Then we'll take the third one off your hands," Charles said. "Even though we've got our tie lines up thanks to your generosity, we'd like to bring up a communications center we can work out of down here."

"Great." Dar said. "Now you can all do me a favor and get your operations groups to take the lid off completing new orders in the rest of the damn country. You're not going to need all those techs here."

"We can," Charles said. "But it's not so much us, Dar. I talked to my ops VP before when you asked, and it's the local exchange. They won't drop the last mile. I've got a call into my counterpart at Qwest and Bellsouth, trying to see what's going on. "

"I heard they'll start releasing that on Monday," Roger spoke up. "Everyone outside the Verizon area, anyway." So at least that's probably good news."

"If it's true," Charles said.

"Come on then." Dar gestured to the door. "Bring whoever you need to take them over. I'd rather get moving before they come with some other request we have to find a way to support." She waited for the men to walk ahead, then joined Alastair and her father as they followed behind.

"Glad we're going to end up getting somewhere from this," Alastair said. "But I can't say I'm enjoying the ride."

"That was pretty scary," Dar admitted. "I'm not sure what the rules are anymore."

"I ain't sure there are any," Hamilton said. "Listen, Maestro, no one loves your ass kicking attitude any more than little old me, but I'm not sure even this Louisiana lawyer could dig you out of the spook's palace so do me a little old favor and keep a sock in it, will ya please?"

Dar was silent for a moment, then shook her head. "I'll do my best." She finally muttered. "But this is getting down a dark road I'm not sure we want to be on."

They emerged into the dust filled, overcast street, and pulled their masks on. "I'm not sure we've got any choice left," Alastair said. "I thought we might get some good press out of it, but after what you told me about them giving that story about the systems being fine, I'm not so sure."

They walked down the street, passing firemen and other search workers trudging back in the opposite direction. They got only cursory glances, as the exhausted men went back toward the disaster site, some holding small brown bags in their hands.

One looked up at Dar as he went past, his eyes briefly focusing on the logo patch on her jumpsuit. He lifted the small bag and nodded at her. "Thanks."

Dar had no idea what he was talking about. She lifted a hand and gave him a wave. "Anytime."

They moved on. "Alastair, I'd be happy if we get out of this here thing with our skins intact at this point," Hamilton remarked in a serious tone. "We can write it all off as service rendered. The press may not know what we did, but they're going to have to write one mean non-disclosure if it's going to keep us from telling the stockholders."

"Well, that's true. We do have to book the expense." Alastair said. "Anyway, I'm glad we're moving back up to the office. We can start a triage center for our accounts there. See what we can do for them while your team is getting the rest of this ready, Dar."

Dar was merely looking forward to a shower and a cold drink, at this point. "Sure." She walked on, clearing her throat a little.

The streets around them were covered in dust, as were the buildings, and the cars alongside either curb. But there were a few now that weren't so covered, and in two places it looked like emergency service organizations were setting up shop.

The strangeness was wearing off, she realized. She was getting used to seeing this destruction, just like she was almost used to the rough cotton constriction of her jumpsuit, and the claustrophobic enclosure of the mask she was wearing.

The late afternoon sun could barely penetrate the cloud of smoke and dust, and as she walked, she had a sense they were moving through some strange otherworldly dreamscape, kicking up puffs of dust as they went along in quiet procession.

They had won the day. They were getting what they wanted. Despite all that, Dar felt a sense of unease at how the achievement had been made. Was the Verizon crew leader really in trouble? Or would the city keep him out of the way long enough for them to get what they wanted?

He'd been removed so easily. Dar exhaled, acknowledging that Hamilton's advice had probably been very sound. She had no desire to be in that guy's shoes, despite the fact she felt he was just speaking his mind and heart regardless of what his real motives were.

What did that say about the situation?

"Ah. I think someone's looking for you, Dar." Alastair poked her.

Dar started out of her inner musings and looked up, to find a somewhat short, jumpsuited figure moving toward them out of the gloom. Even in the coverall and mask, Kerry was immediately recognizable. "I think you're right."

Dar sped up her steps and eased between the others watching Kerry's path alter as she was, in turn, spotted. She wondered if her partner had some new problem or whether she just...

Dar was betting on the just. "Hey." She greeted her as they neared. She could see the pale green eyes watching her through the mask, and even through the two layers of plastic, she could also see the smile in them.

"Hey." Kerry responded. "There you are."

"Looking for something?" Dar's brows lifted.

"You."

"Ah." Dar smiled and gave her a quick hug. "C'mon. We're heading back to the bus." She indicated the crowd around them. "We're leaving the sat rigs. We're going to park one near our tech office, and give one to each of our friends here. Then the bus, and us, are heading back to the office."

"Did we make any progress?" Kerry willingly turned and kept up with her.

"Yes. But not the way I'd like to have," Dar admitted. "I almost wish I'd taken your advice and got out the checkbook."

"Really?" Kerry frowned.

"Really. Let's get to the bus, and I'll tell you all about it." Dar glanced casually around. "I think it threw all of us for a loop."

"That doesn't sound good."

"I'm not sure it is." Dar put her arm around Kerry's shoulders. "In fact, I'm pretty sure it isn't. There's a lot more going on under the hood here than we know."

"Ugh." Kerry grunted. "Right now all I want under my hood is a cold beer and a shower."

"I can make that happen." Dar assured her.

"I bet you can."

KERRY LEANED BOTH hands against the tile wall and let the shower beat down over her shoulders. The water felt so wonderful she was contemplating falling asleep where she was, but after a minute, she straightened up and reached for the scrubbie sitting in the stainless steel basket.

She squeezed a blob of apricot scrub on it, and started soaping herself. It felt good to feel the clean tingle, although she'd worn her jumpsuit she'd felt like the dust had formed a film on her skin and she was literally itching to get it off.

It was good to be back at the office away from all the destruction. Kerry rinsed herself off, then applied a good handful of shampoo to her hair and scrubbed her scalp. Up by the hotel, there were people and cars, and a lot of activity, a far cry from the ghostly wasteland they'd so recently left.

With the last of the soap circling down the drain, she shut the shower off and stepped out, wrapping herself in the thick towel that was hanging nearby. Even that felt good and she dried herself off, glancing briefly in the half fogged mirror at her reflection.

Grim. She stuck her tongue out at the disheveled image. Then she got her underwear on and ran a brush through her hair, before she wrapped the towel around her neck and emerged from the bathroom.

It was quiet. The windows were surprisingly sound proofed, and the room itself had a thick carpet, and a comfortable king size bed — not a specially grand space, but right now it seemed like heaven to Kerry's tired eyes.

She pulled on a pair of carpenter pants and a polo, but left her feet bare as she went over to the desk and sat down next to it, picking up her water bottle and taking a swig.

Laying down was an option, but she knew if she did, she'd fall asleep and she wasn't sure she wanted to do that. Dar was down in the basement of their office looking for pipes, and she wanted to wait for her to come back up to the room to see what she'd found down there.

The team — she'd started to think of all of them as one big team — would probably want to gather for dinner. She'd heard them talking on the ride back up from Battery Park, and there was something of a group mind going on that she could appreciate in the situation.

She did appreciate it. However, on a personal level, she would have rather spent the time alone with Dar simply decompressing. Her body wasn't that tired, but her mind was, having spent hours and hours chasing problems around in circles.

"I don't think I'm up to a communicative evening." Kerry remarked to the empty room. "But let's see what happens." She glanced at her laptop, then she extended her legs and crossed them at the ankles, leaving the machine sitting closed on the desktop.

Her cell phone and PDA rested next to it, both blessedly quiet for the moment.

That was good. She was tired of telling people what to do, and getting mostly bad news from all quarters. She wanted to be able to chill out, and not feel guilty that she was letting issues lie without her attention.

There was a point, she had discovered, when you lost the ability to quantify everything you had to do when there was just too much of it. It was like trying to dig a hole in the sand by the ocean — fast as you kept digging, it kept filling.

She'd found that point today, right before she'd shut her laptop and turned off her mic. No matter how many customers she'd talked to, there were more waiting. No matter how many times she explained the situation, there were people that begged the exception and, to their credit, most of them were not frivolous requests.

Never enough.

Kerry took a swallow of her water, then decided she really wanted something stronger. She got up and put the cap on the bottle, then started looking around for some shoes, figuring even a seat in the corner of the bar would probably keep her from falling asleep until Dar finished fiddling.

Maybe they'd even have some decent jalapeno poppers or something. Kerry found her boots and put them on, then tucked her room key into one of her side pockets and slipped out the door and into the hallway.

It, too, was quiet. She passed one other person on the way to the elevator, and rode all the way down in solitary splendor to the floor which housed the bar. This area was more crowded, and she spotted a few familiar faces as she made her way into the dark, wood-lined space. "Hey guys."

"Hey boss!" Mark waved her over. "The big Kahuna was checking one more thing, then she said she'd meet us up here."

"Good." Kerry claimed one of the leather chairs in the midst of her techs. "Someone get me a beer, please. The bigger the better."

"Right you are, ma'am." Shaun got up and trotted over to the bar.

"Long ass day, huh?" Mark asked. "Man, I don't envy those phone guys though. I wouldn't want to be creeping around in that subway at night."

"No way." Another of the techs agreed. "They've got balls." He paused, and blushed. "Sorry ma'am."

"No problem." Kerry sighed. "They've sure got more balls than I do, anyway." She glanced at Mark. "So what's Dar doing now? Did you find a route through the basement?"

Mark shook his head. "No such luck," he replied, mournfully. "I can't even get them to tell me where our damn demarc is. They have to call some guy who was on vacation or something to find out. We couldn't find any easy way to get from the building out."

"Ugh." Kerry accepted the large, frosty mug of beer Shaun was handing her. "Thanks. Where's Kannan?"

"In our room," Shaun said. "He's still pretty freaked out. I told him to order some room service and relax."

Kerry took a sip of the cold beer and swallowed it "Good choice." She complimented Shaun. "And good idea to have Kannan just rest tonight. I have my admin trying to get him a flight out of here tomorrow to go home. I don't think he's really in danger hereafter all, so many people here in New York are from India it's not really unusual— but I understand how he feels."

"Yeah, I know." Shaun picked up his own glass that seemed to be some kind of highball drink. "He's just freaked out by all of it. Sucks too, because he's our best WAN guy."

It did suck. Kerry sat back in her chair and looked around the bar. Aside from her group, there were several others, clustered around the scattered tables or watching the three television sets mounted on the walls.

Ordinarily, the screens would have sports on them, she figured. Basketball, or football, or whatever ESPN was serving up. Now, all three were tuned to CNN, and those sitting around seemed fixed on the pictures that showed again and again the horrific sights she'd gotten to know up close and personal earlier that day.

Shots of the wreckage. Shots of the Pentagon. Shots of a burned field in Pennsylvania. Talking heads. Shots of the president with his bullhorn standing on a mound of debris. More talking heads. Shots of smoke, of the mayor at a funeral, of the barges removing remains to

Fresh Kills landfill along with mounds and mounds and mounds of debris.

Fresh Kills. What a cosmically ironic name. Kerry was truly surprised someone hadn't changed it just to spare everyone the wince. It was Dutch, she'd learned. The old word kille meaning water channel and the place itself was an estuary that drained wetlands into the sea, but in the current context it was ghoulish and she was tired of hearing it.

Certainly, she'd winced. That reminded her of something and she set her beer down, removing her cell phone from her belt and opening it. She looked up a number, pressed the dial, and listened to the ring until it was answered. "Hello, Mother."

"Wh...oh, hello, Kerry," Cynthia Stuart answered. "What a surprise. I hadn't expected to hear from you this evening. Where are you? Still in New York?"

"Yes. Across from our office at Rockefeller Center," Kerry replied. "How are things there?"

"Frustrating," her mother answered honestly. "I have to say it's very difficult talking to people who cannot see past someone with perhaps a different religion, or so on, and who must assume everyone who is from somewhere else is suspect."

"I heard about the attacks," Kerry said. "I'm sorry. We encountered that here. One of our techs is from India and he's had a tough time."

"Terrible." Her mother agreed. "I have to say your being there also makes me quite anxious, however, Kerry. Angela is also concerned. "

"Thanks. It's been a rough day. We were down at the disaster site earlier. We just got back uptown a little while ago."

"Oh my." Cynthia gasped a little. "I had no idea! I saw the pictures on television just before...it seems absolutely horrific. Hold on, Angela, I have your sister on the phone. She seems right in the middle of everything again...what...oh, all right. Yes, hold on."

"Ker?" Angie's voice came over the line. "Are you nuts? Get the hell out of there!"

"Hi, Ang." Kerry gave her tablemates a wry look, and a shrug. "Family," she mouthed. "Get out of here? We're in the lobby bar at our hotel. What's wrong with it?"

"Kerry, cut it out! Why are you guys there?" Angela actually sounded upset. "It was bad enough when you were at the Pentagon, but Jesus!"

Perversely, after being horrified the whole day, now Kerry felt the need to downplay the whole thing. "C'mon, Ang. There's a whole city full of people here. Chill. We had to come here. There's a lot of stuff that needed taking care of. "

"How long are you staying there?" Angie asked. "Have you heard what's going on here?"

"I heard. People are going a little crazy, I think," Kerry said. "We have a lot of customers down here, and there are some things we're doing for the government. It's not just me and Dar, either. Our CEO is here and a bunch of our corporate people. "

"So you and Dar aren't running the planet as usual?"

Kerry spotted her beloved partner entering the hotel, surrounded by men, all of whom were glued on whatever it was she was telling them. "Who us? Nah, we're just little fish here." She watched Dar, hands moving in a decisive motion, dismiss her accolytes who scattered in all directions. "We're just a couple of nerds to these guys."

"Uh huh," Angie said. "Sis, be careful, please? It's easy to get hurt in all the stuff going on."

"I will."

Dar stopped at the front desk and leaned over the top of it talking to the short, well dressed woman behind it.

"Ker?"

"Huh?" Kerry wrested her attention back to her phone. "Sorry, what was that?"

"I said, here's Mom back. Be careful!"

"Here comes Big D." Mark spoke up. "Looks like she could use a beer too, Shaun."

"Hey, you'd think my family were Irish bartenders or something...oh wait. They are." Shaun good naturedly got up and headed back to the bar.

"Kerry?"

"Yes, I'm here." Kerry could see the irritation in her partner's body language, but she smiled anyway, as the stormy blue eyes lifted and found hers. "Listen, I hope everything settles down and people start to think again. I know this has to be a knee jerk reaction."

"I certainly hope so. Will you be there long? "

Kerry considered the question as Dar arrived and took a seat on the arm of her chair. "I think we'll know more on Monday, to be honest. I'll let you know," she said. "I'm sure Dar will want to get out of here as soon as we can."

"Bet your ass." Dar commented.

"I'm sorry, what was that?" Cynthia asked. "Was that Dar? I thought I heard her voice."

"It was," Kerry said. "She was just agreeing with me."

Shaun came back over and offered Dar a glass. "They told me to get this."

Dar eyed him. "They did, did they?" She let her eyes narrow. "Now why would they say something like that?"

"Um." Shaun took a half step back.

"C'mon boss." Mark called over. "Be nice."

A grudging smile appeared on Dar's face and she extended one hand to take the glass. "Thank you, Shaun." She lifted the glass and glanced around the table. "Let's hope this is one day in a million."

"Hear hear." Kerry lifted her own glass. "Mother, we're going to rustle up dinner now, so let me let you go. I'm glad the family's safe there, and I hope things cool down." She listened, then closed the phone and put it down on her knee. "People, you all did an amazing job today."

"Ma'am, we just hung out and watched," Shaun said.

"That's okay, I did too." Kerry bumped Dar's leg with her shoulder. "Dar did the heavy lifting. But everyone hung in there, and now at least we have a plan, and we're moving forward." She glanced up. "Right?"

Dar waggled her free hand and took a sip of her beer.

"Uh oh." Kerry retreated to her own mug.

"We have some challenges," Dar said, after a pause, waiting for everyone to lean forward to listen. "I found out we need to go and take a closer look at the subway tunnels coming under the office tomorrow. Apparently there's more than one set."

"Oh sure," Scuzzy spoke up. "You ain't gonna believe how many tunnels are under this city here. I think there's like ten that come into Grand Central...you remember Grand Central? That's where we met up that time."

"I remember." Dar nodded. "Looked like a maze made by whacked moles fighting blind badgers," she said. "So tomorrow we need to try and scope a path for them to take that cable up into the building so we can cross-connect it to our gear."

"We can't use the copper riser," Mark said. "I didn't find any ground level demarc."

"I'll go with ya tomorrow," Scuzzy said, confidently. "My old man worked here. I used to sleep in some of them little rooms, me and the rats and the bums."

Kerry felt the air in the bar hit the outsides of her eyeballs as they widened.

"Y'know, you never know. They might have coal bins and who knows what down there. We'll find something. But I thought you were telling them to take it out to Roosevelt?" Scuzzy went on. "What's up with that?"

"Kerry reminded me it'd be a lot closer to bring it here," Dar said. "We've got enough pipe here to take at least part of the traffic."

"That sure helps," Scuzzy said, sucking on the straw poked in her colorful fruity drink. "Cause you don't want to be in those tunnels under the East River, you know?"

"I know." Dar agreed solemnly. "Me either."

"Specially since the Roosevelt is like, halfway to China." Scuzzy continued, "It's like, ten, maybe fifteen stories underground, and I got my ears all screwy going up and down from there."

Dar regarded her for a moment, then she looked down at Kerry. "This project lucked out having you in it. I sure as hell am not going ten stories underground to fish fiber cable up."

"Anytime, honey." Kerry leaned her head against Dar's hip. "Though I have to admit I'm not crazy about going ten stories underground right now either."

"That was rough, today," Scuzzy commented. "I thought I seen some bad stuff before but that was bad. Real bad."

"I've asked our real estate branch to find a different location for the technical office there." Dar said, after a brief silence, "I don't know how long it's going to take them to get things going again."

"I feel bad for all the people who live down there," Shaun said. "Like the office folks. They can't go home. That must be terrible on top of everything else."

"Living down there right now would be a lot worse," Scuzzy said. "They're better off staying uptown. I got a cousin who's right on the edge of where they don't let you go no more, and she's thinking of staying with my uncle in Jersey for a while."

"I'm sure most of the people here would rather go somewhere else for a while," Nan said, in a quiet voice. "I know I would. It was horrible in DC, but nothing like this."

Kerry listened to the voices around her, and found a kinship in the mental exhaustion she heard in them. She felt Dar's fingers close on her shoulder and figured they needed a change of scene. "How about we all go find some dinner now. You guys up for that?"

"Hell yes." Mark put his glass down hastily. "I'm starving."

"That sounds damn good to me too." Andrew had been sprawled in a nearby chair. Now he straightened up and studied his neatly laced military boots. "Find us some place we can get some steak and taters."

"Let's go." Dar slipped off the chair arm and offered Kerry a hand up. "Alastair and Hamilton are meeting with some board members, so they'll just have to miss out." She waited for the group to rise and start to file out the door. "With any luck, wherever we find will have ice cream sundaes."

"There's a Ben and Jerry's around the corner," Kerry answered instantly. "Caught my eye on the way in."

Dar chuckled.

"Hey, gotta find the essentials."

"WE'RE GOING TO regret staying out this late." Kerry trailed after Dar down the hallway to their hotel room. "Tomorrow is going to really suck."

"It is," Dar agreed, keying the door open and shoving it inward. "But I don't care. I needed a mindless night out." She trudged inside passing the bathroom and moving further into the space. "We'll survive. Mark has two cases of Bawls in the truck."

"Good point." Kerry closed the door behind them, sat down in the nearest chair and unlaced her boots. "A lot of people were out tonight. I was sort of surprised."

"Hysterical relief." Dar dropped down onto the bed and laid down flat on her back. "Felt a little desperate."

Kerry finished with her other boot, then got up and went over to the bed, sitting down and picking up one of Dar's legs to get at her laces. "I feel a little desperate," she said. "Christ, I want to go home." She pulled a lace loose.

Dar rolled her head to one side and gazed at her. "We will soon."

"Not soon enough," Kerry replied. "I feel so damned overwhelmed here, Dar. I'm not sure why." She pulled off one shoe, then the sock beneath it, pausing to tweak her partner's toe before she got up and went around to the other side of the long legs, and sat down to pick up the other foot.

Dar's eyes followed her. "You don't know why you feel overwhelmed? Ker, you're in the middle of a disaster zone in an unprecedented act of terrorism against our country. How are you supposed to not feel overwhelmed? I was watching those guys out there today. They're just digging, digging, and they had no real idea of what they were digging for. You don't think they're overwhelmed?"

Kerry removed Dar's other boot, and then set her foot down, leaning back along her side on the bed. "I know they are. That's what makes me feel so crazy. I should be able to do my job here because I wasn't a part of all that, but it's just making my brain go in circles." She propped her head up on one hand. "Why can't I be more like you?"

"A single minded idiot?"

Kerry smiled wryly. "Focused," she corrected her partner, "with an infinite capacity for innovation."

Dar turned on her side so they were facing each other. She lifted a hand and stroked Kerry's face with the backs of her knuckles. "You can only focus so long," she said. "That's why I stopped looking for holes in the wall today and took tonight off. Yes, I'll pay for it tomorrow, but I've finally learned the value of chilling out."

"You didn't chill with those darts." Kerry enjoyed the touch, savoring the look of gentle affection gazing back at her. "I can't believe you beat your Dad."

Dar grinned "Neither could he." She gently traced one of Kerry's pale eyebrows. "You weren't so bad yourself."

"It was fun," Kerry admitted, "but I'm glad we skipped the karaoke bar." She clasped Dar's hand with her own, and studied her face, half hidden in the shadows of the dimly lit room. There was a furrow over her brow and she looked tired.

"Hehe, me too," Dar said. "I guess we should get undressed and get some sleep, huh?"

"We should." Kerry agreed. "Especially if we're going to spend tomorrow digging around in office basements." She levered herself up and stood, unbuckling her belt and getting out of her cargo pants, hopping over to one side as Dar did the same.

"Careful." Dar reached over to steady her, as she draped her pants over her suitcase and stripped off her shirt one handed over her head. "Last thing you need is rug burns."

"Thanks, sweetie," Kerry said. "I know I can always depend on you to keep me from falling on my butt."

Dar chuckled, then she moved over a few steps to put her shirt away.

Kerry folded up her clothing and put it to one side of her suitcase, rummaging inside it to remove her sleep shirt. She had it in one fist, when a long arm snaked around her and removed it from her grasp. "Hey."

"Hey." Dar dropped the shirt back on the bag and took her hand instead, drawing her toward the bed. "C'mon. There are plenty of sheets on the bed. You won't be cold."

Kerry felt the faint thrill of unexpected raciness. "I'm not cold already."

Dar glanced over her bare shoulder at her, a faint grin twitching at her lips, as she waggled an eyebrow. "Oh really?"

"Really." Kerry planted a kiss between Dar's shoulder blades, then bumped her gently forward. "Lead on, hot stuff."

"Remind me of that again tomorrow after we're both conscious again," Dar responded, in a wry tone. She continued moving forward, towing Kerry along behind her.

Kerry smiled and followed willingly. "Bet your booty I will." In a moment the room was in darkness and she was under a set of cool sheets rapidly warming her and Dar's bare bodies. And the comfort of the skin on skin touch pushed the day's anxieties aside.

Animal comfort. She wrapped her arm around Dar's waist and felt her exhale. "Dar?"

"Yes?"

"Why do you really think they made that announcement today? About the systems working? Do you think they were playing with us?"

"No." Dar said, after a pause, "I'm not sure why they did it." She added, "maybe so people...so investors wouldn't panic."

"Hm." Kerry nibbled a bit of the skin on Dar's shoulder. "I think they're going to anyway. I bet when that market does open it drops like a rock."

"Nah." Dar shook her head. "People had time to stop and think. Having it closed wasn't a bad idea regardless of what the technical situation was. No knee jerking if you've had almost a week to react."

"But what if we can't actually bring everything back up by Monday? Won't that..." Kerry paused. "Maybe that's why they made that announcement. To put pressure on us."

Dar snorted softly.

"It bothers me. I don't like people playing games when we're going crazy trying to get things done here." Kerry grumbled.

"Yeah, I know." Dar rubbed Kerry's back with her fingertips.

"Sorry I'm whining."

"You're allowed." Dar looked up at the dimly seen ceiling. "Seems like this has been going on forever, huh? It's hard to remember I was in London a few days ago," she said. "Working with those guys...I feel like it's been a year since then."

"I was giving a speech just a few days ago," Kerry replied. "You know, I can't even remember what the hell I said," she admitted. "But I wish that reunion was the worst of my worries right now."

"Yeah." Dar let her eyes drift shut, glad of the thick glass windows that blocked most of the city noise. "I wish the worst thing I had to worry about was playing in that damned softball league and hitting myself in the head."

"Y'know though," Kerry mused, "before this all happened, that visit was turning out better than I expected. I think my mother caught a clue."

Dar gave her a squeeze. "I think your mother values family," she said, "and she wants you to be a part of that." She kissed Kerry on the top of her head. "I don't blame her a bit."

Kerry smiled. "I love you."

Dar's eyes opened again. "Back atcha, but what brought that on?"

Kerry snuggled a little closer. "Because I'm sitting here at three in the morning bitching and you're not telling me to shut up and go to sleep." She could feel Dar's body shudder with silent laughter. "You're so sweet to me."

Dar hugged her a little tighter, still chuckling.

"When we were down at the park today, I was looking out the front window at all those rescue workers sitting there, and it kind of brought home to me just how many blessings I have in my life." Kerry said, after a pause, "the primary one being you, of course."

"Likewise." Dar exhaled. "I'm one of the luckiest people on earth."

"We're both soppy mushballs."

"Guilty."

Finally, Kerry found herself smiling and letting it go, unable to resist the love she could feel wrapped all around her. She closed her eyes and listened to Dar's breathing for a few minutes until the dim shadows faded out and she drifted off to sleep.

Dar stayed awake a few minutes more, enjoying the sensation of Kerry's breath warming her shoulder. They would try and accomplish the task they'd started on, she decided, and then, once that was either finished or failed, they would go home.

They were too close to the center of this. Dar could envision an unraveling ball of requests if they kept going, the pressure to succeed growing greater and greater, as the shadow threat of what might happen if they didn't hung over them.

Too much risk for too little return. Tomorrow she'd corner Alastair, call Maria, make arrangements for them to get transport out and, by the end of the day Monday, she decided, she'd be sitting on her patio playing ball with Chino and listening to Kerry rustling up coffee in the kitchen.

She closed her eyes, and exhaled, nodding her head in confirmation.

Chapter Nine

KERRY BREATHED IN the scent of fresh coffee as she entered the hotel café, pausing in the doorway and lifting a hand to wave hello to Hamilton who was already seated inside.

"Good morning, Ms. Stuart." Hamilton waved back, then waved her over. "Come on over and sit your self down here so I don't have to be talking to the maple syrup will you please?"

Having very little choice, unless she wanted to start the day off profoundly rude, Kerry crossed the parquet floor and joined their corporate lawyer at his table. "Careful what you ask for." She sat down and accepted the menu from young male server as she opened her napkin and put it on her lap at the same time. "Dar's on her way down."

"Honey, even that thought can't stir my grits this morning," Hamilton told her. "You all do know what grits are, right?"

"I know what grits are." Kerry assured him. "I can even cook them."

"Shocked. I'm shocked," Hamilton said. "A Midwesterner cooking grits. What is the world coming to?" He picked up a piece of rye toast and methodically buttered it. "I had the honor of attending a shindig at the governor's place with Al last night."

"He had a party?" Kerry's voice dropped.

"He called it a strategy and planning meeting," Ham told her. "But I will say that was the first planning and strategy meeting I ever have been to that had salmon canapés and whisky highballs." He took a sip of his coffee. "Ah am guessing all those federal people in town needed some catering to."

"Well, we went out ourselves last night." Kerry half shrugged. "I guess salmon and whiskey are about equal to beer and cheeseburgers and a good game of darts."

Hamilton looked up at her over cup. "Now doesn't that sound down home."

"Home would have included my motorcycle and my dog." Kerry glanced up as the server reappeared, hovering politely at her elbow. "Can I have two orders of eggs over easy with crisp bacon, white toast, and one side of blueberry pancakes, please?"

The waiter blinked, then he scribbled it down.

"And coffee." Kerry handed him the menu. "My father used to have meetings like those. The only bright part of them for me were the chocolate mousse cups they always left close enough to the door for me to steal."

Hamilton sipped his coffee again. "Somehow I can easily picture that," he remarked dryly. "We apparently got our selves onto the good boy list in all that hullaballo yesterday. Given my preference, I'd have rather stayed bad."

"Did you get an idea last night of what their motives were? What they really want?" Kerry asked. "Some of the things they were saying and doing were really very intimidating."

"What do they want." The lawyer sighed, and leaned back in his chair. "That's a damn fine question. I do think first of all those men are scared half to death."

"I thought they were acting as though they were embarrassed," Kerry responded. "That this happened. That it was allowed to happen."

Hamilton regarded her. "There is that there piece too," he acknowledged. "I heard a lot about getting back to normal, putting on a tough face, that sorta thing, but you know, honey, there ain't no getting back to normal in a thing like this. It changes people."

"It changes everything," Kerry said.

'Yes, it does." Hamilton nodded. "It will change a lot of things for us. No matter what the outcome is in this thing we're doing, people now understand what we do in a very different aspect. That could end up good, and it can end up bad."

Kerry took a swallow of water from the glass in front of her. "You know, my father was very unhappy about our government contracts. He felt we had too much control."

"I do remember that." Hamilton nodded. "No offense to those passed, but your father was a right pain in my ass."

"Mine too," she answered steadily. "But was he right?"

Her table companion thought about that in silence for a few minutes, then shrugged. "I honestly don't know the answer to that question right now. Not through any fault of ours, understand. We did what we do. But you know, I just don't know."

"Hm." Kerry picked up her fork and studied it. "I'm not sure I do either."

"Good morning, Hamilton." Dar appeared from thin air, even making Kerry start a little as she took the chair to her partner's left. "I hear you and Alastair had a good time last night."

"Well, good morning to you too, Maestro. I was just telling your charming colleague here about it. You seem to have won the approval of the powers that be, unlikely as that may seem to all and sundry."

"Peh." Dar fastened her gaze on the waiter, and reeled him over. "Coffee, please." She glanced back at Hamilton. "I didn't do a goddamned thing. That bastard threatened his way into a solution."

"Only too true," Hamilton agreed. He paused as the waiter returned, carrying a tray full of plates. "So what did you ladies do last night?" He changed the subject, as the waiter put down his breakfast, then tried to figure out what to do with all of Kerry's.

"I took the team out to dinner." Dar reached over and took one of the plates from the waiter, putting it down in front of her. "That goes there, the other plate put between us. Thanks." She took a gulp of her coffee. "Then we found a sports bar that had something other than CNN on and chilled out for a few hours."

"Ah would have traded my salmon canapé for a beer and a pretzel in a heartbeat," Hamilton said.

"Ah, there you all are." Alastair arrived, taking the fourth chair at the table. "Ham, I've already had two calls from the FBI this morning. I don't think I can stall them on the employee lists much further."

"Well, Al, then I'm going to have to file a damn injunction against them in Federal court and that ain't happening till Monday. "

"I don't know..." Alastair shook his head. "This guy is not giving up."

"Tell them we locked the database and no one can get access to it until we've had a chance to file in Federal Court." Dar bit into a strip of bacon.

"Can we do that?"

"Yes." Dar and Kerry answered at the same time.

"And even if we couldn't," Kerry wiped her lips with her napkin, "they have no way of knowing that. It's in a data center in the middle of the Houston campus in a building among hundreds that only four people have access to. What are they doing to do, go room by room tapping on the outside of the servers?"

"Well," Alastair gave her a wry look, "they could arrest me."

"We'll never let them take you alive, Alastair," Dar said.

Alastair sighed. "You all seem to think this is funny."

"I don't think it's funny, I think it's idiotic. What the hell do they want our employment records for?" Dar asked. "Is this all about the damn taps or something again?"

"Just coffee for me, thanks." Alastair told the waiter. "And a glass of grapefruit juice, if you've got it."

"Of course sir."

"Dar, it ain't nothing about taps." Hamilton lowered his voice. "They need a list of all our people who are in government facilities. That part makes horse sense. It's the rest of the records they want that's giving my Louisiana ass a hive."

Dar chewed a mouthful of her breakfast as she studied her table companions. "A list of our people," she said, after swallowing, "in their facilities?"

"Yes." Alastair nodded. "It's a security issue."

Dar folded her hands on the table and leaned forward a little. "Why don't they just run a report in their own damned database?" She asked. "Why the hell do they need our records for??"

"Their database?" Hamilton removed a pad from his pocket and pushed his plate aside. "Dar, have I ever told you just how much I do truly love you more than my luggage?"

Kerry eyed him. "Hey."

"Yes, their database." Dar went back to stabbing her eggs, making them yolk all over the plate. "How in the hell did they think all those people got credentials to work in those facilities? Pulled them out of their asses? They all have security clearances. Issued by the damned GOVERNMENT."

Alastair and Hamilton exchanged glances. "Did you write that database too?" Alastair inquired. "Maybe you could go run the report for them, if you can spare a minute."

Hamilton waved his pen at him. "Al, hush. This'll help I think. Just tell those folks to call me if they call you again." He smiled at Dar. "Always lovely to spend time with you ladies. I'll be off to fence with the Federals now. Wish me luck." He got up and lifted his jacket off the back of his chair. "Al, I'll let you know what I find out."

"Sure." Alastair waved at him as he left. "Well."

"Want a pancake?" Kerry nudged the plate toward him. "It's probably going to be a really long day."

Their CEO gazed at her for a moment, then he reached over and took the top pancake on the stack, rolling it up and dunking the end in the cup of maple syrup. He took a bite. "Can someone tell me why we're doing all the right things, but everything is going to hell anyway?"

"Welcome to our world." Dar crunched noisily on her bacon. "Just wait. It'll start raining any minute."

KERRY PULLED UP the zipper on her jumpsuit, then she went over to the plastic shopping bag on the desk and removed some power bars from it, stuffing them in a couple of the pockets. She then clipped her cell phone, and a new accoutrement—a radio—to her belt.

The masks she gratefully left behind, settling a company logo baseball cap on her head instead. "Okay," she addressed her reflection, "let's see what we can go find in the bowels of the city."

The subway. Kerry shook her head. Dar was already on the lower floor of the hotel talking to the maintenance people. Kerry figured by the time she got down there either they would be ready to move ahead or Dar would be veering off on another path altogether.

She hoped it was a different path. She knew they were far from the disaster site, but she had no desire to be anywhere underground. With a last patting of her pockets she tucked her room key away and headed out the door.

The elevator opened, and she entered, to find Alastair already inside. "Hello, again," she greeted him. "Going to join us in the tunnels?"

Alastair had his hands in his pockets. He had a pair of khakis on, and, surprisingly, a rugby shirt. "I think I'd rather do that than meet with the press. That's where I'm off to."

"Ah. Ugh." Kerry sympathized. "Are we in trouble again?"

"Not this time, apparently. Seems like word got around about our hospitality buses, and our folks taking care of some of the workers down there. One of the local stations wanted me to chat about it."

"Oh. Well, that's great," Kerry said, as the elevator arrived at the lobby and opened. "Isn't it?"

"Any press is generally good press." Alastair followed her out into the lobby. "But, we've been high profile here, and I've got a gut feeling that might not be the best thing in the long run."

"Not after what happened to that guy yesterday." Kerry shook her head. "I'd rather be under the radar myself."

"Exactly," Alastair agreed. "But I suppose giving out cookies and pop can't be too controversial."

They walked across the lobby, and Kerry wasn't surprised to find Dar standing by the coffee stand. She reached for her radio then paused as Dar looked around the lobby, spotting her in a few seconds.

A faint grin appeared. Dar indicated the stand with her thumb, then turned as Kerry nodded emphatically. "Well, good luck," she told Alastair. "We'll try to hold up our end of this."

Alastair chuckled. "Not worried about that at all. I never had any doubts before over what Operations could do, but now I've got a whole new respect for you and Dar. Been a real eye opener."

Kerry wondered what that meant. "Well, we try." She veered off to where Dar was waiting with two big cups of coffee in her hands. "See you later."

Alastair continued toward the front door, and Kerry ambled to a halt next to her partner and her heavenly burden. "I feel like swimming in that coffee." She accepted her cup. "Find anything?"

"Labyrinthine basements." Dar informed her. "Soon as Mark and the boys get back from grabbing flashlights and water, we'll head down there. No one knows where the hell some of the corridors go."

"Great." Kerry sighed.

"Hon, you can stay up here and work on issues if you want." Dar rested her hand on Kerry's shoulder. "You don't need to come spelunking with me." She tweaked a bit of Kerry's pale hair. "There's plenty to do topside."

"I know. But I want to go." Kerry took a sip of her coffee. "And it can't be as bad as yesterday. I thought I was going to have nightmares from that."

"You didn't."

"I didn't. I didn't dream at all, that I remember. I think I was too tired." She spotted Mark and his crew coming out of an elevator. "Or maybe I just dreamed about you the whole time. I felt like I did when I woke up."

Dar turned her head and gave her partner a puzzled look. "Huh?"

"Never mind. Tell you later." Kerry raised her cup toward Mark. "Hey. You guys ready for some exploration?"

Mark looked tired, but he nodded. Shaun was with him, along with Scuzzy and Nan, and Joshua, a tech from the office. "Ready as we'll ever be," he said. "Hope we find something though. I'm whacked from last night."

"Me too." Shaun agreed, stifling a yawn. "What were those drinks we were having?"

"Yo, you're some kinda lightweight," Scuzzy said. "We weren't out there late!"

"Yes, we were." Nan disagreed. "I've still got karaoke ringing in my ears." She covered one. "I've never been in a club that loud before."

"Hey it's the city," Scuzzy said. "People need to blow off steam around here, you know? Been rough this week."

"Hey, I had fun. I'm just tired," Nan said. "You guys had the right idea, heading back." She gave Dar and Kerry a wry look. "I think I had an hour sleep."

Dar took the flashlight Mark was holding out and slipped it into the long pocket along one seam of her coveralls. "Okay, let's go." She pointed to the front doors. "We'll walk down to the office, then find a subway entrance. The concierge said there's one right near by."

They exited the hotel and started down the block, crossing two streets before they neared the rear entrance to their offices. "Can we get to the subway from inside?" Dar asked.

"Sure." Scuzzy led the way into the complex. "They got lots of underground stuff here. You know? Great for when it's snowing. You don't want to freeze your ass off getting coffee in the morning."

"Smart idea." Kerry agreed. "But it makes me realize why all those people from New York moved to Florida. You never freeze your ass off doing anything there."

They walked through the concourse and down a set of stairs passing from the light into the underground part of Rockefeller Center. "Is that where we're going?" Dar pointed to a sign that simply said, 'Subway'.

"Yeah, that's the Sixth Ave, you know? Independent line," Scuzzy said, as they started for the stairs. "You guys are gonna have a big problem getting from there to the IRT, you know?"

"The what?" Kerry asked.

"Don't the tunnels all connect?" Dar asked.

"Well, sure." Scuzzy led the way down the steps. "Like, eventually." She continued, "but not here on Sixth, maybe near the shuttle, like where we met, you know? This subway was built like after the other one. The IRT, that was the first."

"I see." Dar grunted.

"I don't." Kerry chimed in. 'There's more than one subway?"

"Well, not now. Now they're all one system." Scuzzy explained. "But back in the day they were all fighting with each other putting tracks down everywhere."

"Uh huh." Dar looked around the lower mezzanine. "So where do we go from here?"

"C'mere, let me show ya." Scuzzy led them over to big map on the wall sealed behind scratched plastic. "See, we're here." She pointed at an orange line. "This subway, it goes over here, and then over toward Roosevelt, see?"

"Right." Kerry nodded.

"But them guys, they're coming up here, on the East side line." Scuzzy pointed at a green tracing, that wound its way up the map. "'Cause that's the closest to the Exchange, you know? Maybe they're going down the kiosk there, or something. I don't think there's any opening down below the building or nothing."

Dar looked from one line to the other. "Do they connect here?" She pointed at a blue line north of them.

"Well, that's where they eventually come in," Scuzzy said. "They sorta cross around there, but there's like long corridors and stuff and stairs and escalators..."

"Oh boy." Kerry muttered.

"Okay." Dar held a hand up. "First things first. Let's find a way to get a cable from our offices down into one of these tunnels. Is this one the closest?" She pointed at the orange line.

"Sixth Avenue, sure." Scuzzy nodded. "So we can go to the basement of 30 Rock, and go down into the subway from there, and see what we can find. Okay by you? We can ride down to the 53rd, and see if that crosses over, and then get over to the Lexington from there."

"Right. Let's go." Dar paused and looked around at the busy activity underground. She pictured the buildings above them and started off down the corridor. "Mark, do we have a line we can start running down from our offices?"

"I got some guys up there," Mark said. "Kannan decided to stick it out, now that we're hanging around here so he's up doing some prep. I wouldn't try to bring out a fiber line from our side, boss. Melding those pipettes underground is gonna suck."

"I'm glad he decided it was okay to stay," Kerry said. "He's very nice."

"He's a freaking awesome fiber tech," Mark replied. "So I am too, especially since the next guy I could get up here is in Miami."

They walked along the concourse which now sloped downward a bit and widened, gaining shops on either side. "We're under 30 Rock now." Scuzzy announced confidently. "They got some cool shops here now. Not like it used to be, all the windows empty."

Kerry found it somewhat incongruous. She understood the logic of having things underground when the weather above sucked, and also how they had to use pretty much any square footage they could find in an island as small as Manhattan, but she still found an underground shopping center weird and depressing.

Or maybe she was still in a bad mood. She walked alongside Dar and tried to put that aside as they traveled along a thick wall that looked like it had been veneered over more than once. "So our offices are over this."

Dar stopped near a large set of stairs. She peered up them. "Elevator stacks don't go down this far."

"No." Scuzzy shook her head. "I heard this was going to be the big entrance to the subway from the Rock, only the shops kinda died off so they made it into the skating rink and all that stuff."

Dar folded her arms. "Okay, so let's go up one level first and see where we can bring a line down." She started up the steps with the rest of her little group behind her. They ended up in the main lobby of the building where their office was located.

It was full of people. "Doesn't look like anything's here, Dar," Kerry murmured. "Where's the demarc?"

"Mark..."

"I'm on it." Mark headed off toward an information desk.

"There's the entrance to the subway in that corner." Shaun pointed toward the front of the building. "I can see the sign from here."

"Okay. Let's go back downstairs then." Dar removed the radio from her belt. "Mark, we're going back down to find the subway entrance."

"Gotcha boss." Mark's voice crackled back.

Kerry followed Dar back downstairs, trying to ignore the people who were staring curiously at them. She felt a bit like they were going in circles. "There has to be pipes coming in here, right?"

"Sure," Scuzzy said. "Lots of pipes under here, but not the kind we put our stuff in. Big pipes, water, sewer, steam pipes..."

"Steam pipes?" Shaun asked. "For what?"

"Heat."

"Oh." Kerry scratched the bridge of her nose. "Of course."

They crossed the busy concourse and headed over toward the front corner where people were streaming in and out at a rapid pace. Dar dodged several oncomers, then she pulled them all over to one side against the wall.

"Sheesh." Kerry looked back the way they came. "That's going to be tricky to run a cable through."

"When was this built?" Dar asked Scuzzy.

"Thirties, something like that."

Dar's radio crackled.

"Hey Boss?" Mark's voice cackled from the radio. "I found the door to the demarc. You might want to come over here to check it out," he said. "I'm down here behind the stairwell."

"Uh oh." Kerry murmured.

"You folks stay here." Dar motioned to the rest of them. "Think about how we can run a thick cable—the kind we ran yesterday, Shaun—across that floor if we have to." She bumped Kerry. "C'mon. Let's go see what the bad news is."

Kerry willingly went along with her as they crossed the floor, yet again, back the way they came. "We're starting off kinda slow today huh?"

"Ungh." Dar rolled her eyes. "I swear I feel like packing everyone into that damn bus and driving south." She led Kerry around the stairs, spotting Mark behind them near a thick metal door accompanied by a dour looking man with a ring of keys. "Ah."

Mark indicated the door with his thumb. "In there."

"Least you people got the sense to dress fer this." The man with the keys shook his head and sorted through the ring, finally coming up with one of the keys and trying it in the lock. He turned it three times, and then a loud clank was heard. "That's it." He pulled the key out and turned the door handle, pulling the door open to release a puff of musty, dusty air.

It was dark inside. "Any lights in there?"

The man muttered and felt around inside the door, finally slapping at something which resulted in a weak yellow illumination. Then he backed out and gave them a gruff jerk of his head in the direction of the door. "I ain't going in there."

Dar stepped to the entrance and looked around. "All right, lets..."

"Got bit by a rat in there once." The man wandered off. "I'm getting coffee. You're on your own."

"Thanks." Dar had stopped dead, her eyes flicking down at the ground in search of rodents that might attempt to snack on her toes. "Appreciate the warning." She glanced behind her. "Anyone coming with me?"

Only Kerry stepped forward immediately. "Right here."

After an awkward pause, Mark followed her, fishing his flashlight out of his pocket. "I don't like rats."

"I had mice in college." Kerry edged past her partner and entered the room without hesitation. "As pets." She paused and looked back over her shoulder. "Not for lunch." She flicked her flashlight on and went further into the room that was full to the rafters with dust covered wall boxes and wires hanging down low enough to almost brush her head.

Dar twirled her flashlight in her fingers and followed, a faint grin on her face. "Watch your head."

"Mine's a lot lower than yours is, hon. "

Dar ducked under a loop. "Good point."

"Hope those aren't electrical," Mark muttered, bringing up the rear. "This could get way more exciting than we need it to."

THE ELECTRICAL ROOM was a labyrinth on its own. It had several levels that seemed to have been built in different times and styles and, on top of that, the floor itself wasn't level. "Careful of that damn ladder." Dar warned, as Kerry started to climb down one. It was a cast iron pipe with diamond plate steps, and it shifted creakily as she put her weight on it.

"Yikes." Kerry went down it as fast as she could, arriving on a lower level to be greeted by rustlings and a pair of glowing eyes in the dark that vanished when she shone her flashlight in the corner. "What in the hell..."

A huge pipe ran over her head, its width twice her armspan at least. Its sections were held together by huge, riveted collars and its outer surface was covered with thick, peeling paint. She put her hand on it, surprised when she felt warmth against her skin.

Shaking her head, she ducked under the pipe and went past a huge bin with a closed lid, and three more large pipes running up and down vertically. They all seemed ancient, and were thick and heavy cast iron. "What is all this stuff?"

"It's not telecom." Dar was methodically searching the far wall. "I don't care what it is."

"Reminds me of that old cruise ship." Kerry edged through two large black iron posts with rivets in them and ducked under a pipe as she spotted a bit of wood through the gloom. "Is that it back there?"

Dar peered past a large box she was looking in. "Where?" She shone her flashlight into the dark corner. "Mark, over there." She closed the box and ducked under the pipe. "Kerry, you rock."

"Holy shit." Mark crawled out from under a step and got up. "In the back there? Dar, this is nuts! There's power running all over this place. How in the hell does our data not suck here?"

"My engineering can overcome pretty much anything or so everyone keeps telling me." Dar edged in next to where Kerry was standing, and they peered over a big iron pipe to see an old, tattered piece of plywood bolted to the back wall with a familiar set of telephone punch down blocks on it.

They were covered in dirt and dust, so obscured the colors of the wires were completely indistinguishable. Kerry squirmed over close to it and shone her flashlight on a tag, which was completely blank, brown from age, and crumbling at her touch. "Wow."

Dar peered at the electrical board perilously close to Kerry's shoulder. "Ker, don't move back. I think that's a live block."

Kerry froze, then carefully looked over her shoulder shining the flashlight on the cast iron works. "New York Edison Company," she read, "nineteen hundred and one."

"Didn't Scuzzy say this building was built in the thirties?"

"Maybe they reused the hardware." Mark managed to squeeze in closer. "Shit most of this room is older than I am. Hey, there's a door down there...for midgets."

Kerry gave him a sideways look, then she turned carefully and pointed her light at the back wall under the block. Sure enough, there was a door there. "Wow. Midgets for real."

The door was about as high as her knees with a knob near the bottom of it as though a regular height door had been cut in half. "Wonder where it goes? Looks like it's been painted over a few times."

"Probably doesn't go anywhere. They just didn't feel like removing it." Dar dismissed the painted over panel and started exploring the punch down. "I can't believe this is the demarc."

"For the whole building?" Kerry's voice rose in utter disbelief. "No way. No way in hell, Dar. There are hundreds and hundreds of tenants here. This block is barely big enough for a dozen of them."

"Well, the way the guy said it, the big boys have a nice room up one level in back of the elevator stack," Mark said. "We're private line, so..."

"Are you kidding me?" Kerry asked. "Do you mean to tell me they wouldn't let us drop a line into their room, and I'm carrying one of those bastard's entire backbone on my network?"

"Um." Mark's eyes widened.

"Grr." Kerry fumed. "Let me call the office and have those bastards cut off." She started to fish for her phone only to find her arms gently held. "Dar!"

"You're going to electrocute your ass. Hold still." Dar tugged her away from the electrical panel. "Cutting them off doesn't really get us anything, Ker. Money probably crossed hands to get them a new facility. We had nothing to do with it."

"But that's not fair!" Kerry protested. "We pay as much as any of them do for this damned access!"

Mark kept his mouth shut, peering at the blocks instead and trying to read some of them.

"Shh." Dar managed to maneuver her pissed off partner into a clearer space, then she wrapped her arms around her. "Leave it, Ker. Not worth the headache."

Kerry drew in a breath to continue arguing, then paused and exhaled, unable to keep the anger roiling inside the warmth of Dar's embrace. "It's not fair," she repeated. "Look at this place, Dar. They're probably laughing their asses off at us over this."

"Probably. But we're a level under them, and that means we're closer to our goal. Leave it."

"Grr." Kerry sighed, giving in. "And I'm damned well going to get this changed, but yeah, it'll wait until this is over."

Dar gave her a squeeze. "Now let me in there to see what the hell's going on with that demarc." She slipped past Kerry and carefully eased her way between the electrical panel and the iron pylon to get closer to the age scarred wood.

"You tricked me." Kerry issued a half hearted protest before she inched in after her, raising her hand to stifle a sneeze as they stirred the dust around them. "I'm safer in there, Dar. I'm smaller than you are."

"Nah, I'm fine." Dar disagreed, poking her head around a pipe.

"Okay." Mark finally spoke up. "I think there's only six or eight active on here, so we should be able to find ours pretty easy." He peered into the far corner. "Hey, Dar, is that a smartjack? There in the back? That has to be ours."

Dar directed her flashlight in that direction and leaned closer to look, inadvertently brushing her elbow against the electrical panel. She yelped and jumped back, nearly knocking Kerry on her butt. "Son of a bitch!" She grabbed her elbow, which was numb and tingling.

"Live, huh?" Mark asked, weakly.

"What kind of idiocy is this!" It was Dar's turn to be outraged, as she examined the panel. It was floor to ceiling copper strips with clamps at various levels. "You could get killed in here!"

"Easy honey." Kerry patted her hip. "How about we find our circuit and get out of here before we both end up in the hospital?"

Dar muttered under her breath, then cautiously eased back over to the back wall and peered at the box. It was the same dingy gray as the rest of the room, but there were somewhat newer looking cables coming out of the bottom, and a tag that was more white than brown hanging from the front.

She extended her arm carefully and got a fingertip on the top of the box, almost jumping out of her skin when her cell phone rang. "Brpht!"

"I got it." Kerry fished in her partner's pocket and retrieved the instrument. "Hello?"

"Glad you were here." Dar went back to prying the box open.

"Me too." Mark chimed in. "No offense, Big D, I'da let it ring."

Dar paused and looked over at him, then chuckled briefly.

"Hell...ah, is this Kerry?" Alastair's voice trickled hesitantly through the speaker. "I'm sorry, I thought I..."

"You did. Hang on." Kerry tapped Dar on the arm with her phone. "It's Alastair."

"Take a message." Dar was struggling with the box top. "If I overbalance I'm going to be a French fry."

Kerry pulled her arm back and took a step sideways out of the way, and away from the electrical panel. "Sorry about that. Dar's occupied right at the moment. Anything I can do to help?"

"Got it." Dar pulled the top of the box off with a rusty sounding screech of metal on metal. She set the top aside and shone her light on the inside, which had a modern piece of equipment clamped in it, full of blinking LED's and reassuringly clean plastic. "Ah hah."

"That it?" Mark stood on his tiptoes to look over the iron grillwork separating him from the section Dar was inside of. "Damn, look at that thing. That box looks like it should be coal fired."

"Well, it's a smartjack," Dar muttered. "I think that box used to be something else though."

Kerry was torn between listening to the phone and listening to the discussion. "Sorry, what was that again? No, that wasn't a smart ass...no, no we've...we're looking for our circuit in the office...oh, okay." Kerry put her hand over the mic. "Paladar?"

Dar stopped in mid motion and carefully turned fully around, giving Kerry her full attention. "Yes?"

"ABC News is outside. They want to talk to you."

Dar looked at her, then looked to either side at the inside of the grubby, dingy workspace. Then she held up one finger and turned back around, careful to edge away from the copper panel.

"That meant for me, or them?" Kerry asked.

Dar turned back around, one eyebrow hiked all the way up.

"Just checking." Kerry smiled.

"Tell them to kiss my ass." Dar went back to her task.

Kerry gave her a fond look. "Alastair, she's trying to read a circuit tag in a dark room that looks like a medieval torture chamber, and not be electrocuted at the same time. Can they wait a few minutes?"

She half turned and spoke into the phone. "I don't want to rush her. She'd look really strange with curly hair." She waited. "Okay, that's what I figured. I'll call you when we're out of here. Bye."

She closed the phone. "Well."

"23T234X6RZ45R," Dar replied.

Mark scribbled on the back of his hand. "I'm pretty sure that's ours, Dar. It's the right sequence."

"Me too," Dar agreed, pulling her hand back from the box and letting the top close over it. "Glad we found it, but I have no clue in the world how we're going to get the damn cable into this room. I don't think we can cross the shopping center with it."

She backed slowly out of the gap between the iron works and the live electrical panel and joined Kerry near the sloping back of the room. Now that her eyes had grown used to the gloom, Dar looked around at the space and studied the structure.

There was an old iron chute that cut off at the edge of a newer looking wall, and she walked over to peer at it, rubbing her thumb along a set of hammered letters. "Castle Coal," she said. "I don't get it. What's a coal thing doing in the middle of a modern building?"

Mark turned around. "These are steam pipes." He pointed. "We don't really have steam upstairs, do we?"

They all looked at each other, then both Mark and Dar looked at Kerry.

"Don't ask me." Kerry held her hand up. "I assumed we had central air and heat in the building. We never used coal in Michigan. You signed the lease, Dar. Did it mention steam? Scuzzy said there were steam pipes, but sheesh."

"Hell if I remember." Dar shrugged. "Doesn't really matter I guess. Now that we found it, let's go back to the rest of the group and see about a path. We probably need the building management involved."

"Should I get them to bring a router and a fiber hub here?" Mark asked. "We're gonna need to split the signal but..." He looked around. "Wonder if they've even got an outlet for power." He flashed his light around the walls and looked under a few of the boxes. "Crap."

"Can we get an electrician to...well, what am I saying? We'd have to contract Methuselah for that electrical panel. Maybe he's free." Kerry started making her way toward the entrance, scribbling herself a note. "Worse comes to worse, Dar, we can run a power cable in too. This isn't going to be pretty no matter how we do it."

Mark climbed up into another section ducking under the iron supports as he peered along the underside of a large pipe. "Lemme see if I can find something here. Running cable is gonna suck."

Dar leaned her elbows on Kerry's shoulders and whispered into her ear. "How could it possibly be anything but pretty if you do it?"

Aw. Kerry had to smile, despite the surroundings. "Flattery will get you anything you want, you know that?"

Dar chuckled. She felt Kerry's body lean back a little against her, and she savored the moment, nibbling on the edge of her ear . "Did you really think I was flipping you off?"

"No." Kerry tilted her head back and gave Dar a kiss on her jawbone. "I'm just glad I'm here with you and I felt like messing with you a little," she admitted. "This is so insane. What are we doing here?"

"C'mon." Dar bumped her gently. "Let's go see what other bad news awaits us." She put her hands on Kerry's shoulders and steered her toward the door. They had left it open, and the light from outside seemed an odd contrast to the dank, dark, interior of the old closet they were poking around in.

The tangle of pipes and iron bars made their progress slow, but they climbed up the steel steps and onto the platform that held the door just as Mark crawled back out from under an ancient console, his jumpsuit now liberally covered in grunge.

"Anything?" Kerry asked.

"Maybe," Mark said. "But I think the outlet's older than I am. Scary." He dusted himself off as they emerged from the room, blinking a little in the light. The building superintendant was leaning against the opposite wall, and he pushed off to come meet them as Mark pushed the door closed.

"Seen enough?" The man asked.

"We found what we were looking for, yes," Kerry said. "Now we have to find a way to get to it. Do you have a building electrician? We need some work done."

The man stared at her. "Work done? Lady you seen that room? No one does no work in there."

"They put our circuit in there. That's work." Kerry's nape hairs bristled. "Though I'm going to have a word with the management here as to why that happened."

The man held his hands up. "That's not my area," he said. "You want the electrician? I'll call him. He can tell you himself," he said. "You want to wait here? I'll have him come down." He didn't wait for Kerry to nod before he picked up his radio and started speaking into it, turning away from them and lowering his voice. Then with a glance at them, he walked away, heading for a door in the back of the hall.

"I'm going to go grab a router and see what mounting stuff we have," Mark said. "I'll come back here and wait for the electrical guy if you want to go see what's going on."

"Sounds like a plan," Dar said. "Thanks Mark."

"No prob." He trotted off toward the stairs, leaving Dar and Kerry behind.

"You want me to tell Alastair you can talk to the press now?" Kerry asked.

"No," Dar replied placidly. "That's not part of my job. That's part of his job. He's got Hamilton with him, and the entire New York office publicity machine with him, and I've got better things to do."

"All righty," Kerry said. "But honey, even though I love you more than anything on earth, you're going to be the one to tell him that, okay?"

Her partner chuckled wryly.

Dar's phone rang again. Kerry promptly handed it over to her.

Dar took it. "Hello," she answered briefly after glancing at the caller ID. *Not him* She mouthed at Kerry. "Yes, this is Dar Roberts. Who is this?" She paused, folding her free arm across her body and resting her elbow on her fist. "Okay, bu...oh, all right. Okay." She nodded. "So what's the issue?"

Kerry half listened and half watched their surroundings. There were a lot of people walking around, but they all seemed distracted, and the stores she could see had workers in the doorways, mostly standing and watching the passersby.

"So they're fighting over that? What the hell do you want me to do?" Dar asked. "What makes you think that?"

Kerry spotted their team coming out from the entrance to the subway. She waved at them, catching Scuzzy's eye and smiling as they changed direction to come over to where she and Dar were standing. "Here's the rest of the gang, hon."

"I think that's a crock of bullshit," Dar said. "I'll head over there, but only because I want to see the datapath. If you're still there wasting time then I'll see you, but I hope you get your head out of your ass and get working before then."

Kerry patted her partner's hip. "Easy, tiger."

Dar closed the phone abruptly and clipped it back on her pocket as the rest of the crew arrived. "Jackasses," she muttered. "Did you find a route?" She asked the gang.

"We found a lot of mad people," Shaun said. "Boy, people get pissed off when you ask dumb questions in the subway around here. They even got mad at her." He indicated Scuzzy, who nodded.

"Okay. Well, I'd like to ride from here back to where they have to drop the line into the tunnels," Dar said. "They've got some kind of hangup somewhere up there about the cable they want to talk to me about."

"What kind of trouble were they giving you, Shaun?" Kerry asked. "What were you guys asking?"

"Just where the tunnels met and stuff like that. You'd have thought we were asking for the president's fax number," Shaun said. "They're just freaking tunnels. What did they think we were going to do, set a bomb off in them?"

Everyone fell silent after he finished talking, looking at each other awkwardly as the words penetrated.

"Well, ya know..." Scuzzy murmured.

"They might have thought just that." Dar finished, quietly. "Let's go folks. We found the drop and Mark's going to work on getting our end of this set up. We might as well find out how far they've gotten before he goes to too much trouble."

"We can take the six," Scuzzy said. "I'm sure they're up past Brooklyn Bridge station already. We can walk, or take the 8th Ave up to the 53rd."

Dar eyed her. "You pick. None of the rest of us know what the hell you're talking about." She added, "But since the cable's probably going to have to come from underground, we should go the same route."

"You got it." Scuzzy turned and motioned them back the way they'd come. "Let's get a move on, people. We got trains to catch."

Chapter Ten

"ANYTHING?" DAR PEERED out the door to the subway train that was idling briefly in the station. "See anything, Scuzzy?" She glanced at her watch, uncomfortably aware of the rapid passage of time. "This is nuts."

"Not a damn thing." Scuzzy scratched her chin, as she hopped quickly back into the train. "Where the hell are these guys? I thought for sure they'd be at least halfway up to the place by now."

"You and me both." Dar ran her fingers through her hair. "I don't get it. They were all fired up to get this done after that meeting."

"Maybe they got a problem." Scuzzy looked apologetic. "Them guys ain't bad, mostly. They were pretty spooked after that guy got in trouble. My uncle said all of 'em were talking about it. Nobody wants that sorta trouble, you know?"

"Mm." Dar gripped the bars of the train rocking back and forth against them as though her body motion could make the car move with it. She went to the door again and looked out, squinting into the darkness as she peered into the tunnel. "Damn it."

They were in the first car of the train right behind the conductor's booth. Kerry was sitting in one of the seats with her cell phone pressed to her ear and her free hand cupped over the other side of her head.

Dar glanced at her, then stepped back as the doors started to close. "Ker? We're moving again."

"I feel it," Kerry muttered. "Okay, folks, I'm going to lose you again. I'll call you back." She closed the phone as the train rattled forward plunging from the fluorescent light of the station into the darkness of the tunnels again.

Dar sat down next to her and put a hand on her knee. "If this is driving you nuts, you can take off at the next station. Go back to the office and deal with Lansing there." She studied the frustrated expression on Kerry's face, watching the pale lashes flicker a little. "Okay?"

Kerry rested her elbows on her knees her phone clasped in her hands. "No," she said, after a moment. "I want to stay here."

"Sure?" Dar gave her kneecap a little scratch.

"Yeah. I'm just saying the same thing over and over again. It's probably a good thing I keep having to get off the line before I start screaming."

"Ah." Dar leaned back extending her long legs across the floor of the car. She regarded the interior, then shook her head a trifle. "I can't believe I'm in one of these things and it's not freaking me out," she remarked. "Last time I nearly chucked my guts up."

Kerry straightened up and sat back. "Relative levels of things to freak out about?" She suggested. "I know it would take a hell of a lot to freak me out right now, that's for sure."

Dar spread her arm out along the back of the seat behind Kerry, waiting until she felt the tense back relax against her touch. "So what's

Lansing's problem? Can I help?" She rubbed the bottom of her thumb across the top of her partner's shoulder. "Someone I can yell at for you?"

A grudging smile appeared on Kerry's face. "Backups are taking too long. They're still pretty saturated across the northern links and they're running into issues finishing the drive mirroring."

"Are you kidding me?" Dar peered at her. "They're bitching about that?"

"It's causing problems with their autonomic scripts." Kerry tilted her head back to rest on Dar's arm. "Their production jobs aren't kicking off on time and it's throwing everyone off. I understand how frustrated they are, but damn it, Dar, its not like we're hanging out having Daquiris here."

Dar reflected on that. "I could use a Daquiri right now," she said. "Tell them to split the backup into two segments, and run them on alternate nights until we get a little more clear and I can spend some time working the metrics. We'll take the risk."

"I suggested that." Kerry watched Dar's profile. "That's what we were arguing about. When I call them back I'll tell them you said so, and that should end that conversation."

"You make me sound like such a pirate captain."

"Here's the next station." Scuzzy stood up. "They got to be here. This is the freaking last stop on this here train. It's Brooklyn Bridge!"

"Hold that thought." Kerry stood up as they pulled into the station and clipped her phone to her belt as Dar joined her and they both went to the door and peered out. The station was relatively quiet and, as they stepped out onto the platform, the rest of the passengers exited and headed for the stairwells further down.

Scuzzy had bounced out ahead of them, and she was near the very end of the platform, her head poked out into the tunnel as she shaded her eyes. "Okay, so here we are. Where the hell are these guys?"

Dar studied the tracks, not seeing any indication of new cable running through that would hint at the teams passing. "Kerry, get your buddy on the phone and find out where the hell these people are," she said, going over to the cracked Plexiglas covering a subway map and studying it. "If this is Brooklyn Bridge, we're almost back to where we started yesterday. What the hell have they been doing?"

Kerry joined her, phone pressed to her ear. "I don't want to go any closer to where we were," she stated. "We don't have any protection, Dar."

"Right there with you, Ker. They should have been a lot further up by now. This may all be one big damn moot point."

The train behind them was still idling in the station. Scuzzy came back over to where Dar and Kerry were standing, extending her arms out in visible bewilderment. "I don't get it."

"Us either." Dar acknowledged. "I find it very hard to believe these people haven't gotten up this far yet. What the hell are they doing, laying the damn cable an inch an hour?" She went to the edge of the platform and looked down the tunnel, seeing not much other than a few lights off in the distance.

It smelled. A gust of surprisingly cold air blew back down into her face and she stepped back quickly, glancing behind her at the train.

"No, you aren't." Kerry was speaking into her phone. "I'm standing right here, looking at the wall and we're in the city hall station."

Across the platform, against the far wall, Dar could see another, smaller concrete slab that was darkened and obviously not used. She turned around and saw the twin of it against the other wall, then she went again to the edge of the tunnel and peered inside.

The driver had come out of his cubicle and he approached her. "What are you people doin'?" he asked, in a gruff tone.

Dar turned. She held up her ID and credentials, which he peered at. "We're working with the government," she said. "Trying to lay some cable down these tunnels."

The driver looked down the tunnel, then at her. "You're crazy, right? You think you're putting cables down the subway? We got manholes for that." He pointed across at the other, darkened platform. "They're over there, not in the tunnels lady."

"Are they?" Dar looked where he was pointing seeing a rolldown door in the gloom. "Can I get over there to look at it?"

The driver studied her , then he shrugged. "G'wan inside the car. I'll open the other doors. You might need to jump a little."

"Look, I'm telling you I'm right here. No one...what? What do you mean, another city hall?" Kerry motioned Scuzzy over. "Can you talk to this guy? He's not making any sense to me."

"Sure." Scuzzy willingly came over. "He's probably from Brooklyn or somethin'."

Dar entered the car through the open doors and crossed over waiting until the driver entered his cubicle and opened the far set exposing the dark, shortened platform. It wasn't much of a jump, actually. Dar merely stepped across onto it, and pulled her flashlight out to explore.

The platform was filthy. She had the brief sensation of what it might be like inside a coal mine as she walked carefully along the concrete slab glancing up at an old mosaic embedded into the wall. "Brooklyn Bridge," she muttered under her breath.

It was obscured with plaster and a half wall of whitewashed wood forming a crude storage area. Next to that was a door painted black to match the inside walls and battered with years. Dar walked over and turned the knob, fully expecting it to be locked but not entirely surprised when it wasn't.

She pushed the door open and peered inside, and sure enough, she was faced with more cable trunks than she knew what to do with. She entered and looked around, tipping her head back to look up and see tiny chinks of light above her head.

They flickered, then flickered again, and she realized she was looking at daylight. Manhole? She turned and looked at the door, then shook her head and continued exploring.

"Hey, Dar!" Kerry's voice echoed through the station. "Where are you?"

"Over here." Dar examined the huge bundles of cables and thick, riveted pipes that ran along the wall. A rustle of movement made her jump, and she flashed her light into the corner, which now had a pair of glowing eyes. "What's up?"

"C'mere!"

Dar backed out of the room with guilty relief, shutting the door quickly behind her before she turned and found Kerry looking out of the open doors at her. "What's up?"

"What's there?" Kerry countered. "Did you find something?"

"Cable trunk." Dar joined her in the car. "Not sure it helps us. Not sure where it ends up."

"Hey, if you people wanna keep talkin', I got to pull the train around to the other track," the driver said. "You want to ride around? I got no problem with that, since you're with the government and all."

"We're n..." Kerry started to answer, then she stopped. "Sure, that's fine. Thanks." She waited for the door to the driver's compartment to close. "Dar, they told Scuzzy they were in some other City Hall station. She thinks they're in the wrong tunnels."

Dar looked over at Scuzzy, who lifted her hands again. "There ain't no other City Hall station on this line, yeah? They got one over on the BMT though. I think they came down into the wrong stations or something."

"Great." Dar exhaled, pressing her nose against the window as the train started moving. "We're screwed."

"I think it's the stock market that's screwed, hon," Kerry said, pragmatically. "It's not our fault they took the wrong stairs."

"We'll still get screwed over it. No one's going to care if they did the wrong thing. We're the ones who promised we'd fix it." Dar stared grimly out the window, as the train eased into a turn, and the walls shifted from a drab sooty black to a lighter brick.

She got the impression of light, and she cupped her hands against the glass to see better. "Wh..." Her eyes took in arches and brickwork, a flash of mosaic, flickers of light, and outlined in it a group of workers with a familiar spool. "Hey! Hey! There they are!"

"What?" Kerry crowded against her and looked out the window. "Where who...oh...huh?"

"Scuzzy, get this guy to stop, willya?" Dar called out. "There are the bastards. In there!"

Scuzzy was already hammering on the door to the driver's compartment. "Hey buddy! Hey! Hold it up!"

The train shuddered to a halt, jerking and rattling and throwing Kerry against Dar and both of them against the window. Dar grabbed Kerry and the pole she was standing near and got them both upright as the door to the driver's pod yanked open and the driver emerged.

"What in the hell are you people yelling about?" the man asked. "Jesus Christ you scared the shit out of me! You know what it's been like the last couple days? I'm having a heart attack!" He fumed. "What's wrong with you?"

"Hey, take it easy." Scuzzy held her hands out. "We just found the guys we were looking for, yeah? We didn't want to miss them."

"What are you ta..." The driver ducked back inside and looked out his window. "There's no one...oh hell. There are people there. What the hell are they doing there?" He opened the slat and stuck his head out. "What you people doin' out there, huh?"

Dar leaned closer to the doorway. "Can you open the doors?" she asked. "We need to talk to those guys."

"What?" The driver was still yelling out the window. He reached back inside and triggered a switch. "How in the hell did you get in here? They told us this was strickly off limits!"

"We're the phone company, shaddup!" The man on the platform yelled back.

Dar went to the door and stepped carefully over the shoulder width gap onto the platform, turning to hold out a hand to Kerry without really even thinking about it.

Kerry paused in the act of hopping out and eyed her, a faint smile twitching at her lips. She shifted her flashlight to her left hand and reached over to clasp Dar's fingers, squeezing them as she stepped over to the other side and gave her a little bump. "Thank you, sweetie."

Her partner paused, and a tiny wrinkle appeared on the bridge of her nose. "Was I being pretentious?"

"Just charming." Kerry moved past her. "Wow. What is this place?"

Dar glanced around, then headed for the cluster of men around the spool. "Let's see what those bastards are doing here."

Kerry let her go ahead, taking a moment to tip her head back and look around. Scuzzy came up next to her and they both slowed to a halt, and simply stared around them. "Wow."

"No kidding," Scuzzy agreed. "I ain't never seen nothing like this in the subway. that's for sure."

It seemed like it was part of the tunnel itself, which curved around in a big loop, the far end disappearing into the darkness again on the far side of space. But in the center, the ceiling lofted up in a series of gothic arches that culminated in a thin ironwork tracery of windows that allowed the light in from outside to spill across the intricately bricked walls.

It was surprising and beautiful, completely unexpected and Kerry took her camera from her belt pouch and adjusted the flash taking a few pictures of the work. "I guess there were two City Halls." She pointed at a mosaic tile sign on the wall, which held the words. "How weird."

Scuzzy was looking right up at the ceiling. "Whoa," she said. "You know? I think this is like, right outside the freaking entrance to the Hall. I seen those glass things from the top, you know? I asked my brother what they were once and he had like no idea."

"Ker." Dar's voice interrupted their sightseeing.

Kerry put her camera away, turning and heading over to where her partner was standing. "Sorry, what's up?"

"Wrong fucking cable." Dar enunciated the three words in the most clipped tone imaginable.

"Oh Jesus." Kerry pinched the bridge of her nose, as a headache she'd been keeping at bay started up again. "Not what I needed to hear."

"This is what those guys gave us,"the man from Verizon spoke up immediately. "This ain't my fault," he immediately added. "This is the stuff those guys from Jersey brought over, right Mike?"

"Right." Another tech agreed immediately. "So that's what I told that guy, you sure it's this code? I had the code. I told him the code, and he said yeah, it was the right code, but I knew it wasn't no right code because I been laying this cable since I was eighteen years old, and I know what code it should be, and it ain't this code."

"Right. So we told those guys somebody needed to come down here and look at this before we went no further, because this is a lot of crap to go through for no reason," the first tech said. "And my guys gave me a lotta crap about it and just said to go on with it, but ain't no way was I gonna have these here guys run this here cable if it's the wrong stuff."

There was a brief silence. Then Dar folded her arms over her chest. "Right choice."

The tech nodded. "You got that right. So they sending someone down to here now? I ain't got all day to be sitting in this tunnel."

"They sent someone," Dar answered, before Kerry's bristling hackles could make her pale hair fluff out like a Chia pet. "I'll look at the cable."

"You?" The man gave Dar a doubtful look.

"Yes."

"Okay." The man motioned the other techs over. "Unreel some of dat, willya? This here lady wants to see it." He looked back at Dar. "You sure you know what you're looking at?"

"Yes."

"Whatever." The man motioned her forward. "C'mon, c'mon. We ain't got all day."

"Shit." Dar pulled out her flashlight and walked over to the spool where the telco techs were unhitching the end of the cable in the spool and twisting it back for her to inspect. "This was one complication I wasn't expecting."

"Can I punch him while you're figuring out what to do?" Kerry asked from between gritted teeth. "Stupid piece of ignorant pork rind."

"Easy slugger."

DAR LEANED AGAINST the intricately bricked wall, her arms crossed over her chest, her mind racing. In front of her the track was now clear as the train had moved along into its appointed time slot. She had been left to ponder the cable, the techs, and the pit she'd dug herself into.

Shit. She felt like kicking herself. After all the bullshit she'd been spilling about everyone else's lame ass actions she had to face the fact she had screwed up to an intolerable degree by not simply checking what type of cable this half ass vendor was giving them.

Inexcusable.

Kerry came over and leaned against the wall next to her, their shoulders brushing. "Hey." She braced one booted foot against the brick. "Thanks for the advice on the Lansing issue. It worked."

Dar looked sideways at her.

Kerry peered mildly back.

"You're welcome," Dar finally said. "You trying to make me stop kicking myself?"

"Well," her partner plucked at the knee of her pants, "actually I was trying to find something to say to you that wouldn't make you blow up at me."

"At you?"

"You know what I mean. Hon, I know you're freaking out. I don't want to make it worse for either of us."

Dar sighed.

Kerry felt the gentle pressure as Dar leaned against her, a non verbal acknowledgment and surrender she felt a great deal of sympathy for. There really wasn't much she could say, to be honest. Dar was right. She should have checked.

Of course, she could try to take responsibility for that on herself, but if she tried, she knew Dar would go ballistic and, frankly, she wasn't looking for any kind of tension between them since the situation was already more than wretched enough.

Honesty seemed the better route. With Dar it always was, even if her own inclination was to try and make excuses or find some way to entice her lover into feeling better about whatever it was she was kicking herself over. "So it's the wrong kind of fiber."

"Wrong kind of fiber," Dar agreed. "Multimode. The long distance optics are single mode."

"No options?"

"Longest reach multimode will do is 550 meters." Dar let her head rest on the wall. "Eighteen hundred feet."

Kerry did the math, and sighed. "Do they have any other spools?"

"Sure. All the wrong kind," Dar supplied. "Know what that bastard said? Oops."

"Oops." Kerry mouthed the word. "Nice."

"Yeah." Dar acknowledged. "Mongolian clusterfuck, courtesy of yours truly." She gazed up at the skylights, then pushed off from the wall. "Well, screw it." She started back toward the techs, who had been taking a break leaning against the cable spool. "No point in standing around."

Kerry gathered herself up and followed, catching up as Dar neared the work crew. "Hon…"

Dar held a hand up. "Okay, go ahead and keep rolling it out. We'll deal with it on our end." She said, in a brisk tone as she came up next to where the men were lounging. "We're running out of time."

The crew leader turned in surprise. "Yeah? This is the wrong stuff though," he pointed out. "You said so."

"Not a problem," Dar replied steadily. "I'll handle it. Just get the cable rolled out. We've got a solution."

The man studied her. "Awright." He shrugged. "Overtime for us, and not doin what those guys down town from here are doin. Sounds good to me. Okay boys?"

The techs dusted their gloved hands off, most of them nodding. "Better than digging out pipes," one agreed. "At least it's quiet down here, and no dust."

The men got to work, standing up and taking hold of the spool. "Down the line here." The crew leader motioned Dar and Kerry out of the way. "Scuse me, ladies. We got work to do."

"Sorry, we definitely don't want to hold you up." Kerry gave him a smile. "We'll be waiting for you on the other end. Thanks for taking the time to let us know about this, by the way. At least it gives us time to get a solution in place before you get up there."

The man nodded briefly at her. "You the people with the bus?"

Kerry nodded back. "We'll send some snacks down the line to you when we get back. We really appreciate you guys coming through for us with this."

The men reacted to Kerry's charm and sincere tone. They gave her brief smiles, and one of them touched the rim of his hard hat as they rolled the spool by. "See you down at the Rock, pretty lady," he said, giving Kerry a wink.

Kerry gave them all a genial wave. She waited for them to move down the curve of the track before she turned and looked at her partner. "Come up with a plan?"

"Nope." Dar had her hands in her pockets. "I haven't a damn clue what I'm going to do."

Kerry turned her head and looked at the men, then swiveled back to face Dar. Her brows lifted. "Is this something maybe you can come up with a fix for?"

"Probably not."

"Hon? Is there a reason you want these guys to work all night doing this then?" Kerry asked, gently. "I know you hate to give up, so do I , but there's a lot of work they could be doing too, huh?" She laid a hand on her partner's arm to ease any sting from the words.

Dar merely lifted her shoulders in a mild shrug, though. "I can't just tell them to stop," she said. "Even if I know it's probably going to be a waste of time."

"Probably?"

"Well..." Dar removed one hand from her pocket and raked her hair back from her eyes. "I know the physics of it, Ker. But let's go back to the Rock, and I'll get on the phone with some of the eggheads I know up at our network vendor and see what they say."

Kerry studied her face cast in the shadows from the skylight's grill. Even she could see the doubt in her partner's eyes, and from her own knowledge of the technology she faced, the understanding that this time Dar really was just tossing crap in the air.

Sobering.

"Okay." Kerry said, after they were both silent for a minute. "We really don't have much choice, do we?"

"No."

"Then let's boogie." Kerry turned around. "Scuzzy? You around here? We've got to get going."

Scuzzy trotted down a set of steps in the center of the curve. "Man, this is amazing," she said. "I ain't never seen nothing like this place. You know what this is?" She came over, full of enthusiasm and oblivious to the nerdish gloom around her colleagues. "This is like the very first station in the subway."

"Is it?" Kerry looked around again. "It's really interesting."

"Yeah. I found a plaque over there." Scuzzy pointed. "This is where it started, you know? The first station where all the trains left from back in like in 1904. " She looked up. "Man, they used to make things cool, huh?"

"Why don't they use it anymore?" Dar spoke up. "Seems like a waste to leave it here."

"Oh." Scuzzy pulled out her phone. "Hang on a minute, that driver told me to like call him when we needed to get out of here. Walking down the track is not cool." She dialed a number, turning her head to one side and covering her ear as she waited for it be answered.

Her decision made, Dar turned her attention to her surroundings. She walked over to the plaque and studied it, tipping her head back to look at the mosaic sign above. There was an elegance and an architectural beauty to it that surprised her, and she allowed herself to be distracted by the artistry in the tiles and the arches.

She felt a moment out of time, hearing the echo of a different era as Kerry walked quietly up behind her coming to stand at her side, sliding the fingers of one hand into Dar's front pocket.

The silent support in the motion both charmed her, and made her feel more than a little guilty. She glanced to the side, catching Kerry's profile in the dim light from the work lamps.

After a moment, Kerry sensed it and turned her face a little their eyes meeting. "Know what I think?"

"Bet I'm about to," Dar wryly answered.

"I think Heaven is really going to be a plane seat heading home." Kerry tugged her a little. "C'mon, boss. Let's get out of here. I think I hear our chariot approaching."

"Here we go." Scuzzy confirmed it, pointing down the track. "Man, I wish I'd took pictures down here. This was freaking amazing."

"I have some. I'll share." Kerry clasped Dar's hand with her own and started toward the edge of the platform. Ahead of them, on the far side where the track seemed unused, the men were already working their way along, flashlights casting odd bursts of light against the soot darkened walls.

"That's cool." Scuzzy joined them at the edge of the concrete. "I mean, I know this is real serious and all that stuff, but I think New York is the coolest city, and I love seeing stuff like this. Like, you been over Brooklyn Bridge?"

"I have," Kerry responded, since her silent partner wasn't looking likely to. "It's an amazing construction," she added. "I know the head of the office here—who died in the attack—was also a big fan of the city wasn't he Dar?"

"He was," Dar said. "I'm sure he would have loved to have seen this place."

The train pulled slowly into the station, its bright number six prominent in the gloom. Scuzzy tilted her head back and looked up at the skylight. "Like that stuff. Today, we put these lights everywhere. Back then, they were smart. They used what they had, you know? Got all kinds of light in here from that."

"Using prisms." Kerry waited for the door to open, then she hopped inside.

"Prisms," Dar repeated, as she joined her.

"You people done with all this now?" The driver poked his head out. "My boss said I can't do this no more. They got real pissed at me."

"We're done," Kerry said. "Thank you very much for picking us up."

"Yeah, that was really cool." Scuzzy went over to him. "This place is great."

The driver shrugged. "It's just a tunnel." He went back in his cubicle and closed the door, then closed the outside doors and put the train in motion. They sat down as they left the old, unused station and pulled around, shuttling through only a short period of darkness before they were pulling into Brooklyn Bridge.

Dar settled back in her seat to wait out the ride, folding her arms over her chest as she half closed her eyes and thought about light.

And prisms.

Kerry felt her phone buzz, but she left it on her belt content to merely sit and share Dar's space as she let her mind go blank. There would be time when she got back to the office to continue her never ending problem solving.

Right now she could use the tunnels as an excuse to rest her head against Dar's shoulder and think about something trivial, like the pretty mosaics on the wall back there, and how warm her partner's skin was.

There was no real point in wondering what they were going to do about the problem of the cable. If Dar didn't know what to say about it, no one did.

She really had no idea what they were going to do.

DAR RESTED HER forearms on the mahogany wood surface appreciating the sound proofed walls and the stillness of the office.

On the desk was a phone and her laptop which was closed. The rest of the office was fairly sterile and empty, a spare the staff had rapidly found for her when she and Kerry returned from the subway, moving from an active part of the work back to something a bit more administrative.

For once, Dar was glad. She didn't really want to be around the fiber guys and Mark, who were setting up the gear needed to make the connection she knew wasn't going to happen when it was all said and done.

She didn't want to say anything to them, but she was finding it hard. It was an odd mix of embarrassment, anger, and frustration at the situation and self disgust at her part in it.

Ugh.

She looked at the phone, then removed her PDA and opened it, flicking through the address book as she searched for a specific entry. After she found it she exhaled, studying the phone pad for a long time before she made a move toward it.

A knock at the door stilled her hand in the act of dialing. She released the line and put her hands back on the desk. "C'mon in."

Alastair poked his head in at the invitation. "Hello, there."

"Hey." Dar waved him forward, guiltily glad of the interruption. "How was the interview?"

Her boss smiled briefly. "Well, that went just fine. But you know they followed me back here. Really want to talk to you."

Dar made a face. "Alastair, I'm busy."

"I know," Alastair said. "But they're right in back of me, lady. Don't make me turn around and boot them. They're not bad folks. Just want a few minutes of your time."

Silver linings. Dar sighed. "Okay, sure. Might as well get it over with before I get on a conference call." She shifted and rested her chin on her fist. "Bring them in."

Alastair smiled again, this time far more warmly. "Thanks." He drew back for a moment, then opened the door and entered, holding it open for the rest to follow. "C'mon in, folks. Dar's got only a minute, so please keep it brief."

A group of four people entered, two men dressed in khakis carrying cameras with pockets full of technical items, a tall man in a turtleneck and a jacket, and a medium height woman in a leather coat and boots.

"Hi." Dar briefly wished Kerry was in the room. "What can I do for you folks?"

The tall man approached the desk. "John Avalls." He held a hand out. "Thanks for taking the time to talk to us, Ms. Roberts. We won't be too long."

Dar stood and took his hand. "I'd appreciate that. We're in the middle of a lot of activity here."

"This is my colleague, Sarah Sohn." The man indicated his female companion. "And our cameramen John and Barry."

Dar gave them all a brief nod. Then she stuck her hands in her pockets and waited.

The reporters came closer to her while the camera people set up their gear. Alastair loitered in the background perching on a credenza that held a set of glasses and probably hid a large screen television panel.

"Okay." Avalls was flipping through a notepad. "Sorry, Ms. Roberts. It's been a long couple days for us too. I'm trying to get my questions straight here so I don't waste your time."

"No problem." Dar watched the cameramen wrangle their gear. "I can imagine that you folks have been going without any sleep just like we have. "

"Exactly." Sarah nodded. "You almost feel guilty taking a nap, like you're going to miss something if you do." She had a portfolio open, and she took up a position near the short edge of Dar's desk. "For a while there, even going to the restroom felt like that."

Dar nodded. "Can't be like that forever though."

"No," Sarah said. "It's funny you say that because I was thinking that this morning before we met Mr. McLean, I had so many other things to do—personal things, laundry, you know, shopping—that I haven't even thought about since Tuesday. "

"Life's moving on," Alastair suggested. "I know we feel it. Our customers were completely understanding the first few days, but now, their priorities are changing too."

Avalls looked up from his notes and nodded. "I found myself hoping over coffee this morning they'd find me an assignment somewhere else," he said, honestly. "You can just take so much. I felt like going to cover baseball in Wisconsin."

Dar nodded slowly. "Wish I was home in Miami, myself, matter of fact. Alastair and I were in London when it happened, and we've been going full out since then."

"I was at my in-laws in Virginia," Avalls said. "My father in law was having his sixtieth birthday party, and we had the whole family in for a big barbeque." He glanced up from his notepad. "Now he never wants to celebrate his birthday again. "

They were all silent for a moment. "Tough to know who to be mad at, isn't it?" Alastair came over and settled on the far edge of the desk Dar was standing behind. "Anyway, here we are."

"Here we are," Avalls said. "John, you ready?""

"Yeah. I think there's enough light in here not to use ours," the cameraman said, peering into his lens at Dar's image. "We're good."

"This is a high pickup mic," Sarah said, "so we don't need to do the whole stick it in your face thing. It's picking you up fine." She looked at a meter on the device she was wearing over her shoulder. "And it's quiet in here."

"Great." Dar rocked up and down on her heels. "One warning. I'm tired, and I'm not a talking head," she said. "Don't ask any questions you don't want to hear the answers to."

Sarah looked up and smiled at her. "We know. Ms. Roberts, I've been a fan of yours since you did an interview about that ATM breakdown for a colleague of mine. I can't speak for John, but we're not here looking for a headline on the crawler. We just don't understand some things we've seen happening and we'd like to, and we think you have the answers."

"You speak for me,"Avalls said, mildly. "I am just the talking head."

Dar relaxed, sensing a weary doggedness in the little crew she understood at a gut level. She was usually wary of the press, given her recent experiences with them sometimes more than wary, but in this time, in this place, she felt like it was going to be okay.

Alastair, after all, knew her well enough not to put her in front of a couple of antagonistic reporters, didn't he? She glanced over at him, seeing only mild interest on his face. "Nice shirt, Alastair."

Her boss eyed her. "Laundry's in the hands of the hotel, Paladar. I wasn't banking on spending an extra couple of weeks on the road with you."

Dar grinned, then she turned back to the reporters. "So, what can I answer for you folks?"

"Okay."Avalls studied his pad and paper. "Let me put on my weatherman voice and get this started." He cleared his throat. "Ms. Roberts, we all know everyone rushed to New York to help in this time of great tragedy. But what did that mean to you? What are you doing here?"

"Dar, be good," Alastair got in, just as she was taking a breath to answer. "Remember this will probably be national."

Dar merely laughed. Then she sighed. "What am I doing here." She mused. "Well, for one thing, we didn't rush up here. This was our second stop."

"Second?"

The door opened and a familiar blond head poked inside. Dar motioned her partner forward, then returned her hands to her pockets.

"We went to the Pentagon first, physically, but in reality we were everywhere after it happened."

"Can you explain that?" Avalls asked.

"Not without a white board and at least ten colored markers," Dar replied. "In brief, we reached out and connected all of our corporate resources so we could understand what was happening and mitigate the effects when we could, and where we could."

Kerry came over and took a seat out of camera range in one of the comfortable leather chairs to one side of the desk.

"Then, after we got a team on the ground at the Pentagon and resolved their immediate infrastructure problems, we came here." Dar concluded, "and since we've been here, we have been using the resources we have to try and help the city knit itself back together. "

"The city asked you to come?" Avalls asked.

"We came for our people here," Alastair answered. "City didn't have much to do with it."

"But once we were here, and they knew we were, they gave us a priority list and we did what we could with it," Dar added.

"Yet you brought your infamous bus with you." Avalls consulted his pad. "This bus, which I've heard about from roughly everyone including all our production people, has been seen all over the city passing out drinks and cookies." He glanced up. "Was that calculated? Good corporate PR?"

"I'm sure it is good corporate PR. The name of the company is plastered over the outside of the damn things," Dar replied. "But in fact, no. We sent the buses because we knew we had people here who needed help. Not people in general, our people here in the city."

"I'm sure a cynic would doubt that," Avalls said, but he smiled.

"I'm sure they would," Dar agreed. "And in the end, it really doesn't matter because the buses did what we wanted them to do and more. No matter what anyone considered the motive to be, we know better."

"So what now? What are you doing now, and what do you intend to do in the future here?" Avalls asked, after a brief pause. "How long do you focus on New York?"

Dar remained silent for a moment, pondering what to answer to that. "We focus on all our customers," she said finally. "So in that sense, we'll be busy here for a while. We have a lot of facility down that we need to take care of."

"That's not exactly what I meant," Avalls said. "I understand, of course, you take care of business. What I meant was, how long will you be acting in this...well, let's call it philanthropic mode? I'm sure you're not billing Manhattan for the cupcakes."

Dar turned her head and looked at Alastair, her brows lifting.

The camera swung over and focused on the CEO. He had his arms folded over his chest, and a thoughtful expression on his face. "Well now." He mused. "I don't think we ever even thought about it that way. I recall being on our conference bridge and, naturally when I heard about the problems our people were having here, of course we sent our service personnel. It's part of who we are as a company, you know? It's the people."

"The people?"

"The people." Alastair indicated the general surroundings, and then specifically Dar and Kerry. "Our company is our people. It's not the technology and the gew-gaws and wiring. Of course we focus on taking care of the most precious resource we have, and the buses will stick around until we no longer need them. If the city benefits by that, great. I'm fine with funding as many damn cupcakes and cups of lemonade that we can pass out."

"Now," Dar cleared her throat, "will that bring us good PR? Sure. Will people remember the logo on the bus? Sure." She shrugged. "But we'd do it anyway. Our people are as glad to see those buses as anyone else is."

"Okay, cut it, John," Avalls said. "So now let me ask you...shouldn't the city, or the government be out there doing the same thing?"

Dar sat down behind the desk. "Not my area."

Kerry chuckled.

"Not being provocative?" Sarah chuckled also. "The Red Cross is out there. There's nothing in the government really that provides that type of service. That isn't their area either."

"That's true," Kerry responded. "We have to have that facility because, like Alastair said, our people are our most important resource. We have to provide for them so they can do the jobs we need done in situations like this. It's tough to be away from your family and thrown into a relatively dangerous situation."

"Well, we could say the city workers and the military have the same issue," Avalls commented.

"Yes, but they get paid to do public service," Kerry said. "Our people get paid to be nerds. That doesn't usually mean you put your life on the line for your job."

"And yet, here you are," Sarah said. "And from what Mr. McLean said, you were down in the disaster area in the wreckage yesterday where you could easily have been hurt, true?"

"True," Kerry agreed.

"Do they pay you for that, Ms. Stuart?" Avalls asked, folding his hands over his pad.

"No." Kerry shook her head.

"So then why go? I'm not asking to be contrary. I'm curious."

Kerry glanced past him. "Because Dar went," she answered honestly. "And I go where she goes, no matter how crazy it is."

That shut them up. They glanced between Kerry and Dar, as the cameraman fiddled with putting his gear away. "All right then," Avalls finally said. "Thanks for taking the time to talk to us. I really appreciate it."

"Anytime." Dar leaned back in her chair, as Alastair got up from the desk.

"I'll walk you folks out," Alastair said. "Dar, the board's asked for a short recap call, can we squeeze that in next?"

"Sure," Dar agreed.

They left, closing the door and leaving Dar and Kerry alone in the office. Dar turned in her chair and regarded her partner, a wry smile on her face.

"Was that too goofy?" Kerry asked.

"Nah. Wish they'd gotten it on camera," Dar replied. "We might as well get all the good press we can now because you know we're going to get thrown under those damn buses when nothing works on Monday."

Kerry sighed. "So you haven't come up with a brilliant plan to fix the problem yet?"

Dar snorted. "Ker, thanks for the vote of confidence, but even I can't change the laws of physics." She went back to her PDA. "Hang out. You can hear the guffaws of laughter when I ask the guys over in the optics division of our network vendor if they can."

"Yerg."

"Mm."

Chapter Eleven

"HOW'S IT GOING, Mark?" Dar released the radio button and waited. She leaned back against the wall behind the desk where Kerry was seated studiously pecking at her keyboard, the tip of her tongue sticking out as she concentrated.

Dar found the expression adorable and, despite her current aggravation, it made her smile.

"Good news," Kerry said after a moment. "They got all the circuits back up at the Pentagon, Dar. That room is fully operational now." She glanced up at her companion. "What's so funny?"

Nothing." Dar cleared her throat. "That is good news. That should give you some slack on the bandwidth in that area," she added. "I know that was stressing the backhaul carrying most of that on the sat."

"It does," Kerry agreed. "I'm glad, because I told some of the customers we have riding on the sat as primary we'd maybe see some improvement after the weekend." She went back to her keyboard. "Not that it kept them from bitching at me."

"Hey boss, Mark here." Dar's radio crackled."I got the router mounted down here. Had to pay to get some guy to give me power though. They freaked out when I wanted to run a cord over the ground."

"Expense it. Whatever it was," Dar responded.

"He...uh, didn't exactly give me a receipt," Mark admitted, "and I kinda had to pay in cash, if you get my drift."

Kerry turned and peered over her shoulder again. "We're not going to pass the ethics certification this year, are we?"

Dar gave her a wry look. "Expense it anyway, Mark. We'll approve it. We need to get a pull cord run down to the tunnels. Any progress on finding a path?"

There were a few clicks on the speaker before Mark answered. "They're working on it, boss. Kannan and Shaun are down there looking for a way up. Nothing yet."

Damn. Dar tapped the mic against her chin. "Okay. Keep me in the loop."

She clipped the mic and sighed. "I feel like a complete shit head making them go through this knowing it's for nothing," she said. "Just for that, I'm going to pay them all bonuses when we get back."

"Are you going to tell them?" Kerry leaned on the chair arm and studied her partner. "I guess what I mean is, what are you going to tell them once the cable gets here? Mark's going to know when he sees it, certainly Kannan will."

Dar slid down the wall to sit on the floor, extending her legs out. "I know. I don't know what I'll tell them. I'm not going to tell anyone now. Let the damn cable get here, and then...I don't know." She scratched her ear. "I'll be honest I guess. Tell them we were working on a way around it, but it didn't work out."

Kerry got up and walked over, sitting down next to Dar and stretching her legs out alongside her partner's. "This sucks, sweetie."

"It sucks." Dar's cell phone rang. She pulled it out and answered, "Dar Roberts." She listened. "Oh, hey, Chuck. Hang on." She keyed the phone's speaker. "Go ahead, Kerry's here too."

"Hey yeah, hi, Kerry." Chuck's voice echoed. "Listen, they briefed me on what you asked, Dar. I've checked with a few people. That spec won't carry the distance. It can't."

Kerry closed her eyes and pinched the bridge of her nose.

"I'm aware of that, Chuck," Dar said. "Problem is, that's all they got here. You know what's riding on it," she added. "I've been through the specifications with a fine tooth comb and I know it says it's impossible. I want to know what is possible, and whether all it's going to take is a lot of money, which I'm willing to cough up."

"Well, I know, Dar," Chuck answered. "I got fifteen senior engineers here in the white board room looking at this from every angle, but you know it is what it is. At most, they can tweak the modules to go a thousand, maybe twelve hundred meters. That's it."

Dar sighed. "Damn." She exhaled. "You were our best shot, Chuck. You've developed the latest set of optics everyone uses."

"I know," Chuck agreed. "Not to toot our horn, but if we can't do this, nobody commercial can. We're the big dogs."

"That doesn't really..."

Chuck uncharacteristically cut her off. "So, what I decided to do was call in some friends of mine who work over at NASA. My brother is an engineer over at Lockheed Martin, and he's got some contacts on the team who did the Hubble. "

Kerry peered at the phone with renewed interest. "Never thought of that," she murmured. "When in doubt call a rocket scientist."

"All right," Dar answered. "Do you think they'll help?"

"I don't know," Chuck answered honestly. "It beats sitting in this room watching everyone scratch their heads and shrug their shoulders. We can't do beans with this Dar. Maybe they got some bright ideas. It's optics. If anyone can come up with some hair brained idea to make duct tape and mirrors work, it'll be those guys."

"I appreciate it, Chuck," Dar said. "We're at our wit's end here too. The nearest spool of the right stuff is 2,000 miles away and I can't get it here before Tuesday."

"'Ouch," he responded "Well, I have no idea if anything will come of it, but I didn't want to just drop it," Chuck said. "I'll let you know if we find out anything, okay?"

"Thanks," Dar responded. "Later, Chuck." She closed the phone and studied it. "That's not going to happen. We don't have the time."

"You having that cable sent?" Kerry asked.

"Yeah."

"I'm glad he took the initiative without you having to ask." She reached over and patted Dar's leg. "Come with me to get some lunch? It's getting pretty late and we got up pretty early."

Dar sighed.

"Hon, you're doing the best you can," Kerry said, gently. "You engaged the right people, they brought in the right people, and if this doesn't happen, it won't be because we didn't try." She leaned close and captured Dar's eyes. "We can only do what we can do."

"Yeah, I know." Dar picked up Kerry's hand and brought it to her lips, kissing the knuckles. Then she turned it palm up and kissed that. "We have to keep going and see where it takes us." She got up and hauled Kerry up with her pausing to kiss her palm again as they stood.

"Keep doing that and I'll tell you where it's going to take us. Right back to our hotel room, that's where." She slapped her partner on the butt and nudged her toward the door. "Scoot."

Instead of scooting, Dar turned and let Kerry's forward momentum bring them together. She wrapped both arms around her and tilted her head, kissing her on the lips.

Far from protesting, Kerry returned the hug and kiss with enthusiasm. They parted a little after a minute, and she looked up into Dar's eyes, enjoying the frank passion she saw there. "What were we about to do?"

"Go back to the hotel," Dar promptly supplied. "You mentioned something about lunch."

"Hm."

"They have room service."

"Heck with that." Kerry smiled. "We can stop for a hot dog on the way back." She stretched up and stole another kiss, then she firmly took Dar's hands and started leading her toward the door. "C'mon. I need a break. Chances are we're going to end up in some dusty wiring room tonight."

"Hm." Dar sighed regretfully. "Unfortunately I think Alastair scheduled a board conference call. We may only have time to get that hot dog."

"Grr." Kerry thumped her head against Dar's shoulder. "Why can't the board watch CNN?"

"Easy, hon." Dar scrubbed the back of her neck and gave her a hug. "We'll take a break after that. Let's skip the group dinner tonight and chill, okay?"

Kerry kept her head resting against her partner. "I've wanted to do that for days," she admitted. "I know it's anti-social, but my nerves are getting rubbed raw in all this."

Dar leaned against her and kept up her gentle rubbing along Kerry's spine. "We're going home Monday," she said, after a long moment. "I sent Maria a note to make our reservations."

Kerry shifted her head and looked up. "Good," she replied. "That's the best news I've heard all week. I was going to ask you later if we could."

Dar smiled briefly. "So there's a light ahead in our tunnel, Ker. We'll do what we can until then, so hang in there."

"Hanging." Kerry wrapped her arms around Dar and hugged her tightly. Then she let go, and pointed to the door. "So now that my libido is going to be thwarted, I'll settle for lunch. Lead on, Magellan."

Dar did, opening the door and heading out into the hallway.

They, almost literally, bumped into Alastair as the doors to the lift opened. "Ah." Dar stepped back out of the way. "You see our friends off?"

"I did," Alastair said. "Not bad folks, really. I thought that went pretty well. Didn't you?"

Dar nodded. "Far as that sort of thing goes, yeah." She agreed. "Seemed pretty innocuous. I'm willing to bet they were glad to get a soft story for a change after what they've been covering the last few days."

"You got it." Alastair agreed. "Dar, I set the conference call for forty-five minutes. Can I buy you ladies lunch?"

"Absolutely." Dar indicated the door. "We were just heading out for that ourselves. I need to let you in on some technical issues that have cropped up."

"Uh oh."

"I'll translate." Kerry promised. "I've also got some major customer complaints you probably should know about."

Alastair sighed, as he punched the button for the lobby. "Fair trade. The FBI is after us again."

"Great."

"WHY DID I let you talk me into this?" Alastair studied the sushi menu wryly. "Don't tell me you don't eat hamburgers, Dar."

"I do," she replied. "I love cheeseburgers. I also love sushi. Relax, Alastair. It's good for you."

"I even got my mother to go to a sushi restaurant." Kerry added, "She liked it."

"Your mother isn't from Texas." Alastair grumbled. "They have anything barbeque here?"

"Barbeque eel."

Alastair looked up over his glasses at Dar, as stern an expression on his face as Kerry had ever seen.

"I got Dar's father to try it and he liked it." Kerry informed him. "Honest."

"Is that why he turned down going to lunch with us?" Alastair asked, dryly. "I was wondering about that."

Dar chuckled. "He doesn't really like sushi. He eats it to humor Kerry." She explained. "But here, Alastair, just order the beef teriyaki. You'll be fine, unless you're allergic to soy sauce."

"Hm? Ah. I see." Her boss looked moderately pacified. "Well, that looks all right. At least I know what it is."

"Does he really?" Kerry inquired, peering at her partner. "Do that to humor me?"

"Sure." Dar went back to the menu. "Just like you tried sushi to humor me back in the day." She studied her choices. "That worked out a little better though."

"It did." Kerry agreed. "I love sushi." Her eyes flicked up to Dar's profile. "Not as much as I love you, of course, but still..." She watched the pink blush color her ears and smiled. "And really, Alastair, California rolls are pretty innocuous. Rice, crab stick, some cucumber and a little seaweed."

"Seaweed?"

"Seaweed." Dar set her menu down. "So..." She leaned back in her chair. "Here's the mess we're in." She paused as a young waitress stopped at the table, her eyebrows lifting slightly and a pad in her hand. "Everyone ready?"

"Yup." Kerry put her menu down. "Dragon roll for me, please, and some miso soup."

The waitress looked at Dar. "Same for me, and a glass of ice tea, please."

"Of course." The girl turned to Alastair. "Sir?"

Alastair took his glasses off and handed her the menu. "I'll have the same." He announced. "What the hell. You only live once." He settled back in his chair. "And I'll have a glass of wine with that, if you don't mind."

"Certainly sir." The waitress took their menus and disappeared.

Dar folded her arms and exhaled. She felt as tired as Kerry and Alastair looked. They could have stayed at the office and had lunch there, but the noise and the constant questions had driven all of them out into the streets in search of a few minutes peace.

"So," Alastair said, "you were saying?"

Dar wished she wasn't saying. "We have a problem. Verizon sent over the wrong type of fiber optics cable. They didn't realize it until they'd already rolled it part of the way out, and there's none of the right type anywhere near here."

Alastair folded his hands on the table. "I see."

"Aside from that, the path from the subway up to our office is problematical, and we don't know if we can bring the cable from the other subway to the one near the office," Kerry added. "But that's all pretty minor. The cable type isn't."

"Won't work?" Alastair asked. "Or is it just tough to make work?"

"Won't work," Dar said. "Not without optics that don't exist yet." She cleared her throat a little. "I've asked our networking vendor to look into it, but the design cycle for those things is around two years."

Alastair checked his watch, then looked at her. "Doesn't sound good. What's our plan B?"

"We have no plan B." Dar's voice remained quite steady. "If this doesn't work, it doesn't work. I won't have the right cable in until Wednesday, maybe Tuesday night. It weighs half a ton."

"I see." Her boss digested this. "Well. That sure sounds like a problem." He twiddled his thumbs, pondering the news.

Dar waited, watching his face. She'd known Alastair long enough to predict most of his responses, but the situation they were in was so extraordinary she found herself unable to imagine what he was thinking, much less what he would say.

She'd gotten used to the idea that they were screwed. At this point, she really wanted to get it all over with.

"Okay," Alastair finally said. "If it happens, it does. If not, I'll deal with it." He smiled as the waitress brought back tall, fragrant glasses of ice tea. "Thank you, that looks great." He took a sip. "I wish I could work up a froth over it ladies, but to be completely honest with you, I'm pretty much out of arm waving."

"Me too," Dar agreed. "I can't even get mad at the jackass from Verizon. He was scared enough to be wetting his pants. He just wanted out of that room."

"I think he thought he was doing the right thing," Kerry murmured.

"Probably did," Alastair said. "I take it we're going to keep trying, right? I mean, we're not going to walk away from this, are we?" He cocked his head and regarded his tablemates. "I'm not going to say anything to the government people, of course. Let them think whatever they want."

Dar hesitated.

"We'll keep going." Kerry spoke up. "Because you never know until it's over, that it's over. I've learned that the hard way over the past couple of years."

Alastair nodded. "Is there anything more we can do? Anyone I can call and take my frustration out on?"

Dar shook her head. "Me." She added, after a pause, "Since I'm the one who didn't check to make sure they were using the right damn cable."

"You can't idiot proof the world, Dar." Alastair dismissed her admission with a gesture. "Fella who brought the stuff over to his own people to run should have known." He added, "I know we're trying to help out here, but hellfire."

Kerry smiled warmly at him, aware of the vaguely sheepish expression on her beloved partner's face. "We expect everyone else to be as good as we are. We get bit with that sometimes," she remarked. "You get used to people performing at a certain level which our people do, but not everyone else does."

"Exactly," Alastair said. "So Dar, don't be silly. It's not your fault." He peered around, pausing to watch the sushi chef behind the bar. "That's the cook?"

"That's the sushi chef," Kerry said. "We usually sit near the bar at the sushi place near our office down south and watch him work. It's like food art."

"Interesting culture." Alastair commented. "Been to Japan a few times, to our regional office there. They're always wanting me to send Dar over to visit them for some reason."

"Some miso soup?" The waitress was back, with three steaming bowls. She set them down with spoons then smiled and vanished again."

Kerry settled in to enjoy her soup, her eyes drifting idly past their table at the small crowd around them. It was late for lunch, and the restaurant was only a quarter full, most of the tables with one or two occupants either engrossed in their papers or staring off into the distance as they waited for their meals.

"Is this tofu?" Alastair asked.

"Yes." Dar lifted her bowl and sipped directly from it, cradling it in both hands. "I'm not fond of it."

He studied the white block, and then bit into it gingerly, chewing and swallowing with a noncommittal expression on his face. "Hmph. Doesn't taste like anything."

"That's why I don't like it," Dar said.

Kerry let the conversation flow past her. She watched three men enter, and look around, then motion at the hostess. They were heavyset, and all had dark hair and irritated expressions. They pointed at a table, and walked over to it, sitting down as the waitress hurried over with menus.

"Gimme a pitcher of coke," one said. "Then get lost."

Kerry's lip twitched. The waitress didn't seem fazed, though. She brought back a pitcher and three glasses, put them on the table, and walked away without a word. Was it the men being rude? Or was it something typical for New York that the woman was well used to?

"Ker?"

Kerry started, and turned her head. "Sorry. Just thinking." She scooped up a spoonful of mushrooms and tofu and munched them contentedly. Tofu didn't taste like much, it was true, but she liked the texture and the contrast between the silky blocks and the other vegetables in the soup.

"So anyway," Alastair lowered his voice, "after I got off the phone with the guy at the FBI main office, another fella called me and asked for something else, wanted to know if we had any telephone records from our customers."

"Telephone?" Dar's brows knit. "Did it not occur to them to call the telephone company for that?"

"Hell if I know. That's what I asked him. They were looking for something else though, they said something about narrowing the focus."

"But why our customers?"

"Maybe they asked the phone company, and they got what they asked for," Dar said. "And it was a trillion one line entries in tapes delivered in a big box on their doorstep. There's such a thing as too much data."

The waitress appeared with three plates. She set them down and smiled. "Please enjoy."

"Thanks, we will." Kerry glanced around, as the woman left. "Don't they need to have court orders for this kind of thing, Alastair? What's the legal part of this?"

Alastair was studying his sushi roll. "Now, what in the hell am I supposed to do with this?" He asked. "As for the legal stuff, I tossed that over to Ham. I'm not about to cough anything up without a subpoena, but y'know, he heard rumblings that someone told them they didn't need one."

"What?"

"Chopsticks." Dar held them up. "Put them in your hands like this." She demonstrated, watching him try to imitate her. "Or pick the damn things up with your fingers. We don't care."

"Dar." Kerry remonstrated her. "It's not that hard...here...do it this way."

Alastair bemusedly studied her fingers. "That's what Ham said they said." He continued the conversation as he tried to make the sticks come together. "That they didn't need any court order, they had orders from high up to get what they needed, however they had to."

"Wow."

"Scared Ham." Having achieved dubious success, Alastair applied the chopsticks to the sushi roll. "Not much does."

"So what does that mean for us?" Dar asked, fiddling with her own implements. "Is he saying we should...what is he saying?"

"Y'know, Dar..." Alastair studied the bit of sushi. "Now what?" He looked at Kerry.

"Dunk it like this." Kerry motioned with her own piece of sushi, dipping it into the little bowl of soy sauce near her plate. "Then you eat it."

"Then I eat it," he mused. "Ham said he was going to call a friend of his in the government, try to feel them out, see what the real deal is," Alastair said. He dunked the piece gingerly and then popped it into his mouth, chewing resolutely.

Kerry exhaled. "That doesn't sound good." She put her sushi in her mouth and chewed it, glancing past Alastair's shoulder at the table of men behind them. They had their heads bent together, and as she watched, they looked up and over at them, then quickly looked away as they saw her attention.

Hm.

Alastair finished chewing, swallowed, then took a sip of his tea and sat back, looking reflectively at the plate.

"Not good?" Dar hazarded a guess.

"If we can't rely on the law...what the hell does that mean?" Kerry asked. "What are we supposed to do?"

"Well," Alastair said. "That was completely unlike anything I expected." He picked up his chopsticks again. "I like it. Good stuff." He picked up another piece. "Kerry, don't worry yet. I'll let you know when it's time."

"Can't do much about it anyway." Dar plowed through her lunch. "So let's talk about something else. When they let people back down into the tip of the island, they're going to need communications. How do we handle that?"

Kerry was chewing as she eyed her partner.

"How about those Padres?" Alastair blinked mildly. "You like baseball, Dar?"

Dar looked from one to the other, then shook her head and went back to her sushi. "I feel like I'm having lunch with a tableful of abstract art."

Kerry swallowed hastily and smothered a laugh.

Alastair paused in the act of wrangling another piece of his sushi. "Not gonna ask." He concluded. "And none of you say a word to my wife about me having this. She'll think I've joined a cult."

"Cult." Dar mused. "That mean you're going to get a tattoo?"

Alastair stopped chewing and looked at her.

"Just asking."

Chapter Twelve

KERRY TROTTED DOWN the steps, descending to the lower level of their office complex as the crowds were thinning out and the hallways emptying. Outside, it was already dark, and she glanced at her watch as she rounded the corner and headed for the small closet in the back of the stairs.

Time to go. "Hey guys, you back here?"

"In here." Mark's voice floated out.

Kerry ducked inside the doorway to the closet, spotting lights inside. She found Mark and Kannan there, hunkered down next to a box mounted on the wall and a panel full of blinking lights. "How's it going?"

"Not bad." Mark dusted his hands off. "Kannan's finishing the prep on the fiber box."

Kannan looked up from his work. He had a white helmet on with a light in the front, and its beam nearly pegged Kerry in the eyes before she stepped sideways to avoid it. "It is almost done, yes," he agreed. "This will be all right, I think. We left room for them to bring the cable up here, against the wall."

He indicated the path. "Then it is a simple curve into the termination box, here, where we can then connect it up to our router."

The router was on a makeshift shelf, a flash of new steel against old, blackened iron but sturdy enough to hold the square, stolidly blinking device that was already trailing wires that led to the half buried panel they'd found earlier.

"I finished making the hookup." Mark seated a punch down tool in his belt kit. "I think I blurped everyone upstairs, did you see it?"

"Dar did." Kerry's eyes twinkled a bit. "That's how she knew you had to be about done."

Mark grimaced. "She'd probably have done it without a hitch." He groused. "But man, it's dark in here."

Kerry patted his shoulder. "So, we're ready on this end? Ready for them to bring the cable up from the subway, and that's it?"

"Well." Mark sat down on a piece of jutting pipe. "I mean, in terms of connecting it, yeah, that's it. But once it's hooked up, Dar's got to figure out what to do with all those different data streams. I got no clue what's going to come down that pipe and I don't think she knows either."

"Can we get a list of what it is from the Exchange?" Kerry frowned. "That can't be that hard."

"Can't figure out who to ask," Mark admitted. "I talked to a few of those guys down there and they all had different answers. Apparently the people who really knew what was up—I guess two guys anyway—aren't around anymore."

"Ah." Kerry crossed her arms. "Okay, well I'm sure she'll figure it out. But we're done on the physical side."

"Yep." Mark nodded. "Next thing that happens is the cable gets here, and Kannan connects it up to this panel." He patted the structure. "I plug it up, we get blinkies, and then Big D can figure out how to get the bits where they need to go."

Kerry exhaled silently. "What about the other end?"

Mark gathered up his tools. "I figure we can run down and do that end tomorrow. They get any further today? I know you guys were saying they were stuck down there." He edged carefully around the electrical panel which bore a new, shiny clamp with cables trailing from it toward the wall and the equally new socket the router was plugged into.

"They're working on it," Kerry said. "They know what the deadline is. We have to make sure we're ready so we're not the hold up, right?"

"Absolutely," Mark agreed. "C'mon, Kannan, pack up. I'm dying for a beer."

"That sounds good to me too," Kannan agreed. "I think I have enough of these ends to make the connections for tomorrow at the other place. Then I hope they get this done quickly. Once we are finished with this, Ms. Stuart, will we be going back to Miami?"

"Yes," Kerry answered, in a definite tone. "We have a lot to do back home getting our own house in order. I'm glad we're helping out the country here, but we're at the end of our ability to extend ourselves while our own people and customers also need help."

Kannan nodded.

"Too right." Mark tucked his gloves into his belt. "I think these guys are taking advantage of us. We're too freaking convenient. I heard those dudes down at the exchange talking about how they'd get us to do all this stuff for them and then they'd bill the feds for it."

Kerry stared at him. "Are you kidding me?"

"Nope." Mark shook his head. "I've been meaning to tell you about it. I kept forgetting with all this crap going on. I mean," he held one hand up, "like, they're happy we're helping and they think it's great we're doing this, but they're also checking to see how they can line their own pockets at the same time, if you know what I mean."

"I know what you mean." Kerry stepped back and held the door open. "Let's lock this and go get that beer. Dar and I have some work we need to catch up on tonight, so we'll pass on dinner, but she wanted to buy the first round of drinks."

"That is very nice." Kannan shouldered his backpack as he and Mark moved past Kerry and she shut the door behind them. "It is difficult, these things we are doing, but all the same satisfying. It is good to do hard work."

They walked around the back of the stairwell and headed for the steps up to the lower level of offices. Most of the shops were closed, though the restaurants were still open, and there was a small scattering of people still walking around.

Near the entrances, there were National Guard troops standing near the walls and watching the remaining people, their eyes following the odd one walking along as their hands cradled their rifles.

It brought home, again, what had happened. Kerry had realized she'd started to forget, caught up in the moment of doing what they were doing until she was pulled back into focus by seeing one of the guardsman, or hearing someone talk.

Seeing the pictures of the site. Pictures of the dust covered firemen doggedly searching through the wreckage for survivors, or signs of their lost comrades.

Resolutely she turned her back on the guard and led the way up the steps, reaching the lower level and heading to where Dar and the rest of the team were waiting.

The offices above were already quiet. The staffers had gone home — those that could — and the rest were going with them to stay at the hotel until they were allowed back downtown. Alastair had visited the hotel manager and leased out a floor of the place to give the dispossessed a place to call home that wasn't the office they'd been camping in.

Life was moving on. One of the salesmen had commented on it as they'd broke up and closed the office down for the first time since the attack. There was a sense of sadness about that, a grief that was only partially acknowledged, and not yet dispelled.

She could see Dar, leaning against the wall, her hands in her pockets as she talked to one of the New York staff. Her partner looked tired. There was an uncharacteristic slump to her body posture that was visible to Kerry, if not to anyone else, and she felt a moment of impatience that they had to postpone a retreat to their room if even for the best of motives.

Dar sensed their approach and looked up, past the person she was talking to right into Kerry's eyes. Her expression shifted and one brow raised, the message as clear as the crystal goblets in the store fronts she was passing.

Absolutely expressive. Kerry could recall only a few times she'd seen that particular look, usually at the end of a very long day, when the inner door to her office would open, and Dar would be leaning on it looking at her with that look, and saying "Take me home."

Everything went into the to-do folder when that happened. No matter if she was working on who knows what urgent problem, she'd put her phone on voice mail, pick up her laptop, and they'd go. That look was where the line was drawn, and always had been.

"All right, we're all accounted for," Kerry said, as she reached her partner's side. "Let's roll, people." She waited for Dar to push away from the wall and then she put an arm around her, giving her back a little rub with her fingers.

They climbed up the steps and out into the night, crossing the marble courtyard and heading for the streets beyond. Traffic had picked up a trifle, and the streets seemed busier, but Kerry wasn't sure if that was something really different or if it was because it was Saturday night and more people would be out.

Dar's arm settled over her shoulders with welcome warmth. She looked up at Dar. "Tired?"

"Headache," Dar replied briefly. "Looking forward to kicking back and chilling."

"Me too." Kerry exhaled. "I think I'll settle for a bowl of soup for dinner and a bubble bath."

"Mmhg." Dar made a low sound of appreciation. "And ice cream," she added.

"Of course."

They followed the group along the sidewalk, not at the very back, but near it. Kerry was glad the pace was casual, since the long day of running around had tired her out. She also had a slight headache, and the cool breeze felt good despite the city scents in it.

She felt a little sweaty, a little dusty, and another thought crossed her mind. "Hey Dar?"

"Mm?" Dar seemed supremely content to amble silently at her side.

"That hotel has a pool, doesn't it?"

"I think so. Wow. A swim sounds like a great idea." Dar perked up a little bit. "What made you think of that?"

"You in a bathing suit," Kerry answered. She felt Dar twitch a little, then start to laugh. "You asked."

"I did." Dar chuckled, giving her a one-arm hug.

A tall figure dropped back to join them. "Hey there." Andrew greeted them. "What are you kids up to?"

"I was just going to ask you that, Dad," Kerry responded. "We haven't seen you since lunch. What have you been up to?" She tucked her free hand through Andrew's elbow. "I heard some of the guys saying you were yelling at someone before."

"Wall." Andrew made a dismissive gesture. "I been sticking around that coonass. He got himself mixed up with some of them gov'mint fellers and they was giving him a hive over some reports. Fellers were jackass rude."

"Alastair was telling us about the FBI wanting more reports. Was that it?" Kerry asked.

Andrew nodded. "Yeap. Got my back up when they started saying how they were thinking how cause all them boys of yours weren't from here that we were some suspect or something."

"What?"

Dar craned her neck around to look at her father. "What?"

"Yeap," Andrew said. "Don't know where they got that idea, but ah talked to them about it and I think they're all right with it now."

"Huh." Kerry frowned. 'What's that all about? Dar, we've had non US workers on visa to us here for years. You know as well as I do we take every qualified network tech we can find."

"I know," Dar said her expression a little grim. "But I also know there's an isolationist streak in this country a mile wide, and I've got a feeling this disaster is going to give that a chance to show."

"Them folks just ain't been much in the world." Andrew remarked.

"My father was one of those people," Kerry said. "He used to say all the time that we had to watch out for what he called that 'foreign element'."

A siren erupted nearby and everyone flinched. But it was only a lone police car pulling around a corner and racing through the taxi crowded street with lights flashing.

"And a couple days ago, what was undeniably a foreign element, killed a few thousand people and brought down two buildings and part of a third." Kerry went on. "So maybe those people feel justified."

They walked along in silence for a few minutes crossing a street at the light and moving along the block toward their hotel. Their colleagues were walking in a group around them, talking in low voices.

"Country's always had people from other places," Andrew finally said. "Ain't nobody hardly can say they b'long here."

"No one likes to remember that in times like this." Kerry agreed wryly. "My father's family, back in the early nineteen hundreds, came from Scotland." She paused. "My mother's came from Germany. "

"Wall." Andrew scratched his ear. "I believe my folks been here a while longer. Dar's mother's folks came with them Pilgrims."

Kerry turned her head and stared at her partner, one blond brow arching sharply.

Dar shrugged. "She thinks it's funny."

"No wonder she made that crack about the turkey last Thanksgiving," Kerry said. "But anyway, here's the hotel. Let's leave this for tomorrow, and take a mind break. Okay?"

"Sounds good to me." Dar was glad to see the doors to the hotel. Her headache had gotten worse during the walk and even the enticing leather chairs of the bar weren't appealing to her. There was noise there, and people moving around, and she wanted none of it.

"Alastair?" Kerry called out softly, as they entered the lobby.

Their CEO turned, spotting them and pulling up. "Well, hello there. Glad to be at the end of this long day as I am?"

"You bet," Kerry said. "Hey, looks like they resumed the games this weekend."

The bar was relatively crowded with most of the screens shifted from CNN's tense pictures to the colorful flash of football and green grass, and the drone of the stadium. One screen, a large one in the back, had the news going, but most of the patrons were around the bar with an attitude of perceptible relief.

"You a fan?" Alastair asked.

"Not so much." Kerry admitted.

They paused in front of the bar — the big group of them — watching the screens.

"Hey, folks." Alastair addressed them. "Give me an ear, eh?"

Everyone turned to face him. "We've got the whole floor, matter of fact, we took over the concierge lounge up there too. It's got a big screen. How about we all go up there and I'll get some suds in, and we can watch from there."

Big smiles.

"You are a real cool dude," Scuzzy said. "Anyone ever tell you that?"

Alastair managed a brief grin, and then he waved them toward the elevators. "Let's put this plan into action then, shall we?" He waited for the group to start trouping toward the end of the lobby, before he turned to Dar and Kerry. "Feel free to skip the game shindig, ladies. I'm sure you have other things to do."

"Thanks." Dar didn't miss a beat. "We do." She gave Kerry a kiss on the top of her head. "C'mon Ker. You owe me some ice cream."

"Owe you?" Kerry got her arm wrapped around Dar's waist again. "Thanks Alastair. We were hoping for a chance to chill for a while."

He winked at them, and strolled ahead. Andrew chuckled and

joined him, leaving Dar and Kerry to bring up the rear.

Which they did. "He's a good boss," Kerry commented, as they passed the front desk.

"He is. Or I wouldn't have stayed for fifteen years, and in fact he wouldn't have put up with me that long either." Dar responded. "He's as conservative as they come, and yet, he never turned a hair at my being gay."

"Never?"

Dar shook her head as the waited for the elevator. "When he was promoting me to Vice President of Operations, I met with him and warned him I was, and that it would probably cause a problem for him. He said he really didn't give a damn who I slept with."

"You think he meant that though? A lot of people say it," Kerry said.

"Then? I think he said it because he thought it was the right thing to say." Dar acknowledged. "But over the years he grew into that statement, and now I absolutely think he means it."

"He sees value in people." Kerry exhaled. "Wonder if his kids know how lucky they are." They got into the elevator and were quiet for the ride up, exchanging mild nods with the three other guests who had joined them.

The floor was already noisy down near the lounge when they got off, a trickle of television sound coming out along with the chatter of many voices.

"Glad we're down at this end." Kerry waited for Dar to key the door open and followed her in, closing it behind them and shutting out the sound. "Ugh."

"Ugh." Dar repeated, trudging across the carpet to her bag. She opened it and took out her bottle of Advil, opening it and shaking out a few of the pills. A warm body bumped into her, and she turned to find Kerry standing there, hand outstretched.

"Share." Kerry bumped her again.

Dar did, and then put the bottle back and rooted in the bag for her swimsuit. She took it out and paused at the credenza, picking up the bottle of water there and uncapping it. "Want some?" She took a swig and passed it over.

Kerry swallowed her handful of pills and wandered over to the book of services, opening the front page. "Dar? Where is the pool?"

Dar pointed up.

"Wow." Kerry went over to her bag and opened it to retrieve her suit. "Glad I got into the habit of always packing mine like you do." She commented. "You don't know how many times I've thanked you when I was traveling and ended up in some business hotel with a nice pool and a nice bar and this suit made me pick the virtuous path."

Dar's warm chuckle surprised her with its closeness, and she turned to find Dar standing behind her, already in her suit. "Holy cow how did you change so fast?"

"Lots of practice with you taking my clothes off." Dar gathered Kerry's shirt in her hands and started easing it over her head. "There are robes in the bathroom. We better take them before we end up being entertainment for that crowd in the other room."

Kerry stifled a giggle as Dar's fingers brushed her bare ribs. "Go get the robes," she said. "I'll get changed and we can head down."

"Up." Dar tickled her navel, and then she backed off and headed for the bathroom.

Just ten minutes ago, she'd been toast. Kerry quickly shed her pants and underwear and got into her bathing suit. Ten minutes ago she'd been a little down, a lot tired, and wanting nothing more than to crash.

Now? Kerry looked up from adjusting her strap to find Dar leaning in the doorway, a knowing look in her eye. She felt a surge of sensual energy, a clean, powerful sensation that made her smile. "Ready?"

"Always." Dar tossed her the other robe and held a hand out. "Let's go. I want to get wet."

"Me too." Kerry answered, with a frank grin. "Let's hope no one else in the hotel does."

"Let's hope they don't have lifeguards."

THE WATER FELT unspeakably good closing over her as she dove in. There was that moment of silence, quickly overwhelmed by bubbles as she headed for the surface and felt the agitation next to her of Dar's tall form plunging in one step behind.

She surfaced and sucked in a lungful of chlorine-tinted air, blinking droplets out of her eyes as she flipped over onto her back and relaxed. "Ahhh."

Dar emerged from underwater next to her, shaking her head to clear her hair from her eyes. "Not overheated. Nice."

"Nice." Kerry agreed, enjoying the pleasantly cool liquid cradling her body as she floated. The pool was reasonably large, a rectangle of clear water against a painted blue background with lanes marked on the bottom.

There were no slides to go down, or diving boards to tempt Dar's quirky daredevil side. Just a placid expanse of water inside a glassed in space that would be pleasantly sunny in the daytime but now was full of watery shadows and highlights.

Around the pool were chaise lounges, and on one side was a bar that was currently closed.

That was fine with Kerry. It was nice to have the pool and Dar to herself. She rolled over and dove under again, pulling herself along with her arms and kicking from one side of the pool to the other, the chlorine only stinging her eyes a little as she swam along.

She rose to the surface again and exhaled, then turned when she heard splashing behind her.

Dar was swimming along the length of the pool with smooth, efficient strokes, barely creating any wake as she reached the end of the pool, disappeared underwater to turn, and then surfaced again still in motion.

Kerry didn't feel so ambitious. She stroked forward slowly in a lazy frog motion, blowing bubbles as she meandered around in a circle, going from side to side as Dar turned and came back again.

She took a breath and ducked underwater again, diving down to the bottom of the pool and swimming along the bottom, enjoying the silence and the sensation of weightless gliding. She reached the wall and turned, heading back across the width of the pool in the other direction.

Halfway there, she felt something snag her suit. She turned to find Dar turning with her underwater, those blue eyes glinting with mischief.

Kerry twisted free and shook a finger at her mockingly and headed for the surface as she ran out of air.

Dar went with her and they broke the surface together inches apart. "Hey, it's a fish." Dar smiled.

"Was that a fishhook that caught my suit?" Kerry splashed her a tiny bit. "Boy this feels great."

"It does." Dar agreed. "Wish it was in the pool back home, but I'll take it." She eased over onto her back and stretched her arms along the pool edge, gripping the tile rim with her hands.

Kerry swam slowly around in a circle, the sound of her displacing water the only echo in the large space. "So, where's the first place in Europe we're going to visit? You want to go the Alps?"

Dar's face relaxed. "Thank you for not talking about work," she replied, simply. "I can't take any more thinking about it right now."

"Me either." Kerry paddled over to her. "So, where?"

"Where do you want to go?" Dar countered. "It's going to probably be near your birthday."

"Oo." Kerry put her hands behind her head and floated, bumping Dar gently and then moving away. "Where do I want to be for my birthday this year? Let me think."

Dar was content to do just that. She tilted her head to one side and admired Kerry's lithe body, glad to enjoy the moment.

"Dar?"

"Uh?" She straightened up and stifled a grin at Kerry's raised eyebrows. "Sorry. Drifted off there."

"Ah hah." Kerry looked skeptical. "Maybe it was mentioning it earlier, but you know, I think I'd like to go to Scotland," she said. "Could we start there?"

"That would be cool." Dar agreed. "I'm up for that."

"That's what I'd like to do for my birthday this year. Go to Scotland and have a blast with you. Climb some mountains, see some castles, and just hang out. I hadn't really thought about it before, when we were talking about the Alps and everything. That would have been fun too."

"But?"

Kerry gazed up at the glass ceiling, the smoked surface barely showing the fuzzy outline of the moon overhead. "But I don't know. It would be so easy to go to all those ritzy places. We could afford it."

"We could afford damn near anything we want." Dar agreed. "You'd look good in a Swiss chalet."

Kerry smiled. "That's the point, I think. I want to be touched by the places we go to, not just by a nice vacation. I think that'll happen in Scotland." She turned her head to look at Dar. "I'd like to see Antarctica, and maybe the Sahara desert."

"How about climbing Everest?"

Kerry's brow twitched. "Ahhhh...no." She grinned briefly. "That idea doesn't thrill me. I don't mind working for my fun but that's way too much work, hon."

"Phew." Dar chuckled. "For me too. I'd like to see the Mayan ruins in Central America though." She paused, thoughtfully. "It's hard for me to think about going somewhere for a month. There are so many places I'd like to go."

Kerry rolled over and swam back. "You know what the truth is, Paladar?" She went nose to nose with her partner, stretching her hands out and bracing them on either side of Dar's head. "Just going with you anywhere for a month is something I very badly want to do."

Dar released the wall and settled her arms around Kerry instead. "Me too. We need to do this," she added, in a softer tone. "I wonder how many of those people in those towers were telling themselves someday I'll do that."

Kerry remained still and quiet, listening.

"Someday I'll see that." Dar went on. "Someday. Bob wanted to buy a sailboat someday, he told me."

"No more somedays." Kerry let her forehead rest against Dar's. "We so easily could have been in harm's way in this, Dar. I want to savor every minute living my life with you from now on."

Dar kissed her. "Scotland it is." She promised. "That's going to be a blast. Maybe I'll get a suit of armor there to match that old sword I've got."

"Maybe we'll try haggis." Kerry suggested.

"Maybe we won't." Dar smiled anyway, and then paused. "Or what the hell. If Alastair can try sushi, I can try oatmeal in sheep innards." She kissed Kerry again, and then she nipped her nose and surged forward, taking them both underwater.

"Bwwflhh..." Kerry spluttered, as they surfaced. "Dar!"

"Tag." Dar pinched her in a sensitive spot. "You're it."

"Yowch!" Kerry yelped, grabbing for her partner who was no longer there. "You pissant!"

Dar took off, diving under the water to escape, barely eluding Kerry's outstretched fingers. "Slowpoke!"

"Oh, I don't think so, madam." Kerry plunged after her. "This ain't no forty foot piece of ocean." She dove under the water and swam after her elusive tormentor, reaching for skin or any bit of bathing suit.

The moon slid behind the clouds overhead, wisely hiding its eyes.

"I'VE GOT WATER in my ears thanks to you." Kerry hopped on one foot, as they waited for the elevator to deposit them on their floor. "That was fun though."

"It was." Dar felt very pleasantly tired after two hours of water horseplay. She put a hand on Kerry's back to steady her, as the elevator slowed to a halt and the doors opened. "We're here."

Cheers echoed through the hall as they exited, and they could see the doors to the lounge still open. "Sounds like a good game," Kerry said, as she removed the room key from the pocket of her robe. "Glad everyone's enjoying it. They needed a mind break."

"Yeah." Dar agreed. "Tomorrow's probably going to be rough. I'm glad Alastair thought of it." She glanced down the hall. "Speaking of."

Alastair had just come out of the lounge, and was heading toward his room. He saw them and paused, then continued past his door and approached them instead. "Well, what have you two been up to?"

"Really want to know?" Dar asked, folding her arms over her terrycloth-covered chest and leaning against the wall.

He paused and considered. "Am I going to have to speak to the hotel manager tomorrow because of it?" he asked cautiously.

"Probably not." Kerry ran her fingers through her wet hair somewhat self-consciously. "We were swimming in the pool."

"Ah." Alastair nodded. "That sounds pretty innocuous." He leaned against the wall himself. "Game's about done. I'm going to let all these kids finish the night out. I'm bushed." He stifled a yawn. "Good bunch there."

"Glad they had a chance to relax," Dar said. "I think tomorrow is going to be a little different."

Alastair eyed her shrewdly. "Even with our challenges?"

Dar shrugged. "Who the hell knows? Maybe we'll get lucky." She straightened up and started for their hotel room door. "Anyway, good night, Alastair. See you in the morning."

"Bye." Alastair waggled his fingers and turned to head back to his own room.

Kerry opened the door and held it for Dar to enter, and then followed her inside. The room was dimly lit, and she caught the scent of chocolate wafting in the space, along with something a little spicier. "Did you send a telepathic message to room service again?"

Dar was by the desk, investigating the tray resting there. "Sorry to disappoint you, babe. I used the phone by the pool while you were doing that last set of laps. Hot chocolate, Thai chicken soup, and baked Brie with some crackers and fruit. Sound all right to you?"

Kerry detoured to the desk and liberated a grape from the bowl, popping it into her mouth and biting down. It was juicy and sweet, and she gave her partner a one armed hug for it. "Yum," she agreed. "I'm going to go change out of my suit."

"Me too." Dar untied her robe and eased it off. "Last thing I need is to catch a damn cold at this point." She draped the robe over a chair and wandered into the bathroom.

Kerry stole another grape and followed suit, shivering a little as the draft from the air conditioner hit her damp skin. "Dar, could you...thanks." She caught the towel coming at her face one handed, and then she got undressed and rubbed herself dry.

Dar came around behind her and draped a shirt over her shoulder, then kissed the back of her bare neck, making her shiver for a completely different reason. "Thanks." Kerry ruffled her hair into some sort of dryness.

"For the shirt?"

"That too." She put the cotton garment on, and ran her fingers through her hair to straighten it. "You know, that really was a great idea to go to the pool. I can't believe I'm saying this, but I really miss our gym time."

Dar paused and peered over her shoulder, one eyebrow lightly raised.

"When we're there, we focus on something other than whatever problems we're dealing with that day." Kerry clarified. "You get out of that mind space."

"Ahhh."

"You know what it is? I'm not physically tired." Kerry sat down and pulled over one of the bowls of soup. "My brain is exhausted." She took a spoonful of the spicy broth. "It's like those people downstairs at the bar. You can't keep watching those pictures."

Dar sat down opposite her picking up her cup of hot chocolate and sipping from it as she considered what Kerry had said. It was an odd feeling. In her, unlike Kerry, it manifested in a sense of intolerant impatience that made it difficult for her to concentrate on what she was doing.

The swim break had been a relief. Being silly and chasing Kerry around the pool had let her buzzing brain relax and now that they were back in the room, she was content to concentrate on what was on the tray and leave worrying about work until tomorrow.

She pulled her soup over and fished out a chunk of chicken. It tasted of coconut and lime and both she and Kerry were quiet as they chewed. The silence was comfortable though. Dar put some of the Brie on a cracker and put it on Kerry's plate, then assembled one for herself taking a bite as Kerry reciprocated by putting a handful of grapes in front of her.

She looked up, and their eyes met. Kerry's expression eased into one of tired affection, and she reached out with her free hand capturing Dar's fingers and simply clasping them.

The warmth of it made her smile. The sweetness of the moment made her focus intently on it, savoring the strength of Kerry's fingers curled around hers, and the spicy scent of the soup and the knowledge that there were hours and hours left before the sun would rise and bring another day.

Time to hoard every moment of it.

Chapter Thirteen

A FLARE OF brilliant light and a crash brought Dar awake with a painful suddenness. The echoes of the sound ringing in her ears as she instinctively reached for Kerry just as another flash lit the room followed instantly by a window rattling boom.

Without really thinking, Dar bundled her nearly startled witless partner in the sheets and rolled off the bed, landing them both on the floor on the side away from the window.

"Hey!" Kerry yelped. "What the hell is going on?"

Dar frantically tried to untangle herself from the sheets as her brain finally woke up and placed the sound, and the lights, and the rumble into a familiar context. Then she stopped, and slumped to the floor, her head thunking against the carpet as she let out a groan. "Son of a bitch."

Thunder rumbled again, and Kerry struggled up onto one elbow, raking the hair from her eyes as she peered around. "Thunderstorm?"

"Thunderstorm," Dar confirmed, as she listened to rain pelt the window. "Sorry about that."

Kerry sat up cautiously untangling her legs from her partner's. Aside from the bursts of lightning, it was dark inside the room and a glance at the clock confirmed her suspicions that it was far from dawn.

She groaned, and settled back down on her side, pillowing her head on Dar's stomach. She could hear Dar's heartbeat slowing and she closed her eyes, willing her own to stop racing. She thought she might have been dreaming, though she couldn't really remember anything.

She had that odd sense of disassociation that usually meant she had been though. Not a bad one—probably one of those hazy, weird dreams she sometimes had where she was running around in a forest chasing rabbits.

No idea what that was all about but Kerry greatly preferred them to the darker ones that made her wake shaking or in tears.

Bleah.

She felt Dar's fingers slide through her hair and scratch gently across her scalp. "Well, that sure wasn't the way I like to wake up."

"Me either," Dar agreed mournfully. "I don't know what in the hell I was thinking."

"You were thinking there was a bomb going off outside and we needed to be out of the way which we are. But now that it's just Mother Nature scaring the crap out of us, we can probably get back up where it's more comfortable, huh?"

"Yeah." Dar pushed herself up into a sitting position, as Kerry did the same. They got to their knees and stood up. Kerry crawled back into bed while her partner pulled the covers back up off the floor and settled them over her. "I see my PDA flashing. Let me see what's up since I know that's not you."

"Not me." Kerry agreed, snuggling back into a comfortable position and wrapping one arm around her pillow. She watched Dar walk over to the dresser and pick up the flashing device, her body outlined in flashes of silver from the window.

Mm. "What's up?" Kerry asked.

Dar brought the PDA back over to the bed and sat down on it, handing it over to her partner before she got under the covers and reclaimed her pillow. "Hurricane Gabrielle, crossing Florida."

"Great." Kerry thumbed through the message. "Glad we're not in Disney World. I forgot all about the damn storm. It won't come up here, will it?"

"With our luck?" Dar put her arm around Kerry and snuggled up to her. "Probably be a category five with a tidal wave." She exhaled. "Damn. Now I've got a headache from waking up like that."

Kerry studied the PDA. "Hon, you got another message here. I think it's from our network vendor buddy." She passed the PDA over her shoulder.

"Read it to me." Dar nuzzled the back of Kerry's neck. "I'm sure it's bad news anyway."

Kerry cleared her throat. "Dar—I'm in Bethesda at Lockheed Martin. I had a five-hour meeting with the folks here, and once they got past asking me not if I was crazy, but how crazy was I, not to mention how crazy you were, we got to talking."

"Sounds like fun." Dar mumbled.

"It gets better." Kerry promised. "Sort of." She scrolled down. "Everyone agrees there's no way to develop an optics that'll handle the specifications of multimode over that distance."

Dar lifted her head. "That's better?" she asked, her voice rising.

"Put a sock in it, Roberts. Let me finish." Kerry chided her. "Here we go. But when I told them what the stakes were, they called in a couple of specialists who agreed to see what they could come up with."

"Peh." Dar put her head back down. "In two years we'll hear of some military application for an optic that can go ten miles on multimode."

"One of these guys," Kerry went on, undeterred, "is the guy who figured out how to make the Hubble work after they sent it up with a bad shaped mirror."

"Peh."

"Anyway, I'll know more in the morning. I'm gonna go get some coffee and find a chaise lounge somewhere. Hope you all are doing good up there." Kerry finished and half turned, putting her hand on Dar's hip. "Honey, at least he's trying. It's 4:00 a.m., and he's at some think tank working to get help for us."

"I know." Dar relented. "I'm just in a bad mood. My head hurts and I feel like a moron for pulling us both out of the bed. And I was having a nightmare."

Kerry set the PDA aside and turned over, facing her partner. She gently pushed the unruly hair from Dar's eyes and stroked her cheek. "Want some Advil?"

Dar's expression shifted and she produced a mild grin. "Got everything I want right here in bed with me."

Aw. Kerry was charmed both by the sentiment and the almost shy look in her partner's eyes. "You know what? I just remembered. I was dreaming about you when you woke me up."

"Me?"

"Mmhm." Kerry traced one of Dar's eyebrows with a fingertip. "We were celebrating something in some cabin somewhere. I have no idea what. But you gave me this really pretty carved wooden bird, and we were laughing like crazy about it."

"What was so funny about it?" Dar asked. "Did it have two heads or something?"

"I don't know." Kerry put her head down on the pillow. "There was a fire in the fireplace, and I could smell the trees outside, but I don't know where we were or why that bird was so funny," she admitted. "You have such a beautiful laugh."

Dar's brow wrinkled a little. "No I don't."

"In my dream you did." Kerry disagreed. "And you really do. I love your laugh."

Dar stretched and relaxed against the bed. "Trying to make me feel better?"

"Working?"

Dar's brief grin altered into a true smile. "The thunder was worth it." She tucked her arm under her pillow and let her body relax, hoping her now buzzing brain would settle down and let her get a few more hours sleep.

She felt Kerry's hand touch her cheek and with no further words, the gentle stroking against her skin spoke as loudly as her partner ever could.

What a gift. Dar closed her eyes, feeling the faintest of stings. How many people had woken together last Tuesday, had a little pillow talk, gotten up, gone to work and then hours later found themselves forever sundered from this gift they probably hadn't thought twice about when they'd left the house.

"Dar?" Kerry's touch became firmer against her cheek and there was a rustle of bedclothes as she shifted and brought a comforting body of warmth into the sudden chill around her. "Hey."

Dar opened her eyes. "Sorry." She didn't bother to dissemble. "Just freaking out a little."

"About the fiber?" Kerry sounded confused, and a touch distressed.

"No."

Kerry eased over and put her arms around Dar. "Did I do something?"

"No." Dar returned the embrace. "It just hit me." She paused, as her throat tightened. "All those people who had people they loved never come home that day."

Kerry's breath caught. She swallowed audibly.

"Could have been any of us," Dar whispered. "What a crappy world this is sometimes."

"Sometimes," Kerry finally replied, her voice rough. "Do you know how glad I was it was you who told me what was going on? That we were on the phone no matter if you were thousands of miles away? "

"Wish you'd have been there with me," Dar said. "I was so damn scared something would happen to you before I got back."

Kerry buried her face into Dar's neck feeling a shiver go down her spine. "Likewise. I don't know what I would have done if anything had." Tears welled up that had been trapped inside her for days. "Oh my god, Dar."

Dar returned the hug. "Longest few days of my life." She drew in a shaky breath. "Damn, I can't wait to go home. I want out of this." She couldn't quite stifle a sniffle.

"So do I," Kerry whispered. "It's been making me crazy."

They were both quiet for a moment. Then they both exhaled at almost the same time. "Wow." Dar cleared her throat. "Sorry this got so lousy."

Kerry shook her head a trifle. "I'm not. I'm glad I said that to you. I've been wanting to before we let this all pass. We've been up to our eyeballs since it happened and I've got all this stuff bottled up making my guts ache."

Dar slid her hand up along the back of Kerry's neck kneading the muscles there with gentle fingers. She felt the warmth as Kerry exhaled against her skin, and blinked her eyes to clear the tears from them.

She didn't cry often. Dar suspected the stress wasn't doing her any favors and she could feel the shivers rippling through Kerry's body. "Let's table it for a few hours." She pulled the covers over both of them. "We'll be okay."

Kerry relaxed against her. "When I'm right here, I'm always okay. Hope I find out why that bird was so damned funny." She closed her eyes and kissed Dar on the collarbone. "Love you."

That made Dar smile again, finally. "Love you too." She tuned out the muted sound of the air conditioning and the far off grind of elevator machinery letting the darkness and the rhythm of Kerry's breathing lull her back into sleep.

Maybe, she mused, it was a cuckoo bird.

"NOT A GOOD morning." Dar followed Alastair into the conference room that already had a half dozen people in it.

Angry looking people. Dar gathered up the gruffest of her attitudes and put them in place before she took a seat at the end of the table, while her boss circled and went to the center. She put her forearms on the mahogany surface clasping her hands together.

"All right folks. Let's sit down and talk." Alastair took the middle seat and waited for the rest of the people in the room to follow suit. "I understand everyone's pretty upset."

"Upset?" The man directly across from him leaned forward. "McLean, that's not close to what I am. My business is dead in the water, and what do I see on the news last night? You giving cookies to firemen."

Dar propped her chin on her fist and decided to remain quiet. She had certain sympathy for the customers who had come to complain, but she also had sympathy for Alastair, and couldn't really think of anything to say that wouldn't piss off either one or the other.

She wasn't even really sure why she'd accompanied Alastair, except that he'd asked her to, and it delayed her needing to go take Mark aside and confess about the fiber before he caught up with the cable layers, or went to the Exchange and found out for himself.

"I can understand that," Alastair said. "But the fact is I'm not the fella who's going to fix your problem, so I don't really see what the harm is in my answering questions about our community relations group." He added, "it's not as if my being interviewed is stopping anyone from working."

"That isn't the point." The man stood. "All I am hearing about is how you're helping the government, helping the rescuers. I hate to be crass, but what about us?" He pointed at himself, then at the rest of the people who apparently were content to let him speak for them. "When do we get help?"

"Well..."

"Come on, McLean," the man said. "You've been here for days. It was all over the news. When do we get some attention? Or are you all about the publicity and kissing the governor's ass?"

Alastair looked over at Dar. "Wanna give me a hand here?"

The tableful of people turned and looked over at her.

"I could undress and pose on the table." Dar suggested. "That help any?"

Alastair had the grace to look scandalized. "Dar." He sighed, missing the sudden reactions to the name from the rest of the table. "It's not funny."

"I wasn't joking." Dar shifted and rested her weight on her elbows. "Listen," she addressed the customers, "if there was something we could do to fix everyone's issues, don't you think we would be doing it? You think we like being in this room getting yelled at?"

"But what about what you're doing for the government?" One of the other men spoke up. "Why can't you do that for us? My business is on the line between the closed zone, and they told me I wouldn't have service for months. Months!"

"Because we haven't done that much for the government," Dar replied. "Who are, by the way, as much our customers as you are." She stood up and circled the table ending up next to Alastair. "Do you know how much damage was done around the area of the Towers? Do you know how much infrastructure, electrical, telecom, plumbing, you name it, was destroyed down there?"

"Of course," the man said. "I watch CNN same as you."

"Have you been down there?" Dar asked.

"They won't let us," the first man answered, frustration evident in his tone.

"Want my advice?" Dar sat down next to her boss. "Get your asses out of there. I've been in the area. Cut your losses. Find other space."

The men looked at her.

"I'm not kidding," Dar said. "If you want me to tell you I can put a satellite rig in there to get your systems up, and backhaul your traffic that way, I will. I can do that." She looked at each face in turn. "But if you want your business to survive, if you depend on walk in traffic, on people coming to you, then get out. "

"But..." the leader said, and then fell silent.

"Thousands of people died there," Alastair said quietly. "I was down in the area myself, along with Dar here...and by the way, sorry. My manners went out the window. This is our Chief Information Officer, Dar Roberts." He paused. "In case you didn't guess."

"I guessed." The man murmured.

"How are we supposed to just move?" the second man asked. "Don't get me wrong, Ms. Roberts. You're not the first person who's told me that, but we've been there for twenty years! How do we leave our customers behind like that?"

"Some of them will be moving too," Dar said. "It's a matter of survival." She looked at them with some sympathy. "Come up here. I'm sure Alastair can negotiate good rates here at the center for our valued customers. Right Alastair?"

Alastair's wry look said it all. "I'd be glad to work on that, absolutely. I know they've got some vacancies here, and we've got bargaining leverage with the management." He paused. "Let me know what kind of space you're looking for, and I'll do my best."

"That's crazy. I can't afford these rents," the second man said. "I don't think I can afford you now."

A silence fell after he finished talking, and the men on the other side of the table looked suddenly uncomfortable. "Well, matter of fact, I've been leaving messages here about that subject." the spokesman said. "Haven't gotten a call back. Is Bob in the office? I'd like to talk to him."

Alastair's jaw shut with a click and his nostrils flared. "Sorry," he said, in a clipped tone. "He's not in." He folded his hands, tension showing in his knuckles.

"Oh, well..." The man didn't seem to notice. "I guess I can talk to someone else about it. We need to defer your bills. I can't afford to pay when I'm not getting paid myself. Someone filling in for him?"

Alastair let out a careful breath. "Not yet."

"Well, he should at least put an out of office message on." The man went on, "if that's not too much to ask I..." His voice finally trailed off as he caught Dar's glare. "What?"

"Our sales team was in the towers during the attack." Dar reached over and put a hand on Alastair's shoulder. "Bob was there. He didn't make it."

The spokesman stared at them in shocked silence.

"I'm sorry," the woman next to him said. "We didn't know that."

"We're also missing some people." Dar responded quietly. "So if you're wondering, that's why we're here. We don't really give a rat's ass about the governor."

Alastair lifted his clasped hands and rested his head against them.

"Well hell," the spokesman muttered, after a pause. "Why didn't you say something? For Pete's sake people. Now I feel like a prize jackass."

Dar half shrugged. "You have a right to be here, asking us what you are asking us. You're our customers."

"Yeah, but..." The man exhaled. "Sorry. We're just so frustrated."

"So are we." Dar picked up the desk phone and dialed a number.

"This is Dar. Is Nan out there? Send her to the small conference room, please."

Now everyone looked uncomfortable, trying not to stare at Alastair's silent figure.

The door opened and Nan stuck her head in. "Ms. Roberts? You asked for ..." She stopped, her eyes flicking from the customers to their CEO. "Is something wrong?"

"Could you please take these people to one of the reception areas? They need to discuss space requirements, maybe relocating to this area. See if Kerry can talk to them, get some details."

"Yes, ma'am." Nan responded instantly, opening the door the entire way. "Could you come with me please?"

The customers scrambled to their feet and headed quickly to the door. "Thanks. We'll work it out," the spokesman muttered. They followed Nan out the door and she closed it behind them, leaving Dar and Alastair alone.

It was quiet for a few minutes. The air conditioning cycled on and off, and very far away, a siren was heard. Finally Alastair dropped his hands to the table and looked sideways at Dar, appearing as tired and as human as she'd ever seen him. "Sorry about that. "

"Don't be." Dar studied his face. "Kerry and I both lost it last night." She glanced away. "It's too damn much to keep dealing with."

Alastair sighed. "I want to do the right thing by everyone, but damned if I know what the right thing is right now." He tapped his thumbs on the desk. "That was a good idea, telling them to find other space by the way."

"They haven't been down there." Dar leaned back in her chair. "Or they'd have thought of it themselves."

A knock came at the door. Alastair sat back and hitched one knee up. "C'mon in."

The door opened, and the secretary poked her head in. "Sir, there's someone here to see you." She looked apologetic. "He's very insistent."

"Jesus." Alastair looked plaintively at the ceiling. "Sure. Bring him in. Dar, stick around, willya?"

Dar merely kept her place, letting that be her answer as the door opened again and a tall man in dark khakis and a leather jacket entered. He crossed to the table and set down a briefcase leaning on the surface and looking right at Alastair.

Dar herself could have been a coffee machine in the corner for all the attention he gave her.

"McLean? My name is Jason Green. I work for the Department of Defense. I'm going to cut to the chase. Your people have been stonewalling me, and it's going to stop, right now. I want a list of your people in our facilities and I want it now."

"Why?" Alastair asked.

"What?"

"Why?" He repeated. "I know Hamilton's talked to you. You all have the information you need in your own systems. Why do you want mine?"

"You don't really need to know that," Green said.

'Sure I do." Alastair remained calm. "They're my employees, and I have a responsibility under the law to protect their information and their privacy."

"You don't get it do you?" Green sat down. "McLean, I'm not your enemy. I don't honestly want to be here jerking you around. You don't have a choice. You have no recourse. You can't ask me what I want this for because I've been given the authority to do whatever I need to do in order to get what I think is important."

"Regardless of the law?" Alastair asked.

"Law doesn't mean anything. You ever heard of martial law? We're in it. They just haven't announced it to the press." Green told him. "I could throw you in jail as a suspected terrorist and you'd spend years in some hole without contact with your family or anyone else. So do you and me a favor and just give me the damn list."

Alastair steepled his fingers and tapped the edges of his thumbs against his lips as he studied the man. Then he turned and glanced at Dar. "What do you think?"

Green turned, as though noticing Dar for the first time. His eyebrows rose.

Dar rested her hands on her knee. "I think if my father was here, he'd kill this guy." She remarked. "That's what I think."

"Who in the hell are you?" Green asked.

Dar ignored him pulling her laptop over. "But I'm not going to sit here and watch you get dragged off to some gulag on account of a database, Alastair." She opened the laptop. "I'll parse a file for them. They won't know what the hell to do with it. They won't be able to read the format, their program will spit out a pile of crap when it tries to ingest it and there's no information in there they don't already have, but what the hell." She rapidly logged in to the machine. "I'll give it to him and he can go weenie waggle somewhere else."

"Hmph." Alastair grunted. "Well, if you think that's a good idea…"

"Do you have something to put the file on?" Dar looked up at the man. "Or do you want me to pour raw packets down your goddamned underwear?"

Green stared at her. "What?"

"Did you bring a portable hard drive?" Dar asked. "Or did you bring a truck to haul off the five hundred pounds of paper it'll take me to print out eighty thousand records?"

"W…"

"You came here and asked for something." Dar enunciated the words. "Do you have any idea in hell what it is you're even asking for?"

Green turned to Alastair. "I don't appreciate being spoken to in that way, McLean."

Alastair regarded him for a moment. "Too damned bad," he said. "Answer the woman if you want your list. If not, hit the road. We're busy people."

The man sat back in his seat bracing his hands on the table. "Did you not listen to a word I said?"

"We did. We just don't care," Dar said bluntly. "All we've heard from you people since this whole damn thing happened is pointless demands and threats. You have no idea on the planet what to do with what you're asking for, and your people can't use the data I give you.

But what the hell. To get you out of here I'll go ahead and produce it, but you've got to cough up something to put it on or carry it away with, and do it fast."

"I'm sure you have something..." Green blurted, half standing. "You can't expect me to..."

"No, I don't," Dar said. "We don't allow portable storage devices in our facilities. It's a security issue." She rattled some keys. "And these databases are protected by encryption, so I hope what you've got can handle it, not to mention interpret the structure. "

Green leaned on the table. "You're interfering with National Security." He spoke the words emphasizing the capital letters.

"I'm just telling you the truth." Dar stood up, stretching to her full height. "You want us to break the law? You threaten us with jail? You stand here and talk nothing but utter bullshit, you waste of my taxpayer dollars." She put her hands on her hips. "Who the hell do you work for?"

"Listen, lady."

Dar circled the table with surprising speed. "You listen, jackass." She let her voice lift as she closed in on her target, missing the widening of Alastair's eyes behind her. "Get your boss on the phone. I want to talk to him and tell him what a complete idiot he has working for him."

The man stood up. "You want to speak to my boss? All right. I'll arrange for that." He stepped back from the table and pushed the chair into place. "Don't go far." He turned and walked to the door, leaving and closing it with surprising gentleness.

Alastair rested his chin on his hand, his elbow propped on the table. "I think we just got ourselves in trouble, Paladar."

"You care?"

"Not really." Her boss shrugged. "Let me warn Ham. He's about ready to disown us anyhow. With any luck maybe I can get them to throw us all out of the city and we can take everyone out of here." He stood up and picked up the phone. "I'll warn the board they may need to post our bail too. That should start their morning off right."

Dar smiled briefly. "Let me go talk to my people. Call me if you need me." She headed for the door, as Alastair raised a hand and waggled it at her in farewell.

Not a good morning, at all.

"SEE, HERE'S THE deal." Mark was sitting on the floor with a thick loop of rope over his shoulder. "We figured we'd track back, and get a rope down to where those guys have to bring the cable so we can haul it when they get here."

"Like a giant pull string." Kerry was crouched next to him, a flashlight held in one hand.

"Yeah." Mark nodded. "Problem is we're kinda stuck getting out of this freaking room." He looked around the old, small space. "I don't know what the hell we're gonna do."

Kerry backed out of the room and looked across the floor toward the entrance to the subway. The space was filled with people crossing back and forth. "Well, with enough arm twisting we can run it across the floor I guess."

Mark joined her. "They're gonna freak."

Kerry shook her head. "It's dangerous. That's a big cable. Everyone's going to trip, they're going to have to put a shield over it or shut this floor down."

"Guess they'll have to." Mark agreed. "Let me get hold of that maintenance guy and give him a heads up. I bet we're going to have to go up the chain for it."

"Probably." Kerry agreed. "I'll go talk to the building management. I think I just booked them a couple thousand in rentals so I've got some good points in the bank with them at the moment." She dusted her hands off. "I'll be back."

"You got it boss." Mark dropped his loop of rope and started off toward the back of the hall.

Kerry slid her flashlight into the side pocket of her coveralls and moved in the opposite direction, climbing up the steps and crossing the floor toward the management office for the second time that morning.

It felt like she was being constructive. The morning session on behalf of their customers had been almost pleasant. She was bringing more business, and the complex was glad not to have someone asking for exceptions, or rent deferrals.

She pushed the door to the office open and returned the brief smile of the receptionist. "Hello, me again. Is Tom available for a quick moment?"

"I'll ask, Ms. Stuart." The girl got up and disappeared into the inner maze of office hallways as Kerry went over to the courtesy counter and started fixing herself a cup of tea.

One thing about New York. Kerry selected a fragrant bag from a box of assorted teas and dispensed hot water over it. People liked their comforts here. She stirred the cup and took a sip, turning and leaning against the wall as she waited.

The girl came back. "Right this way, ma'am." She smiled, waiting for Kerry to join her before she led her back into the managing director's office. "Here you go."

"Hello there again." Tom Brooks waved her in. "What can I do for you, Kerry?" He was an older man, with a close-cropped beard and salt and pepper hair.

"Well..." Kerry came in and took a seat across from him. "I wish I could say I've got another dozen tenants we'll guarantee for you, but this time I'm here to make trouble."

"Oh no." The man behind the desk didn't look overly alarmed. "How much trouble can a nice young lady like you cause anyhow?"

"You'd be surprised." Kerry remarked, dryly. "Just ask my boss. Anyway, here's the problem we have." She went on, "as you know, we've got an emergency project going on for the city government."

"I didn't, but it doesn't surprise me. Every little thing these days is an emergency."

Kerry toasted him with her cup of tea. "Point made. In this case, there are a bunch of telecom wiring people running a big piece of fiber cable from the New York Stock Exchange to our demarc down in the dungeon here — lower level."

Tom blinked at her. "Seriously?"

Kerry nodded. "Seriously."

"Jesus." He shook his head. "How in the hell are you going to do that? There's no opening from that area near the steps to the subway." He thought a minute. "You'd have to bring it up through the station and cross the concourse with it."

Kerry nodded.

"You want to do that?" Tom's voice lifted sharply. "You kidding me?"

Kerry shook her head.

He leaned back in his chair and tapped his pen on the desk. "Wow." He mused. "That could be a big problem. There are a lot of people down there," he warned. "I don't know if we can run a cable across the floor. Maybe we can run it along the wall or something."

Kerry grimaced a little. "That's a long way."

"Well, it's coming from a long way. I don't think they'll let us cross the concourse due to safety reasons. Let me take my guy down there, and we'll look at it. What size cable are we talking about?"

"Two inch round," admitted Kerry. "We know it's a hassle, but the project we're working on really is a number one priority for the government."

"Surprised they're not in here telling us what to do then." Tom got up. "I'll see what we can arrange for that, Kerry. I know you all have been working down there. My facilities chief has been bitching about having to leave the door open. I'll let you know what I find out."

"Thanks." Kerry got up. "Believe me I know we're asking a lot. We're trying to get this working and there's a lot riding on it." She took his proffered hand. "Thanks, Tom. I really, really appreciate it."

"Save that till I can do something about it." Tom warned. "And you folks be careful of that room in there, okay? There are some dangerous pipes and things in there."

"We know. Dar nearly got knocked on her behind from that electrical panel." She followed him out of the room and down the hall. "Do we really use steam heat here?"

Tom chuckled. "Sure as hell do. Glad we don't have to turn those pipes up with you all in there. I'd have to charge you for a sauna bath." He held the outer door for her. "After we get through this, let's talk about moving your connections someplace else."

"How did we end up in there anyway?" Kerry waited for him to catch up to her and they walked across the floor together. "Dar was wondering about that."

"Long story. We'll get it straightened out." He started angling away from her. "Be in touch with you, Kerry. Let you know."

"Thanks, Tom." Kerry headed for the steps, her cup of tea still clasped in her fingers, feeling another, though minor, sense of accomplishment. She didn't envy Dar, who was floors and floors above her, dealing with the press, the government, and the board.

She'd heard Dar yelling in the conference room, and then a man had stormed out of the office, nearly knocking down people on his way out. Department of Defense, Dar had told her afterward, and probably a lot of trouble headed back their way.

Ugh.

She trotted down the steps and headed back to their little dungeon. Shaun was seated outside with a piece of pizza, and Kannan was sitting cross-legged sipping from a steaming cup. "Hey guys." She greeted them. "Mark back yet?"

"Not yet." Shaun shook his head. "Ms. Stuart, we want to go down to the other end and do the setup there, but we're kinda not sure how to do that. I don't think they'd just let us in there, you know?"

Kerry took a seat next to him. "Good point." She took a sip of her tea. "Well, tell you what. Once Mark gets back, I'll go round up Dad and one of the trucks and we'll all go down there together. That work?"

"Sure," agreed Shaun. "Maybe we can even do the whole cross connect, if they got the other end of that cable up in the right spot."

Ah. Kerry turned and looked inside the room. "You mean the connection box, like that?" She indicated the new panel.

"Yes." Kannan spoke up. "It would be good to get the melding down and the connectors polished and ready. Then we have only this side to do when the other end of this cable arrives here."

Kerry felt a little awkward, not entirely sure of whether she should spill the beans now, or wait until they arrived downtown. Part of her wanted to tell the techs the truth, but she also felt that Dar had wanted to keep it under wraps, and she wasn't sure if this was the place or time for her to countermand her lover's wishes.

She didn't mind disagreeing with Dar. They did sometimes. But she was sensitive about doing it in front of people who worked for them because she never wanted to give the impression that she was leveraging their relationship to appear to control her partner when it really wasn't anything like that.

Oh, well. Kerry drank her tea, allowing the silence to continue. Well, she did leverage their relationship, all the time, but not really to control Dar, more to find a consensus when they were on opposite sides of any particular question.

She knew that Dar would listen to what she was saying, even though she didn't agree with it, just because Kerry was who she was, and they were what they were to each other. There was no way around that. Dar often blew other people off and refused to take them seriously. With Kerry, that was never the case.

Dar always took her seriously. She always took Dar seriously. Sometimes they compromised. Sometimes they didn't, and Kerry would accept Dar's opinion. Sometimes Dar would listen to what she had to say, and then change her mind and agree with Kerry's view.

But they would never have gotten that far if there wasn't total trust between them that gave her that edge in dealing with Dar's mercurial, restless nature.

Speaking of. She heard a set of distinctive footsteps approaching and looked up just as Dar came around the corner of the stairwell, trailed by Mark and Andrew. Her partner looked frustrated and she felt the glower just before her eyes met Kerry's and she headed their way. "Here comes trouble."

"Uh oh." Shaun started chewing faster. "Better suck that up fast, Kan. Her nibs looks pissed."

"There you are." Dar addressed Kerry.

"Here I am." Kerry agreed, patting the floor next to her. "Come. Sit. You look mad."

In the act of turning and accepting the offer, settling gracefully next to Kerry, Dar managed to somehow lose most of the frustration in her attitude and ended up merely looking bemused. "What's the scoop here?"

Mark crouched down next to the two techs, and they started talking in low tones. Andrew picked a spot on the wall and leaned against it, crossing his ankles as he waited for everything to shake out.

"Scoop." Kerry offered Dar the remainder of her tea. "Well, I talked to the building about our running cable across the floor. I don't think they'll go for that, but they're looking at alternatives."

"Uhgh." Dar grunted.

"The team wants to head down to the Exchange and make the connections down there. " Kerry kept her voice neutral. "So I thought I'd take Dad and help them get in there and get set up."

"Ah." Dar grunted again with a completely different inflection. "Okay." She took the cup and finished the beverage.

"But I wanted to discuss that with you first," Kerry said. "I know you have some concerns." She put her hand on Dar's thigh. "But if you want, I can handle that end of it for you."

Dar studied her, a faint smile appearing on her face. "Thank you, Kerrison."

"What are friends for?" Kerry smiled back. "You take your share of tough calls, sweetheart. I don't mind shouldering this one for you."

"I know," Dar uttered softly. "One of the many reasons I love you."

Aw. "Any fallout from the DOD?" Kerry leaned closer, lowering her voice. "Do you want me to pander to my genes and call my mother to see if she can help with that?"

"No." Dar set the cup down. "Hamilton advised me to get the hell out of the office and go hide somewhere in case they show up to drag me off. I'll take the team downtown. I know you don't want to go back down there."

"Any word from Lockheed?"

Dar shook her head.

"Let's both go," said Kerry. "Let's go, and we can lay it out for everyone, and just do everything we can do. Okay?"

Dar studied her laced fingers, then looked up and over at Kerry. "All right. You and me, all the way." She reached over and clasped Kerry's hand. "Let's go."

They stood. "Okay, team," Kerry said. "Let's get our gear together and go down to the other end of this situation. Dar and I have some information to give you, and then we can get what we need to get done taken care of. "

The techs were already scrambling to their feet, and Mark had ducked inside the room for his backpack. "Hey." He poked his head out. "We taking the bus? I threw a bunch of the gear in it, and it's got three cases of Red Bull."

"Sounds like a plan," Dar said. "It's going to be a long night."

"Ain't they all?" Mark disappeared inside the room again as they got ready to move out. "But hey, we'll make history, right?"

Dar stuck her hands in her pockets and regarded her father. "I think sometimes making history's overrated."

"Yeap." Andrew agreed. "That is the truth, rugrat. That is surely the truth." He clapped her on the shoulder. "'Specially since history ain't always your friend."

They gathered up their gear and headed off, walking up the steps and out into the afternoon light into a street full of people and sirens and cool, dusty air.

KERRY BRACED HER hands on the sides of the doorway leading from the main part of the bus into the driver's compartment. Ahead of them the road was relatively clear, though the sky was hazy with smoke and the dusting of ash remained on almost every surface.

There was still an air of desolation present. Here and there, she could see where a car had been removed, or boxes were now piled on the sidewalk, and scattered here and there were people walking slowly, looking around as though in disbelief.

"Just opened the east side here to people," said the driver. "Just this side of Broadway."

Now that he'd mentioned it, Kerry started noticing figures moving around in the distance. She could see flashlight beams in windows, and it brought back the memory of the big power outage they'd suffered in Miami not that long ago.

She'd used a similar flashlight to stumble through the darkness of the condo, the stuffy closeness driving her outside and down to the Dixieland Yankee's cabin where the boat's batteries and a solid charging from the engines kept her and Chino comfortable through that very long night.

So many people hadn't been nearly as lucky. She'd heard the stories at work the next day. Just like so many people here now weren't lucky. People were rooting through dust covered belongings and cleaning out putrid refrigerators while they cruised by in their air conditioned bus.

"What a mess." Dar had come up behind her, and now Kerry could feel the warmth along her back as her partner came into her space. "These people are coming back to Hell." She leaned back into her partner's chest. "What a nightmare."

"Reminds me of Hurricane Andrew." Dar let her hands rest on Kerry's shoulders. "We sent a bunch of people down south to help clean up. Some of our staff lived down there. Total disaster."

"Did you go?"

"Sure," Dar replied. "Ended up puncturing my hand with a rusty nail and getting hauled off to the first aid station. They have picture of me sitting there with two guys hanging on to my paw with a three inch piece of iron sticking out of it."

Kerry turned her head and stared at her. "You didn't pass out?"

"Only by a whisker." Dar overturned her left hand and flexed it. "Only my ego kept me upright. I wasn't going to take a dive in front of half the company." She looked up to find Kerry gazing indulgently at her. "It was damn close though."

Kerry could imagine it. She knew how squeamish her partner was about injuries and she could just picture the stubborn set of Dar's jaw as she fought to remain unfazed. It had nothing to do with courage. Dar had more of that than most. "You poor thing." She leaned over and gave Dar's palm a kiss. "Too bad I wasn't there to take care of you."

"Mm." Dar glanced past Kerry as the bus came to halt and the air brakes blasted out a hiss. "Here we are." She drew in a breath, and then let it out. "Time to pay the piper."

Kerry turned all the way around and bumped Dar lightly with her fists. "I'm right with you, tiger." She followed Dar down the aisle to the center of the bus where the team was getting their masks together and testing radios.

Dar took up a position near one of the doors and folded her arms over her chest. "Folks, listen up."

Kerry stuck her hands in the pockets of her jumpsuit and stood just a half step behind her boss, underlining her support. She watched the faces of the techs as they stopped what they were doing and turned toward them.

"We've had a major screw-up." Dar got right to the meat of the matter. "Those guys running the cable are running the wrong kind."

The techs all blinked in surprise. Mark put his backpack down and leaned on the bar. "Huh?"

Dar nodded. "We found out after they'd already started rolling it. The right stuff won't be here until Tuesday at the earliest."

The techs looked at each other, then at Mark, then at Dar.

"How wrong is it?" Mark asked. "The wrong micron?"

"Multimode," answered Dar.

"Oh no." Kannan groaned. "That will not be good."

"Shit." Mark looked nonplussed. "What are we doing down here then? We'll just have to do it again on...like on what, Wednesday? You going to tell them to stop?"

"No." Dar shook her head. "We're going to make the connections as though the cable was the right kind. I knew they were using the wrong type yesterday, and told them to keep going."

Even Mark looked at her with confusion and disbelief. "Bu..." He started then stopped. "Bu..." He started again. "Boss, that's not gonna work."

"I know."

Kerry decided to keep quiet. She edged a step closer to Dar and leaned against the wall, looking steadily from face to face, mildly wondering what Dar was going to tell them.

"There really isn't any option," said Dar. "They expect this to work tomorrow. I know it won't work until Wednesday at the earliest...if they can get that other cable run. But at least we'll have all the connections in place and ready to go."

"But..." Mark hesitated. "Won't they be pissed? I mean, I heard them talking, boss. This is serious shit."

"They'll be pissed," Dar agreed. "But that's not your problem. That's mine and Alastair's problem."

"Mine too." Kerry piped up. "I'll walk the plank with you, Captain Roberts."

That got a nervous smile from the techs. "And," Dar shrugged lightly, "we've got some people looking at the technology to see if there's anything to be done."

"That will be very interesting if they discover anything," Kannan said. "It will be very difficult I think."

"Very interesting," Dar said. "So just go in there, and make like everything's normal. Set up the connections and put the patch in. Don't talk about the cable being a problem. Let's get in and get our part of this done, and get out of here. "

"Right." Mark nodded. "Sounds good, boss. You guys got all your gear? Let's get moving." He shouldered his pack and slipped the smaller of his two masks over his head to nestle under his chin. "You think we need the full ones?" he asked Andrew, who was lounging nearby.

"Figure you should take it." Andrew held his up. "Sure as hell if you don't, you'll need it."

The techs trooped out the door and down onto the sidewalk, all with laden backpacks and leg pockets stuffed with tools and water bottles. The bus driver came up behind them as Andrew started to follow.

"I'm going to park it here. The cops say that's all right," said the driver. "I'll pop out the SAT dish and see what I can pick up in the way of news." He held up a radio in one big hand. "I'll let you know if anything stirs up."

"Thanks." Dar glanced out the door where the techs were gathering. "Hopefully this won't take long." She patted Kerry on the hip. "C'mon pirate. Let's get this done."

Kerry followed Dar down the steps and blinked her eyes already stinging a little as she drew in a breath of dusty air. "Ugh." She slipped on her mask and adjusted it, hoping it would block out the stench an errant puff of air brought her.

Dar adjusted her credentials and edged through the crowd. "Let's go." She started for the steps to the Exchange, aware of the armed guards at the top of them. "Ker?"

Kerry dodged around Mark and joined her. "They took that pretty well." She uttered in a low tone as they trotted up the steps to the building.

"There's an advantage to having everyone too scared to disagree with you. Sometimes, when you really need it, they just shut up and do what you tell them to."

"Dar," Kerry patted her side, "they always do what you tell them to. If you told them to wrap our building in twisted pair cabling and paint Alastair's car pink, they'd do it."

"You wouldn't." Dar gave the guards at the top of the steps a brisk nod, and went right past them, reaching out to open the door and hold it open.

"Paint Alastair's car pink? I might."

"Ma'am?" The guard moved to intercept her. "This is a restricted area."

"Damn well should be." Dar presented her credentials. "If they didn't put us on the access list they will as soon as we get in there. Excuse us." She motioned the crew through. "Kerry, go in there and find whoever's in charge and get them to give this gentleman the right data."

"Yes, ma'am." Kerry marched past without hesitating watching the guard try to untangle his tongue as they slipped past and into the building. "I'll get right on that."

"Ah. But...ah..." The guard glanced at Dar's credentials. "Oh, well, okay, I'm sure that's fine," he said. "I think I remember some people from your company here earlier, right?"

"Right." Dar agreed. "Thanks." She pointed at the bus. "There are hot drinks and snacks in there if you get tired of holding the wall up out here." She went past into the building and let the door shut behind her catching sight of Kerry waiting patiently not far away.

"See?" Kerry commented to the techs waiting nearby. "It's like having a beautiful animated can opener sometimes."

Dar stopped in her tracks, both eyebrows shooting up. "Excuse me?"

A loud argument down the hall distracted them, and Kerry was saved from answering as they turned and looked toward the noise. A group of men were coming out of a room all talking at once. They were dressed in business shirts and slacks, most carrying jackets.

"Move!" The man in the front ordered them. "What in the hell are you people doing up here? Get back to where you belong!" He was relatively short, but had bristling gray eyebrows and hair, and a pair of what would be extremely shiny patent leather shoes if they weren't currently covered in dust.

Kerry saw her partner's eyes narrow, and she instinctively put a hand out, catching Dar's arm as she moved back against the wall to let the men pass. "Dar, hold on."

She could feel the tension as Dar stood her ground. "Dar, c'mon. These people aren't worth it."

The man pulled up short, since Dar was standing in the middle of the hallway effectively blocking it. "Did you hear me?"

"Listen, sir, we're doing all we can." The man behind him caught up to him and grabbed his arm. "You don't understand what's gone on here. What these people have been through."

"I don't give a shit what these people have been through." The man in the lead turned around, throwing the hand off his arm. "This place has half the liquidity of the planet tied up in it. You fed some bullshit to CNN but if it doesn't open tomorrow morning, everyone's head's gonna roll." He turned back around. "Move out of the way or I'll toss you on your ass, lady."

Dar grinned with absolutely no humor and a good deal of delight.

"Lord." Andrew shoved his way back down the hallway. "Can't leave you for a minute, can I?" He took the man by the shoulders and shoved him past Dar. "G'wan, blowhard. Git your ass out before you done get hurt."

"What? Get your damn hands off me! Police!" The man yelled, thrashing around.

Andrew gave him a final shove then he put himself between the angry figure and Dar's tall form, his bigger body blocking the hallway with even more effectiveness. "Git!"

"Sir!" The other man dashed after him, taking hold of his arm. "Whoever you people are you better get lost. Now!" He hurried the man past, before he could recover and say anything at all, and they disappeared around the corner toward the door.

Dar sighed. "There goes my fun for the day." She turned back to the rest of the men, who were standing there gaping. "Who is that?" She indicated the now vanished man.

"Marcus Abercrombie." The young man nearest her answered promptly. "The second richest man in the world. He's just really upset about the market. We just heard they're having problems with the systems."

"We're the ones trying to fix it," Kerry told him "We don't appreciate being yelled at."

"Well, sure. No one does." The young man agreed. "Hi. I'm Barry Marks." He offered Kerry his hand. "I'm the trading floor coordinator." He glanced past her. "Are you the technical people? Our director said they were expecting some people here to look at the computers."

Dar joined Kerry, now that it appeared the excitement was over. "We're working on the problems, yes. I heard the CNN report too — that guy didn't buy it?"

"Nope." Marks shook his head. "He came in the back and started snooping around and figured out that it wasn't working. He said he'd keep it to himself, but I bet we see it on CNN in ten minutes. He's probably telling his chauffeur about it right now."

"Great." A man behind him sighed. "Like we don't have enough problems. I don't want all those damn Federal guys shouting at me again." He looked at Dar. "Can you fix it?"

"Ultimately? Yes," Dar said. "There's nothing in technology enough time and money can't fix."

"By tomorrow morning?" Marks asked.

"That's an open question." Dar pointed down the hallway. "Let's go downstairs, team. We're wasting time."

They filed past the brokers who looked dubiously at them, and shook their heads. "Tomorrow's going to suck," one said.

"No matter what happens." Marks agreed. "Let's go get some coffee. My mouth's dry as a bone from the damn dust."

They headed in the opposite direction. Dar was glad to be rid of them, as they walked down the hall and headed down the steps to the lower level of the building. "Did you call me a can opener?" she asked Kerry.

Kerry chuckled under her breath.

"Manual or electric?"

Chapter Fourteen

ANOTHER DUSTY, CONCRETE room. Another raised floor. Another long stretch of time between humming black racks of equipment that gave off the faint scent of ozone and plastic.

Kerry lifted herself up off the floor, pulling her head out of the space under the floor and resting her weight on her elbows as she waited for the blood rush to fade. "Can't see anything."

Kannan and Shaun were over by the wall against a sheet of plywood that was as age worn as Kerry felt at the moment. They had a black box partially assembled; their heads bent over thin strands and tiny posts, their tools gathered neatly around their feet as they sat there cross-legged.

"They had the end right there." One of the techs from the Exchange was sitting on a desk nearby. He pointed at the hole in the floor. "Then those guys pulled it back, I guess. It disappeared."

Kerry folded her hands, and studied her knuckles. "Didn't occur to anyone to anchor the cable?" She inquired.

"It's not our stuff." The tech shrugged. "No one told us what they were doing."

Kerry silently counted to ten. "Boy, that's a shame." She shifted her flashlight and inched herself forward, extending her head down under the floor again. It smelled dank and musty, and she had to keep convincing herself she didn't smell anything worse than mold.

It was uncomfortable, and it gave her a headache hanging upside down as she was. She pushed that aside and extended her arm down into the space, turning on her flashlight and examining the underside of the floor.

It was full of trays and pipes, the cabling so dense she could barely see past it. She squinted hard, peering past a clump of metal and dust and spotted a stretch of the cabling that was scraped free of the grime. "Ah."

"Found it?" Shaun asked.

"Found where it was." Kerry pulled her head back out and moved down two squares, picking up the aluminum floor puller and thwacking it down against the surface. She wiggled it then she leaned back, hauling the floor tile up off its frame and sliding it out of the way.

She got down on her belly again and continued her investigation. She could see the scrape marks traveling over the piping and squirmed further into the opening, shining her flashlight under the next section of floor.

Eyeballs reflected the shine. Kerry stifled a yelp and somehow kept herself from scrambling out of the opening by sheer will.

"Something wrong ma'am?" Shaun looked up.

"Um. No." Kerry bravely resumed her search. She looked for the eyes, but there was nothing in that back corner now except some hanging cable.

She was about to move on, when her eyes registered something unusual, and she looked back at the spot, carefully craning her neck to one side and narrowing her eyes. "Oh crap."

"Ma'am?"

Kerry got up and crawled over two more squares to where she'd seen the eyes, and then she slapped the floor puller into place and settled back, both hands on the device. "You might want to get back." She told the tech. "I saw something move under here and it's too small to be one of us."

The tech didn't need to be told twice. He jumped off the desk and went around it, backing away from Kerry. "You're crazy to be opening that up. Could be anything under there. Someone said there were snakes."

Kerry took a deep breath and yanked her shoulders back, pulling the tile up off its seating. She rocked back onto her heels and pulled the tile with her, tensing her thighs a she prepared to have to jump clear just in case.

Nothing stirred. She slid the tile to one side, and shone her light on the cabling underneath. "Look at that."

The tech got up on the desk and peered over it into the space. "Holy crap."

Shaun and Kannan scrambled to their feet and approached, staying cautiously behind Kerry's kneeling form. "Oh wow," Shaun said. "That's all chewed up!"

Exposed now in the light, there was a thick bundle of cabling, a lurid blue color that was marred by a huge clump in the center that was chewed all the way almost to the bottom of the bundle, resulting in tangle of butchered wires. "Sure is." Kerry examined the hairball. "Well, this didn't happen in a week, did it?"

The tech circled the desk and knelt next to her warily, looking at the cables. "That's new." He said. "For sure, because I know where that bundle goes and that stuff was working before all this happened."

"Wow," Shaun said again. "That's a...what a mess."

"For sure," Kannan agreed. "That will take many hours to fix."

"Guess you guys better get started then," the tech said. "Cause this stuff will never work if that's not connected."

"Us?" Kerry looked up at him. "This isn't our wiring."

The tech shrugged. "It's not our wiring. We just do server management here. That's all. We don't touch any of the infrastructure stuff."

"Who does?" Kerry asked. "And where are they, by the way? "

The tech shrugged again. "Some company that some big guy here owns a part of. They got a couple of guys and a truck, and they come in when we need new cables run and stuff like that. They monitor everything remotely."

Kerry counted to ten again. Then she counted to twenty. Then she gave it up and started to put the tile to one side, her temper flaring.

A bang issued from the space. It put a cap on her reaction, and made everyone jump. "What the..."

Another bang and she started to get up and away from the hole, which suddenly started to issue flashes of light.

"Oh my god." The tech jumped back, bumping into the desk and falling into it, then bouncing off and lunging back across the open hole, his arms flailing. "Ahh!"

Kerry succumbed to latent heroism and grabbed him, throwing herself into him and taking them both to the other side of the open floor just as a loud sound emerged and the hole erupted with a flurry of brown forms.

"Holy shit!" Shaun let out a yell, jumping backward and grabbing Kannan by the shoulder as rats boiled out of the floor scattering in every direction.

Kerry hit the floor with a painful jolt and rolled clear of the tech unable to place the sounds and hearing the alarm in her people's voices as she smelled a deep, raunchy stench come into the room. She wrenched herself around and got her hands under her, shoving her body away from the floor and nearly pitching herself right back onto it when a rat ran over her hand toward the server cabinets.

She bit her tongue, and got enough command of her body to get her feet under her and stand up, fiercely resisting the urge to jump up onto the desk. "Nice." She croaked. "What the hell brought that on?" She grimaced a little, as her ribs protested her impact with the floor.

The tech jumped onto the desk. "That's it. I'm getting out of here. All that overtime ain't worth it. That's a freak show." He walked to the end of the desk and hopped off, then disappeared out the door without a backward glance.

"Nice." Kerry looked around. The rats had all disappeared. She walked cautiously over to the hole and crouched down at a respectful distance, peering inside. As she watched, the end of the cable she'd been searching for inched into view, with a loud scraping sound and a clinking of the metal ends that protected it. "Ah."

"Hey. It's the cable." Shaun had eased warily up behind her. "Where'd that come from?"

"Someone has found it." Kannan came over and knelt right next to the opening, reaching down without hesitation and taking the end of the cable in one hand. "I am going to pull this now." He called down. "Be relaxed."

He braced one foot and pulled gently on the cable end.

"Don't pull too hard." Shaun advised. "We have to get it back under the floor over to the wall." He came out from behind Kerry and knelt down by his teammate's side.

Kerry eased slowly upright, as a sudden motion caused a jolt of pain. She bit off a curse and stepped back, getting out of the tech's way and moving back over to desk.

"Got it?" A voice echoed softly up to them.

"Got it." Shaun called back. "Was that Mark?"

Kerry perched on the edge of the desk pressing her elbow against her side. "I think it was." She agreed, removing the radio clipped to her shoulder. "Mark, this is Kerry. You there?"

She heard a crackle of noise on the speaker, then Dar answered, her deep tones roughened with the radio's interference, but comforting to Kerry's ears nonetheless.

"We're here," Dar said. "They get the end of that damn cable? We had to push it up back through a bunch of garbage and through a damn access pipe."

"We got it." Kerry acknowledged. "You chased a bunch of rats up here with it."

"What?"

"And, we've got another problem." Kerry went on. "Dar, you better come up here and look at this," she paused, "and I think I..." She stopped, aware of the techs listening. "If you're done there, come on back."

"Be right there." Dar's voice had taken on an edge and Kerry exhaled, as she clipped the radio mic back on her shoulder.

Breathing hurt. She figured that meant nothing good, but she decided to remain where she was, watching the techs work the cable under the floor toward the wall. She saw Kannan examine the end closely and nod, but neither he nor Shaun said anything about it.

Good people.

"That was crazy, huh?" Shaun looked up. "This place really is crazy."

"It is." Kerry agreed. "I don't know what we're going to do with that cable mess in there. We keep having everyone else's problems dropped in our lap."

"That's a mess." Shaun agreed. "That's probably a hundred cables that need to be fixed."

"Not too good at all." Kannan said.

There were footsteps in the hallway, and suddenly the door was filled with Dar's tall form. She stopped in the opening and looked around, focusing on Kerry. "Hey." She crossed the floor to her partner's side, ignoring the open sections, the mass of screwed up cable, and the two techs.

Her jumpsuit was covered in dust and grime and she brushed her hands off as she arrived in front of Kerry. "You okay?"

Kerry managed a brief smile. "What makes you think I'm not?"

Dar moved closer. "You're white as a sheet. What happened?" Her voice dropped, taking on a concerned tone. "Ker?"

"Sorry." Kerry waited for the pain to ease. "I did something stupid crazy. When you were pushing the cable back in here a bunch of...I guess those big rats. They came up through the floor." She took a shallow breath. "Anyway, the other guy that was here was falling into the open hole and I grabbed for him and we both landed on the floor."

Dar put a hand on her knee. "And?"

"Caught my ribs on the edge of the tile," Kerry admitted. "Think I cracked something." She saw Dar's reaction start as she was saying it and she reached over to grab her hand. "Not bad, at least I don't think so."

"Cracked anything isn't good." Dar glanced around. "C'mon. I'll take you over to the hospital. They can take some X-rays."

"No, c'mon. I don't think it's that bad." Kerry protested. "I just got the breath knocked out of me." She amended her diagnosis. "Just a bruise. Chill."

Dar's brow arched sharply.

"You would say the same damn thing," accused Kerry.

"So, because I'm an idiot, you have to be an idiot?" Dar asked.

Kerry thought about that. "Yes."

Dar gave her a dour look. "Go back to the bus, and catch your breath," she said. "I don't want you to bruise anything else."

"Dar..."

"That wasn't a request." Dar's voice sharpened unexpectedly.

Kerry tilted back a trifle and studied her companion, seeing the storm in the blue eyes glaring back at her. "Okay," she responded. "Boss."

Dar stepped out of the way to let her leave, and she did, swallowing against the lump of unease in her throat. Dar didn't pull rank on her often, and even less so in situations like this that crossed into their personal lives, but it stung every time, and this was no exception.

Even if she knew Dar was right, and she was being stubborn, it didn't help. She kept her elbow near her side as she made her way down the steps; the hallways eerily empty, as were the sidewalks when she emerged.

The bus door opened as she approached though, and she climbed inside to find a quiet oasis waiting for her completely bereft of staff or visitors. As the door closed shut behind her, the air even cleared and she felt her shoulders relax. "Thanks, Alan." She called into the driver's compartment. "Quiet today huh?"

"Yes, ma'am." The driver called back. "I'll just be here reading my paper. Let me know if you need anything."

Kerry removed her mask and tossed it on the table wincing as the ache in her side started throbbing uncomfortably. She walked over to the courtesy kitchenette area and opened the small refrigerator. Inside there were milk chugs. She took one out and opened it.

"Ow." The twisting made a jolt of pain go all the way down through her groin. "Stupid idiot." She went to her pack and fumbled out the bottle of Advil, opening it and then tossing down the handful of pills with a swallow of the milk.

It tasted good and soothing against the roughness in her throat. Kerry took the chug with her and carefully sat down in one of the leather chairs, leaning a little on her good side to take the pressure off her ribs.

The pain eased. She exhaled, reaching up to unclip the radio mic and pausing.

Call Dar? Find some excuse to reach out and make that contact? She felt the urge to do that, to smooth over the moment's anger between them before it festered and yet, she didn't want to interrupt Dar in front of the rest of the staff for something silly.

Something she knew Dar knew would have nothing to do with what she was calling for.

"Ugh." Kerry let her hand drop and sipped her milk instead. "Dear God I wish it was tomorrow already." She decided she'd rest here for a few minutes, and then go back to the data center and make her amends in person.

Her side did hurt. A lot. She concentrated on breathing shallowly and put her head down on her arm as she waited for the medication to kick in. "Rats." She muttered. "What in the hell else is going to happen to us here?"

Her radio crackled softly, its speaker right near her ear. Then it clicked off, much as she had only moments before.

Kerry closed her eyes, and managed something almost close to a smile.

DAR KNELT BESIDE the open floor, working hard to focus her mind on the problem in front of her. She stared at the cable mess for a long minute before she glanced over at Mark giving him a half shrug. "Our options are fix it, or tell them to fix it."

Mark nodded. "Shaun said the guy in here said their network people are somebody's cousin."

"Great." Dar rested her elbow on her upraised knee. "All right," she finally said. "Get a couple of the LAN guys down here with a kit. I'll go find the idiots running this place and see if I can get them to take responsibility for it."

"Think they will?"

"No," Dar said. "But I want them on the record refusing to." She stood up and stepped carefully over the open space. "Stupid bastards."

"This is a lot of crap." Mark got up. "Crap on top of crap if you know what I mean."

Dar looked past him, silent for a moment. Then she looked back. "Yeah. I'll be back." She ducked out of the computer room and looked both ways, and then turned right and reluctantly headed further into the building.

Reluctant, because her conscience was really driving her in the opposite direction, back to the steps, and the door, and the bus where her partner was supposedly resting.

She felt bad about ordering Kerry out. Even if she was right, and even if she knew her partner knew she was right, it put her guts in a knot remembering the imperfectly hidden hurt in Kerry's eyes when she left.

Stupid, really. Dar prowled the hallways, poking her head into the doors on either side. Most were empty—given that it was Sunday and getting late—and she suspected finding a responsible person who'd be willing to help her was going to be unlikely.

Also stupid. Really.

She paused before a barred window and stared out of it. Maybe Kerry was really pissed at her for what she'd done. She watched the shadows move past the glass. Her partner knew her well enough to give her ten minutes to chill, and then usually she'd be back around her, nudging and poking and putting her in a better mood.

She'd expected that this time. But an hour had passed and her partner had remained in exile, and Dar was starting to feel very unhappy about it.

"Shit." She turned and put the window behind her. "Grow the hell up, would you?"

She climbed up the steps toward the large inner doors and pushed them open, emerging into the trading floor that was now dark, silent and empty.

It smelled. She wrinkled her nose. Not of dirt and decay as the basement below had, when she'd worked with Mark to push the cable back up, but of wood and paper, oil and dust, with the scent of stale perspiration just at the edges of everything.

The room was vast, but seemed far less so with the strips and outlines of cable supports that criss-crossed over the endless series of kiosks and connected them with miles of wires.

Without the clutter, it would have been grand, reminding Dar just a bit of the Grand Central terminal she'd visited on her last trip to the city. But with all the machinery and trappings of modern technology it seemed more like a cyber junkyard.

Dar studied it, reflecting on how much her life had been influenced by the goings on here. Then she shook her head and turned, walking out and back down the stairs.

"Oh, Ms. Roberts?"

Dar paused and waited as a young man caught her up. "Yes?"

"Hi," he said. "Barry Marks. We met earlier?"

Dar turned and faced him. "Yes?"

"Listen," Marks looked both ways, and then back at her, "my boss just called me. "

"I don't care," Dar said. "I've had it up to here with everyone's bosses calling everyone's bosses trying to make people kiss their asses. I'm over it."

"Wait..."

"I don't care who your boss is, or who he called, or what he's threatening, or what he says some other jackass is threatening. I just don't care. Either the damn thing will be fixed tomorrow or it won't. Not a jack thing you can do about it."

Marks stuck his hands in his pockets. "Boy, you're a tough cookie. Okay. I just wanted to pass along a warning, that's all."

Dar rolled her eyes.

"The governor is on his way here." Marks added. "I guess he's spoken to Abercrombie." He gave her an apologetic look. "Sorry about that. Everyone's kind of losing their mind about tomorrow. Any idea what we're going to do?"

"Postpone the opening." Dar leaned against the wall.

"We can't do that."

"Better figure out how to do this the old fashioned way then." Dar indicated the doors to the big room. "I'm not going to tell you it's going to be all right, buddy. It's a clusterfuck. There are parts of this thing ripped up and I can't even find someone from here to go fix it."

"Well..."

"You know whose cousin does the wiring here?" Dar pressed him. "Maybe you can have him call me, since no matter what we do with the uplink it's not going to help with the pile of cable chewed up by rats in there."

"Rats!"

"Can your boss find whoever's cousin it is?" Dar persisted. "Because that would help a lot more than sending me some ridiculous warning."

Marks held his hand up. "I'll call him. He knows the guy who's in charge of the facilities here. Probably some friend of his. Want him to come see you?"

Dar turned and started walking. "Have him see Mark Polenti in the computer room. He knows what to do." She called back over her shoulder. "I've got a...something more important to take care of."

"Right." Marks shook his head and headed for a small office nearby. "Knew I should have just taken the train up to Niagara this morning. Screw this."

Dar heard the echo, and felt a certain sympathy with it. But she kept walking, down the hall and down the stairs to the street, ignoring the guards and the people walking down the side walk as she focused on the bus door.

It opened as she approached and she waved a hand in the direction of the driver as she climbed inside, glad when it closed behind her and she was sealed inside the quiet peace of the bus.

Very quiet. Dar found herself stepping cautiously as she went through the front part of the bus to the back, spotting Kerry immediately. She circled the chair, finding her partner fast asleep against one arm, her breathing slow and even.

So that was the reason she hadn't come back outside. Dar felt both relieved and a touch embarrassed. She went over to the storage compartment and removed a small lap blanket from it. She opened it up before she returned and settled it around Kerry's sleeping body.

She waited a moment to see if that would wake her. When it didn't, she knelt down and carefully loosened the laces on her partner's hiking boots, and easing them off her feet.

She set the boots down, then straightened up and went to the refrigerator removing a chocolate chug and leaning back against the counter to drink it.

It was very quiet. Even the sounds outside had fallen off, except for the beeping of cranes and the sound of heavy machinery in the distance. She could also hear a fading siren, but around the bus there wasn't much going on.

She felt her PDA go off, bringing a welcome distraction. She put the chug down and pulled the device out of her pocket, opening it and reviewing the messages. "Ah." She muttered softly, taking out the stylus and touching the top one.

Hello Dar. Good news and bad news. Bad news first. They've looked at all the existing optics and nothing we've got can be altered to work over MMF at that distance, even with some classified stuff they have here.

Well, that was bad news. Dar found herself shrugging, having expected the message. She had decided they were going to have to wait until the new cable got here.

So, now the good news. They have an experimental optic here they're putting together for the space station and they think maybe they could see if it could be adapted. My guys are working on building an enclosure for it, so if they hit pay dirt we'll be able to fit it in the chassis you guys have there. It's a pretty slim chance.

Dar blinked at the message. Pretty slim? It was a hell of a lot more of a chance than she'd considered possible.

So anyway, that's the news. We'll be burning the midnight oil — let you know if anything looks promising. Hope it's worth something by the time we're done.

Wow. Dar tapped the screen to respond.

We're burning the midnight oil here too, just in case. Slim chance or not, this is the only hope we have, so whatever you come up with will be better than what we've got now. Whatever the cost turns out to be for this — bill me for them. If you come up with a solution, name your price. DR.

She sent it, then folded the PDA cover down and slid the device back in her pocket. Could they do it? At least they were trying. Dar picked up her chug and drank it slowly, the cold, sweet beverage easing the ache in her throat.

What next? She glanced over to where Kerry was still sleeping soundly. With a sigh, she set her empty chug down in the garbage and retreated to the door of the bus, opening it and emerging outside quickly, shutting the door behind her.

No sense in waking Kerry up, after all. Better she get some rest. Dar was glad of the decision a moment later when her cell phone rang, making her jump a little. She glanced at the caller ID, and then opened it. "Hello, Alastair."

"Dar. Where are you?" Her boss sounded exasperated.

"At the Exchange. Outside," Dar replied. "What now?"

"Well, do me a favor lady, and take all those people you got down there and pile them in that bus and take off," Alastair said. "The governor is on his way down, and I just told him to kiss my ass."

Dar leaned back against the bus, finding a smile somewhere. "You did, huh? What happened?"

Alastair exhaled. "Jackass. Someone got wind of their little game with the test yesterday and says they're going to tell the press. So the bastard told me he was going to cut them off and tell them we screwed something up and now we're trying to fix it."

Dar blinked. "Fuck him."

"Pretty much what I said. So gather the troops, Dar. Put them on the bus and head back up here. We're out of this."

"Just like that?" Dar asked.

"Just like that. I told him he could tell the press whatever he wanted, but then again, so would I," Alastair said. "I've had it up to my eyeballs. I already told the board."

It suddenly occurred to her that she wouldn't want to cross Alastair, not in this mood. "You got it, boss. I'll go get the team and tell the driver to get ready to move. I don't want to be here when that jackass gets here and starts yelling at me."

"Damn right," Alastair said. "See you back here in a little bit."

Dar closed her phone, and exhaled. "Well." She tossed the phone up and caught it. "So much for that." She headed for the door, then halted, turned, and went back to the bus. She keyed the door open and trotted up inside, heading over to where Kerry was napping.

The blanket was now tucked around her, her fingers clasped lightly in it, and there was the faintest of smiles on her face.

Dar knelt, and put a hand on her shoulder. "Ker?"

The green eyes fluttered open at once, and the faint smile grew into a real one.

"How are you feeling?" Dar asked. "Sorry I was a bastard before."

Kerry drew in a breath, and then grimaced. "Ow." She muttered, sheepishly. "Don't apologize. I should go get this checked out. It's killing me." She extended her hand and clasped Dar's. "Thanks for the blanket." She added, "I figured you were the only one who could have done that and not wake me up."

"Well, we've got time to go do that now. Alastair just pulled us out. I wanted to wake you up before I got the rest of the crew in here rattling around. We're going back uptown."

Kerry blinked. "Really? What happened?"

"Long story. Tell you when I get back." Dar stood. "We could be heading home sooner than I thought." She stroked Kerry's head as she circled the chair. "Hold down the fort, okay?"

"Sure." Kerry eased to a sitting position as the door closed behind Dar. She wrapped the blanket around her shoulders and tried to find a comfortable position, wiggling her toes as she blinked the sleep out of her eyes. "It's over?" She looked over at the television screen that was showing scenes of the Pentagon. "Wow."

She felt a sense of relief. Her head fell back to rest against the leather surface and she imagined herself stepping off a plane into Miami's muggy heat. "Awesome."

DAR RESTED HER elbows on her knees glad she'd sent the bus on ahead to the office. The medical examination was taking longer than she'd expected it to, and she was starting to get nervous flutters in her guts.

Not that it was her guts being examined, but still. She was hoping Kerry's injury was nothing serious, but experience had taught her that the longer they poked, the more they generally found. It was the reason she avoided doctors when she could, and even though her better sense insisted that Kerry's ribs had to be looked at, her animal anxiety wished they'd just kept driving.

"Ms. Roberts?"

Dar lifted her head quickly, turning to find a nurse at her side. "Yes?"

"Could you come with me please? Your friend asked to see you."

Friend. Dar took a breath, and then she stood and waited for the nurse to move forward so she could follow her. There were places, she reasoned, where making the point about their relationship wouldn't have gotten a second's hesitation from her.

Here, in the waiting room of St. Vincent's hospital, surrounded by dozens and dozens of people who were sitting there, in crisis, waiting in vain and hoping that a loved one who had gone to work on 9/11 would come straggling in...this wasn't a place to make a personal point.

She followed the nurse down the hall and past a set of sliding doors. There were rooms on either side, with old wooden doors and wooden sills, and the desks were age worn Formica when they weren't buried under paperwork.

The nurse paused before one of the exam rooms and gave her a brief smile. "In there." She stood back so Dar could enter, and then left.

"Hey." Kerry was lying on an examining couch, halfway reclined.

She had her boots and her jumpsuit off, but was fully clothed otherwise.

"Hey." Dar glanced around, finding them alone in the room. She crossed over to her partner and studied her. "You okay?" She found the lack of blinking and beeping machines, needles, or other medical equipment encouraging, so she took Kerry's hand in hers and clasped it, feeling the chill under her fingers quickly warm.

"Yeah, I will be." Kerry looked more than a little chagrined. "I did crack a stupid rib on that damn tile. Dar, that's freaking embarrassing," she complained. "How am I supposed to explain to everyone that I hurt myself escaping from a bunch of rats while falling into a raised floor?"

"You want me to tell them you actually saved me from falling off a balcony or something?" Dar asked. "I'm cool with that. After all, you told everyone I saved you from a shark." She chafed Kerry's hand, seeing the unusual pallor of her skin. "Hurts?"

Kerry nodded briefly. "They wrapped me up, and they're giving me a pain prescription. Not much else they can do. The doctor said it was just a hairline fracture, and that I was lucky as hell." She drew in a cautious breath. "Pain's making me sick to my stomach though."

"Does that mean I get to take you back to the hotel and put you to bed?" Dar's eyes twinkled gravely. "Now that we're not on the hook anymore?"

"God, that sounds like heaven. It's so hard for me to wrap my head around the idea that we're just walking away from this. What about you?"

Dar shrugged. "You want to know the truth?"

"You want to go home." Kerry studied her face intently. "The guys want to go home. I heard them talking. They don't really like being here. The only thing that's been keeping them on the job is you."

"Me?" Dar looked honestly surprised.

"Oh, honey please." That brought a smile to Kerry's pale face. "We'd all walk over hot coals for you and you know it."

Dar's brow creased. "Do you seriously think I'd let you walk over coals?"

Kerry was prevented from answering by the return of the doctor. "Hey doc."

The doctor, a middle-aged man with curly gray hair and a kind face, bustled in with a clipboard and a folder. "Well, hello there again, young lady. I think we've about got you wrapped up here. This your friend?"

"Yes, it is." Kerry nodded. "Dr. Ames, this is Dar Roberts."

"Hi," Dar responded warily.

"Hello, there." The doctor gave her a smile. "Well, here's what I've got." He handed Dar a big envelope. "These are her X-rays for her doctor at home."

Dar took them. "Okay."

"Here's her prescription. It's pretty strong." The doctor handed over a smaller square of paper. "If you want my advice, don't let her sleep lying down. Find a recliner and use the arms for support until the bone starts healing."

"Okay." Dar repeated feeling slightly bewildered. "I'm sure we can do that."

"Good. Take care of her, she's a cutie." He patted Dar's shoulder and left the room, whistling softly under his breath.

Dar turned and looked at a bemused Kerry. "Does he think you're my lover, my kid, or my puppy?"

Kerry started laughing, then immediately regretted it. "Oohh." She held her side. "Honey, don't make me laugh, please. It hurts like hell." She moaned.

Dar set the envelope down, stuffed the prescription in her pocket, and carefully got her arm around Kerry's shoulder. "You ready to go be coddled unmercifully?" She could feel a chill under her touch, and put her other arm around her partner cradling her gently.

Kerry relaxed, and exhaled. "They gave me a muscle relaxant. I'm a little loopy. I think that's why the doctor was letting your brain do the work for me."

"No problem." Dar kissed her on the top of her head. "Let's go. We'll grab a taxi outside and be back at the hotel in no time. I'll call the hotel and have them buy a recliner while we're on the way over."

Kerry chuckled faintly. Then she swung her legs off the couch and got up, helped by Dar's firm grip. "Want to hear the good news?"

"Sure." Dar left her arm around Kerry as they made their way to the door.

"My blood pressure was on the low side of normal." Kerry didn't quite manage to keep the smug tone out of her voice. "Even after all the crap we've been through."

Kerry experienced total shock when the nurse had glanced up and patted her shoulder, releasing the cuff and taking the stethoscope from her ears. "Perfect," the woman announced. "I love to see nice, healthy women."

Amazing. Kerry had almost forgotten about her damn ribs in her delight. The injury was painful and annoying, but finite and her blood pressure wasn't. She was glad to hear the recent stress hadn't resulted in a reading that would guarantee to cause her far more anxiety.

"Now that's awesome." Dar agreed. "I'll take that news any damned day." She looked both ways as they exited from the room, and then eased out into traffic. "Probably a good thing they didn't take mine while I was waiting for you."

"Aw." Kerry was content to shelter in Dar's arm, as they dodged the quiet crowd in the waiting area on the way out. "Why were you so stressed? I think we both pretty much knew what they'd say." She glanced to either side as they reached the door.

"I hate hospitals." Dar muttered.

Kerry patted her stomach. "I know, hon." She caught the eye of a woman standing just outside the hospital entrance, her hands full with a stack of colored paper. The woman came forward and held out one of the sheaves.

"Oh." Kerry took it instinctively. She looked at it, seeing a round face with a fringe of dark hair looking back at her.

"This is my husband," the woman said. "Have you seen him? He went to work on Tuesday. I know he must be here somewhere. Please look at it. Have you seen him at all?"

Kerry felt Dar's body shift and she stopped walking, touching her partner on the arm as she bent her head to study the page seriously. "Dar, look. Did you remember seeing anyone like this?"

Thus called, Dar tilted her head and focused her eyes on the sheet. The man's face was ordinary and unremarkable. He had a golden skin tone, and in the picture he was smiling broadly at whoever was taking the picture.

Could have been anyone.

"Anything, Dar?"

Dar put her photographic memory to work, flicking through pictures of the last couple of days, above ground and below, going along streets, and standing on the steps of the Exchange, riding in the subways, walking around their hotel.

Down in Battery Park.

'I don't think I have," Kerry said finally, in a regretful tone. "Dar?"

"I didn't see him." Dar lifted her eyes and met the woman's squarely. "I'm sorry."

The woman wandered off without answering, going up to the steps to greet the next people to come out from the hospital with her colored paper, and her eternal hope.

"Jesus." Kerry murmured. "My god, Dar. These people have no freaking closure." She watched the woman plead. "Did you hear the news? I was listening while I was waiting for my X-ray. They think four thousand people are missing, and they've only found a hundred and eighty bodies."

'Yeah." Dar guided her to the curb, and turned to watch for a cab. "You don't have closure."

Kerry turned and looked up at her. Then she leaned into Dar's body. "Sorry."

"Don't be." Dar signaled a cab. "My father's waiting for us at the hotel. If ever I had to have it beaten home to me what a lucky son of a bitch I am, you just did it."

They got into the cab without further conversation. Kerry leaned against Dar's shoulder and watched the streets go by, feeling a sense of separation from the world around her.

She wished they were home already. She was tired of the crowded chaos of the city. She no longer wanted to help out, or deal with the problems, or face the impatient antagonism they'd been subjected to by pretty much everyone they tried to help.

She'd just had enough. She felt bad for all the people here, she felt bad for their customers who were in the affected area, and she felt bad for her country and about the future that had suddenly become very, very murky.

But she'd had enough. It was time to let someone else step up and take care of things, and respond to the government's demands. They had done their part. She had done her part, and had a cracked rib to show for it. "What time's our flight tomorrow?"

"I have Maria trying to change it for the morning," Dar said. "It's one something right now."

"Wish there was a flight tonight." Kerry mused. "I'd love to be home right now, on our comfy couch, petting Cheebles."

"Me too," Dar agreed. "I miss my milk dispenser."

Kerry snorted softly, trying to stifle a laugh. "You're so bizarre sometimes."

The cab pulled up in front of their hotel. Dar paid the fare, and they walked inside, not really surprised to find the rest of their team gathered in the bar. "Let's say hi." Kerry nudged her partner in that direction. "And I'd love a beer before I start taking those drugs."

Dar hesitated, and then she surrendered. They walked into the bar, crossing past the service area to the pit of chairs filled with their staff. "Hello, folks," Dar said.

"Hey!" Scuzzy waved. "How are you guys?"

"How's the ribs, boss?" Mark was seated next to Scuzzy, a frosted beer mug in one hand. "You look kinda washed out."

"I feel washed out." Kerry eased into a seat. "I have a cracked rib."

"Ow."

"Ooh." Scuzzy made a face. "Man that hurts, huh?"

Dar rested her hands on the back of the chair. "Someone please order Kerry a beer. I'm going to go arrange for her drugs."

"Hey. I've got a cracked rib. Not broken vocal cords." Kerry reminded her. "Scoot. I'll get you a Kahlua milkshake."

"Mm." Dar patted the back of the chair, and then headed off toward the concierge stand. The lobby was relatively empty, and she found the concierge ready and willing to help her. "I have a prescription." She produced it. "Can you get it filled for me?"

"Of course," the man said, immediately. "May I ask what it's for?"

Dar studied the paper. "Painkillers?" She handed it over. "My partner has a cracked rib."

"No problem." The man accepted the slip and briefly looked at it. "Do you have a preferred pharmacy? We've got one right around the corner, but it's local and might not take your insurance."

"Just get whatever's fastest." Dar waved her hand a little. "I don't care what it costs."

The concierge smiled at her wholeheartedly. "Now, there's a woman after my own tastes. Ma'am, just leave it with me. I'll have it brought to your room as soon as it's filled. You're in 1202, correct?"

"Correct," Dar said. "And while you're at it, I could use a few other things up there. Got a pad?"

The man whipped a pen and paper out faster than her eye could follow.

Chapter Fifteen

"SO, THAT'S WHAT happened." Kerry cradled the mug of beer in both hands. The twinge of holding it, she decided was worth its cold comfort. "I can't figure out what the rats were doing there."

"I got that cleared up." Scuzzy held her hand up in the air as though she were in class. "I was talking to these guys here, in the hotel? They got a place down near where the towers were. They said it was all full of rats when they went down there today. They came up from the sewer."

"From the sewer?" Mark cocked his head. "For what?"

"They said, from all that stuff that happened down near the towers." Shaun spoke up. "I heard the guys at the Exchange talking. They're in all the basements."

"Ugh." Kerry grimaced.

"I am glad we are not going back there." Kannan spoke up. He was seated in one of the big chairs, his slim form almost swallowed by it. He had a steaming cup in his hands that he'd been sipping from. "That place disturbed me very much."

"Me too," Kerry said. "I think I have too much of an imagination."

"The big cheese has big brass ones to pull us out of here," Mark said. "Those guys down there couldn't believe we were just leaving. They thought we were bullshitting."

"No bullshit," Kerry shook her head. "They finally pushed Alastair too hard."

"Someone call my name?" Alastair entered the bar and went over to the service area taking a seat on a barstool. "Ladies and Gentlemen, you have my greatest admiration and gratitude for the work you've done here."

"Include yourself in that, sir." Kerry told him. "Teamwork gets you nowhere without good leadership to go along with it."

Alastair looked exhausted, but that made him smile. He lifted his newly poured beer in their direction. "To being homeward bound."

"Yeah!" Mark lifted his mug. "Café con leche at the airport's on me!"

Dar returned and perched on the arm of Kerry's chair, picking up the cup on the table in front of her and taking a sip from it. She let her free hand rest on Kerry's shoulder, and listened to the chatter of the group around her.

It felt good. They had done their best.

Now they could move on.

KERRY PAUSED AND leaned her hands on the back of the room's chair, staring at the bed. "Dar."

"Yes."

"What in the hell is that?"

Dar wandered over and stood next to her.

"If you say it's the bed, I'll bite your arm." Kerry warned her. "What did they do to that bed?"

Dar studied the piece of furniture in question. The top of the bed was literally covered in pillows, some stacked against the back, some arranged long ways down the mattress, a few dotted around apparently as decoration. "Well," she cleared her throat a little, "they said they didn't have time, or the space to get a recliner."

Kerry turned her head slowly to look at her partner. "Did you actually ask them to?"

"Yes, I did." Dar responded in perfect seriousness. "So anyway, this was what they came up with. G'wan up there and see how good they did."

"Let me get undressed first." Kerry demurred. "Because I have a feeling once I sit down in that nest of feathers, I'm not getting up again." She went over to her bag. "Did you say the drugs got here?" She unfastened her pants and let them drop off her.

"They did." Dar opened a bag lying on the dresser and removed a bottle, examining the label. "Ready for some?"

"Oh yes." Kerry exhaled, wincing as the throbbing got a little sharper. "I'm glad we spent some time with the team, but I'm paying for it." She removed her sleep shirt from her bag and draped it over the chair. "Be right back."

"Yell if you need help." Dar patted her on the hip as she eased by. "I have some goodies here too."

"Thank you, Doctor Dar." Kerry had to smile, as she made her way into the bathroom. "Have we gotten paged for anything?" She called back. "It seems too damn quiet."

"Jinxer."

"Well, it does." Kerry carefully washed her face trying not to move around too much. The water was startlingly cold and she let it run a moment, turning on the warm water until it was bearable. In Miami, she never had that problem. The cold faucet produced, at best, lukewarm water in all but the coldest weather.

She brushed her teeth and rinsed, then studied her reflection in the mirror. "Ugh." She put her toothbrush back into its glass and returned to the room, finding Dar already in her T-shirt, standing there with Kerry's shirt bundled up in her hands.

It felt amazing to know she could just change, despite the relatively early hour, and then go sit quietly for as long as she wanted. "Thank you." Kerry unbuttoned her shirt and let Dar strip it off her. She stood as Dar got her into her sleep garb with careful, gentle hands. "You make me almost forget how much of an idiot I feel like getting hurt the way I did."

"I popped my knee falling in a sinkhole, got smacked with a baseball bat, and got bitten by a fish. You want to have a dumbass injury competition with me?" Dar inquired. "Go sit on the bed, Kerrison."

"Yes, ma'am." Kerry went over and sat down on the soft surface, carefully squirming into the nest of pillows until she was leaning against the ones in the back with her elbows tucked into the ones down the middle. "Ah."

"Comfortable?" Dar was busy at the tray.

"Yeah. Matter of fact." Kerry crossed her ankles. "I am." The support took the pressure off her ribs, and the pain eased. She leaned back and relaxed, letting out a long sigh of relief. "So no calls?"

"No." Dar brought a tray over. "I have our phones forwarded."

"Oh. I see." Kerry tilted her head so she could see what was in her immediate future in terms of edible items. "Wow. What is that..."

"This is lobster." Dar regarded the tray. "Cut up in nice bite size chunks with appropriate things to dunk them in."

"Mm."

"These are corn fritters." Dar went on. "These are green beans because I knew you'd yell at me otherwise, and this is a chocolate fondue."

"Wow."

"With cheesecake to dip in it along with strawberries."

Kerry had been pretty sure she'd entered the hotel room convinced she wasn't hungry, but at the moment, her body wasn't buying that. "This is for both of us right?"

"Yes. Hang on. Let me get the bubbly."

Kerry folded her hands over her stomach as Dar got up to retrieve a bottle and two glasses. Despite the long day, and her aches and pains, the solicitous attention could only make her smile and she did, tilting her head a little again to take a sip from the glass her partner offered.

A little sweet, a little fizzy, a little spicy. The champagne tickled her tongue and she settled back to enjoy as Dar squiggled herself into a comfortable position on the bed and commenced delivering lobster to her.

Perfectly cooked, chilled just right. Kerry licked her lips. "I think I know why emperors had servants now." She accepted another bite of lobster, neatly dipped in butter sauce and a touch of lemon. "This is lovely."

Dar chuckled softly, taking a piece for herself before she offered Kerry a bite of corn fritter. "I just wanted something simple I could handle with my fingers. I'm too tired to mess with silverware. Ready for your pills?"

"Just my luck." Kerry sighed happily. "You know what?"

"What?" Dar delivered a sip of champagne to her.

"Save the pills for tomorrow when we fly." Kerry leaned on her pillows and accepted a mouthful of lobster. "Right now, I feel great." She gazed lovingly at the angular face next to her. "Thanks."

Dar kissed her. "Anytime."

Kerry took another sip of bubbly to clear her mouth. "Dar, how do you really feel about us walking out like that? Do you regret it?"

Dar sipped her champagne, set the glass down, then picked up a piece of corn fritter and bit into it. She chewed slowly, thinking about the question. Then she handed over the other half of her fritter to Kerry's waiting lips. "Yes."

Kerry chewed, and swallowed. "Yes, you regret us backing out?"

Dar nodded. "I hate quitting. You know that. I don't blame Alastair for a minute for what he did, but yeah. I do regret it, a little. But on the other hand..." She offered Kerry more lobster. "Now if it doesn't work we don't have to stand there looking like jackasses either."

"You think that's why he did it?"

"Maybe. I might have. He knew what the deal was. Might have been a calculated decision. This is going to cause a huge wave, but from that standpoint, better than public failure."

"Hm." Kerry cautiously reached for her glass of champagne and took a sip. "That actually makes sense. You really don't think we'd have been able to do it?"

"No. Ultimately we'd have gotten everything in place, but there's no way they could have worked the optics. We'd have been standing there when that bell rang with a lot of egg on our faces. That's why I didn't say anything to Alastair when he told me. He's right."

"That really sucks though." Kerry selected a green bean and ate it. "It sucks that they put us in that position." She paused. "Or did we put ourselves in it?"

Dar extended her legs along the bed and stretched out on her side. She lifted her glass in Kerry's direction in a wry toast.

"Mm." Kerry took a sip of her champagne and set the glass back down. "Can you reach me a bit?"

"Sure." Dar produced a chunk of lobster. "So tomorrow, let's work on wrapping up things here, and get a task list we can throw at ops in Miami. See what we can do for our customers aside from letting them camp at our doorstep."

"Sounds good." Kerry chewed and swallowed. "I can start looking at the capacity we have here. We can find out what we need to do if we need to start mounting SAT rigs on people's roofs."

"With solar panels." Dar suggested. "Maybe we can have the gang down at integration start putting together mobile kits."

Kerry settled back and licked her lips. The pain in her side had subsided to a mild throbbing, and she was perfectly content to lay here nestled in her pillows, enjoying the chance to just sit and talk to her partner.

She hoped the rest of the team was having as quiet an evening as she was.

ALASTAIR SAT DOWN in a leather chair in the empty floor lounge, glad the rest of the team was off resting—he hoped—or enjoying some time off. He glanced over at the door where a secret service agent was standing, his attention fixed on the hallway rather than inside the room.

He thought, perhaps, he should be more nervous than he was, having been called out of his room for this meeting on just a few minutes notice. But he'd discovered he was just too tired, and too over it to be anything more than mildly thirsty.

Fortunately, the lounge was equipped for that. He got up and went to the sidebar holding a self-service beverage station, selecting a teabag and setting it into a china cup. He poured water over it and let it steep, even when noise behind him indicated he was no longer alone in the lounge.

"Hello, Alastair," a voice sounded behind him.

"Hello, Dick." He added a touch of cream and a cube of sugar, stirred, then took the cup and returned to his seat. "If you're here to yell or threaten me, give it up." He sat down, and regarded the man standing across from him. "I'm not in the mood."

The vice president took his hands from his pockets and sat down. "Won't waste my breath" he responded. "We've known each other too long. When you tell someone to fuck off, it's usually for a reason."

Alastair took a sip of his tea. "So what are you here for then?"

"I want to understand. What the fuck you think you're doing, putting everything you worked half your life for at risk here. This is big, Alastair. There's no going back from this. Either you're with us, or you're not, and those that are not, might as well move to Japan."

Alastair regarded him benignly. "Y'know, funny thing. Tried sushi for the first time just the other day, matter of fact, I liked it. Why don't you tell me something? Why are you letting all these jackasses scrambling around like idiots treat people like me like a hired hand? I've spent the last week being smacked around by your lackeys and threatened with everything from jail time to being taken into a back room somewhere all because we're here doing you a fucking favor."

The vice president pursed his lips. He was dressed in a pair of dark slacks and a dark windbreaker, in an apparent pitch to avoid notice. "People are tense. You can't blame them."

"I sure as hell can blame them." Alastair shot back. "Just because every jack one of you got caught bare assed is no reason to take it out on me."

"Alastair," the man shook his head, "you're not doing yourself any favors."

"I'm not looking for any favors."

The vice president exhaled. "You always were such a hard ass," he complained. "Al, this needs to happen."

Alastair shrugged. "Maybe you should have thought of that before you told everyone it was working yesterday."

"Figured I was safe. They told me you were handling it. We have to show how little this affected us. You know that."

"I know that," Alastair said. "So, back to my original question. "

"Oh for Pete's sake," the man said. "Give me a break, Al. Every single department in the whole government was thrown into a high speed reactive mode and told to not let anything stand in their way. This was no joke. This was not some half assed tornado we were responding to. People died."

"Some of mine did," Alastair said quietly. "I lost a good friend down there."

The vice president sighed. "So you won't do this?"

Alastair took the time to sip his tea again. "No. We've done what we could."

"You know you'll get blamed for this. You'll have to stand there and explain why you walked out on helping your country in this time of disaster." There was a perceptible touch of irony in the words. "You really want to do that? Do the people you work for really want that spotlight? You've got a lot of contracts with us, Al. More than most companies."

"The board's been advised." Alastair shrugged. "They agree with my decision."

His visitor looked surprised. "Would your stockholders?"

Alastair shrugged.

"I don't get it."

"Maybe I just don't like being pushed around." Alastair gazed steadily at him. "I'll be there. I'll be glad to stand by my decisions, and my people. If that frustrates you, Dick, sorry. Nothing personal. For what it's worth, I think we did a damn fine job for you through this."

The vice president nodded slowly, shrewd eyes watching Alastair's face with sharp intent. "Nothing personal, Al. I know our wives are close. But we'll bury you for this." He got up and waved, then headed for the door, zipping his jacket up as he gave the secret service man a nod. "Let's go."

Alastair lifted a hand and waved back. Then he let his hand fall to his knee and took a sip of his tea.

After a long moment's silence, the doorway filled again, and he looked up to see Dar's tall form leaning against the sill, arms crossed, pale blue eyes watching him with intent question.

"Tea?" Alastair raised his cup in her direction.

Dar crossed the room and went to the credenza, opening the refrigerator and removing a chocolate milk. She brought it back over and dropped into a chair next to him, extending her long legs and bare feet across the carpet before crossing her ankles. "We in trouble?"

"We?"

Dar opened the milk and drank from it, swirling the liquid around in the container as she waited him out in silence, one eyebrow fully hiked.

"Nah, we'll be fine."

Dar's other eyebrow hiked to join its mate.

Alastair toasted her wryly with his tea, his face creasing into a rueful smile.

DAR WASN'T SURE what made her wake up. She lifted her head off the pillow, looking around in the darkened room. The clock on the bedside table blinked 4:00 a.m. She cocked her head to listen to see if some sound had broken through her dreams.

Nothing. It was quiet. Some soft mechanical sounds were evident— the cycling of the air conditioning and the working of the elevator down the hall—but nothing else seemed to be stirring.

Dar turned her attention to her sleeping partner. Kerry was propped up half sitting against her nest of pillows with the blanket tucked around her, and her face relaxed in slumber.

Seemed like a good idea. She started to compose herself to go back to sleep when the dryness of her mouth annoyed her enough to spur her to get up and do something about it.

With a soundless sigh, she eased out of the bed, stood up, and then moved quietly across the room to the credenza. She sorted through the choices there, not finding anything to her liking.

Being a milk fanatic sort of sucked when you didn't have ready refrigeration. She picked the room key up off the counter and palmed it along with her PDA, giving herself a cursory glance at her reflection in the mirror, before making her way to the door, opening it and slipping outside.

The hallway was, not unexpectedly, empty. She crossed it and went down to the lounge where the big screen television was playing mutely to the audience of couches and chairs.

They'd left the sports on, but at this time of day it was soccer. Dar glanced idly at the screen as she headed for the service fridge, opening it and retrieving a bottle. She took it back over and sat down on the couch, the leather unexpectedly cold against the backs of her thighs. "Urg."

She opened the milk and set it down and turned her attention to the PDA that had displayed the stuttering red light indicating she had messages. She flipped the top open, wondering if it was her mother sending one of her infrequent notes.

Her eyes scanned it, and then scanned it again, more slowly. Then she took a deep breath, and released it. "Son of a bitch."

Hey Dar! Just a got a second to drop you a note before I head for the airport and a flight out there! Tried calling, your phone went to voice mail. But they did it! Those boys worked until their eyes were bleeding, and got that thing working. Couldn't believe it! Still can't! Got some special refractive diamond mirrors in the damn things, but I saw it myself, saw it link up at over a mile!

Shit. Dar knew a moment of total dismay.

Figure to land there around 8, realize it's cutting it close as hell, but it's the best they could do for a flight. Anyway, see you then, and I can't wait to see this thing work!

Dar set the PDA down on her leg and rested her elbow on the arm of the couch, leaning her head against her hand. Then she looked up, and tapped her fingers against her lips, staring blankly at the silent screen.

There had been very few moments in her career when she'd been caught in so complete a quandary as she was now, faced with a situation she hadn't really believed was going to happen. Of course, she could simply do nothing.

Let it all be for nothing. But she knew she should have called when Alastair pulled them out and told them to stop working on it and she hadn't. Hadn't even remembered, focused as she had been on Kerry's injury and taking care of her.

On a human level, she knew that was the right thing. Even if she told the men that, they'd agree. Family did come first and Kerry was her family.

Didn't make it any easier to take though. Dar rubbed her eyes, and exhaled. "Shit." She opened the PDA and tapped the reply key, pausing with the stylus held between her fingers as she tried to compose an answer.

"Couldn't sleep, boss?"

Dar's head jerked up and she looked at the door as Mark entered. He was dressed in shorts and a T-shirt, and he'd obviously also been sleeping. "Got thirsty." She held up her milk. "What about you?"

"Ops woke me up." Mark trudged over to the counter and took out a can of Coke returning to the seating area and dropping into a chair with it. "Freaking accounting jobs didn't run again. I hate those damned scripts."

Dar gave him a wry look. "Want me to rewrite them?"

He paused in mid sip. "Those are yours?" he asked, his eyes widening.

Dar let him wait for it, and then she smiled. "Nah. But if you want I'll redo them anyway."

Mark relaxed. "Man, you had me. I should have figured they weren't. They suck." He took a swallow of his soda. "They crap out at least once a week and we have to restart them. This time they tanked Duk's reporting and he bitched out ops."

"Reporting shit definitely rolls downhill." Dar commiserated. "Speaking of which," she held up her PDA, "c'mere."

Puzzled, Mark got up and edged over joining her on the couch. "What?"

Dar opened the message and showed it to him, watching his face for a reaction. His eyes widened again and his body shifted, as he turned to look back at her.

"Are you kidding me? Is this guy for real?"

Dar sighed. "Apparently he is." She leaned back. "So now this guy's on the way here, ready to save the world and he's going to run right into a pissing match he had no part of."

"Wow."

"Yeah, wow." Dar closed the PDA. "Guess I'll wait until he lands then call him."

"Ouch." Mark murmured. "That's gonna suck." He glanced at his boss. "You didn't think they'd do it."

"I didn't think they'd do it," Dar confirmed, nodding. "Not only that, I didn't bother to tell them to stop trying once we did." She sighed again. "So I suck twice."

"You were kinda busy. I know if it had been my wife who'd broken a rib I wouldn't have thought a half second about work crap. So how's Kerry feeling, anyway?"

"Right now, hopefully she's not feeling anything since she was asleep when I came out here," Dar said. "Probably a good thing, since I know she'd be as freaked as I am about this note."

Mark remained silent sipping his soda. Then he cleared his throat a little and watched his boss out of the corner of his eye. "We could go do it, if you want."

Dar looked at him.

He shrugged.

"Alastair pulled us out. I respect that decision."

"Yeah," Mark agreed. "But we can do it. I know he had heartburn with the governor and all that stuff, but man, if those guys went to the wall for us, it sucks if we can't get it done. And it's really gonna suck for him tomorrow when that bell goes off and nothing happens."

"He knows that."

Mark shrugged again. "He's pretty cool. He's been all right to have with us here. I wasn't sure about it at first, but he's a good guy." He considered. "So we could make his morning, if you catch my drift."

Dar thought about that. It put the question into a different light than she'd been looking at, and she felt herself becoming attracted to the idea. "Alastair is good people," she finally said, in a quiet tone.

"He really likes you. He was talking to me and your pop yesterday and he was telling your pop how lucky he was to have a kid like you."

Dar blushed mildly. "I'm sure my father loved hearing that."

Mark laughed. "Yeah he did. He's a great guy."

"My father?"

"Yeah."

Dar took a sip of her milk. "We're surrounded by good people. You know that?" She mused, and then fell silent for a long moment. "You want to go do this?"

"Yeah," Mark said, without hesitation.

They both half turned at a sound at the door to find Andrew entering. He was dressed for the outside, unlike the two of them, and he slid the hood down on his hoodie as he crossed the carpeted floor. "Lo, there. You people never heard of sleeping?"

"Hi, Dad." Dar watched as he went to the refrigerator, retrieved a milk, then came over and sat down across from them. She lifted her own milk and toasted him with it. "Mark and I were just going to grab our tools and go fix the damn cables. Wanna come?"

Andrew paused in mid sip and lowered the milk. "Excuse me?"

Dar stretched her bare legs out and crossed her ankles. "Our vendor and his friends came through. They duct taped something together that's going to work."

Her father blinked. "I thought you all said you weren't doing this no more?"

"Me too," Dar acknowledged. "But they did it, and I don't want to waste that. Those guys wore their asses to the bone for us."

Andrew studied his daughter's profile—despite the difference of age and gender—very much like his own. "So you all going to go do this thing, no matter what that flannel feller says?"

"Mmhm."

"What about all them gov'mint people? They were some pissed off at you all."

"I don't care." Dar was now at peace with her decision. "These people have been shoving us around since we got here. Maybe they have a good reason, maybe they don't, but I'm just going to take my team, and go do what we do, and at the end of it someone else can decide if it was the right or wrong choice."

Her father produced a wry grin. "Paladar, do you know ah once said something just like that. Turned out all right, I suppose, so ah will surely be going along with you to do this crazy thing."

"Thanks, Dad." Dar smiled at him "Sorry to make your retirement so contentious."

Andrew studied her and then burst into laughter, genuine and real, a happy sound the echoed off the walls of the lounge.

"Well, I'm gonna go wake the troops up." Mark got out of his seat, taking his coke can over and disposing of it. "Meet you back here, boss?"

"I'm going too." Dar got up. "Let me let Kerry in on what's going on and see if I can talk her in to staying here."

Andrew snorted. Mark shook his head. "Good luck with that, boss." He escaped out the door ahead of Dar's reach.

Dar tossed her milk chug and tucked her PDA in her pocket. "Don't tell Alastair if you happen to see him, Dad." She paused at the doorway. "He's setting himself up to take a fall for us, and damned if we're going to let him."

Andrew smiled at her. "G'wan, rugrat." He stretched his legs out. "Ah couldn't sleep fer nothing no how. Too noisy in this here place."

Dar waved briefly. She ducked out of the room and crossed the corridor, spotting Mark down the hall knocking on a door. She keyed her own open, and slipped inside, closing the door behind her and walking over to the bed.

Kerry was still sleeping. Her breathing was slow and deep, and Dar lowered herself to perch carefully on the edge of the mattress, reluctant to disturb her. She knew in the long run that it would be better for her partner to stay here, comfortably resting.

However. Dar reached over and took Kerry's hand, squeezing it gently. "Ker?"

After a moment, Kerry's fair lashes fluttered open, and her fingers returned the pressure. She blinked a few times, and then focused on Dar, taking in the darkness of the room with some alarm. "What's wrong?"

"Nothing." Dar leaned over and let her head rest against Kerry's thighs. "But something unexpected happened."

Kerry blinked a few more times, clearing the sleep from her eyes. "Like what? Are you okay? Did something happen to one of the staff?"

"No." Dar squeezed her fingers gently. "Those guys who were trying to help us? They did it."

"Huh?" Kerry's brows creased. "What guys?"

"Our network vendor."

Kerry was momentarily silent, and then her eyebrows lifted sharply. "They did it? They came up with something that works?"

"That's what they say." Dar nodded. "So they're on their way here."

"B..." Kerry started to sit up then bit off a curse, her eyes going wide. "Oh shit."

"Easy." Dar got up and reversed her position, putting her arm around Kerry's shoulders and supporting her until she could get upright again. "Forgot about that, didn't you?"

"Ooof. Yes." Kerry recovered her breath. "Stiffened up I guess. So...but Dar, why are they coming here? We didn't do the runs. They're going to do that for no reason." She paused, and then looked up at her partner, seeing the grave look in the pale eyes. "Uh oh."

"I told Mark about it. He wants to go for it. He's waking the guys up." She put her hand against Kerry's cheek. "You do not have to get out of this bed. I just wanted you to know what's going on."

There was a curious mixture of emotions on Kerry's face. "That's not fair letting you guys do all the work. I don't want to just sit here wondering what's going on."

"Honey." Dar stroked her cheek. "Please don't be an idiot."

"I'm not." Kerry frowned. "Give me those drugs. Let's see if they do anything useful."

"Ker."

"Don't Ker me. I've been through this whole thing with you. Don't ask me to sit out now." She took a cautious breath. "At least I can just go and be with you. I won't pick anything up."

"You're going to make it impossible for me to concentrate." Dar objected. "C'mon, Kerry. This isn't anything to joke about. You could get really hurt."

"Don't give me that." Kerry reached up and took hold of Dar's jaw. "Please don't even try that after what I've seen you go through in some of the crap we get into."

Dar sighed. "Now we're back into that if I'm an idiot realm again, huh?"

"Dar."

"Kerry, we're going to be crawling on the floor splicing cable. Is that something you really want to be a part of?" Dar asked, practically. "Tell you what."

"You're right." Kerry interrupted her. "I don't want to be on the floor splicing cable."

"Okay." Dar regrouped. "Well then..."

"I want to be with you." Kerry cut her off again. "Can I just go and watch?"

Dar sighed again.

"Besides, you never know. You may need someone to make a phone call, or type a message, or call a relative who happens to be in Congress." Kerry negotiated skillfully. "Besides, now that you woke me up, there's no damn way I can get back to sleep again."

Having known beforehand the argument was going to be moot, Dar was relatively satisfied with the compromise. "Okay." She kissed Kerry's shoulder. "Can't blame me for trying."

"I don't." Kerry responded with a smile. "Dar, I'm glad."

Dar rested her cheek against Kerry's arm. "Glad? That we're doing this?"

"That we're not just walking away. Even if it was for the very best of reasons." She patted Dar's cheek, and then kissed her on the nose. "Thanks for waking me up."

Dar gave in, nuzzling her and exhaling and enjoying a last moment of peace before the craziness started up again. "I'm glad too. Which makes us all nuts."

"Cashews."

"Gesundheit."

KERRY CLIMBED UP the steps to the bus, its engine idling in the quiet of early morning. She paused inside, spotting a familiar figure behind the wheel. "Hi Dad. You driving?"

"Yeap," Andrew said. "No sense getting that feller up out of his bunk. I know where that place is right well by now." He pushed a button, jerking a little as the windshield wipers turned on. "Whoops."

"Have you ever driven a bus before?" Kerry asked.

"Naw." Andrew pushed another button, resulting in the bus's hazard lights coming on with an orange blare. "Drove me a tank a few times though. Can't be that different."

Kerry studied him. Then she walked over and gave him a kiss on the cheek, straightening carefully and retreating to the midsection of the bus before he started experimenting with anything else. Kannan and Shaun were already there, the two of them dressed in dark jeans and navy blue hoodies with equipment belts buckled over the top of them filled to the brim with nerdish jewelry.

"Hello, ma'am." Kannan looked up from stuffing cable ties in a pocket. "How are you feeling?"

"Not too bad, really." Kerry went over to the far side of the bus and opened the door to the small office in the back. Her laptop was already inside and set up. She walked around behind it to find a handful of chocolate kisses on the keyboard, along with two bottles of green tea and her bottle of drugs resting nearby. "Aw."

"Something wrong, ma'am?" Shaun called in.

"Not a thing." Kerry sat down slowly in the chair, testing her rib's reaction to the motion. The chair had nice, padded arms just like her bed cushions had, and she rested her elbows on them in relative comfort. "This'll work."

The door opened again, and she heard Dar's voice trickle back into her little haven. With that as a reminder, she unwrapped one of the kisses and put it in her mouth, humming softly under her breath as she booted up the laptop and waited for her login screen.

On the desk she also had a radio, and her PDA, and she grabbed for both as the bus lurched unexpectedly into motion. "Whoa."

"Everyone hang on," Dar said. "Dad's driving."

"Is that a bad thing?" Mark's voice cut in.

"Let's put it this way," Dar said. "If my mother were here, she'd be calling in an airstrike on the bus to stop us from getting hurt.

Kerry pinched the bridge of her nose and tried not to laugh. She made a note to relate the conversation to Ceci when she saw her, as she knew her mother-in-law would find it worth a chuckle knowing well her husband's method of driving.

Such as it was. "Glad you didn't inherit that part, Paladar." Kerry remarked in a voice loud enough for her to hear.

"So's my mother," Dar responded. "She threw a party when I got my driver's license."

"Wow," Mark said. "All righty then. Everyone got all their gear? Shaun, you concentrate on that Ethernet rat's nest and I'll help Kannan finish the fiber uplink."

"What about the stuff on this end?" Shaun asked. "Those guys weren't finished running the cable, were they?"

"First thing's first, since we're done on this end with the connectivity," Mark said. "That rat's nest'll take us longer than our end will."

"Not only that, the later it gets on that end the more people we have to contend with." Dar said. "I want to get in and get out and then we can deal with the rest of it."

"What if they just quit and left it there?" Shaun asked. "Under the ground in that tunnel?"

Kerry wondered the same thing herself. She had no idea if the workers had been told to stop what they were doing, or if, like their vendor, they'd just kept working in ignorance.

"We'll deal with that when it comes to it," Dar answered, her voice coming closer to Kerry's little den. "I don't want to split up at this point. It's dark and we don't know what we're going to run into." She appeared in the doorway, studying Kerry intently. "You okay?"

"I'm fine." Kerry held up a kiss. "Thank you Dr. Dar."

Dar grinned unexpectedly. Then she shrugged and turned back to the rest of the team, presenting Kerry with an attractive view of her bare shoulders emerging from her tank top as she lounged in the doorway, resting a hand on either side of it.

The bus lurched into motion again, rocking back and forth alarmingly as its tires apparently climbed up onto the sidewalk as Andrew got them underway. "Dar, do we have insurance on this bus?"

"Not my area." Dar glanced over her shoulder. "Should I rig seatbelts in there?"

Kerry settled back in her padded chair for the ride, the motion making her a little seasick when she looked down at her keyboard. She rested her elbows on the chair arms and looked past Dar, seeing the first hint of gray tingeing the windows of the bus.

No sense in looking at the laptop anyway. There was either too much or too little for her to do, especially at this hour of the morning, so she abandoned any pretense of work and simply relaxed as best as she was able for the ride.

A blaring horn and a sudden lurch of the bus made her close her eyes for good measure; glad she wasn't up in the front.

Chapter Sixteen

DAR SWUNG THE door open and flipped the lights on, not surprised to find no one else in the area as she stood aside to let her team in. "Where was that pile of cabling?"

"There." Kerry walked over and tapped the toe of her hiking boot against a square. "I won't forget that any time soon."

"Got it." Mark grabbed a tile puller and thumped to his knees on the floor. "Lemme get this up. You get ready to start clipping, Shaun."

"Watch out for the rats." Kerry said, just as Mark pulled the tile up.

He froze, and then he peered cautiously into the opening he'd just made. "Thanks boss."

Kerry backed away from the space, taking up a perch on the desk. Dar had circled it, and was kneeling down next to Kannan, plugging the configuration cable from her laptop into the router resting on the floor.

Mark carefully shone his flashlight into the opening, and then pulled his kit over and settled on the floor. "C'mon, Shaun. No critters." He removed a set of cutters, an Ethernet crimper, and a handful of ends and mounded them on the floor near his knee, studying the mess to see where to start.

Shaun sat down on the other side of the open tile and removed his own tools.

"Who the hell prepped this router?" Dar asked.

"Uh oh." Mark eyed her. "Why?"

"It's the wrong damned image. Would have truly sucked if they showed up here and we didn't have the right code to support an optics module, wouldn't it?"

Mark made a face, but he kept his mouth shut, his eyes focused on the task at hand.

Dar sighed "Kerry...would you..."

"Mind using the bus's satellite hook up to download you the right image? Of course not, hon." Kerry gazed fondly at Dar. "Which one do you need?"

Dar handed her a slip of paper. Kerry took it and headed for the door, glad she had a task to take care of. Sitting there watching everyone work, while it fulfilled her promise to Dar, wasn't really to her liking.

She walked down the darkened corridor past the closed doors in the nearly silent building. As she came close to the door though, she could see an outline of gray light, and hear the sounds of the city waking up around them.

Not much time. She eased out the door, surprising the guard standing there. "Sorry." She gave him a brief smile. "Need something from the bus."

The man nodded. "All right, Ms. Stuart. But I have to tell you, my boss isn't going to be happy you people are in there. I know you got those passes and all, but no one's supposed to be near this building at this hour. Got a lot of important people showing up soon."

Kerry didn't even feel annoyed. "I understand." She patted his arm. "We'll try to do what we need to do and get out of here, before we can get ourselves and you in any trouble." She walked down the steps and crossed over to where the bus was parked, its door already open.

She entered and grimaced a little as she felt a jolt in her side. "Hi Dad."

"Hey kumquat." Andrew appeared from the back of the bus. "You all doing all right?"

"Yeah, just getting something for Dar." Kerry made her way to the small office and sat down behind the desk, carefully leaning forward and trying not to breathe deeply. She put the piece of paper on the desk, and logged in to her laptop waiting for it to give her desktop image.

"Had some fellers come by here." Andrew had followed her inside. "Think they were them secret service type people."

Kerry kept her arm on her injured side tucked against her side, and typed one handed on the keyboard. "What did they want?"

"Ah do not know that. But they were asking a lot of questions and ah do think they will be back here."

"What did you tell them?" Kerry pecked out a website, waiting for the slow satellite link to return the page to her. Then she logged into their image repository and slowly typed Dar's request into the search box.

"Told them ah was just a tour bus from Japan."

Kerry stopped typing, and looked up over the laptop's screen at Andrew. His scarred face tensed into a grin, which she returned. "You did not."

"Naw. Just told him you all were doing some work for the gov'mint in there. That's all." Andrew relented. "You all want some water or something?"

"Do we have any coffee?" Kerry clicked on the result of the search, and watched it start downloading. She fished in her pocket for a thumb drive, and plugged it into the side of her laptop. "My drugs are making me a little sleepy."

"Ah think we might." Andrew moved away, rattling around in the kitchen area of the bus and leaving Kerry to watch her creeping progress bar.

While she was waiting, Kerry clicked over to her mail program that was sorting itself out in the background. She scanned the new items relieved that nothing seemed really urgent, and her cleaning of the box on Friday hadn't resulted in a cascade of new mail over the weekend.

In fact...She clicked on one, a rare personal note from her sister.

Hey sis.

Mom said you were right in the thick of everything as usual. I hope you're safe, and Dar's okay. I thought it would be better to send you an email because I didn't want to call and interrupt you. I have some good news that I wanted to share though.

Kerry perked up. Good news? "Damn. It's been so long since I've gotten good news in my email I'm not sure what to do."

Brian proposed.

"Holy molasses!" Kerry blurted, straightening right up and then regretting it. "Ow!"

Andrew ambled in at a deceptively high rate of speed given his bulk. "What's the matter, Kerry?" he asked, his eyes flicking over her in concern. "You doin' all right?" He put the cup of coffee he was holding down and rested his big hands on the desk.

"Oof." Kerry tried to catch her breath, closing her eyes as the stars faded. "Wow." She exhaled. "Who'd have thought a little crack would hurt this much." She eased her eyelids open, to find Andrew looking at her with an expression so familiar it made her smile.

Dar's image; that concerned glower facing her, right down to the twitching fingertips resting on the wood surface. Kerry reached out and patted one hand. "I'm okay. I just got a surprise from my sister, that's all."

"Uh huh."

Kerry relaxed as the pain faded. "No, really. Brian proposed to her."

Andrew studied her for a moment, and then hitched up one knee and perched on the edge of the desk. "That the feller who's the daddy of that little boy?"

"The one named for you? Yes." Kerry nodded.

"Took him long enough."

Privately, Kerry agreed. "Well, you know that was complicated. I mean, Angie was married and all that."

Andrew snorted. "I'd a been her daddy that feller woulda stepped up a lot sooner."

Kerry got lost in a moment of wondering what her life would have been like if Andrew had been her daddy. Then she shut that out deliberately, as a pang stung her chest. "I bet he would have. But I'm just really glad he did, no matter how long it took."

"Hmph," he grunted. "Let me go see what's going on outside. Heard me some noises out there." He nudged the cup. "Made that like I do Dar's. Figured it would do."

"Absolutely. Thanks Dad." Kerry turned her attention back to the mail as he wandered out, leaning forward cautiously again and studying the screen.

I can hardly believe it. He came over last night and after we put Sally and Andrew to bed we were just talking and we ended up in the solarium, and the next thing I knew he was kneeling down and taking a box out. I almost freaked!

Kerry smiled quietly. "Good for you, Brian."

He said what happened this week made him realize the world isn't a sane place. That you have to do the right things at the right time and not worry about the future. Maybe he's right. You know, I thought I didn't care, but I found out last night I really did.

So anyway. Will you be my best lady? Maid of honor sounds so stupid. I want you and Dar and Dar's folks to be there. We're planning for a Christmas ceremony, but Mom's freaking out because it's so short on time. She's glad though.

"Sure." Kerry rested her chin on her fist. "I'm sorry I didn't ask you to be mine, but I don't think you were in a space where that would have happened then, Ang." She flipped over to the download, then back to the mail.

"Thanks for making my morning a lot brighter, though." She clicked the reply button, and started to type. "And if it's any consolation to you, Dar freaked when I proposed to her, too."

DAR CLOSED HER laptop. "That's it." She watched Kannan finishing up the delicate task of fusing the fiber ends to the patch panel. "Mark, how are you guys doing?"

"Sucky." Mark grunted. "My eyeballs are coming out of my head keeping track of these damn cables."

Dar studied him for a minute, and then she slid over across the floor. "Got a spare set of crimpers? Let me in there."

Mark handed over a tool without comment, and Shaun squirmed out of the way as Dar joined them at the hairball, pulling her legs up and crossing them underneath her as she settled down. "You just putting...oh, okay. I see."

"Terminating them male and putting couplers in," Mark said. "Easier than me trying to put a splice rack in there, no space."

"Good thing they didn't chew them completely apart." Dar muttered, as she sorted out one set of mangled wire, and clipped out the chewed parts. She tightened a zip tie against one end of the cut wire, and started working on the other. "What a pain in the ass."

"Ms. Roberts?" Shaun cleared his throat somewhat timidly. "Can I ask you something?"

"We're sitting on the floor over a hole that could throw rats at us at any minute. You can call me Dar." Dar didn't look up form her task, as she pulled the insulation off the wire end and separated the pairs, sorting them with expert fingers.

Mark muffled a smile. "You still remember how to do this?" he asked his boss.

"Do you still remember how to do this?" Dar countered, clipping the wires off and inserting them to a clear, plastic end. "How in the hell can anyone forget?" She examined the work critically, then clipped the end into a coupler and went on to the other part of the cable.

"Okay. Uh. Dar," Shaun said. "Is this really going to work?"

They could hear voices in the corridor outside, but so far no one had come inside the room. Now, two, loud, angry male voices erupted just outside, the words so stumblingly fast they could hardly make them out.

"Damned if I know," Dar said, after a moment's listening. "But I think we better get hustling."

Mark checked his watch. "Kannan, if you're done there, wanna give us a hand?"

"Surely." The fiber tech was packing up his gear. "I would be most glad to."

"I find it very hard to believe," Dar stripped the end of the cable, "that this all happened between Tuesday and Friday."

"I don't know...I heard those rats can chew through a car tire in a day," Mark replied. "I saw them down in there Dar. They're big as your dog."

"Mm."

Just then the door opened, and Kerry's poked her head in. "Hey," she said, looking a bit harried. "Dar, you need to hurry up. They're evacuating this lower level because they're bringing some big shots in."

"Give me a break." Dar was clipping the other wire. "We have authorization to be here."

"No, we don't," Kerry said. "They specifically told them no one, especially our company, was allowed in here. They're coming back in ten minutes and they said if we're not out, they're arresting us and taking us to the federal prison."

"That again?" Dar rolled her eyes. "C'mon."

"This time it's no BS, Dar," Kerry stated flatly. "This isn't those bozos we were dealing with before. They scared the hell out of me."

Dar looked up, and saw in the set of Kerry's jaw, and the tension in her posture how serious the situation really was. "Okay. Everyone just do as much as you can in nine minutes and then we're out of here." She looked up. "Can you stall them if they're early?"

"Do my best." Kerry promised. "We got that ten minutes because of Dad." She ducked back outside the door.

"Great." Dar sped up her motions, as Kannan slid into place next to them, already reaching for cables with his slim fingers.

"Wonder what that's all about." Mark snapped a cable into place and reached for another one. "Shit I wish these people would make up their damn minds."

"You must realize," Kannan spoke up, after a moment's quiet. "We must come to this place, once again, when the technical people we are expecting arrive. We must install the optic unit."

"Worry about that when it happens." Dar reached for another coupler. "Let's just get this done. Or as much of it as we can. If some things don't come up, well, they'll just have to deal with it." She snapped the coupler in place and selected her next target.

Focusing intently, her eyes fastened on the cables, her hands making the motions of stripping, and sorting, and ordering automatically. Kerry's warning still ringing in her ears, she crimped the ends on, then coupled them and reached for the next set.

"Jesus, boss." Mark eyed her with respect. "You really didn't forget how to do this did you?"

"Shut up and cable."

KERRY EASED HER hands carefully into her pockets as she emerged into the pearly gray of an early dawn. She looked quickly in both directions, relieved not to see the black SUV's pulled up onto the sidewalk anymore.

Her nerves were wracked. More because she'd seen Andrew's nerves wracked by the agents than by what they'd said to her. Dar's father was one of the most unflappable, bravest people she knew, and to see him shook up by mere humans scared the poo out of her.

"They coming?" Andrew dropped out of the bus, seeing her.

"Nine minutes." Kerry checked her watch. "Seven now."

"The hell." The ex seal exhaled. "Ah do not want any of us to be here when them fellers come back, Kerry."

"I know, Dad." Kerry bumped him very gently with her shoulder. "Dar knows. She'll get back here."

There were already some people on the sidewalk. Not many, several policemen in their distinctive black uniforms, and cars were beginning to park along the street, shadowy figures busy behind the wheels.

They were running out of time. Kerry felt a prickle go down her back. Not only because of the government agents. "C'mon Dar."

"Them people are trouble," Andrew said, unexpectedly. "Them are the kind of people who don't have to account to no one for nothing, you understand me, Kerry?"

Kerry studied his face. "You mean they're above the law?"

"Yeap."

"My father thought he was too." Kerry spotted motion in the distance. "Uh oh."

Andrew turned and saw the trucks coming back. "Shit." He looked up at the entrance. "Let me go get them people."

"Dad." Kerry caught his arm. "Get the bus started. I'll stall these guys if they get here." She nudged him toward the bus. "Dar said she'd be here. Two more minutes."

"Kerry, you do not understand." Andrew protested.

"I do," she insisted gently. "It's okay. They're part of the government, Dad. I've lived with part of the government most of my life. I know where their buttons are. Please. Just leave it to me, and let's get ready to go."

Andrew studied her for a brief moment, and then he nodded and disappeared back up the steps to the bus, leaving Kerry standing alone on the sidewalk.

Kerry took a careful breath and released it, hoping she hadn't pissed her father in law off too much. She then turned and watched the approach of the black SUV's that appeared to be heading directly for them.

She checked her watch and leaned against the bus, feeling the rumble as its engine started up and nearly scared the wits out of her as the air brakes hissed suddenly.

The lead SUV pulled into the next block, and the one behind it continued on toward her. She could see the man behind the wheel, and the one in the passenger seat, both in black jackets, neither of whom were smiling.

The passenger pointed at her, and looked at something.

Oh boy. Her heart started to race. She kept her calm posture though, her ear cocked for the sound of her partner and their team approaching. "Maybe I should call my mother sooner rather that later."

A weak card and she knew it. "You may think you're outside the law, but I bet your boss really hates to be embarrassed."

The SUV pulled into the curb just behind the bus, and the men prepared to get out. One was talking rapidly into a radio, glancing at her all the while.

"Here we go." Kerry prepared herself for the confrontation, deciding a gentle approach to start would be a good idea. "I don't understand officers. What's going on?" She muttered under her breath. "We're just here taking care of a problem, I'm sure this is just a misunderstanding."

The men got out and headed her way. One took a baton out and was holding it.

"On the other hand, screw you asshole works too." Kerry readied a retreat route, and pushed away from the bus, getting her center of balance over her boots. "And so does calling for help."

Loud voices suddenly erupted. Kerry half turned and then turned all the way around as the door burst open and Dar rapidly took the stairs two at a time, the techs right behind her with their eyes wide.

"Get in." Dar ordered Kerry. "Dad, get ready to move."

Kerry didn't waste any time. She climbed onboard just a whisker ahead of Dar's rapidly moving form and moved inside to make room for the rest of them. Just as she got to the far wall, the bus surged into motion, the air breaks releasing and the door hissing shut almost in the agent's face.

Dar grabbed hold of her as they lurched to one side, cradling Kerry against her as they swung around a corner and lots of things went flying, including the techs and a fair assortment of hand tools. Dar had a good grip on the doorway into the back office and didn't get thrown.

"They are laughing at us." Kannan was looking out the back window. "Those men."

"Nice." Kerry had no intention of protesting the hold. Her chest hurt, and the thought of holding herself in place made her grimace. "Did you guys finish?"

"Not quite." Dar braced herself against the doorframe as the bus swerved again. "The building infrastructure people finally showed up."

"Oh, that somebody's uncle company?"

"I think it's Uncle Guido's company," Dar said. "They jumped all over us. They were pissed we were touching their stuff, not that we were in the building though. I wasn't going to stick around to argue about it."

"Yeah." Mark had gotten himself and his gear into one of the armchairs. "Lucky for us big D was there to kick their asses."

Kerry glanced up at her partner. "Did you?" She muttered under her breath, watching Dar's face take on an almost adolescent expression that held its own answer. "Oh boy."

"Yeah, especially since we're going go need to get back in there when the module shows up." Dar said. "Or else this is just a pointless waste of a morning."

"I've never seen anyone kick someone like that." Shaun looked up from gathering his scattered supplies on the bus floor. "That was pretty cool."

Kerry looked back up at Dar, her eyebrows lifting in question.

"They were blocking the door and not letting us out," Dar explained. "Not sure that was intentional, but you said ten minutes and I didn't have time to explain to the stupid bastard... Whoa!"

The bus was turning completely around now, leaning over to a scary degree as the horn blared. Both Dar and Kerry were thrown against the doorsill, and Kannan kept his feet only by the slimmest margin.

"Holy crap!" Mark yelped.

"Hang on back there." Andrew yelled. "Got to get this thing heading back straight."

"Jesus." Kerry tucked her elbow against her sore ribs and tucked her other hand around Dar's waist. "Maybe we should go sit down."

Then the bus straightened up and started going forward, settling down into a more regular movement. "We back on the main road, Dad?" Dar called out.

"Yeap."

"Okay." Dar cautiously released Kerry. "Everyone get your gear together. We've got a lot of work to do when we get to the office. Kerry, can you arrange for Skuzzy to pick our guys up at the airport?"

"Already did." Kerry stayed where she was, tucked along Dar's side. "I sent her and Nan the flight details. She's tracking them too, she'll let us know if they're late."

They rolled along in silence for a moment. Then Dar sighed. "This is insanity."

Mark looked up from zipping his tool bag. "Yeah, but in a good way, right?"

Dar leaned back and put her arms around Kerry again, as the sun started to rise and flash through the curtained windows of the bus, splashing them all intermittently. "We'll find out soon enough, I guess."

"WHERE DID THEY leave it?" Dar had her hands on her hips.

"It's below in the tunnels," the building manager said. "The guy with it said it wouldn't reach any further."

"Oh crap." Mark echoed the words sounding in Dar's skull. "You gotta be kidding me."

The building manager shrugged. "I wish I was. He left the message with me, said he didn't have time to wait for you guys to wake up."

Dar snorted. "Yeah. Thanks." She let her hands drop. "Okay, let's go see where they left it. Maybe they were lying." She motioned Mark and the others to follow her, unclipping her radio from her shoulder as she walked. "Ker?"

The radio hissed, and then crackled. "Right here, go ahead. Scuzzy reports the flights on time, Dar."

"Everything else isn't," Dar said." Cable's still down in the subway."

"Jesus."

"And they think it's too short."

"Oh, man." Kerry's voice reflected the frustration she was feeling. "Dar, I don't..." She stopped. "What's your plan?"

"I don't think we're going to make it either." Dar turned and headed down the steps. "Just... could you grab someone, maybe two people, and see if you can find a pipe, something, anything, in that damn hole our dmarc's in that I can shove a cable through?"

"You got it. On the way." Kerry clicked off.

"This is gonna suck." Mark tugged at the collar of his jumpsuit. "I knew we shouldn't trust those guys. They gave off bad juju."

Dar rolled up the sleeves on her own jumpsuit as she trotted down the steps. She dodged past the hurrying figures of people coming up out of the subway, and paused only when she got to the ticket turnstile. "Damn it."

"Machines over here." Mark had started toward it. "What do we need, four? I'll get em."

"Thanks." Dar put her hands on the bar and peered through them. "Kerry has my wallet." She ignored the stream of people coming out of the turnstiles, studying the wall and stairwells on the other side of the gates until Mark came over with four squares of cardboard.

She took hers and they passed through, walking past the fare booth and going down the steps to the level where the trains were. There was a train on one side of the platform, so Dar went to the other side, and looked up and down it. "Which one would it be in?"

"Um." Mark went to the map in the center of the platform and studied it. "They'd have to be in the tunnel from...here?" He traced a line with his finger uncertainly. "Man, where's that native woman?"

"Fetching our world savers." Dar went over to the map and looked at it. "Yeah, this is the cross over from that other line so it has to be this way." She pointed up the tunnel the train was in. "Let's wait for this thing to leave and go look."

Mark eyed her. "Go into the tunnel? Boss, that's sorta dangerous. We touch that live rail and we're all toast."

"They had to be in there." Dar reminded him. "There's a ledge along the wall here. We can walk on that."

"Oh, my goodness," Kannan murmured.

"Dar?" Kerry's voice crackled faintly on the radio. "You there"

"Yeah." Dar keyed the mic. "What's up?"

"The secret service was just here." Kerry's voice sounded tense. "They asked Alastair to go with them down to the Exchange."

Dar glanced around. "Just giving him a ride?"

"Well." Kerry exhaled audibly. "They made it sound like a polite request."

"That sounds kinda crappy." Mark muttered softly.

"Yeah." Dar clicked the radio a few times. "All right, Ker. Thanks for telling me. See what you can do to find me that pipe."

"Will do." Kerry clicked off.

The train hooted, and the doors shut, then it pulled out of the station, disappearing down the tunnel with a whoosh of dank air behind it.

Dar walked immediately to the edge of the platform and climbed over the rail, getting her boots on the small ledge and walking along it with confidence. She didn't look behind her to see if anyone was following, leaving it to their individual conscience.

It was dark in the tunnel, but this close to the station there were lights against the wall just barely glowing from the layers of soot and grease covering them. She climbed up a few steps onto a platform that faced a set of closed doors, the faint hum from behind them audible to her.

The platform had steps back down to the ledge, she paused, as the wall dipped into a darkened angle as though a wedge had been cut into it.

Dar pulled out her flashlight and turned it on, flashing it down to the tracks to see a set of them diverging from the main ones and heading directly into the wall. The gap they made was far too wide for her to jump, and she wasn't really sure which one of them was live in the dim light.

Jumping down seemed like a bad idea. Dar turned her flashlight to the wedge instead, playing it against the walls. There were old pylons there, branching off to go with the tracks but it all ended up in bricked off wall.

"Over there, boss." Mark spoke up. "See the cable? It's coming down...where the hell does it go?"

Dar flashed her light over to the edge of the tracks and spotted the thick cable. "Yeah." She examined the ground beneath the platform she was on, seeing piles of litter and eyeballs reflected back at her. With a sigh, she gathered her courage and stepped off the concrete, falling through the air for a few seconds before she landed in the trash, sending cracklings and squeals in every direction.

"Yow." Mark stayed where he was.

"You know something? I went into information technology so I'd avoid crap like this. I should have stuck with the damn Navy." She edged carefully along the platform into the shadows, spotting a much bigger bulk in the darkness in the very corner of the wedge.

"Careful, boss."

Dar lifted her light and moved forward into the gloom, pausing when she heard a frantic rustling just near her right foot. "Oh boy," she muttered. "Glad I have boots on." She scuffed her feet forward, and felt her toe impacting something soft and moving.

Expecting a squeak, she was shocked at a hiss instead, and froze in place, her senses on momentary overload.. "Holy shit! I think there's a damn snake down here!" She trained the light down at her feet and searched the litter.

Then she felt something strike at her boots and instinctively she kicked out with one of them, impacting a body and sending it flying.

"Boss! Dar!" Mark scrambled off the platform. "Hey!"

A loud yowl made them both freeze.

"That's not a snake," Mark said, after a nervous silence.

"No." Dar felt her heart about to come out of her chest. "I think it's a cat."

"Kitty cat or wildcat?"

Dar heard motion again and prepared herself to be attacked, but a furry form dashed past her, eyes glinting in the flashlight, and disappeared into the darkness of the tunnel. "Okay." She moved a little further, and then stopped as her thighs bumped into something big. "Oh."

"Wh...oh." Mark peeked past her at the big spool blocking the way. "Hey, good job, boss. You found it."

Dar leaned over and examined the remaining cable, and then straightened. "They're right. Not enough. Barely get to the damn stairs in the station."

"Shit." Mark peered at the cable. "Now what?"

Dar started searching the walls with her light. "I don't know. I honestly don't goddamned know."

KERRY STOOD BACK as they opened the door to the old storage closet that they'd used as a demarc. "Thanks," she told the custodian.

"We really appreciate it."

The man grunted and walked off, shaking his head.

"What a nice guy," Scuzzy said. "A real New Yorker." She looked inside the room. "So what are we looking for?"

"Wow. What a place." Nan entered, shining a big flashlight around. "Good grief, Ms. Stuart. Don't tell me this is an actual telecom demarc."

"Kerry, please." Kerry poked her head in. "Unfortunately, yes, it is. Here's the problem. They have the cable for this thing down in the subway tunnel, and it's too short for us to bring up the steps and across the floor there. Dar wants us to find a pipe or conduit that might go down there so she can bring the connection up."

"Oh. Wow." Nan peered around. "Are we still trying to do this? I thought we were giving it up last night." She looked back at Kerry. "It's almost eight o'clock."

"Yeah." Scuzzy looked at her watch. "I gotta get going to the airport, yeah? Bring this guy right back here?"

"Right back here." Kerry agreed. "Okay, Nan, Robert, let's see what we can find." She entered the room cautiously with the office applications support specialist behind her. "We're looking for a pipe."

"Plenty of them in here." Nan said.

"Keep clear of that one, it's steam." Kerry pointed. "And don't touch that panel. It's live electrical."

Nan stopped, and turned around to look at her.

"Dar found out the hard way." Kerry took a careful breath, and edged along the wall, inspecting everything within reach of her flashlight. She'd passed on wearing her jumpsuit, since the idea of struggling into it was just too much for her at the moment.

Dar had insisted on her boots though, going so far as to put them on her, in a moment of exasperating over protectiveness, in front of the staff standing there waiting for them.

Goofball. She found a pipe and tapped on it, shaking the rust off the outside and exposing the old lettering. "Water. No, that won't do it."

"These are huge pipes...steam you said?" Nan was moving around the other side. "They're big."

"We have steam heat," Robert said. He was kneeling on the floor near the front of the room looking at the pipes protruding through the concrete. "What are we looking for, Ms. Stuart? Will they be labeled? I think these are electrical, they say Edison."

"What we're really looking for is an empty pipe that might go down." Kerry stepped carefully over their router and the fiber patch panel Kannan had just finished. "Something that might be going down into the subway from an office building."

"Well." Nan slid between two of the bigger pipes, her slim form almost obscured by them. "This one says fire alarm system...it's going down."

Kerry abandoned her search and made her way to the other side of the closet, easing her head between the pipes since she was pretty sure the rest of her wouldn't fit. "Okay...oh." She turned her head sideways. "Telegraph conduit. Telegraph?"

"There used to be fire boxes on the street," Robert explained. "Connected to the fire department. It worked by Morse code or something."

Kerry unclipped her mic. "Dar? You there?"

A loud rushing sound answered her and she pulled the mic away from her ear. "Yow."

"Sorry." Dar clicked in a minute later. "Train going by. What's up? You find anything?"

"Are you in the tunnel?" Kerry asked. "Where the tracks are? Holy crap, Dar!"

"That's where the cable is," Dar reminded her.

"Be careful." Kerry felt her stress level rising. "We found a pipe that is supposed to be for the fire alarm system. It says 'telegraph' on the outside. Can you find one down there?"

"Bang on it," Dar said. "Get something and keep banging on it and we'll look."

Nan nodded. "Good idea." She looked around. "There's a piece of brick...maybe that'll work." She squeezed over near the wall and retrieved it, and then came back over and started banging on the pipe.

"Hear that?" Kerry asked over the radio.

"Hang on."

Kerry held the mic with one hand, keeping her other elbow pressed against her side that had started to ache again. "Good catch, Nan." She complimented the woman. "Last thing we needed was to be stuck in here for a long time."

"Ker? I can hear it." Dar answered back. "Just keep banging. We'll try to find ya. Good job."

"Thank Nan." Kerry backed away from the pipe. "Robert, can you find a brick and spell Nan when she gets tired? I don't think my ribs are going to be up to me whacking something."

"Sure," Robert agreed instantly. "Boy that took a lot less time than I thought it would."

"How are we going to get the cable inside the pipe up here?" Nan asked over the pounding. She whacked the pipe at one-second intervals; making a low, gong like sound that wasn't quite pleasant. "There's no hole in the pipe."

No, of course there wasn't. "Hey Dar?" Kerry keyed the mic. "I'm going to need someone up here with a hacksaw."

"Send them up when they're done here," Dar answered, her breathing sounding a bit strained. "Get back to you in a minute."

Kerry released the mic, trying hard not to turn tail at once and go chasing down the stairs to see what her partner was up to. "Boy, that was a lot shorter than I thought, too," she commented. "We may make this if Dar can find that pipe."

"They're making a big deal out of the Exchange this morning." Robert straightened, with a small section of pipe in his hands. "The vice president's going to be there, and a bunch of other people. I hear they're going to have one of the firemen ring the opening bell."

The underlying hypocrisy made Kerry's eyeballs twitch. She turned and looked around searching out a path for the cable to come up once it came out of the pipe. The floor was crowded with mechanics but she traced out a route with her eyes, taking the cable along the floor and past the dangerously humming electrical panel.

Yes, that would work. She eyed the bend the cable would have to make to get to the router, and while it was steeper than Dar probably would have liked, beggars in this case certainly could not be choosers and they'd just have to try and make it work.

She was just relieved they'd found a solution. She checked her watch. Quarter past eight. They had really an hour to get everything hooked up and tested before the exchange opened at nine thirty. If the modules got here in time, it was do-able.

Just.

"Ker?" Dar's voice crackled through, sounding tired and irritated.

Uh oh. "Here," Kerry answered. "What's up?"

"We can't get at that damn pipe." Dar answered. "It's inside an equipment room behind some locked doors."

"Well..."

"Which Mark already picked. Someone decided to dump a load of unwanted concrete in the closet and it's covering the pipes. They're inside the concrete."

Shit. Kerry clicked the mic, looking over at the others, who were looking back at her in dismay. "All the pipes in that area?" She looked around. "They're all on that wall, Dar."

"All of them," Dar confirmed. "Every last goddamned one of them buried inside a pile of rock with construction worker's graffiti marked all over it.

Nan stopped pounding, and let the brick fall to her leg. "So, now what?"

"Good question." Kerry exhaled. Slowly she let her eyes wander over the inside of the room. "Damned good question."

"QUARTER TO NINE." Kerry wiped the back of her hand across her forehead. She was kneeling on the dirty concrete, as Nan squirmed under the consoles looking for something, anything they could use to solve their current problem.

"I don't see anything," Nan said. "Just a lot of dirt."

"Son of a bitch." Kerry exhaled. "This stupid piece of shit room. If I had a stick of dynamite I'd just blow a damn hole in the floor."

Nan eyed her, a trifle nervously.

"Is there anything I can do other than hold this flashlight?" Robert asked. "I feel a little useless standing here letting you ladies do all the dirty work."

Kerry lowered herself carefully down until she was lying flat on her belly on the ground. She slowly moved her flashlight around every inch of the floor, ignoring the throbbing pain in her chest.

"Ker, I think we're about out of time." Dar's voice crackled softly over the radio. "I can't find a damn thing down here."

Kerry cursed under her breath. "Hang on." She keyed the mic. "I'm going to have one last look here."

"Okay." Dar responded. "Good luck. We're not having any."

"Thanks hon." She released the radio and continued her inch-by-inch search, running her flashlight over the back wall past the electrical panel, over the painted over wooden half door, over the brick...

Wait.

Kerry moved her flashlight back. She focused on the long sealed half portal, her eyes flicking over it with startling intensity. "Robert?"

"Yes, ma'am."

"Get me a sledgehammer. Immediately."

"Yes, ma'am!"

Nan squirmed over to see what she was looking at. "What are you going to do?"

Kerry pointed. "That was a door once. It went somewhere." She rested her flashlight on the ground and her chin on the flashlight, trying not to breathe too deeply. "It's lower than the level of the floor."

"You think it goes somewhere?"

"Haven't a fucking clue." Kerry keyed the mic. "Dar, I found something. Give me two minutes, and then see if you hear me knocking."

"Will do," Dar responded. "Got my damned fingers crossed."

Nan studied Kerry. "You people from Miami curse a lot. No offense. It just sounds weird."

"We have a lot to curse." Kerry edged forward, now regretting that she'd declined the jumpsuit. She could feel the chill of the concrete against her belly as she angled herself under a large metal shelf toward the door. "It's either hot and steamy, or it's a tropical storm, or it's bad drivers, corrupt politicians, and roads under perpetual construction."

"Oh." Nan watched her. "You want me to do that? You must be hurting like crazy crawling around like that."

Kerry turned her head and looked at her. "Can you swing a ten pound sledge hammer underhand?"

Nan blinked. "Um...you know, I never tried, but I'm more into marathons than weightlifting."

"Well." Kerry squirmed a last few inches. "I can, and I'm short enough to get in here." She arrived in front of the door. There was an alteration in the floor there, a pour of concrete that had settled into a depression three feet wide. It made the floor in front of the half door a good twelve inches lower than what she was laying on. She ran her fingers over it. "Stairs?"

"Hard to say." Nan looked up over her shoulder at the door. "Found one?"

"I did." Robert came forward. "The custodian was there. I just paid him twenty bucks and he handed it right over." He edged toward where Kerry was. "You want it there, Ms Stuart?"

"We must be in New York," Nan said, in a wry tone.

"Like Washington doesn't know anything about bribes?" Robert jibed back.

"Can you get the head of it here, next to...yeah." Kerry curled her fingers around the shaft of the sledgehammer and steeled herself, tucking her right arm up against her side to support her ribs. Then she lifted the hammer and smacked the head against the door, making a loud cracking boom.

"Whoa." Nan squirmed back out of the way. "Let me get outta here before splinters start flying."

Kerry smacked the door again, then again, and again. It didn't seem to be moving, but she could see the paint cracking along the sealed edges. "Hope Dar can hear that."

"Ker. " As though in answer, Dar's voice sputtered near her ear. "What the hell are you do...where is that? Mark! Mark! Where in the hell is that coming from?"

Kerry felt a jolt in her side, and she took a quick breath against it. She kept up her attack, feeling some of her rage at the situation coming out as she swung against the door harder and harder. "Stupid." Bang. "Piece." Bang. "Of crap." Bang.

"I think the edge is breaking there." Nan had slid over under the back section of piping to get a better look. "Yeah, it is."

"Should be." Kerry grunted, slamming the hammer against the wood as she felt the burn in her triceps. "Glad for all those hours in the gym now."

"You guys actually have time for the gym?"

"We make time for it." Kerry paused and studied her target, and then she selected a different spot and slammed the hammer against the edge of the door near the frame, seeing flecks of brown wood under the black paint.

"Nine o'clock," Robert said. "Ms. Stuart, they're back with that part...upstairs just paged me."

"Go down into the subway and get Kannan and Shaun back up here." Kerry felt her breath coming fast, and her heartbeat hammering against her chest. "Tell them to get ready."

"Yes, ma'am." Robert disappeared again.

"C'mon. C'mon." Kerry closed her eyes and just concentrated on the hammer, blocking out the pain and the burn in her arms. She banged the tool against the wood again, and again, and again, and again.

Faster.

Slam.

Slam.

Slam.

"KERRISON! STOP!"

Kerry almost jumped and smacked her head against the pipes, the voice so loud in her ears it hurt. She dropped the hammer and let out a gasp as the surface she'd been pounding disappeared into a black hole and gust of cold, oil scented air blew hard against her face.

She stared at the opening until Dar's upper body appeared, her arms resting on the depressed floor. "H...hi."

"Sorry I yelled," Dar said. "But one more smack and you'd have gone through the damn door and knocked me off this stack of crates and old railroad ties I'm standing on." She disappeared. "Hang on."

Kerry was very glad to stay completely still, blowing her hair out of her eyes with a puff of relieved breath.

"Wow," Nan said. "Just, wow."

"Here." Dar reappeared with something in her hand. "Feed this in." She got a good look at Kerry's face, and then shifted her focus. "Nan, grab this please. Pull it forward to the rack." She had a cable end in her hand and now she fed it through under the rusted iron pipe work.

"Got it." Nan took hold of the cable and squirmed backwards. "Got it, got it...whoa!"

"Hey!" Shaun skidded to a halt, breathing hard. "There's the cable! Kanny! Move it, buddy!!"

The cable slithered forward as Dar fed it up, past Kerry's shoulder. "That's enough," Dar called back. "Tie it off for strain relief, Mark."

"Doin' it!" Mark called back. "Dar, for Christ's sake don't fall, okay? I don't think I can catch you and we're both gonna end up across those freaking tracks!"

"I'm all right." Dar leaned on the sill again. "You okay?" She focused on Kerry.

"Absolutely not." Kerry reached over and extended her hand which Dar clasped. "We're not done. The part's here, Dar. We've got to get it down to the exchange."

"I know," Dar said. "And I've got to be here to configure this end of it when the traffic starts coming down. I told the router on that end to send me everything. I'm going to split it up here."

"We're insane." Kerry rested her head against her arm. "I'll get the part and go to the Exchange. If they won't let me in, at this point, I'm going to start biting and kicking people so get the bail money out."

"Ker, we can send someone else," Dar said. "I'll send Mark."

"Who do you think has the best chance of getting in there?" Kerry kept her eyes closed. "Honestly."

Dar sighed.

"You're taking me to dinner at Joe's Stone Crab tonight, Paladar."

Dar pulled her hand closer and kissed her knuckles. "Ker, I'll buy Joe's Stone Crab for you if you want, but...ah...can you move back out of the way?"

"Huh?"

"Gotta jump up here." Dar looked behind her.

"Boss! Watch it!" Mark yelled suddenly. "Watch it!"

Kerry's eyes popped open. "Honey you're not fitting through here. Dar, wait...no wai...Dar!"

With a sudden surge, Dar hauled herself through the opening. "Mark! Move!"

"Outta here boss!"

There was thundering huge crash behind her, and far off, the sound of alarms going off. "I think we just blocked the tracks." Dar reviewed her options in the tiny, cramped space. "I think I'm gonna end the day pissing a lot of people off."

Kerry was wriggling backwards as fast as she could, trying not to kick Shaun and Kannan who had descended over the cable and were working furiously.

"Guys?" Dar said. "Stop."

Shaun looked up. "Ma'am?"

"Pull Kerry out of there." Dar pointed. "Just grab her legs and pull gently before she passes out." She looked up, then jumped and grabbed a pipe, pulling her body up and over the top of it. "C'mon people, we're out of time."

Chapter Seventeen

KERRY BOARDED THE subway train with Andrew right behind her, her hands pushed into the front pocket of her hastily donned hoodie. One hand clutched the optic device as she was shepherded to a seat by her tall companion.

"This is a crazy thing." Andrew sat down next to her in the half full train.

"It is." Kerry was aware of every minute ticking by. "But Scuzzy said it would be faster to do this, than try to drive down there with everything going on. I trust her to know New York."

"Some right." Andrew acknowledged. "Lots of traffic now up there."

"Lots." Kerry sat back, feeling utterly exhausted. Part of that was the drug she was taking for her ribs she knew, but there was a bone deep tired along with it she hadn't felt for a long time. "You know, I said to Dar I was glad we were doing this."

"Not so glad now?" Andrew asked, watching her from the corner or his eye. "You don't look so hot."

"I don't feel so hot," Kerry admitted. "I think besides my ribs I'm coming down with something. I've got that ache all over feeling." She exhaled carefully. "Just my luck."

Andrew patted her shoulder. "Hang in there, kumquat. This here thing's about done ah think."

"I'll be glad to get on that darn airplane, that's for sure," Kerry agreed. "Bet you will too."

Andrew let his big hands rest on his knees. "That is a true thing. Place here's got some of the same things I saw some places I been." He continued in a reflective tone, "a lot of fussing with folks haids. Mad. Crazy. Sad. Hating."

"You mean places you've been deployed?" Kerry asked, after a pause.

"Yeap."

The train rattled through the tunnel, and pulled into a station. A few people got off, a lot of people got on. Most were quiet, as they settled in seats, or took hold of the bars. Andrew scanned them, and then he remained seated, pulling his boots in a little to keep them from tripping anyone.

Kerry checked her watch, and then shook her head.

"WELL, DAR, WE knew it would be down to the wire but..."

"Sh." Dar staked out a spot on the floor behind where Kannan and Shaun were feverishly working. "Don't get me wrong," She paused and looked over her shoulder, "I am deeply grateful to all of you for doing this, but if we don't get finished, it's not gonna mean much."

"Sure." Chuck found a spot near the wall. "Mind if we watch?" He indicated his companions; two men in khakis with tucked in short sleeve shirts and actual, real pocket protectors. They had glasses, and that intense look that rocket scientists have.

"No." Dar plugged her laptop into the router and started it up. "Sit down, it'll be a while." It was already stuffy inside the room without the extra people in it, and she felt the sweat gather under her jumpsuit adding to an already significant discomfort. "Hell."

"Dar?" Mark's voice erupted near her ear. "I've got good uplinks...you want me to...what do you want me to do up here?"

"Hang on." Dar unzipped her jumpsuit and pulled it off her arms and shoulders, exposing her tank top covered upper body to the sluggish air. She tied the sleeves off around her waist and retrieved the mic. "All right, listen. We're taking the whole stream from down there so when it starts up I'm going to have to parse it by IP and set up sub interfaces to route it."

There was a long moment's silence. "You're going to do that on the fly, boss?"

"Do you have another suggestion? Cough it up."

"Um."

"Aside from not trying this at all?" Dar exhaled. "I just hope we've got existing gateways to where this stuff's going." She scrubbed the hair out of her eyes with one hand.

"Wow." Mark said, after another long pause. "You want me to..."

"Capture everything so we can put it all back if this tanks? Sure." Dar logged into her laptop. "Wish me luck? Sure."

"Okay, will do." Mark responded. "I feel kinda lame up here. "

"Just hang tight," Dar said. "It's all in Kerry's pocket right now anyway." She set up her monitoring tools, opening a console to the router in one window and several sessions with the routing systems in the Miami office in others.

"Think we can get a case study out of this when we're all done, Dar?" Chuck asked, as he clasped his hands around his knees.

Dar gave him a sideways look.

"How about you keynote our next tech convention?"

"ONE MORE STOP." Kerry stood up as the train lurched into motion. "Ready, Dad?"

"Right with you, Kerry." Andrew stood behind her, one hand resting lightly on her shoulder. They waited for the train to stop, then were the first ones out of the door dodging the rest of the travelers as they reached the steps and headed up them two at a time.

It was loud and bustling under the ground and Kerry got through the exit turnstiles yearning for a sight of the open sky again. She evaded crashing into two men rushing for the entrance and got to the steps outside, running up them and emerging into the open air.

It was gritty and dusty, but there was no time to worry about a mask as Kerry broke into a run toward the exchange. The jolting of her own footsteps sent shocks up and down her side, but she ignored them and focused on the gothic front of the now familiar building a short distance away.

There were people clustered in front of the main entrance. She saw police there, and the military. The streets were blocked off.

Men were yelling. There were two people being held by their arms. "Kerry that does not look good." Andrew was keeping pace with her. "Gonna be a fight."

It was. Kerry could see it. She glanced at her watch and knew they had no time for it. Twenty after nine.

A policeman spotted them running, and pointed. Two military men reacted, and started forward. Kerry took it all in a series of vivid impressions. She realized she had no time to make a decision; her forward momentum was taking her toward the main steps as fast as she could run.

Soldiers ran toward them. "You...have a card you can show them Dad?" Kerry felt her breath coming shorter, and the pain made flashes of black and red on the backs of her eyeballs.

"Lord." Andrew didn't sound happy.

Kerry prepared to haul up as they were intercepted, when a motion caught her eye and she looked down the street to the back entrance, spotting a cluster of suited figures shuffling from a set of black cars.

One moment. One view. Instantly, Kerry changed course. "Hold 'em off." She called back as she bolted down the side street.

"Lord." Andrew dug in his pockets for his identification as he came to a halt in front of the military men. "Whoa there, fellas, Hang on."

Kerry kept going. She ducked between two wrecked cars, her boots tossing up puffs of ash dust as she powered along the sidewalk toward the group of people. The guards at the top of the steps spotted her and turned, and the group on the steps turned to see what was going on.

"Watch it! Stop her!" One of guards yelled. A policeman standing nearby lunged at Kerry, but missed her as she ducked past. "Hey! Stop! Stop!"

The guards pulled their guns off their shoulders, one hopping over the railing and falling to the ground with a grunt as he tried to get in between this oncoming threat and the people on the steps. "Stop!"

"Kerrison!" Cynthia Stuart blurted in surprise, as Kerry closed in on them. "What on earth!" She pushed to the front of the crowd. "Wait, stop. That's my daughter!"

The guards hesitated, just long enough for Kerry to slide past them and get to her mother's side. "Wait... ma'am!"

"Mother." Kerry got hold of Cynthia's arm. "I have to get inside. There's no time to explain." She uttered. "Trust me, please."

Cynthia stared at her for a long heartbeat as their eyes met. Then she blinked. "Well, of course. We must go. Excuse us gentlemen. Sorry for this disturbance. I'm sure Kerrison just didn't want to be late for the opening."

Nine twenty five. Kerry barely held her impatience as they filed in the door among the group of senators, most of them looking at her with varying levels of surprise and distaste.

No time. Kerry broke from them the minute they cleared the inner door, past the guards, past the security in black jackets, past the secret service stationed carefully long the walls. She dodged a set of outstretched hands and went down a hallway, hearing yells behind her.

Ignoring them. Down a set of stairs, around a corner, and she was in the lower level again. Two doors down on the right, and she was throwing her shoulder against the surface as her hands turned the knob, almost falling inside.

Men inside. Startled, they turned, hands outstretched.

Kerry avoided them, her eyes focused on the setup in the corner, the one they'd left there, blinking quietly untouched.

Untouched.

The men were yelling at her, but all she could hear was her heartbeat thundering as she dropped to the floor and slid the last few feet, her hands wrenching at the static wrapping around the module she'd brought.

Footsteps. "Don't touch me!" Kerry yelled in warning, as she felt people closing in and her fingers felt cold steel instead of plastic. She got the optic out and shoved it into place, then grabbed for the patch cable as hands grabbed her.

Digging her boots in she leaned against the yanking, almost blacking out as a jolt of fire went through her chest. "Ahhhh!"

The pull relaxed for an instant, just enough for her to fall forward on to the router and get the end of the cables into place, shoving them home with a set of soft, unremarkable clicks.

So close to her eyes, she couldn't make out the features. For a moment, nothing happened.

"What the hell is that crazy woman doing?'

Then a soft, green light came on. It lit her face up, and as she blinked sweat out of her eyes she swore she could almost taste the green on the back of her tongue.

"Leave her be." Andrew's voice cut in, loud and uncompromising. "Let her loose fore I rip your damn arms off and choke you with 'em."

Nine twenty seven.

Kerry felt the grip come off her, and she rolled over to sit on the floor, legs splayed, breathing hard, and flashes of red in her vision timed with her heartbeat. There were three men in the room aside from Andrew, and they were in logo shirts and pressed chinos.

"It's that crazy lady," the tech who'd been in the room when she'd gotten hurt blurted. "What in the hell are you doing?"

Kerry licked her lips. "Finishing what we started." She got to her knees and then had to stop.

Andrew came over and held his hands out. "Here." He took her hands and lifted her up. "You done now? This thing working?"

Kerry turned to look at the router that was now flashing with a lot of activity lights on the front. "Something's going through. Whether it works or not is in Dar's hands now."

"Wait...are you saying you're fixing this thing after all?" One of the other men stepped up. "They told us you weren't. Some guy came in here and said...there was an FBI agent here asking questions, said they were...that you..."

The tech was looking at something on his screen. "Well, something's happening because all of a sudden this stuff's trying to work," he said. "So if those guys are going to arrest these people they probably should wait a few minutes."

"I should call them..." The man hesitated. "But if you're fixing it..."

Kerry held her hand up. "Spare me the details," she said, exhausted. "We're doing what we can." She turned to Andrew. "Let's go find my mother again. She's going to kill me for using her like I just did."

"Wait, you can't leave." The supervisor started to block the door, then found himself against the wall, pushed there by Andrew's big fist. "Okay. Maybe you can."

"Smart feller." Andrew opened the door and guided Kerry out.

"LINK!" SHAUN BAWLED, shocking everyone in the silence that had fallen as the minutes ticked away to nothing. "LINK! We got a link!"

Dar felt like a bucket of cold water had been dumped on her head. She took a steadying breath and then dove into the console session, seeing the port come active and quickly surge with a stream of traffic.

Many streams of traffic. Dar threw a flow filter in place to sort it, searching for the largest ones first. She clipped and pasted into a notepad file as she found them, her mind registering the networks involved. She dialed her cell phone and put it into speaker mode. "Mark, you there?"

"Here boss." Mark answered. "We got data?"

"We got." Dar rattled the keys. "Get ready for a set of IP's, see if we've got gateways. I'm setting up the interfaces."

"Dar, we've only got like two minutes."

"You're wasting them." Dar concentrated fully on the screen, blocking out the distractions of the room, and the men watching, the heat, and the pressing of the ticking clock against her shoulder blades.

"Okay ready," Mark answered in a chastened tone.

"That's going to be interfaces zero one, zero two and zero three."

"Got it. They're starting the speech up there," Mark answered. "Got gateways."

"Clear the ACL's for it."

"Done."

"Bringing the interfaces up." Dar muttered. "Ready for the next set?"

"Ready."

THE BUZZ OF voices was almost overwhelming. Kerry came in to the gallery pausing in the entrance and looking around to see if she could spot her mother.

On the floor below, the kiosks and stands were filled with traders, the atmosphere frenetic and with an air of almost desperation. She spotted her mother on the far side of the gallery. On the other side, she saw a group of men clustered tightly within the confines of heavy security.

Alastair was there. Outwardly as calm and composed as ever, seeming to ignore the presence of the security agents spaced around where he was standing.

"Kerr...y."

Kerry turned to find her mother approaching. She walked forward to meet her, Andrew right at her heels. "Sorry, Mother," she said, as they met. "I had to get something done."

"Good grief!" Cynthia whispered. "What on earth are you involved in? Someone just told me the FBI has your company under investigation? What's going on?"

Kerry held a hand up. "Give it five minutes, Mom. Then I'll explain everything."

Cynthia looked at her, and then glanced at Andrew. "Oh. Hello, Commander."

"Lo," Andrew responded.

"Well." She turned back to Kerry. "I'm sure there must be an explanation. This is all so..." She fell silent as the speaker went to the gavel across from them, and rapped for attention. "But I agree. Let's see this through, then we can discuss it."

They moved to the rail to listen. Kerry rested her hands on it, so tired it was hard to concentrate on what was going on.

Hard to stand there, and not know what was going on at the other end of the cable. No way was she going to call Dar, and break her concentration, or cause any seconds more delay in what had become the worst of her worst nightmare of a circumstance.

She could feel Andrew behind her, and her mother came to stand at her side, the other senators and dignitaries clustering around them.

"May I now have two minutes of silence," the speaker said and bowed his head.

It went absolutely silent. The only sound was the air conditioning and the soft squeak of a chair moving somewhere in the distance.

An American flag fluttered lightly in the fan breeze, rustling against the stone wall.

Kerry kept her head up and she let her eyes slowly scan the crowd, watching the traders below, heads dutifully bowed, but anxiety for the trade showing in the shifting of shoulders and clenching of fists.

On her level, the dignitaries all were standing in solemn silence, the men with hands clasped before them, and heads bent, the women mostly clasping their hands just over their hearts, some with lips moving in silent prayer.

Behind the pedestal, a group of firemen in their turnout coats waited, too tired to pray.

Kerry turned her head a little and found her gaze caught by a pair of gray ones in the cluster of business suits to one side of the podium. Alastair cocked his head just slightly in question, and she managed a tired grin in response.

What was he thinking?

One more minute. Kerry looked down at her hands, rubbing her thumb across a scrape that stung as she touched it.

One more minute.

"SIXTY SECONDS, BOSS."

Dar barely heard him. She focused completely on the screen,

instinct driving her typing more than conscious thought. Flows and errors flashed in front of her, and she forgot where she was, and who was watching.

Focus.

She typed, and exported, and filtered and watched results as she fought to make the data streaming into her monitor go where she wanted it to go, alerts and warnings flashing by so fast they hardly registered.

"Forty seconds."

Routing. Rerouting. Redistributing directions from the machine under her hands to the big routers sitting quietly in the first floor of the Miami office that Dar would have teleported to if she could have.

Protocols stuttered and skewed, probably affecting traffic across the breadth of their network. Dar didn't have time to worry about it.

"Thirty seconds."

Too much data, trying to get to too many places, all of it critical. Dar muttered under her breath as she recycled the router for the nth time, and waited for it to boot. "Cross your fingers."

"Got everything including my eyebrows crossed," Mark said, nervously. "Twenty seconds."

They waited. Dar gazed at the blinking cursor as the boot screen scrolled across her laptop, checking ROMS and ASICS in a process that seemed glacially slow.

"Ten seconds."

Router prompt. Dar rattled in a command, reviewed the results.

"Five seconds."

Another command and a refresh. Then five keystrokes and a slamming of her enter key so loud it startled everyone watching.

DING, DING, DING. The fireman released the striker, and let his hand fall, as a burst of noise suddenly exploded through the tall space.

Chattering. People's voices. Traders. The rattle of printers.

An LED sign burst into action, spewing out ticker symbols.

Everyone clapped.

Kerry felt her hands start to shake on the ledge, feeling lightheaded. Anxiously, she searched the crowd, but the traders had gone to work and blocked out their watchers, busy at kiosks, busy in clusters, busy at terminals, busy at the business of making money.

Completely anticlimactic. Like nothing was wrong at all.

"All right now, Kerry." Her mother turned to her. "What is all this about?"

"Excuse me." Alastair's voice intruded.

Kerry turned and faced him. "Hi." She started to take a breath, then paused as she was enfolded in a heartfelt hug by her ultimate boss. She could feel the catch in his breathing, and felt the sting of tears in her own eyes, and it was all just so crazy and stupid.

She blinked a little."We couldn't let it go," she whispered. "We just couldn't."

"Meant a lot more than you think it did," Alastair uttered back. "Tell you all later."

"McLean?"

Alastair released her, and they turned to find the vice president there, with several of his entourage. "Well, hello, Dick." Alastair's voice was calm, but its usual amiable tone held a distinct edge. "Nice moment there, with the fireman."

"Beautiful, "the politician responded, aware of all the watching and listening ears. "Real testament to the resiliency of the American spirit. Can't keep us down."

"Absolutely."Alastair agreed. "I couldn't agree more."

The vice president turned and put his hands on the ledge. "Everything's in good working order I see." He studied the busy floor. "As it should be."

"Why yes, it appears that it is," Alastair said. "As you say, you just can't keep us down."

The politician turned back to him, eyeing him sharply. He straightened up and fixed his tie, notching it a bit closer to his neck. "Glad to see everyone pulled together to make it happen." He dismissed them. "Excuse me." He moved past them and joined some of the senators standing nearby trying to catch his attention.

Alastair and Kerry both exhaled at the same time. Then Kerry leaned back against the wall, as her knees started to shake. "Wow," she said, and then fell silent.

Cynthia cleared her throat. "Is...everything all right? I'm sorry, is it..." She peered at Alastair. "Mr. McLean? I believe I have seen you on the business news."

"Ah. Yes." Alastair nodded. "You must be Kerry's mother." He held hand out. "It's good to meet you."

Kerry let it all go past her. "I need to go make a phone call," she finally said. "Excuse me."

Alastair took her arm gently. "I think we all have to make that same phone call," he said. "Senator Stuart, would you care to come with us? I'm sure you have some questions about all this."

"Absolutely." Cynthia looked around to where her colleagues were clustering around the vice president, and the press. "I'd be glad to. Let's go, this way. It's shorter, and I believe, with less people."

"Damn good idea." Andrew finally spoke up. "Bet you got one of them limo cars outside there too."

"Well, yes, actually...it's shared but..."

"S'allright, we'll just borrow it," Andrew said, firmly. "Excuse us."

Kerry let herself be guided to the stairs, completely spent and wanting nothing more than a chair, her partner, and a drink; too tired to even feel triumph or satisfaction at a job well done.

DAR SLOWLY STRETCHED her cramped fingers, listening to the sounds of raucous yelling coming from the speakerphone. She turned her head slowly and looked at Chuck after a moment, letting out a long exhale. "Congratulations," she said. "You made that happen."

Chuck chuckled wryly. "Dar, these guys made that happen." He pointed at the optic unit attached to the router. "And by the way, fellers, what you just saw was the IT equivalent of this woman flapping her arms and flying to the moon."

The two visitors had settled cross-legged on the floor. "I've been in enough bullpen situations to know that was one of those two seconds to blastoff kind of things," one said, pushing his glasses up on his nose. "Pretty neat."

Dar closed her laptop. "Let's go upstairs," she said. "I need a drink."

"Boy that sounds good." Chuck got up, and they all left the little closet and emerged into the shopping level.

Outside, the world coursed past them completely oblivious to the drama in their midst, only giving a passing glance to the engineers and the scruffy looking woman in a tank top and coveralls trudging past them.

"Long day, huh Dar?" Chuck asked.

"Long week." Dar admitted, as they headed for the elevators. She could feel her shoulders slumping, and she mostly watched the floor as they boarded the car, pausing only to punch the button for their level. "But you folks really did the job. That's an amazing feat of engineering."

"Well, thanks," one of the engineers said. "My name's Orin Wellings, by the way." He offered a hand, which Dar took. "We were glad to help. We found out some things that might help us in some other research, so it's all good." He added. "This is my colleague Doddy Ramirez."

Dar extended her hand. "Thanks."

"My pleasure." The man shook her hand. "Talk about down to the wire."

"Mm." The doors opened and Dar led them out, past the receptionist's desk. She pushed the glass doors open and headed down the hall to their client presentation center, marked by a set of teak doors and frosted glass windows. "C'mon."

They followed her inside. "Coffee and soft drinks over there." Dar pointed without looking. She headed for the couch on the far side, dropping into it just as her cell phone rang. "Help yourself to whatever you like." She didn't even check the caller ID. "Yeah."

"Hey." Kerry's voice sounded every bit as drained as Dar felt. "We're on our way back there. Me and Dad, and Alastair and my mother."

"I'm sitting on a couch in the press center waiting for you," Dar said. "But you can't bring the other three on the couch with you. They have to sit somewhere else."

Kerry managed a wry chuckle. Then she fell silent.

"You okay?" Dar asked after a moment.

Another hesitation. "I've been better," Kerry admitted. "Had a bit of a problem getting that part in."

Dar felt a jolt of concern that chased away the fog of exhaustion. "Want me to meet you at the hospital instead?"

"No." Kerry answered immediately. "I just want to go home. We can go to Doctor Steve's as soon as we land if you want, but I'm not spending another day here."

Dar nodded to herself. "Hear ya."

"Have some chocolate milk waiting for me?" Kerry added, with a sigh.

"You got it." Dar waited for the line to hang up and then she closed the phone and rested it on her knee. "The rest of our team's on the way back. Our CEO's with them, I know he wants to thank you guys in person."

The engineers took seats across from her with cups and plates and pleased expressions.

Mark entered with Kannan and Shaun, tired, but visibly happy. "Hey boss. Welcome back from the pit."

"Hey." Dar lifted a hand and waved. "Good job, people."

Scuzzy entered. "Hey! You guys did it!"

"We did it." Dar agreed, gesturing around to include the rest of the room. "You did it." She pointed at Scuzzy. "Everybody needs to slap themselves on the ass for this one."

Chuck chuckled. "Boy, I tell ya, I don't get to hear that very often." He admitted. "Mostly it's can you give me a bigger discount, Chuck, or your damn service center blew me off, Chuck, or your competitors are doing more for less, and what about that, Chuck."

"Yeah, we get that too." Mark brought a bottle of soda back to the seating area and took a chair near where Dar was sprawled on the couch. "Dar, there was only one or two streams we didn't have a gate for. I called the endpoint owner and threw a tunnel up for them, and they're good now."

"You know what the sad part is?" Dar stretched her arm out along the back of the couch. "We're the only ones who are going to know we did this."

"Who the hell cares?" Mark slid down and took a swig from his bottle. "I don't. I know I did it. That's all that matters to me."

Dar watched them all gather, and she let the conversation flow around her, as the rest of the team straggled in. She was tired, but at some level satisfied, glad the circumstances had arranged themselves to allow her to end this day with a sense of personal triumph.

It felt good. She was glad they'd done it.

She realized she must have faded out for a minute, because she looked up at the doorway just in time to see Kerry enter with her mother, and Andrew, and Alastair right behind her.

Dar got up off the couch as they approached, opening her arms up as Kerry walked right into them pressing her body against Dar's with a soft, guttural moan. She enfolded her partner in a gentle hug, oblivious to the room. "Hey babe."

"Ungh." Kerry rested her head against Dar's collarbone. "Get the jam, Paladar. I'm toast."

Dar stroked her hair. "You look it. Sit down on the couch and I'll get you your milk."

Kerry didn't move an inch. "Actually a protein shake would probably do me more good. Any chance of that?" She tilted her head and looked up. "My body's really bitching at me."

"Your wish is my command." Dar gazed down into her eyes, a faint smile shaping her lips.

Kerry's nose wrinkled just a little. "You couldn't care less if the whole room is staring at us, could you?"

"Nope."

"Me either." Kerry pulled herself up and gave Dar a kiss on the lips. "Fantastic job, boss. You brought it home."

"Likewise." Dar returned the kiss and then released her and bumped her very gently toward the couch. "Let me get you something to put in your stomach." She watched Kerry settle on the couch, and then turned to find Alastair in front of her. "Hey."

Alastair put his hand on her shoulder and just looked her in the eye.

Dar winked at him. "Sorry to ruin your martyrdom, Alastair."

She was not overly surprised when Alastair pulled her into a hug. She returned it without reservation, feeling a moment of true personal happiness. "Bastards."

"We need to talk later," he uttered just loud enough for her to hear. "But thank you, Dar. From my heart, thank you."

Dar patted his back and released him. "No problem."

"No problem." Alastair clasped her shoulder, and made his way to an overstuffed chair, which he sunk into with a long, tired exhale. "Anybody got a cup of coffee?"

Dar started to turn, only to find her father there with a bottled protein shake in his hand. "Ah. Thanks Dad. Did you..."

"Heard the kumquat ask you for it," Andrew said. "Think she's hurting. Was a hell of a thing getting to that there place, I will tell you, Paladar. That woman should be in a doctor's office."

Dar glanced at her partner, who had collapsed on the couch. "I know. But I promised we'd go home first. She said we can stop at Dr. Steve's on the way from the airport."

Andrew grunted.

"I'm not hypocritical enough to argue with her. Thanks for helping out, Dad."

Her father clapped her on the back. "Didn't do squat rugrat. Kerry done it all."

Dar took the bottle and returned to the couch, sitting down next to Kerry and opening it. "Here you go." She put her arm over Kerry's shoulders and sighed, as Cynthia Stuart finally got through the crowd and sat down on a chair next to the couch. "Hello again."

"Hello, Dar," Cynthia said. "I'm very worried about Kerry. She seems quite sick."

"Me too." Dar glanced down at her partner, who was sucking at the protein shake, her body pressed against Dar's. "She has some cracked ribs."

"Oh my goodness!" Cynthia blurted. "Kerry! Why didn't you say something?"

Kerry looked up from her shake licking her lips a little. "Didn't have time. Sorry. I guess we need to fill you in on everything else too." Her voice was husky. "Mom got me into the Exchange, Dar. They weren't letting anyone in the front door."

"Thank you." Dar looked at Cynthia. "We were running out of time."

"Well...yes, I could see that...but what exactly were you doing?"

Kerry's mother asked. "I kept hearing the oddest things, about some accident, and some problem or something." She added. "I was even told you were under some kind of investigation!"

Dar looked over at Alastair and raised an eyebrow.

"I think that was really more of a misunderstanding," Alastair said, drawing Cynthia's attention. He put his hands behind his head, interlacing his fingers. "We got it sorted out...I hope."

"They asked us to help out with some connections to the Exchange," Dar offered.

"Yes, I remember Kerry telling me that." Cynthia returned her attention to them. "Some cables or something was it?"

Dar nodded. "We ran in to a lot of issues, and had to get these engineers from NASA to help us." She indicated the two men. "They came up with a solution at the last minute. That solution was what Kerry was carrying into the Exchange."

"Oh!" Cynthia looked at her daughter. "My goodness!"

Kerry gave her a brief smile. She turned slowly and put her legs up on the couch, putting her head down on Dar's lap. "Yeah, it wasn't really a well thought out plan, but we were out of time," she admitted. "I'm really glad I spotted you going in. Wouldn't have worked otherwise."

"Oh, well." Cynthia looked more than a little confused. "Well, of course I was glad to help, but it was so curious that you were having problems with them letting you inside. Didn't they want this problem addressed?"

"Now there's the sixty-four thousand dollar question." Alastair mused. "I tell you, Senator. There were a lot of conflicting motives in that building today."

"Goodness." Cynthia turned toward Alastair again. "But why would that have been, Mr. McLean. Please explain it to me, because I can see no reason for this strange confusion, and I want to understand since I am sure this will come up between me and my colleagues."

"Well..." Alastair drew her attention, giving the pair on the couch some time.

Dar draped one arm carefully over her partner's body. "Feeling any better?"

Kerry turned her head a little, peering up at Dar. "A little." She lifted one hand and rubbed her eyes. "I just feel so damned washed out. It's driving me crazy. I can't think straight," she answered, in a low tone. "Not to mention my guts hurt." She put a hand on her chest. "And I can't get a deep breath because of it."

Dar smoothed the hair back out of her eyes. She could see a glaze in the green eyes looking back at her, and she frowned in concern for a long moment before she pulled out her cell phone. "Okay." She dialed a number from the memory. "Second opinion time."

Kerry closed her eyes and let her cheek rest against Dar's belly. It felt good to be lying down, and even better to be lying down on top of her partner. She wrapped her fingers around Dar's arm and concentrated on breathing shallowly, as she listened to the phone conversation.

"Hey, Sheryl. It's Dar." Dar watched the twitching tension across her partner's face. "Is the doc in? Can I talk to him for a minute?" She waited through a few moments of Gloria Estefan hold music, and then a familiar voice answered. "Hi, Dr. Steve."

"Hey Dar. What's up? Where are ya?"

"New York. Listen, Kerry's here with me and she ran into some trouble."

Their family doctor chuckled wryly. "You're rubbing off on her."

"She got a couple of cracked ribs." Dar went on. "They said it was hairline, but she's feeling pretty bad right now. Says she feels drained and can't think straight."

"Where is she?"

"Lying in my lap," Dar admitted. "But I don't think that's causing it." That even got a smile from Kerry, who opened her eyes and peered up at her. "She's white as a sheet."

There was a bit of rattling and a scuffing noise. "Hang on," Dr. Steve said, his voice a little more serious now. "You know which ribs they are?"

Dar looked down at Kerry who shrugged faintly, and then casually unbuttoned her shirt.

"Go ahead and count. You can see where the bandages are." Kerry closed her eyes again feeling a bit of a draft from the room on her now exposed skin. "Glad I decided on a sports bra this morning."

Dar gently counted up from her waistline. "Six from the bottom," she spoke into the phone. "Somewhere around there."

"Uh huh." Dr. Steve grunted. "They said it was a crack?"

"Just a hairline fracture according to the guy at the hospital. He said to have her sleep sitting up and gave her a prescription for the pain. He sent the X-rays back with us."

"What drugs he give her?" Dr. Steve asked.

Dar pulled the bottle out of Kerry's pocket and examined it. "Oxy-Contin. We picked it up yesterday."

"Honey, throw that in the trash," Dr. Steve said immediately. "Where the hell are you? I'll call you in something else. That stuff's a pile of problems. She having any trouble breathing? Dizzy?"

Dar could feel Kerry's ribcage moving under her hand, and it seemed to her to be doing so with more effort than usual. "I think so."

"Don't let her take any more of that," their doctor said. "How long you going to be there?"

Dar felt a sense of relief. "We're heading back home at one. Can I give her some Advil until we get back?" She looked down into Kerry's inquisitive eyes. She held up the pill bottle and rattled it. "I'll make sure she doesn't take any more of this."

Kerry's face relaxed a little.

"You can do that, rugrat," Dr. Steve said. "I'll see you when you get here, right?"

"Right. Thanks Doc." Dar hung up the phone. "He doesn't like the script."

Kerry blinked a little. "That makes sense," she said. "I didn't start feeling this crappy until after I started taking it. When I got back from the hospital I was fine the whole night." She stifled a yawn and let her cheek rest against Dar's body again. "I'll be fine here until we leave."

Dar tucked the bottle of pills into the cushion. She glanced up as Cynthia returned her attention to them, apparently done with Alastair. She saw the woman's eyes fall on her partner's half bared chest and belatedly realized her tattoo was showing, the snake's head saucily exposed.

Covering it with her shirt would be only too obvious. Dar rested her hand on Kerry's bare belly instead, rubbing lightly the skin just over her navel.

"Kerry, is that..." Cynthia leaned closer. "Is that a tattoo?"

Kerry's eyes went wide, and her nostrils flared. Her hand twitched, as it lay right next to Dar's, and her breathing sped up.

"Isn't it gorgeous?" Dar gallantly came to her rescue. "It's an oraborus, a symbol of eternity, curled around my name." She lifted her hand and traced the design, moving the edge of Kerry's sports bra over so her mother could see it better. "Look at those scales."

"Ah." Cynthia edged closer and peered, not without hesitation. "How interesting." She cleared her throat. "Angela did mention something about that."

"I can always count on Angie." Kerry now dared turn her head and peek at her mother. "She saw it when I stayed at her house last week. Was it last week?" Her brow creased. "Seems like a long time ago."

"Yes, it does." Her mother recovered. "It's quite intricate."

"You don't like it," Kerry said, in a mild tone. "It's okay if you don't."

"Well," Cynthia said, "no, I don't. I don't think it's right for a young woman to mark herself up in that way." She paused. "So, no, in fact, I do not like it."

Kerry felt refreshed by the honesty. "That's okay. I didn't expect you to," she replied with equal candor. "A lot of people don't."

Her mother paused for a long moment, and then shook her head. "Why did you do it then? I am curious."

Kerry looked back up at Dar. "Why did I do it?" She mused. "I think I just wanted that statement, that emotion to be as vivid on the outside of me as it is on the inside." She closed her eyes again and exhaled, another wave of lethargy passing over her.

"I see," her mother murmured.

"I heard Angie's good news." Kerry decided a change in subject was probably a good idea. She could hear her mother struggling to keep her thoughts to herself and she had no desire to spark an argument at the moment.

"Yes." Cynthia sat back, with a genuine smile. "I'm so pleased." She seemed glad of the change as well. "It was a great surprise, but a very welcome one."

Dar cleared her throat gently.

Kerry forced her eyes open to see the raised brows. "Brian proposed to my sister. Angie was as freaked out as you were when I proposed to you."

Dar produced a big grin at that. Then she glanced up at Cynthia. "Congratulations."

"Thank you," Cynthia said, taking a deep breath. "Well, I'm glad these things worked themselves out. I believe I must go back and meet with my colleagues, and then perhaps we might attend a working dinner with the vice president."

"By then we'll be home." Kerry exhaled. "Thank god." She turned her head and opened one eye. "Hope it turns out okay for you."

"And a safe trip to both of you as well." Cynthia concluded. "I'm sure we'll be speaking, Kerry. Angela has told me she wishes you to stand with her at the wedding."

Kerry nodded. "I told her absolutely," she said, getting a smile from her mother. "I'm really happy for her."

"As am I." Cynthia stood up. "Hope you feel better soon, Kerry. I'm sure you're well taken care of here." She gave Dar a nod. "And it was nice meeting you, Mr. McLean. Thank you for explaining things to me."

"My pleasure." Alastair was still sitting quietly in his chair. "Nice meeting you too."

Cynthia gave them all a wave and turned, making her way out of the room.

Dar gently buttoned up her partner's shirt and settled her arm protectively over Kerry's middle again. "Take a nap, champ," she told her obviously groggy companion. "I'll wake you up when it's time for us to leave."

"Gotta..." Kerry muttered. "Damn this stuff's kicking my butt." She gave in to the desire to sleep, as Dar's fingertips gently massaged her temples. "Dar, I'm gonna have to come up with something more radical."

"Huh?"

"I'm outta things to shock my mother with."

Dar chuckled faintly, and that was the last thing Kerry remembered before she let the room slip away.

Chapter Eighteen

CYNTHIA CROSSED THE lobby of the building and approached the front door. She paused, when she spotted Andrew Roberts entering. "Oh, Commander." She waved at him.

The tall ex-seal altered course and intercepted her. He had two overnight bags slung over his shoulder. "Lo."

"I just wanted to bid my farewell to you," Cynthia said. "I assume you are heading home as well."

"That's true." Andrew glanced around. "You want a cup of coffee fore you go? Ah just saw pictures of them people back at the exchange and it's crazy there."

Cynthia hesitated, and then she nodded. "I could use a cup of coffee," she admitted. "There's a nice café, will you join me?"

"Sure." Andrew followed her over to one of the seats and they took over one of the tables in the little café to one side of the lobby. It was before lunchtime, so it was still quiet, and a waitress scooted right over to them when she saw them sit down.

Andrew set the bags down and exhaled. "Biggest cup of coffee you got," he told the girl, who nodded.

"Do you have tea?" Cynthia asked. "I'd prefer that, please."

"Sure, be right back." The waitress left, still scribbling.

"You look tired, Commander. I know it must have been a long week for you as well."

"Yeap," Andrew admitted. "Ah will be glad to get home to mah wife and mah boat, I will tell you. I do not regret coming here to help the kids out, but ah will be very happy to see that there airplane shortly."

"I do understand." Cynthia commiserated. "I didn't want to come here, you know. I wanted to stay in Michigan, dealing with the issues we have there. But I was told it would be highly unpatriotic if I did not come to support the city, so I did."

Andrew snorted. "Patriotism. Most these people round the gov'mint don't know how to even spell that word less what it means."

Cynthia studied him. "It's so interesting that you say that." She looked up as the waiter arrived, and deposited their drinks. "May I also have, perhaps, a tuna on croissant?"

"Sure." The waitress looked at Andrew expectantly.

"Ya'll got hamburgers?" Andrew asked.

"Sure."

"Have me one with cheese and some fries."

"No problem." The waitress whisked off, in a better mood.

Andrew took a sip of his coffee. "You going back home today?"

Cynthia sighed. "Probably tomorrow. As much as I am not enjoying this position I accepted, one does have to stand up for it, you know."

"Yeap."

"Though, I have to admit, I do not think it matters whether or not I go. I am not going to continue in this post, and therefore, the decision really should be mine."

"Yeap," Andrew agreed. "Thought I had to live up to stuff fore I almost lost everything I ever had for that. Don't go there no more." He shook his head. "Figured out I love my family more than my country."

Cynthia smiled. "That's so charming. And you know, I do think you're right. I believe I will change my itinerary, and leave this afternoon as well, since I have so much to do back in Michigan."

"Hear you got a wedding coming." Andrew sat back and sucked his coffee. "Glad that feller stepped up."

The woman across from him lifted her teacup in his direction. "Thank the lord," she said. "I was so disappointed with Brian, really. It's been very hard on Angela, though surely she had to take the same responsibility for her actions." She studied his scarred face. "I did think that was going to be quite awkward between Angela and Kerrison."

Andrew chuckled. "Kerry was some pissed at that boy. Thought he wasn't doing right by her sister."

"Oh," Cynthia said. "Well, yes, I suppose she would feel that way." She sipped her tea. "After all, she'd met Dar by then, hadn't she?"

Andrew smiled. "She done that." He allowed. "Dar said they got to be sweethearts right off."

They were both quiet, as the waitress came back and set their plates down, then left again to attend to the customers now coming in for lunch.

"That...ah, never bothered you, did it?" Cynthia asked.

"Naw." Andrew cut his burger in half and selected the left side of it. "Never had to worry about no feller coming by and doing her wrong while I was out there overseas, anyhow."

"Oh." Kerry's mother sounded surprised. "Well, I never thought of that." She picked her way through her tuna croissant. "At any rate, I am glad she's happy, and that she and Dar are so very fond of each other."

"Me, too." Andrew ate a fry. "Your kid's good people. I am damn glad she's part of mah family."

Cynthia smiled wryly. "I would imagine she feels the same," she murmured. "I know she's had a trying time with her own."

Andrew finished his burger. "Wall, ah think y'all will be all right in that way." He wiped his lips. "She's right fond of you all. Just take some time. Y'all got that."

"Yes, we do." Kerry's mother smiled a little more easily. "As terrible as this past week has been, it has given me hope that my family can find a way to come together again. Kerry has invited me down to see their home and meet their friends."

Andrew chewed his fries as he considered this. "Got a nice place," he finally said. "Ah like that little place they got down south better than the fancy one, but it's all right too."

"Do you mean the cabin? Kerry showed me pictures. It looks so charming." Cynthia sipped her tea. "I'm looking forward to seeing it. She even showed me photos of their pet."

"Hairball." Andrew chuckled softly. "Cute dog." He amended.

"Yes," his table companion said. "Kerry told me..." She hesitated. "I never actually knew what had happened with her little Cocker Spaniel."

Andrew merely grunted.

"I feel terrible now about it. Roger wanted to get her another one, and I convinced him not to." Cynthia said a pensive look on her face. "I just didn't want to have to deal with a puppy. All the mess...I just never knew how much it meant to her or what..."

"That feller who done that was a wrong-headed man," Andrew said quietly.

"Yes, he was," Cynthia said. "Do you know, the police finally closed that case they were investigating about it?" She watched his face intently. "They decided it was an accident after all."

Andrew lifted his eyes and met hers squarely. "That man got what was coming to him. Ah only wish it'd come to him twenty years b'fore then so he did not have no chance to do what he done to your daughter."

Cynthia took a breath, and released it. "Roger finally realized the things Kerry had said weren't lies." She lowered her voice. "It upset him so much. He sent Kyle away while he investigated, and the night he got so sick...it was after he finally spoke to Kerry's old doctor."

Andrew cocked his head slightly.

"You know, I had never seen him cry before," Kerry's mother said simply. "It astounded me. I had no idea why he was so upset, and then...well, then he had this meeting he had to go to and after that...it was too late and he couldn't tell me."

"Lord."

Cynthia wiped her lips slowly with her napkin. "Terrible," she murmured. "I am glad Kyle died. It is not a Christian thing to say, but it's true." She watched Andrew slowly nod. "I do like to think he got what he deserved."

"Ah do believe he did," Andrew said. "Might be he even knowed that fore he died."

Cynthia exhaled. "May the Lord grant that he did." She reached over and patted his hand. "Commander, thank you for taking the time to have lunch with me. It's always lovely talking to you."

Andrew's eyes took on a humorous glint. "Ya'll be sure to let mah wife know when you're coming down our way. We can go have us some conch fritters together."

"I certainly will." She stood up, as the waiter came over. "Here, I believe this will cover it. Thank you." She handed the man a folded bill. "Commander, thank you for letting me buy you lunch. I hope you have a wonderful trip home."

"Same t'you." Andrew lifted a hand and waved it at her. "And call me Andy. I ain't in the Navy no more."

Cynthia smiled. "I will do that. After all, we're family, aren't we?" She turned and left the café, heading for the front door again.

Andrew shook his head and chuckled briefly. "Lord."

DAR WAS CONTENT to sit quietly on the couch providing a pillow for Kerry's sleeping form. The room had gotten crowded with both New York staff and their visiting team, and a pile of boxes had just been deposited on the conference table filling the air with the scent of cheese and garlic.

Kerry was oblivious to it all. Someone had brought a blanket up from the bus and she had it tucked around her, and around Dar's arm that was draped over her body.

Alastair came over with a plate. "Piece of pizza, Dar?" He offered her a slice. "Probably won't have much at the airport."

"Sure." Dar maneuvered the big slice with one hand, getting it folded between her fingers before she nibbled at the small end. It was hot, cheesy, and had a nice crisp crust that tasted a touch smokey. "Mm."

"Sometimes you like life's simple pleasures." Alastair took a bite of his own. "This is one of them."

Dar had to agree. "Bet your wife is looking forward to you getting home, huh?"

"Lady, you know it." Alastair settled back in his chair, balancing a can of root beer on the arm. "We can share a ride to the airport. Get a few minutes of private chat time."

Dar nodded. "You talk to the board?" She glanced up to see the door open and Hamilton appear. "Ah. Lawyer's in the house."

Alastair turned his head. "Hey, Ham, over here." He called out. "Grab yourself a piece of pie and sit down."

Their corporate lawyer complied. He laid two pieces on a paper plate and came over to join them. Atypically, he was dressed in jeans and a polo shirt rather than his usual suit, and he settled into the chair across from Dar with a weary grunt.

"Got your tickets?" Alastair asked.

"Hell yes." Hamilton answered. "I've had enough of the neighborhood to last me a coon's birthday." He bit into his pizza. "I'm on your flight back to Houston, Al. I've got so much paperwork to dig through I might as well take up your space to do it."

Alastair grunted and nodded.

"Where are we with all those government demands?" Dar asked.

"Don't go there, Maestro." Hamilton waved his pizza at her. "Do not ask about any of that. Just please go back to Miami and continue being brilliant and let me do my job."

Dar blinked at him. "Sure. All yours."

"Let's just say I had my hands full the last couple of days," Ham said. "Al, you owe me a damned fine steak dinner out of this."

"No problem my friend." Alastair took a swig of his root beer. "That's a debt I'm glad to pay. We've got a lot of work ahead of us in the next few days."

"Got that right."

Dar could feel Kerry's gentle breathing under her hand, and she was reassured by the easy rhythm of it. She could sense a feeling of relief in the people around her, both the natives and the visitors, and even a few smiles from the New York staff as they joined their teammates in the pizza and drinks.

She wished she could go to sleep along with Kerry. The thought of going through the hassle at the airport and then the flight home was absolutely exhausting.

"Hey, Maestro."

Dar looked up at Hamilton. "Mm?"

"Good job." The lawyer toasted her with his soda.

"Thanks," Dar answered. "Was it worth it?" She indicated the television screen in the background that had CNN on. "Market's dropped how many hundred points?"

Hamilton shrugged. "My daddy, who I will tell you thought I was coming down in the world when I went to law school, advised anyone who would listen that only fools lost money in the stock market. Everyone else just recognized a fabulous buy opportunity when they saw it."

"Our stock's up," Alastair remarked dryly.

"Airlines are dropping," Hamilton added. "That's why I want to get my Louisiana lily white ass out of here before they go bankrupt and stop putting fuel in the tanks before they take off."

"Think they will?" Alastair asked. "People won't stop flying."

"Won't they?" Hamilton asked. "Who's to say it won't happen again. People don't like dying. It ruins their day, Al."

They all went quiet for a moment. "Well." Alastair half shrugged. "I'm not walking back to Houston so I guess I'll risk it. Bad enough I almost ended up having to swim from the Bahamas or get sailed in by Captain Roberts, here."

"What?" Hamilton stared at him.

"Oh, didn't tell you about that part, did I." Alastair rested his head on his fist. "So damned much has happened I'm losing track." He pondered that. "I need a vacation."

"C'mon down by us." Dar offered. "I'll teach you to scuba dive."

Hamilton chuckled. "I'd love to see that." He leaned back in his seat. "See some octopus chasing your ass around the ocean.

Alastair rolled his eyes. Then his cell phone rang and he set his pizza down to answer it. "Now what?" He opened the phone. "Hello?" He paused, listening. "Well, hello, Governor."

"Even if I had grits, I wouldn't let that cheap excuse for a catfish kiss them." Hamilton indicated the phone. "He's got nothing but everyone's worst interests in mind."

"Well, thanks, but we...No, I don't really think we've got the...ah, sure, but..." Alastair removed the phone from his ear and stared at it. "Well, goodbye to you too." He studied the instrument, and then folded it and returned it to his pocket.

"And?" Dar asked.

"The governor has a list of things he wants us to do," Alastair said. "He's on his way over here with a group of something or other and intends on staging a press conference and setting up a task force center."

"Guess he figured out which side we were on," Dar mused.

"Guess he wants everything for free," Hamilton added dryly.

"Guess he can kiss my ass." Alastair stood up and put his hands in his pockets. "Ladies and gents, please listen up."

The room got quiet quickly and everyone turned to face him.

"I'd like to thank you all for everything you've done in the past week. We've done a hell of a job here, despite a lot of personal struggle and tragedy, and believe me when I tell you I personally appreciate that more than I can say."

Tentative smiles appeared. "It's been good having you here, sir," one of the New York staff said. "We really appreciate all the support we've gotten. Everyone's been so wonderful."

"Thanks." Alastair smiled at them. "But right now, what I'd like you all to do is get your things, and pack everything up, and leave the office, quickly as you can."

Everyone stared at him in some surprise.

"Sir?" the man asked. "Is there something wrong?"

"Not a thing," Alastair assured him. "There are some folks coming down here to try and ask us for something I don't want to be around for. So let's get moving, please. Those of us who are visiting are about to head for the airport anyway."

Everyone stirred and started to leave the room, still obviously puzzled. "Paid time off, of course," Alastair added. "Chop chop."

Hamilton had his head tilted back to watch the CEO. "You're becoming an ornery old bastard, Al," he commented. "How's that going to look if the governor shows up here, and no one's home?"

"No one's here, he can't ask anyone, can he," Alastair retorted. "Get a move on, Ham. Get us a car ready and let's scoot. Move it."

Hamilton got up and bowed, then headed off toward the door, chuckling under his breath. Alastair turned to Dar, his brows hiking "You ready to go home, lady?"

"More than," Dar said. "Dad just got back with our bags, so we're ready to go soon as I wake Ker up." She glanced down at her partner. "You sure you want to piss this guy off again?"

"Bastards were threatening to have us all picked up as terrorists and held without counsel, Dar. You want to spend any more time here?"

"Would they have really done it though?" Dar started to gently scratch Kerry's stomach, to get her to wake up. "Or was it just a bluff?"

"I had federal agents on either side of me with handcuffs in that Exchange," he said. "They were all set to announce to the press that they'd uncovered a terrorist plot to overthrow the government by co-opting its information technology."

Dar stared at him. "You're serious?"

"As a heart attack," Alastair said, with commendable calm. "So wake up your sleeping beauty, and let's get outta here. I only hope they don't give us a hassle at the airport." He turned and watched the room empty, except for Andrew who was perched nearby on a chair arm, the bags on the seat next to him. "Ready to move out, commander?"

"Surely, genr'l," Andrew responded. "Sooner we get out of this place, better for us."

"You got that right." Alastair headed for the door. "Move it people! Move it!"

"ALL RIGHT, LET'S GO." Alastair got into the limo and settled across from Dar. "Feeling any better, Kerry?"

"Eh." Kerry was wedged in the corner of her seat, her hands tucked inside the pocket of her hoodie. "My ribs are killing me, but my head feels a lot clearer. The nap helped."

The limo started moving with the bus right behind it where the rest of the team was riding. Kerry and Dar were alone with Alastair and Hamilton, and Kerry almost wished she wasn't. She had a feeling she was going to be hearing things she wasn't going to like.

Dar was seated next to her stifling a yawn. She had her briefcase next to her and a bottle of water in one hand, and she looked both tired and distracted. "You think they'll...what do you think they'll do when they get here and the office is closed?" she asked.

"Beats me." Alastair put his hands behind his head. "I'm sure he'll call me, and I'm sure I'll think of some lie to tell him. Maybe I took the office out to Central Park for buggy rides."

"Al." Hamilton tsked.

"Sorry Ham, I just don't care. I'm not spending one more minute here getting beaten to hell by these bastards. I'll exit the contracts, all of them."

Even Dar blinked.

"I figured," Alastair cleared his throat, "I figured they'd pin me, when I told them we weren't doing the work for them. I figured we'd get bad press, and I'd be pretty embarrassed on television, but hell. How bad could it really be, right?"

"But that wasn't going to happen," Kerry spoke up, her voice still slightly husky. "Was it? I heard the technicians in the Exchange talking about the FBI."

"Found out when I got there that it was a lot worse," Alastair said. "They figured they'd out us as plotting against the government, the company, that is. Had it all laid out. The fact we snuck into the country, all the exceptions we asked for, the guard fracas down by the river, you name it. They had so much detail on so many things they could twist to make us look like the bad guys...hell."

"But none of it was true," Kerry said. "We did nothing but good for them."

"Truth didn't matter," Alastair said. "They wanted a big splash on CNN, big scandal, show they were on the ball, they'd uncovered a plot..."

"They didn't fall down on the job like they did last Tuesday?" Dar spoke up for the first time. She smiled grimly as Hamilton pointed both index fingers at her.

"But really," Kerry said. "They have to prove things like that."

"No they don't," Hamilton said. "That's what changed. They passed a law that gives them the right to hold anyone they think's a terrorist for however long they want, wherever they want, without no charges, or no lawyers."

Kerry stared at him. "What?"

"Ask your mother," Hamilton said. "They said it was necessary so they could find more terrorists planning other atrocities here."

"But we're not terrorists," Kerry said.

"It doesn't matter." Alastair exhaled. "That's what I finally understood, standing there on that damn platform with those damn smug jackasses all around me, telling me exactly what they were going to do because they knew I couldn't do anything about it."

"All that mattered was the spin," Hamilton said. "They told me that when I was looking to file those lawsuits. Told me to not even bother. The law didn't matter right now."

"So anyway," Alastair picked the ball back up, "there I am, standing in the middle of hell wondering how I'm at least going to warn my wife I won't be home when I spot Kerry standing there with a gaggle of senators, and I'm wondering what on earth's going on."

Kerry managed a smile. "I walked into the building with my mother," she said. "It's the only way I was going to get in. She ran interference with the guards, but she had no idea what was going on either. I just had time to get to the server room and put the optic in place before I got upstairs."

"So you knew they were up?" Hamilton asked.

Kerry shook her head. "I knew the link was up, and I knew the rest of it was up to Dar." She looked over at her partner. "She had about two minutes to do what I guess was about three hours work."

Dar shrugged modestly. "I type fast." She gazed over at Alastair. "So you're telling me after we did what we did at the Pentagon, and after all we did for them up to the Exchange, they were going to railroad us?"

Alastair nodded. "Honestly, Dar, it wasn't personal." He saw both women make a face, and glance at each other. "The VP and I go way back. In their minds it was a case of what they thought was right for the country versus a bunch of nerds from some company giving them a hive."

"Scary," Dar murmured.

"It was," Alastair admitted. "I was standing there kicking myself for making a stupid decision and knowing we were all going to pay for it. I didn't want us to be a public failure. Instead, I almost walked us into the end of the company."

"Except we got lucky," Dar said.

"You really think that was luck?" Alastair asked with a smile. "I think it was just people who refuse to stop until they hit the end zone."

Dar shrugged again, lifting her hand in the air and letting it fall. "We made it happen," she acknowledged. "I'm very proud of our team."

"So am I," Alastair said.

"What are you going to tell the board, Al?" Hamilton asked.

Alastair gazed out the window for a few moments in thoughtful silence. "Haven't decided yet. They know I turned them down. I told them I'd take the fall and they were all right with that."

"Morons," Dar commented.

Hamilton snickered. "Al, you have to tell them the whole deal. Lay it out. They gotta know in case this comes back at us."

"Beh."

"Have Dar tell em," the lawyer persisted. "She can get on that call with her typical badass attitude and tell them 'Hey morons! Listen up!'" He gazed fondly at Dar. "You'd do that for Al, wouldn't you, Maestro?"

"Sure," Dar readily agreed. "But I think he's right. I think you should tell the board exactly what happened, Alastair. Everything, including the threats because I think we'll need to decide what the hell we're going to do with our being the government's IT Siamese twin."

Kerry nodded, but kept quiet.

"Half our business is U.S. Government," Alastair stated. "Might get tough."

"If we disband the company," Kerry spoke up at last. "I vote we open a clam shack down in Key Largo where the highest tech item is a wifi hotspot on the tiki roof."

"You ready to retire already?" Hamilton asked her with a smile.

"Right now, yes," Kerry answered. "In a heartbeat."

"I'm with you on that one," Alastair responded, surprising them. "I'm going to have a hell of a time going in to work behind that damn desk after what we all just went through."

Kerry felt that at a gut level. The experience had changed all of them, to a more or lesser degree. She glanced past Dar out the other window as she heard the faint rumble of an airplane taking off. "Almost there."

Dar turned to look too. The entrance to the airport was guarded, and the limo slowed as they reached the checkpoint. "Let's hope they don't have orders to throw us in a paddy wagon." She sat back as the driver opened the windows for the guards to peer inside.

"Hello there." Alastair remained in a relaxed pose his hands still behind his head. "Just catching a flight."

The guard studied them, then turned away dismissively and waved them on. The window closed and they pulled into the airport terminal. "Guess we didn't look dangerous." Hamilton commented. "Little do they know, the poor suckers."

"They're going to freak with the bus." Dar predicted. "We still have half a ton of gear in the back lockers."

"Let's hope they don't," Kerry said. "Dad's back there."

They got to the curb and eased out of the limo onto a sidewalk that was eerily quiet. There were guards stationed along the walk, but only a few cars were there discharging passengers. Alastair signed for the limo driver, and then they stepped back and stood together for a moment.

"Here comes the bus." Hamilton indicated the big vehicle now winding its way toward them. "We should go in as a group. I think our tickets are booked on one big itinerary.'

"They are," Alastair confirmed. "Bea took care of it."

Kerry stood with her hands tucked into her hoodie pocket, watching the bus unload itself of its human and luggage cargo. The techs were all in good moods, glad the work was over and even more glad to be headed home.

She certainly was. She drew in a careful breath and let it out, wincing against the throbbing ache in her side. It felt raw and very painful, as though the bone was creaking in there and every movement almost made her bite her lip.

She felt Dar's hand settle on her shoulder. "Hey," she murmured.

"Doing okay?"

Kerry pulled the hand on her good side out and waggled it, then returned it to its nest. "I'm glad I don't feel like a zombie anymore but boy, this hurts."

"I've got some Advil. Dr. Steve said you could take that." Dar offered. "Let's go inside and get through security and I'll get you some."

That sounded great to Kerry. She followed Dar into the building with the rest of the group as they entered the terminal and started across the worn carpet toward the check in area. It wasn't that busy and they all went up to the counter at the same time.

Kerry stood quietly just behind Dar's shoulder as her partner handed over both of their identifications and declined the offer to check their luggage. It all sounded very normal, and Kerry wondered if it had been that normal for the hijackers as they had checked in not quite a week ago.

The gate agent asked Dar if she'd packed her own luggage. Dar answered that she had, and that no one had given them anything to take on. But that wasn't true, really, since Andrew had packed both their bags.

Should Dar have said that? In this case, of course, it didn't matter because it was her father. But what had the terrorists said in response?

Had they smiled?

Were there more of them right here in the terminal, just waiting for their chance? Waiting for everyone to relax again?

"Okay, c'mon, Ker." Dar handed her a folder. "Here's your boarding pass."

Kerry took it and stuck it in her hoodie pocket. She followed Dar through the winding lines around the corner and into another line, this time for security. "Hope they don't ask to frisk me," she said. "I can't hold my right arm out."

"Why in the hell would they want to f...no, let me rephrase that." Dar settled the straps of both their bags on her shoulder. "I totally understand the desire to frisk you. They better not think about it."

Kerry chuckled faintly. "You're so funny." She sighed, as the rest of their group caught up to them in line. "Hey Dad."

"Hey kumquat. You doing okay?" Andrew had his bag over his shoulder, and he eyed the ones Dar had but didn't grab for them.

"Eh." Kerry moved forward in line as they approached the security station. "I'll be happy when the plane lands."

"You got that right, boss," Mark agreed. "Thanks for making a deal to get those trucks back, Dar. I really didn't feel like driving back tonight."

They got to the front and filed into the security line. Kerry was guiltily content to allow Dar to put all her stuff on the belt, as she waited her turn to go through the X-ray machine. She stepped through and heard no tell tale beeps, but she looked at the guard anyway in question.

He took her boarding pass and looked at it, then waved her through. Gratefully she went to the belt and reclaimed her overnight bag and briefcase just as Dar appeared behind her. They got their stuff and continued on moving down the hallway and then pausing to wait for the others.

Andrew was being held up in the line. Dar watched as her father produced a card then waited, his arms crossed as it was examined. "He's got metal plates in him."

"I know. I remember when we went into the Federal building during my father's hearings," Kerry said. "Should we go help out? Oh, here he comes."

Andrew shook his head, and picked up his bag. He slung it over his shoulder before he joined them. "Can you take it out?" He mimicked the guard's question. "These people are some idiots sometimes. I swear."

Kerry smiled. They walked slowly toward their gate, the rest of the techs in a group behind them. They all stopped at one gate, and then Alastair, Hamilton and Nan started their goodbyes to go on to their own.

"I can't say this was fun," Nan said to Dar. "But it certainly was something I will never forget." She shook Dar's hand. "Thanks for letting me be a part of it."

"Thanks for volunteering," Dar responded. "I know the Virginia office will be glad to get you back."

Nan moved on and faced Kerry. "I hope you feel better."

"Me too." Kerry worked her left hand out of her pocket and reached over to squeeze Nan's. "Take care, Nan. I know I'll be talking to you on the phone." She paused. "And make sure you get your brother's resume in."

Nan blinked. "You remembered that? Wow." She laughed a little in surprise. "I feel like it was a year ago when we had that conversation."

Kerry smiled. "I have to catch the details." She waved at Nan as she walked toward her gate. "Have a good flight."

She turned to find Hamilton standing there. He reached out and put a hand on her shoulder and gave her a wry grin. "Boy, I hope we don't meet like this often," Kerry stated, catching sight of Alastair giving Dar a bear hug nearby.

Hamilton laughed. "You and me both, Kerrison Stuart." He patted her gently. "Take care of the Maestro, will you please? I owe her one for this little shindig."

"I will." Kerry watched him step aside then she was being gently hugged by Alastair. "What a week." She gave him a one-arm hug back. "Hope you have a safe trip back to Houston, Alastair. Come visit us soon, okay? I want to see Dar teach you to scuba dive too."

Alastair chuckled. "You're on, Kerry. You all have a safe trip home too." He gave the group a wave, and then he followed Hamilton down the hallway toward the next set of gates.

Kerry exhaled, as she turned and Dar put her arm around her shoulders. She looked up at her partner, seeing the exhaustion in her face. "I like Alastair."

"Me too." Dar agreed. "He's seriously thinking of retiring," she added in a quiet tone. "That's what he just told me."

"Wow." Kerry looked back down the hallway. "I don't blame him, but..."

"Yeah, but." Dar mused. "I don't want to work for anyone else."

"Me either."

"Dar, they're starting to board." Mark came over and touched Dar's arm. "I know you guys want to get on and sit down."

Kerry was glad to head for the jet way. She was glad to hear the beep as her boarding card was processed and the motion under her feet as she walked down the ramp to the airplane door and passed inside, greeted by the flight attendant who stepped aside and indicated her path to her first class seat.

They all had them. Dar had told Bea to book the whole team as first class, so she settled into her leather seat surrounded by the chatter of the techs and Dar's low, burring response as they filled the first class cabin.

"Can I get you something to drink, ma'am?" the cabin attendant asked. "Some coffee maybe? You look a little tired."

Kerry looked up at her. "How about some warm milk?" she asked. "Can you manage that?"

"Sure."

She sat back in her seat, resting her elbows on the arms. She was in the front row of the plane, and she could see the cockpit, a crude metal plate hastily covering it and it reminded her all over again of what had happened less than a week ago.

Were they safe? She looked around the first class area, which was mostly full of their people. What if there was a bad guy, or more than one in the back? She watched the crew. They looked wary and worried, their eyes taking in everyone and everything.

Including Kerry and the rest of them here in first class, who she realized, included Kannan's exotic features, and Andrew's scarred intimidation. Was the crew worried about them? Should they be?

The flight attendant returned with a steaming cup. She set it next to Kerry's hand, and set down a small dish of warm nuts next to it. "Here you go."

"Thanks," Kerry said. "Terrible week for you guys, huh?"

The attendant made a face. "The worst ever," she said. "You live in New York?"

"No." Kerry indicated the people around them. "We're from Miami. We work for ILS. We drove up to help out, now we're going home."

"Oh." The attendant looked around the first class cabin. "Are these people all with you?" She glanced back at Kerry, who nodded. "That's good to know. Every time I fly now, I wonder; who are these people? Are they crazy? Are they going to hurt me? I never felt like that before."

"I think we all feel that way now," Kerry commented, as Dar returned to her seat and dropped into it. "Hey. You got that Advil?"

"Sure." Dar got up and rummaged in the overhead bin, pulling the bottle out of her backpack. "Can I get some coffee?" she asked the attendant. "Before we take off?"

"Sure." The attendant gave her a friendly smile. "Be right back."

Kerry watched her return to the service area and talk to her colleague, who had a list in her hand and was reviewing it. She looked at the list, then out at them, and then nodded, a look of perceptible relief on her face.

Wow. Kerry leaned back, as Dar handed her some pills. She popped them into her mouth and swallowed them down with a sip of her warm milk. What would it be like to go to work every day and worry about someone trying to kill you and everyone around you?

It would be like being at war, she guessed. Or being somewhere that bombs going off were an everyday occurrence.

Welcome to the rest of the world, America.

Dar took her seat and reached over the divider to take Kerry's hand curling her fingers around her partner's and letting out a tired sigh. The attendant closed the door to the airplane and they were on their way.

At last.

Chapter Nineteen

"ALL RIGHT, YOU little scamp. Stay still a minute."

Kerry did, closing her eyes as she heard the hum of the X-ray machine. She was flat on her back, the chill of the table cool against her bare shoulder blades and her skin still just a little warm from the sun outside.

The sun of home. The achingly hot sun and the thick, swampy air that coated her with sweat not ten steps outside the door to the Miami airport they'd landed at shortly before.

Heaven.

"Okay, got it." Dr. Steve stepped around the X-ray shield and came to Kerry's side. "That's a hell of a bruise you got there, spunky."

Kerry glanced down at her side. "Yeah. It was so stupid, Dr. Steve. I tripped trying to keep some guy from falling on his face and ended up halfway under a raised floor."

Their family doctor put his fingertip on her nose. "Next time let the guy fall on his head. Don't cause yourself such pain, huh?"

"Twenty-twenty hindsight." Kerry accepted his hand up and swung her legs off the table, easing off it to stand next to the doctor in her jeans and sports bra. "It still hurts like hell. But at least I'm not all foggy from those drugs they gave me."

"Hon." Dr. Steve put his hands on her shoulders. "That stuff could have killed you." He told her bluntly. "You were lucky you were running around like a crazy woman because you could have sat down somewhere and nodded off, and not woken up."

Kerry stared at him.

"I am not kidding. Not only wasn't it the right thing, but it was too big a dose for you. That size dose is for someone like Dar's daddy. You are not the size of Dar's daddy. I am going to call up that doctor and read him the riot act."

Kerry took a breath, and then released it. "I don't think he did it on purpose."

"That's not the point. We're doctors. We're supposed to know what the hell we're doing and not deliberately try to kill people. It's called the Hippocratic Oath. Ever hear of it?" Dr Steve seemed truly outraged. "I'm sure that guy didn't do it on purpose, he was just in a hurry."

"Well." Kerry picked up her T-shirt, holding it in her hands. "It's a good thing Dar called you then, huh?"

"For once, she did. If it had been her, I bet she wouldn't have." Dr. Steve patted her shoulder. "Now, go on in there and keep her company while I develop these. After that prescription, I want to make sure you don't have a tennis ball inside there or something he might have missed."

"Okay." Kerry walked out of the X-ray room and down the hall of the small family practice, passing two occupied rooms with nurses busy at their work. Dr. Steve had cut off the bandage she'd had on, and as she passed the reception desk, she saw the doctor's daughter glance over and wince.

"Yow." The girl stood up and came over. "Wow, looks like you got hit with a baseball bat."

"Yeah." Kerry smiled as Dar jumped up and headed over. "Hon, give me a hand with the shirt. The doc's looking at my X-rays."

Dar took the garment and gathered it in her hands. "If I'd known your ribs looked like that two days ago we'd have been home way before now." She frowned at her partner, getting the clothing over her head and settling it around her carefully.

"I don't care what they look like." Kerry leaned against her. "I just want to go home and spend a few hours in our hot tub, have something scandalously decadent delivered for dinner, and crash with you in our waterbed after that. "

Dar paused and looked slightly overwhelmed. "Boy that sounds great," she said, after a minute. "No laptops, no pagers, no pain in the ass government officials..."

"You guys had a rough time up there, huh?" Sheryl commiserated.

"We did," Kerry said. "We're glad to be home."

Dr. Steve came out of the hallway, and crooked his finger at them. "C'mere, kiddies."

Dar and Kerry joined him in his small office, where he put the X-rays up on a screen and turned it on. "Look here." He pointed at a curved shadow on the picture. "That's your rib, Kerry. You have not one, but three hairline fractures." He indicated three things that looked like scratches. "A little more pressure and that would have been a real fracture, and probably caused you a hell of a problem."

"Yow." Kerry grimaced. "So what do I do?"

"Nothing," Dr. Steve said. "They're already healing, see here?" He indicated a blur on one end. "We wrap you up and you go home and relax, which I gather is what you want to do anyway."

Kerry nodded vigorously.

"I will give you something to take the edge off." Dr. Steve continued. "Can I talk you into taking a few days off as well?"

"Absolutely." Dar answered for her. "We're both taking the rest of the week off."

The doctor stared at her suspiciously.

"Thanks boss." Kerry gave her a kiss on the shoulder. "Can we go out on the boat?"

"Absolutely." Dar agreed.

"Let me get you wrapped up before this pipe dream disappears." Dr. Steve waved Kerry out to the hallway. "I should take an X-ray of her head, the way she's talking."

TWILIGHT FOUND KERRY seated on the porch, a tall glass of ice tea by her side, and a Labrador at her feet. She rocked the swing chair back and forth with one foot braced against the railing, and savored the salt tinged air wafting past her face.

It was so good to finally be home. She reached down and scratched Chino's ears. "Hey Cheebles. You glad we're back?"

Chino stood up and licked her knee, laying her chin there and staring soulfully up at Kerry. "Gruff."

"I'm glad we're back too." Kerry told her pet. "I missed you." She watched Chino's tail wag, and felt like wagging her own in response. "Thanks for being good for your grandma."

The sliding door opened and Dar appeared, wandering over to join her and stepping over Chino to take a seat next to her.

"Ahhh." Dar propped her feet up on the rail, and put her hands behind her head. "Damn I'm glad to be here."

"Me too." Kerry took a sip of her ice tea. "Listen to those waves."

The ocean was crashing up against the beach and the seawall, and they could hear rollers coming in. "Dad just called. He and Mom just made it back over to South Point," Dar said. "He said we should get together for dinner sometime later on this week."

"Sure." Kerry leaned a little and kissed Dar on her bare shoulder. "Whatever you want to do is cool with me."

Dar put her arm over Kerry's shoulders and let her head rest against her partner's. "I want to put you in the hot tub," she said. "I have some cold apple cider chilling next to it and a bowl of cherries."

Kerry was more than ready for that. She was already in her swimsuit and she joined Dar on the steps to the tub, easing down into the heated water as the scent of chlorine rose around her. The warmth stole into her bones and she felt a sense of relief as she settled in place and the bubbles rumbled around her soothingly. "OOohhhh."

Dar slid into place next to her. She tipped her head back and looked up, to see a partly cloudy sky just starting to show a few stars scattered around. They usually visited the hot tub at night when the shadows and indirect lighting let them dispense with the swimsuits, but it was very nice to just float weightless in the water as the sky turned dark. "Feel better?"

Kerry let herself relax, and felt the tension drain from her as the bubbles flowed gently over her body. Her muscles relaxed, and even the ache in her ribs subsided a little as she no longer bore weight on her chest. "That feels wonderful," she admitted.

"It does. If you didn't have cracked ribs I'd suggest we go out for a night dive."

"Ooh." Kerry imagined the immersion and the rich twilight. "Stupid damn ribs."

"We have time." Dar offered her a glass of cider. "We can just be beach bums this week."

Kerry sipped the cold, fizzy drink. "You were serious? We're taking the week off?"

"This week, and next week if we want to," Dar responded. "They just got a month's worth of hours out of us in six days. We're due."

"Good." Kerry set the cup down and closed her eyes. "I want to sleep in tomorrow. I told Mayte to just tell everyone who calls I'm on sick leave."

Dar rolled onto her side and nibbled Kerry's ear. "I told Maria to say our offices are closed for the week," she whispered, "and not to save the voice mails or emails."

Kerry eased over onto her side facing her partner. She rested her hand on Dar's hip and leaned forward kissing her on the lips. "We're going to regret these suits, aren't we?" She savored the sensual rush as Dar's arms gently encircled her pulling them together.

"Just this once I wish we'd put on bikinis," Dar admitted. "Or waited until it was dark."

Kerry had to admit she agreed. "Twenty-twenty hindsight." She settled a little closer and kissed Dar again, the rush of the water over her skin now equal parts comforting and erotic. She blocked out the recent past and concentrated on the body pressed up against her, fingers already itching to slide the strap of Dar's suit down her shoulder.

There was no pressure against her ribs and though she still ached, she could breathe with some comfort in the weightlessness of the water. Even the ache faded as Dar's hand slid along the back of her thigh and their lips met again for a longer exploration.

It was so strange not to feel anxious. Kerry gave in to her inclination and slid Dar's strap down feeling a faint chuckle against her lips as she did so. So strange not to have all that tension and the ticking clock hanging over them.

The warm water suddenly swirled against her bare breasts as Dar neatly extracted her upper body from her suit before she even realized it was happening. She shoved aside her thoughts and focused on the teasing touch against her nipples, the gentle tweaks wringing a guttural sound from deep in her throat.

It was still twilight, but she didn't care. She got Dar's other strap down and they worked their suits off in something like harmony, motions slow and easy, ending in a rush of passion as their bare bodies met and brushed against each other.

Dar's hand stroked lightly down the inside of her thigh and Kerry forgot about everything except the desire she felt and the craving of her body for that touch. She half rolled onto her back as Dar's attentions became intimate, her hands sliding down Dar's sides in response.

The sensations built so fast she barely had time to take a breath. Her body felt like it was on fire and she surrendered to the wave of intensity just holding onto Dar to keep herself from slipping under the water.

Her body tensed and convulsed, her grip tightening instinctively and then slowly loosening as her heart hammered incessantly in her ears. She let her head fall back and looked up at Dar who was gazing lazily down at her, a sexy, knowing smile on her face.

The whole world could have changed around them, but it didn't matter. Kerry cupped the back of Dar's neck and pulled her head down for a kiss, her other hand making its way down her partner's belly.

They mattered. This mattered. Being in love mattered. Let the world go crazy. She couldn't give a damn.

DAR SURVEYED HER handiwork on the tray, trying to decide if there were exactly enough grapes surrounding the crab claws and shrimp or if she needed to add another handful. Eventually she selected a few strawberries instead, and settled them in place. Then she picked up the tray and headed into the living room with it.

Kerry was sitting in one of the plush leather chairs in her pajamas, her feet up on an ottoman, and a colorful dive magazine in her hands. She looked up as Dar entered her face creasing into an easy grin. "Oh my gosh, Paladar. What do you have there?"

"Dinner." Dar set the tray down on the table between the two chairs. "You wanted decadent, you got it. We've got seafood platters with a half dozen things to dunk stuff in, hush puppies, corn fritters, conch fritters, spicy fries, corn on the cob, a token bowl of cream spinach so you don't spank me, and Baileys mocha milkshakes."

"Ahhh." Kerry surveyed the feast. "Where do I start?" She picked up the milkshake and sucked on it. "Mm." She pointed at the magazine with her pinky. "We should go on a dive boat, Dar."

"We own a dive boat, hon." Dar curled up in the chair across from her partner. She picked up a crab claw and dunked it in a few things, then sucked the flesh from it with a low gurgle. "Mm."

"Yes, I know." Kerry selected a shrimp and scooped up a thick coating of cocktail sauce. "But I think it would be cool if we go somewhere the Dixie can't take us, like Australia or Papua New Guinea, and do a diving live aboard there."

"Hm." Dar nibbled on a corn fritter. "That could be fun. Is there a package advertised in there?" She pointed at the magazine. "Gimme. I'll book us."

Kerry tossed the magazine over. "Page 74. It's a nice looking boat, and they got good reviews."

Dar examined the page while she sucked on a crab claw. "You got it," she said. "They've got a ten day going out end of October. Want that for a birthday present?"

"Yep."

"Done."

Kerry grunted in contentment, carefully lifting her plate over and resting it on the arm of the chair as she dug into its contents. "That's going to be so cool."

They hadn't talked about work since they'd gotten home. Dar had no intention of changing that trend. "How's your side feeling?"

Kerry chewed her shrimp and swallowed before she answered. "It hurts," she admitted. "If I breathe the wrong way, it's painful, and if I move my arm around a lot. It's not that bad though." She went back for a crab claw. "It feels a lot better just being here in our home."

Dar nodded in agreement. She stretched her legs out and propped her feet on the ottoman, reaching with her other hand for the remote control. "What are you in the mood for?"

"Crocodile man," Kerry said. "Anything except news and sports."

"Gotcha." Dar found the channel and set the remote down. "After we wake up tomorrow I'm going to go down and spool the boat up. Maybe we can do sunset on the water tomorrow night. I'll have the club cater the galley."

"Sounds great to me." Kerry took a sip of her milkshake. "You think the seas are still up from that storm?"

"Hurricane Gabrielle?" Dar chuckled. "I'll check the marine forecast, but it should be all right if we head south."

"Head south." Kerry mused. "Want to go to the cabin? Chino'd love that, wouldn't you, Chi?"

The Labrador's head popped up, ears perked. Her tail started sweeping the tile floor.

"Yeah, I do," Dar said, after a brief pause. "I want to get lost for a few days. Hard to do that here."

Kerry looked up and studied her partner's profile for a moment. Dar didn't seem upset, just somewhat thoughtful and quiet, and she wondered what was going through her head. She almost asked, and then decided to be patient and see if Dar would start talking about it instead.

They ate in silence for a little while watching the antics on the screen. Kerry took a few forkfuls of the spinach and munched them, enjoying the fresh, green taste that cut the richness of the fritters and the tangy taste of the cocktail sauce.

The items were familiar to her. She and Dar often shared fresh seafood, which they both liked, and she'd gained a taste for the sweet spiciness of the fritters and the rough texture of the corn. She dipped a fritter in the spinach and chewed it, washing the whole thing down with a mouthful of milkshake that tasted almost as bad for her as she figured it probably was.

Who cared? She picked up another crab claw and dunked it in the butter sauce. "Did I dream it, or did I actually show my mother my tattoo?" she asked, glancing at Dar. "I sort of halfway remember something like that."

"You did." Dar agreed. "You pulled your shirt off in the conference room and your mom was right there. I was counting your ribs."

"Jesus." Kerry laughed softly. "Oh well. Worse ways for her to see it I guess. All in all, she really wasn't that bad for all this, even before it happened. I think I was more of a jerk to her than the other way around."

"She's had her moments." Dar demurred.

"No, I know." Kerry worked on cleaning her plate. "Nothing's going to change what happened between us, it happened. I know that, and I think she knows that. But I really was a bastard those first few days, Dar. I'm kind of ashamed of that."

"But you're such a cute bastard, Ker." Dar didn't seem fazed. "Anyway, it all ended up pretty much okay, didn't it? I thought she reacted pretty well to the tattoo. She didn't freak out. Dad said she told him she was happy she'd been invited down here."

Kerry munched a fry. "Yeah," she said, after a moment's thought. "She came through for us at the Exchange. She had no idea what was going on, but she just went with what I was asking." Kerry remembered the moment. "Maybe there's hope for us."

"I'm thinking we'll find out at your sister's wedding." Dar said, dryly. "I hope you get to pick your own dress, and you don't have to wear one of those creepy bow front things."

"I'll pick my own dress. They know better." Kerry smiled. "I'm glad for Angie."

"Me too," Dar said. "I was hoping they'd get together. I know your mother had them move in, but two kids to take care of can be tough. I know my mother had a rough time with just me."

"Just you?" Kerry looked affectionately at her partner. "Honey you're equal to triplets in anyone's book." She finished the last of her fries and sat back. "Whoof. I'm stuffed." She rested her chin on her fist, her elbow propped on the chair arm.

"Too stuffed for key lime pie?" Dar eyed her.

"Hm."

"That's what I thought."

KERRY IDLY WATCHED a seagull wheel over the dock, peering hopefully down at the tall figure wandering back up the beach. She was ensconced comfortably in the big hammock on the porch of their cabin, her bare feet dusted with sand and her skin slightly tight with sun and salt air.

It was Friday. She was several shades bronzer, a few pounds heavier, and her ribs had subsided to an ache she could manage with Advil. They had spent most of the week just lazing around the cabin, swimming in the surf and taking walks down the beach together since the weight of their dive gear was too much for Kerry's injured side to handle.

They had spent time shell hunting instead. Kerry now had quite a collection of them, and she was pondering what to do with them as she swung in the languid air. Maybe some jewelry? She'd found several tiny olives she imagined would make pretty earrings, at any rate.

She wondered if Dar would like them. She knew some of her work colleagues would. Maybe she'd make a few for Mayte and Maria before they went back. There was a place down the road that she knew would have the settings for them, and a goldsmith's shop she could get chains at a little further south.

"Hey." Dar arrived on the porch, tweaking one of Kerry's toes as she dropped into a chair nearby. Chino trotted up after her shaking herself free of salt and sand, before she went over to a large bowl near the door and lapped thirstily.

"Hey." Kerry amiably replied.

"You decided yet?" Dar leaned back and laced her fingers behind her head.

Kerry studied her partner. Dressed in a tattered pair of shorts and a tank top, her dark hair windblown all to hell, it was very hard to imagine her willingly going back to their maroon offices in Miami encased in a business suit.

Or, was that just rationalization for what she wanted to do anyway? Eh. Kerry smiled. Who cared? "I want to stay here. We can do a little work from our offices back there."

"Great decision." Dar complimented her. "Especially since we're getting a couple of visitors next week. Alastair's dropping by for his scuba lesson."

"Really?" Kerry rested her hands on her stomach and twiddled her thumbs. "That should be fun. Is he bringing his wife?"

"Yes. They're going to stay in one of the resorts down the road," Dar said. "We're going to have a board meeting while he's here. Get some stuff resolved. Talk about the market. The whole world is in a tailspin."

"Okay." Kerry wriggled into a slightly more comfortable position. "Sounds good to me. I still don't have to look at email until Monday, right?"

Dar gazed at her, a faint grin on her face. "Nope."

Kerry closed her eyes. "Good." She wiggled her toes. "I've almost got my brain to the fully flushed point, where I maybe could start thinking of dealing with all the crap again by Monday."

Dar got up and circled the hammock taking hold of the edge and lowering herself into it next to Kerry. She snuggled up next to her partner and sighed happily. "I vote we move the company down here. What do you think?"

"Mm." Kerry pondered that. "We'd have a hell of a time in hurricane season, honey." She mused. "But yeah, I would love to leave the traffic and the chaos behind for a while."

"Well." Dar rested her head against Kerry's. "It'll depend which way the company wants to go. If we pull out of the government contracts like Alastair was talking about, that's one thing. But I got an email from Gerry."

"Uh oh."

"Apparently," Dar cleared her throat, "that little bit of weenie waggling Alastair did had the reverse effect than he was looking for. He got some major mojo points for telling those bastards to kiss his ass."

"Oh for Pete's sake." Kerry rolled her eyes. "Why in the hell would we want to get involved with them after what they did, Dar? They tried to screw us to the wall!"

"Huge amounts of money," Dar replied. "Unlimited budget. Unlimited resources. Gerry's happy as a clam. He apparently thinks I should be too."

"Are you?" Kerry turned her head to study Dar's profile.

Dar looked up at the porch overhang for a little while as they swung together. "I'm a moderately patriotic person," she said, finally. "My father's a retired career military officer. I grew up on a military base. I came very, very close to joining the service."

"I remember when you got that medal," Kerry said. "You couldn't have stood up any straighter if you'd been a soldier. "

Dar nodded. "I've always been very proud of the fact that our company handled...no, protected so many resources of our country. I felt it was...it was always sort of a way I could be a part of that world even though I decided against it way back when."

"And?" Kerry asked, after a period of silence.

"And now, after what we just went through with the people representing our government I feel ashamed to admit to anyone we have anything to do with them." Dar's voice was gentle, and reflective. "I feel betrayed."

"When I was down by the battery, I gave one of those firemen working there some ice tea," Kerry said. "He said the same thing. He felt betrayed." She curled her fingers around Dar's. "See and I always came at it from the opposite direction, Dar. I always felt betrayed by our government because I lived with it. I saw it from the inside."

"Mm." Dar grunted. "I never thought of you like that."

Kerry chuckled. "I know. I think you see me as a lot more innocent than I really am," she said. "I don't show you my bastard side."

"You never did. Even when I was going to fire you."

"No." Kerry admitted. "You never gave me a chance. I fell in love with you the minute I saw you and the worst I could be was indignant. God, how confusing that was for me. I wanted to be so nasty to you and I think the worst thing I ever said was..."

"That you hoped I was going straight to hell because that was where I belonged." Dar interjected.

Kerry was quiet for a moment. "Yeah. Right before you saved my ass from being robbed, and maybe raped, and probably killed. So much for my ability to judge people, huh?"

"Meh." Dar shrugged, chuckling under her breath.

Kerry exhaled. "What are you going to do, Dar?"

"I don't know. I just don't know. I want to talk to Alastair, find out what he thinks, and tell him what I'm thinking. I know we talked about starting our own company before but..."

"But now maybe we mean it," Kerry finished, in a soft tone. "I could make a change. I like what I do, but sometimes it's like looking at a never-ending train track of problems just coming at you. I don't know how you did it as long as you did."

"You know what our biggest problem is?" Dar pondered the ceiling again. "For one thing, I know they'll put me under a non-compete clause if I resign and for another, if I open a consulting firm the first people who are going to be banging at my door will probably be the government."

"How long for the non-compete?" Kerry asked.

"A year, probably. That's the standard," Dar replied. "But in return for that I get all my accrued vacation time, my pension, stock options...it's a bribe, but it's a pretty good one."

"So can we go traveling around the world for a year?" Kerry asked. "Just seeing stuff?"

Dar cocked her head thoughtfully. "Now, that doesn't sound bad at all," she admitted. "Is that something you'd like to do? You want to just blow everything off for a year?"

"Are you kidding me?" Kerry eased over onto her left side and wrapped herself around Dar's body. "Yes. I would very much like to do that. Maybe after Angie's wedding we can just take off and go everywhere. Anywhere."

"That would work," Dar said, after a brief pause. "Because we'll need to give them a couple months to find our replacements." She smiled. "Wow. I can't believe how good it feels to say that."

Kerry gave her a kiss on the cheek. "Thanks."

"For?" Dar nibbled her earlobe.

"Not making me ask you to fire me."

Dar looked at her in surprise.

"I'm halfway kidding," Kerry admitted. "It's just been so nice to be able to do whatever I wanted this week instead of what I felt like I had to do." She traced one of Dar's ribs. "I guess seeing what happened to so many of those people made me realize how precious every minute is."

Dar captured her hand and lifted it, kissing the knuckles. "Yeah. That's pretty much how I feel too. I don't want to waste all my life minutes on broken routers." She went nose to nose with Kerry. "We need to have more fun."

Kerry grinned. "Of course, every time we try to have fun..." she reminded Dar. "We get our asses in trouble."

"That can be fun too." Dar cupped her cheek, and then kissed her on the lips. "You up for a walk on the beach before dinner? I think we're going to have a nice sunset."

They rolled carefully out of the hammock and paused long enough for Kerry to duck inside and get her camera and a couple of bottles of beer. Then they sauntered down the steps and headed off across the sand with Chino racing ahead of them.

"You think I could make shell jewelry Dar?"

"Sure. Why not?"

"But would you wear it?"

"Sure."

"Even if I made you a pair of three inch round sand dollar earrings?"

"No."

"You wouldn't?"

"No."

"How about a shark's tooth necklace?"

"Now you're talking."

OTHER MELISSA GOOD TITLES

Tropical Storm

From bestselling author Melissa Good comes a tale of heartache, longing, family strife, lust for love, and redemption. *Tropical Storm* took the lesbian reading world by storm when it was first written...now read this exciting revised "author's cut" edition.

Dar Roberts, corporate raider for a multi-national tech company is cold, practical, and merciless. She does her job with a razor-sharp accuracy. Friends are a luxury she cannot allow herself, and love is something she knows she'll never attain.

Kerry Stuart left Michigan for Florida in an attempt to get away from her domineering politician father and the constraints of the overly conservative life her family forced upon her. After college she worked her way into supervision at a small tech company, only to have it taken over by Dar Roberts' organization. Her association with Dar begins in disbelief, hatred, and disappointment, but when Dar unexpectedly hires Kerry as her work assistant, the dynamics of their relationship change. Over time, a bond begins to form.

But can Dar overcome years of habit and conditioning to open herself up to the uncertainty of love? And will Kerry escape from the clutches of her powerful father in order to live a better life?

ISBN 978-1-932300-60-4

Hurricane Watch

In this sequel to "Tropical Storm," Dar and Kerry are back and making their relationship permanent. But an ambitious new colleague threatens to divide them --- and out them. He wants Dar's head and her job, and he's willing to use Kerry to do it. Can their home life survive the office power play?

Dar and Kerry are redefining themselves and their priorities to build a life and a family together. But with the scheming colleagues and old flames trying to drive them apart and bring them down, the two women must overcome fear, prejudice, and their own pasts to protect the company and each other. Does their relationship have enough trust to survive the storm?

Enter the lives of two captivating characters and their world that Melissa Good's thousands of fans already know and love. Your heart will be touched by the poignant realism of the story. Your senses and emotions will be electrified by the intensity of their problems. You will care about these characters before you get very far into the story.

ISBN 978-1-935053-00

Eye of the Storm

Eye of the Storm picks up the story of Dar Roberts and Kerry Stuart a few months after Hurricane Watch ends. At first it looks like they are settling into their lives together but, as readers of this series have learned, life is never simple around Dar and Kerry. Surrounded by endless corporate intrigue, Dar experiences personal discoveries that force her to deal with issues that she had buried long ago and Kerry finally faces the consequences of her own actions. As always, they help each other through these personal challenges that, in the end, strengthen them as individuals and as a couple.

ISBN 978-1-932300-13-0

Red Sky At Morning

A connection others don't understand...
A love that won't be denied...
Danger they can sense but cannot see...

Dar Roberts was always ruthless and single-minded...until she met Kerry Stuart.

Kerry was oppressed by her family's wealth and politics. But Dar saved her from that.

Now new dangers confront them from all sides. While traveling to Chicago, Kerry's plane is struck by lightning. Dar, in New York for a stockholders' meeting, senses Kerry is in trouble. They simultaneously experience feelings that are new, sensations that both are reluctant to admit when they are finally back together. Back in Miami, a cover-up of the worst kind, problems with the military, and unexpected betrayals will cause more danger. Can Kerry help as Dar has to examine her life and loyalties and call into question all she's believed in since childhood? Will their relationship deepen through it all? Or will it be destroyed?

ISBN 978-1-932300-80-2

Thicker Than Water

This fifth entry in the continuing saga of Dar Roberts and Kerry Stuart starts off with Kerry involved in mentoring a church group of girls. Kerry is forced to acknowledge her own feelings toward and experiences with her own parents as she and Dar assist a teenager from the group who gets jailed because her parents tossed her out onto the streets when they found out she is gay. While trying to help the teenagers adjust to real world situations, Kerry gets a call concerning her father's health. Kerry flies to her family's side as her father dies, putting the family in crisis. Caught up in an international problem, Dar abandons the issue to go to Michigan, determined to support Kerry in the face of grief and hatred. Dar and Kerry face down Kerry's extended family with a little help from their own, and return home, where they decide to leave work and the world behind for a while for some time to themselves.

ISBN 978-1-932300-24-6

Terrors of the High Seas

After the stress of a long Navy project and Kerry's father's death, Dar and Kerry decide to take their first long vacation together. A cruise in the eastern Caribbean is just the nice, peaceful time they need—until they get involved in a family feud, an old murder, and come face to face with pirates as their vacation turns into a race to find the key to a decades old puzzle.

ISBN 978-1-932300-45-1

Tropical Convergence

There's trouble on the horizon for ILS when a rival challenges them head on, and their best weapons, Dar and Kerry, are distracted by life instead of focusing on the business. Add to that an old flame, and an aggressive entreprenaur throwing down the gauntlet and Dar at least is ready to throw in the towel. Is Kerry ready to follow suit, or will she decide to step out from behind Dar's shadow and step up to the challenges they both face?

ISBN 978-1-935053-18-7

OTHER YELLOW ROSE PUBLICATIONS

Brenda Adcock	Soiled Dove	978-1-935053-35-4
Brenda Adcock	The Sea Hawk	978-1-935053-10-1
Brenda Adcock	The Other Mrs. Champion	978-1-935053-46-0
Janet Albert	Twenty-four Days	978-1-935053-16-3
Janet Albert	A Table for Two	978-1-935053-27-9
Georgia Beers	Thy Neighbor's Wife	1-932300-15-5
Georgia Beers	Turning the Page	978-1-932300-71-0
Carrie Brennan	Curve	978-1-932300-41-3
Carrie Carr	Destiny's Bridge	1-932300-11-2
Carrie Carr	Faith's Crossing	1-932300-12-0
Carrie Carr	Hope's Path	1-932300-40-6
Carrie Carr	Love's Journey	978-1-932300-65-9
Carrie Carr	Strength of the Heart	978-1-932300-81-9
Carrie Carr	The Way Things Should Be	978-1-932300-39-0
Carrie Carr	To Hold Forever	978-1-932300-21-5
Carrie Carr	Piperton	978-1-935053-20-0
Carrie Carr	Something to Be Thankful For	1-932300-04-X
Carrie Carr	Diving Into the Turn	978-1-932300-54-3
Cronin and Foster	Blue Collar Lesbian Erotica	978-1-935053-01-9
Cronin and Foster	Women in Uniform	978-1-935053-31-6
Pat Cronin	Souls' Rescue	978-1-935053-30-9
Anna Furtado	The Heart's Desire	1-932300-32-5
Anna Furtado	The Heart's Strength	978-1-932300-93-2
Anna Furtado	The Heart's Longing	978-1-935053-26-2
Melissa Good	Eye of the Storm	1-932300-13-9
Melissa Good	Hurricane Watch	978-1-935053-00-2
Melissa Good	Red Sky At Morning	978-1-932300-80-2
Melissa Good	Storm Surge: Book One	978-1-935053-28-6
Melissa Good	Storm Surge: Book Two	978-1-935053-39-2
Melissa Good	Thicker Than Water	1-932300-24-4
Melissa Good	Terrors of the High Seas	1-932300-45-7
Melissa Good	Tropical Storm	978-1-932300-60-4
Melissa Good	Tropical Convergence	978-1-935053-18-7
Regina A. Hanel	Love Another Day	978-1-935053-44-6
Maya Indigal	Until Soon	978-1-932300-31-4
Lori L. Lake	Different Dress	1-932300-08-2
Lori L. Lake	Ricochet In Time	1-932300-17-1
Lori L. Lake	Like Lovers Do	978-1-935053-66-8
K. E. Lane	And, Playing the Role of Herself	978-1-932300-72-7
Helen Macpherson	Love's Redemption	978-1-935053-04-0
J. Y Morgan	Learning To Trust	978-1-932300-59-8
J. Y. Morgan	Download	978-1-932300-88-8
A. K. Naten	Turning Tides	978-1-932300-47-5
Lynne Norris	One Promise	978-1-932300-92-5
Linda S. North	The Dreamer, Her Angel, and the Stars	978-1-935053-45-3
Paula Offutt	Butch Girls Can Fix Anything	978-1-932300-74-1
Surtees and Dunne	True Colours	978-1-932300-529
Surtees and Dunne	Many Roads to Travel	978-1-932300-55-0
Vicki Stevenson	Family Affairs	978-1-932300-97-0

Vicki Stevenson	Family Values	978-1-932300-89-5
Vicki Stevenson	Family Ties	978-1-935053-03-3
Vicki Stevenson	Certain Personal Matters	978-1-935053-06-4
Cate Swannell	Heart's Passage	978-1-932300-09-3
Cate Swannell	No Ocean Deep	978-1-932300-36-9

VISIT US ONLINE AT

www.regalcrest.biz

At the Regal Crest Website You'll Find

- The latest news about forthcoming titles and new releases

- Our complete backlist of romance, mystery, thriller and adventure titles

- Information about your favorite authors

- Current bestsellers

Regal Crest titles are available from all progressive booksellers including numerous sources online. Our distributors are Bella Distribution and Ingram.